# The
# Sistahood
# of Shopaholics

ANTHOLOGIES

St. Martin's Griffin ✻ New York

# The Sistahood of Shopaholics

Leslie Esdaile, Monica Jackson, Reon Laudat, Niqui Stanhope

Design by Susan Yang

Interior title art illustration by Jonathan Bennett

ISBN 0-7394-3796-8

# Contents

# Shameless

## LESLIE ESDAILE

# Chapter 1

*Hotlanta, Georgia. July.*

Della Mitchell clutched the steering wheel of her silver SUV and closed her eyes. The anticipation of one more shopping hit riddled her body as she tried to calm herself and prepare for her first solo mission back into the world. A whole year and twelve nearly impossible steps had led to this moment of freedom. The excitement within her almost brought on delirium. They'd told her it would feel like this when it was her turn for a furlough.

Her group had also cautioned her to remember what had sent her into a close brush with financial catastrophe. The thought stilled her as she opened her eyes and looked across the expanse of lot-bound cars toward Lenox Mall's shopping epicenter. Yeah, she had to keep things in perspective.

Silk was her nemesis, and only methadone for what she really needed in her life. Her addiction to lingerie had nearly bankrupted her. Della shook her head and got out of the vehicle, holding her designer Fendi bag close to her body. Not today. She would not OD on the luscious garments that made her feel sexy and wanton and sensually female. Nope. She could handle a first walk through paradise . . . Victoria's Secret.

Today, her hands would not tremble like a junkie's when she fingered the fine fabrics and thought of what they felt like next to her skin. Uh-uh. Even though her fellow shopaholics claimed that once an addict, always an addict, she was healed. She had dredged and exorcised her demons.

The mall entrance was in sight, and she fixed her mind on the past while holding her head high. All right, so what, she'd married for every wrong reason in the book. Robert had been dependable, degreed, consistent—and controlling. Okay, that was then; this was now. But his ass was still cheap enough to make an eagle scream. Della felt her strides widening with purpose as her heels clicked against asphalt. She chuckled.

As Della approached the megacomplex of pure hedonism, her eyes tried not to drink in the liquid pleasure of chrome and glass to the palace entrance, where soon marble would be underfoot. What had possessed her to drive all the way from Roswell to be back on Peachtree Road? she wondered. Maybe she just needed the long drive to build anticipation, like foreplay—or just to clear her mind before she did this solo reentry thing? That was her motto these days, "Pace yourself, sister, 'cause it ain't going nowhere." She only wished, twice a day now, that she'd taken more time before deciding to marry Robert.

What had started off as a socially acceptable date with Robert turned into a consistent but unimaginative tryst with a logical lover. But the group told her that had been her own choice—no excuses. True. Her biological clock had ticked until the alarm went off, so his sterile proposal ("Why don't we just get married?") had sounded like a rational offer then. So had the little chip of a diamond, which he'd haggled over with the jeweler in front of her. It hadn't been the size of the ring that bothered her; it was the spirit in which it had been given: begrudging, complaining. Sadly, she'd accepted it, totally unaware of what that would really mean. A banker—what had she expected? She wanted to cry but made herself laugh instead, a survival mechanism developed over the years. Laugh, sister, because you are too crazy.

She took a deep breath and entered through two large glass doors and allowed the different smell of in-mall ecstasy to wash over her. Oh, God, it felt so good to be in here one more time. Determined to pace herself, she found a bench and sat, needing the time to contain her emotions before deep immersion.

Della watched the people going by. Some were hurried; some were strolling in a lazy, wealthy fashion. Thank God it was still too early for the teenage crowd to have descended upon the mall. She glanced around and noted that some of the early-morning shoppers were focused, as if they were on a mission, while others walked and gabbed and scolded children as they passed. Children. For the sake of her heart's deepest desire, at age thirty she'd sold a part of her soul to a man who had no generosity of spirit. Now, at thirty-five, she had the one gift she'd always thank Robert for, even if he didn't appreciate it himself—Claire. For the sake of her child, she still held on to her ex-husband's name, and for no other reason. That was love sublime.

The thought was so sobering that Della almost left the mall. Claire coming into her life had brought everything into exquisite joy, as well as painful focus. When she'd carried that breath of God up under her heart, inside her body, everything that had annoyed her about Robert Mitchell had become unbearable. His snide comments about her free, easygoing manner had irked the doo-doo out of her. His insistence that she adhere to a strict diet, lest she gain an ounce more than she should, ripped at her self-esteem. The way he threw a fit if she bought a stuffed animal (or anything else he considered nonutilitarian for their baby on the way) used to send needles into her brain. And the way he'd looked at her ripening form with disgust rather than with pure awe had shattered her heart and almost broke her spirit. Screw him—now and forevermore—she was going shopping!

Feeling the breath evacuate her lungs made her take two long sips of air to replenish the void. Weight crushed her chest as her hand inadvertently went to her finally flat stomach. Beauty had been inside her and was never fully appreciated. All her husband had seen was bulk and stretch marks. Her widened hips, rounder behind, and more pendulous breasts remained after Claire was born, a badge of motherhood. No denying that fact. Instead of seeing lushness, he'd compared her with the dead, skinny-girl images within glossy pages of magazines.

She might have endured his disdain, but there was no forgiving the man for looking down at their perfect newborn *girl*, still damp from delivery, his sigh one of pure disappointment rather than joy. He'd wanted a son. Even the nurses had turned away from him and studied Della with sad, mute expressions before their eyes blazed with quiet rage. The child was perfect—a gift, a blessing. She'd been born gorgeous, alert, whole, healthy, and hale, and this bastard was still complaining and measuring the gift of life like he measured everything else, with a warped yardstick.

She told herself that she had to move, had to stop thinking about the moment that she could remember like it was yesterday. In the middle of the mall, Della could feel a panic attack about to sweep through her. She was still so very angry. The OB-GYN had even glanced over his mask at her husband, and then quickly pulled his focus away to keep his eyes trained on the post-birthing task at hand. Yeah, even the doctor was *through*, but the man was professional enough to stay out of the province of marital counseling. However, the delivery team's eyes spoke volumes. Robert was a fool. Wouldn't even go to counseling or church, convinced that his position was logical and righteous. Pullease.

Della swallowed hard and studied her hand, which no longer bore

Robert Mitchell's pitiful ring. Two professionals—a banker and a marketing executive—a match made in Hell. Through the sudden moisture in her eyes, Della almost laughed again. Maybe she wasn't ready for a maiden flight back into a shopping venue? She could feel the old rage bubbling within her, threatening to drown her.

The group just didn't understand what it had been like having every task in the house measured according to a fifty-fifty division of labor—*on paper*, no less! Before she went to the market, Robert insisted on developing a list that was adhered to, lest she pick up an extra cut of meat that wasn't sanctioned. He'd been so infuriated when she sometimes forgot to use the coupons he'd clipped that he'd taken to going to the market himself. And her friends had thought it was because he was such a nice, responsible, helpful guy. Absurd.

How could she explain to them what it was like to have all the household duties posted on the refrigerator weekly with names beside each task, and if she should get busy at work, or later with Claire, then Robert would cross off one of his own chores and put her name beside it to keep the score *exactly* even? Just like he made love. Exacting. Even. There were some things she hadn't been able to tell the group.

The mall felt like it was closing in on her. Anxiety threaded through her veins. Della glanced up and down the long expanse of glistening corridors. Okay, so fine. No excuses. She'd been all wrapped up in the prospect of getting married, like any newly engaged woman would, and filled with joy that she could finally have the big day in white. There was no measure for the look of completeness on her parents' faces. And, yeah, she'd been so busy building her career in year one that all these little Robertian foibles seemed minor. She hadn't worried about them.

Year one, she was still in bliss. Then came year two, and much of the euphoria had burned away by the time she became pregnant and they'd bought the house. The real fights started then, too. As did her recognition that these weren't little spats, but serious issues . . . but by then, Claire was firmly in her womb.

Della pushed herself up to stand, blinking back tears. The group had been good to her. With them, she'd shed twenty-five pounds of Michelin tire from around her waist, face, and arms, albeit she still had twenty to drop from her big butt, thick thighs, and hips. With the group's assistance to stay on a strict financial diet, she'd cleaned up the ten thousand dollars of credit-card debt and had lived like a nun. Abstinence in every way. No splurges, no men, no nothing—just take care of Claire, work off the debt, rebuild a career. Focus. Yeah, having support was a good thing. A necessary thing. It numbed a sister up like Novocain.

The support group had taken some of the sting out of the pregnancy aftermath: a year of listening to her husband's sarcasm about her figure, a year of him giving her his back in bed because her body had changed and a part of it still belonged to her little girl, a year of buying beautiful lingerie to make herself feel pretty, a year of hoping he'd cut the bull and just be nice to her, a year of socially acceptable self-destruction from frustration (good food, gorgeous fabrics). Finally letting him take the lion's share of property just to be done struggling with him once and for all. Yeah, she'd been addicted to a very private joy—feeling pretty for herself—and even that had gone awry. The cost was prohibitive at her levels of indulgence.

Headed for a sure crisis, like an epileptic fit, she knew she had to get out of the mall, *now*. Thinking of Robert was not a good thing. The girls were wrong. Thinking about Robert required morphine, not methadone. Thinking of that asshole and his skinny, high-yella secretary was going to make her melt plastic, big-time. Fry it at the register. Thinking about all the cutting words, the two years of struggle to get away from him—the bitter contention being about property, not custody—could possibly spiral her into a twelve-hundred-dollar binge. She could feel it coming. Her hands were literally shaking.

Della reached for her cell phone and called her coach. As soon as Gillian's voice filled the receiver, Della blurted out the truth. "Gurl, help me. I need an intervention. I'm in the mall. I'm staring down at my purse. Victoria's Secret is fifty feet away, and I'm not ready."

"Okay, okay, okay, lady, think. Get to a calm place in your head. You can do this."

Della paced before the bench as her knuckles went white around the tiny black phone. "A year with him bitching at me, then almost a year with him while pregnant—complaining, hovering, making me feel horrible about natural body changes—and two years to battle my way out of that trap called a marriage with a cheap SOB, Gil! Oh, my God, a year to clean up the credit-card carnage of trying to find a little joy in silk, and to redecorate an apartment—my daughter is three, and I'm a statistic. I'm thirty-five. I've just relocated to Atlanta. I've got this new, high-pressure job, and all my family is back in Philly. I had to sell the house, give up sex—"

"Stop," Gillian urged in a soothing tone. "Remember why you got into trouble. Inner rage at the lack of appreciation, anger, feelings of deprivation, and the shopping was *only* a temporary fix. Remember our work in healing the woman within? But now, you have a new start. You're making healthy personal choices nowadays. You are working for a premier soft-drink company—"

"I know, I know," Della rushed in. "Thank you for everything. If your headhunting firm hadn't gotten me out of Philly . . . Oh, girl."

"Listen," Gillian pressed on. "I didn't say that about your new job to make you feel guilty. You couldn't have landed the job unless I had something to work with. You don't owe me. The company paid me well to place a good candidate who is a successful single mother, who just so happens to be a good friend. You're beautiful, young, attractive, dynamic, and you have value. You're free, and you have no one but yourself and your child to please, and you have your own apartment. You don't need to binge. You don't need a toxic relationship to fulfill your desires—not as long as they make D batteries. You are strong."

Growing steadier, Della closed her eyes and took a deep breath. "You're right." A sad chuckle escaped Della's throat. "Duracells and lace. Yeah. I remember the pledge. Nothing toxic. I was just having a silk hysteria attack. It's been so long. In fact, I think I'm going to walk out of here right this moment. I've already got every color of silk—from faux virgin white to vampire black, and every shade in between. I don't need a thing. So, I'm set. I already have enough lingerie, and haven't had a soul to wear it for in like . . . uh . . . damn, girl, years."

"Buy some more batteries," Gillian said with an easy giggle. "I can hear the strain in your voice."

"No. I'm fine. Just had a moment."

"We must be honest with ourselves, Della. You are a sensualist. It is a part of your nature. The feel, the smell of new silk, the way it makes you look, the sound of it as it moves against the sheets while you sip champagne and eat chocolate."

Della shut her eyes. "Gurl, it's been too long. Please, don't even talk about it. That was BC: before Claire. I'm a mom now. I *can't* go into that store. Not yet. Too many pre-Robert memories of what silk can do, okaaaay. I'm not ready."

"Don't live in denial, embrace that part of you that makes you, you—don't suppress her, just give her limits."

For a moment, neither woman spoke as Della collected herself. Gillian broke the silence with gentle laughter.

"Right. Right," Della finally whispered, joining in Gillian's good humor. "I remember what the facilitator said. Like Ramona's shoe thing . . . when she had to take back the five pairs of Pradas and select just one." However, Della's breath came out in a hard rush as she opened her eyes and stared at paradise not fifty feet away.

"Exactly. Okay, now. You can do this. Today is supposed to be a happy day. A chance to show yourself that you have limits that *you* control and can set. If you turn back now, you'll just break out one night without an intervention call, and you'll binge because you'll really feel deprived. Now, listen, I've got Claire for the day. You march yourself in there, buy a couple of items, have a healthy lunch, stop at a drugstore for some Ds, and then go home."

Gillian's laughter continued to pour through the cell phone, and it made Della giggle harder at her own craziness.

"Right. That's true. Yeah. I can do this."

"Pray for strength," Gillian said, her tone soft but firm. "Call me before you get to the register, though. The first time back in is really difficult."

"All right. I will," Della replied on another long exhale.

"Say it with me: Help me change the things I can change, and to release the things I can't, and to have the wisdom to know the difference between the two."

Della nodded, allowing her voice to join with her friend's in the Serenity Prayer. The two fell silent for a moment once more. She added in her own private lament: *Lord, help me find some joy, real passion, and fun that's not detrimental to me or my baby girl.*

"You okay, lady?"

"Yeah," Della said. "I'm going in."

.  .  .

He hated malls. But there were some things a man just had to do. Okay, so if he was going to break up with Vanessa, he'd at least go out with a righteous apology. Why he felt like he owed her one was still unclear in his mind. She'd been like all the others—well pedigreed, educated, long-legged, beautiful, and a total barracuda. As long as he had the pockets, he had a date. And that had begun to feel like he was paying for an elegant escort service. No matter.

He wasn't buying this one a ring, either. In fact, it was his firm oath to stay away from any jewelry as gifts. He'd learned that early on. Byron Fulton did not do the diamond thing. First it would be a tennis bracelet, or earrings on a special occasion; then by the time a big holiday came around, the sister would open the box and the argument would always crop up about the next step, blowing the groove. In his mind, there was no *next step* for a sister trying to lay a bear trap.

Why was that so extreme? His position had never wavered; he'd always been honest. They knew he was a pilot, and that he traveled. He always told them up front that he was not interested in settling down. And, as long as they were riding first class, shopping till they'd dropped, they didn't seem to mind. What he could never figure out was the shift. Byron took long determined paces through the mall, dodging slow-walking patrons as he contemplated that undefinable thing that made women go from the easygoing level one, to def-con five.

The change was always an imperceptible thing, too—it happened almost overnight. Initially, he'd be a trophy, and so would they; a mutual understanding would be in full effect. You attend my job functions, and I'll attend yours. You call me when you need some, and I'll oblige the call, if you oblige mine when I'm in town. Simple. Not complicated. Marriage was a long way from a booty call.

By thirty-eight, he was probably too old to go that route anyway.

Until he found what his brothers and sister had found, he wasn't going out like that. They had what his parents had had. It was something rare, tangible, and money or title couldn't buy it . . . and their love had lasted almost fifty years, and still hadn't perished, even when his dad passed on. That's what he was holding out for. The real McCoy. The real diamond of life forged by time, the ability to go through good times and bad times, something genuine. Not a sister who grasped at title, salary, the right real estate, and the four-carat rock to simply show off to her sorority friends.

Byron's heels ground out his resistance to the popular convention of getting married by a certain age. No. He was a bachelor for life. So, yeah, he'd just find something nice for Ness, hand it to her over dinner, and then launch into the conversation that had needed to be had for a long time. His gaze swept the array of store choices. Perfume? Nah. He no longer wanted to be that close to smell the fragrance against her café au lait skin. A nice handbag? Sorta impersonal, given that they'd been lovers. Shoes? Crazy. He wouldn't have a clue. A household knickknack? No. He chuckled. She might use it as a weapon. Okay, then what? Maybe something to say that he still found her attractive but wished her the best in her quest to dragnet a husband.

The pink store interior drew his attention. Nice lingerie? Maybe. But nothing too suggestive, because that could sidetrack the conversation. Vanessa did have a way of doing that to him. In fact, that had been the delay. Despite all her manipulative ways, the woman was talented. He let his breath out hard. Cold turkey was the only cure.

Standing outside the store, he studied his options and then got real. Lingerie. The gift would be personal enough to say she'd meant something at one point—sort of a peace offering now that it was over. Yeah. Vanessa had technique but not an ounce of passion within it. Everything was a performance, down to the last shiver. Well, maybe

not the last shiver . . . His ego couldn't allow him to go there. A sad
chuckle found its way up and out of his throat as he shook his head,
because the truth had a way of getting past the ego shield. He knew.
Had always known that about her.

A brother who'd been around the block a few times could always
tell.

# Chapter 2

More grounded now, Della took her time to enter the sumptuous haven of lingerie splendor, and she respectfully waved off the attention offered by one of the register ladies.

"No, thank you," Della murmured, "I'm just looking."

The young woman returned a knowing gaze. One pro could always identify another.

"Then, ma'am," the store agent drawled in a deep Georgia accent, "you just call on me if you need anything."

Della nodded. The girl smiled. They both walked away from each other. This was the dance. The wondrous fragrance of the store made Della slow her steps and take in the new row of color she hadn't seen before. It drew her like a magnet. Something fragile and a shade between midnight blue and violet pulled at her, made her wind a seductive path through burgeoning aisles to get to it. They'd come up with a new hue of sapphire and violet—and her size area on the racks was filled. Heaven help her. It was on.

There, in a brand-new display, every black-violet undergarment matched in a suite of private adornment. Her fingers touched lace, and she carefully lifted a wisp of negligee from the tall kiosk. She studied the line of the garment as she raised it for inspection. Jesus . . . a full-length gown, slit up the back, with a dangerously low mesh bodice that V-ed to her V, and studded by teeny clusters of embroidered satin leaves. It was gorgeous blackened sapphire upon darker sapphire-violet that threatened to cover just the right places to allow modesty to prevail, with a swath of sheer leaves down the hip to also indicate the lack of underwear beneath the gown. No back, just six strands of cord. Pure brilliance of design, lightweight material extremely expensive in feel—even the underside hosted finished French seams. And the color . . .

Della brought the fabric to her nose, closed her eyes, and inhaled. She could feel her eyes cross beneath her lids. Unable to stop it, she heard a quiet moan of total satisfaction pass her lips. She didn't care what this piece cost—today, it would be hers.

He knew he should have gone home to change out of his uniform first. In a joint like this, he was a sitting duck. But thankfully, it was early enough in the morning not to be crowded, and he'd been able to get the ladies at the counter to back off so he could browse. They couldn't help him; he didn't know what he wanted.

Byron glanced around sheepishly. Okay. This could be a quick in and out. A couple of old ladies gave him the eye, and there was only one sister over by the racks. But man . . . *baby had back.* All right, focus. In and out. No lingering. No big game hunting. Just in and out. Start with color. Vanessa liked hot pink. But dang . . . the sister over there was fine.

Maybe if she liked that color, he could just go over and at least check out a style. Yeah, that made sense, he told himself as he walked through the aisle to where the tall, classy sister stood. But as he approached her, he was not prepared for the look on her face.

He had to admit that the sister's rear view had been a part of the gravitational pull toward her. The way her black pants stretched over her ample behind and flared slightly at her curved calves had bent his decision to walk in her direction. The color of her tank top matched her skin, giving the illusion that she was bare from the waist up, and had also factored in. He'd wanted to see her face. That part of her had been impossible to detect behind her mane of shoulder-length mahogany hair. As he drew close enough to get a respectable glimpse, he'd been blown away.

Her eyes were closed, her lush lips were parted, and the look of sheer ecstasy in her expression made it hard for him to breathe. It had been way too long since he'd seen that kind of honest pleasure on a woman's face. If lingerie did that to her, then *dayum*. . . .

Dumbfounded, his gaze discreetly appraised the roughly five-foot-eight beauty made taller by her thick-wedged sandals. Even her toenails were polished in an elegant French manicure that matched her delicate hands. . . . The way she touched and stroked the silk made him swallow hard again. High exotic cheekbones, long throat, breasts the size of cantaloupes . . . in a tank top, no bra strap showing, could only mean she was doing strapless to hold up that amount of sensuous weight, torso pulled tight into a narrow waist only to gradually expand into brickhouse hips and thick, succulent thighs with no space in between them. His line of vision swept over the amber skin she exposed—flawless, save a perfectly placed beauty mark on her shoulder. Had to be God's imprint of perfection. Heaven help him, this woman was seriously fine.

When she opened her eyes, he quickly cleared his throat. Caught off guard, he tried to muster something plausible to say, while her startled, deep brown irises practically drank him in.

"Uh, I'm sorry. Didn't mean to frighten you. Just saw you over here, and you seemed to know more about picking out this stuff than me . . . so, I thought I'd ask your opinion. I have no idea where to begin."

• • •

Either the angels above had heard her prayer out in the mall or the devil had followed her into the store. But since angels didn't necessarily do lingerie, this apparition definitely had to mean trouble. Della forced herself to smile, even though it took a second to get her bearings. How was she supposed to process six feet four inches of Hershey's chocolate fine, in a uniform, flashing a smile that gave the lights in Victoria's competition, and smelling fantastic? *Get thee behind me, Satan.* A man in a lingerie store had to be somebody's husband or lover, or he was gay.

"Uh," Della stammered. "What does your wife like?"

"Oh, I'm not married," he replied quickly. Too quickly.

"Yeah, okay. Well—"

"No, really. I'm not."

"Okay, then, what does your girlfriend like?"

When he hesitated, she found herself smiling. Bingo. All right, let's do this.

"Special occasion . . . anniversary, engagement, her birthday?" Della rattled the questions off like a physician making a diagnosis. Whoever was getting this hunk's attention was surely blessed. Nonetheless, she wasn't buying or trying.

"Umm, well, it's sort of an appreciation gift." He cringed as the words came out of his mouth. He was nuts to be in here, trying to pick up this woman. No. He had to chill. This was insane. But the wider she grinned and the more amused she became at his ineptitude, the more he wanted to find out about her. He looked at the sheath of fabric she held. Dang, whoever the lucky brother was to see her in that, he was blessed.

"Appreciation gift?" Della could feel an eyebrow cock despite her decision to stay out of this man's business.

He chuckled. "Yeah. Long story."

Whew. She had to get out of there. His Southern drawl was pouring over her like hot butter on a biscuit, as were his eyes.

"Everybody's got one." She laughed. "Get her a nightgown."

"What's your favorite color?"

"What?" Thoroughly taken aback, all she could do was stare at the man.

"I mean, you know. What colors do women like?"

Nice save. The brother was smooth. "It doesn't matter what color *women* like. The question is, what color does *she* like?"

This sister had class. He loved it. She wasn't giving an inch, and rightfully so. She'd looked straight past his uniform, glanced at his wings, and offered an expression that told him she was thoroughly unimpressed. *Cool.*

"You're right," he murmured. "Hot pink."

"Then you're in the wrong aisle."

He laughed now. "I know. My bad." But he also hadn't moved.

"Try a pink nightgown," she said with a smirk, and motioned to where that color of gown could be found.

What could he say? He'd been dismissed. A brother had to have some pride, after all.

"Good choice," he said, and meant it. "Your husband is a very lucky man."

"*Was* a lucky man," she said softly, and turned her attention to a matching robe to go with the gown she'd slung over her arm.

"I'm sorry he passed," he heard himself say to her, not sure why.

A lazy, lopsided grin crept out on her face as she glanced up. "The man didn't die. Just walked. What made you think I was a widow? I look that bad standing in the black-gown section?" Then she laughed again and shook her head.

An earnest, ripe laugh flowed out of her mouth and brought warmth that kicked his pulse up a notch. Her voice . . . Wow.

"Naw," he said in an casual tone. "Figured the man had to be dead, if he wasn't still with you." It was time for him to go. He'd just kicked the corniest, high-schoolish line his embattled brain could think of, and the woman had put one hand on her hip. He had to laugh at himself.

"All right, all right, sister. I know. Don't shoot. It's just that I was supposed to be in here buying a breakup gift, and here I am, in trouble. I'ma go tend to my business—but you should know that you just made a grown man act stupid. Have a nice day."

She stood there, watching him take long strides across the store. He loped, more than walked, an easy glide, shoulders back, chin held high, his athletic body working beneath navy blue. He'd tipped his hat like a Southern gent, flashed a to-die-for grin of self-deprecation, went to a rack, glanced at it, snatched off a garment, and in two seconds was at the front of the store. Daaaayum. Nobody had rolled up on her like that in years. Just flat-out got in her face with pure animal magnetism, openly flirted, and then backed off. Deep. She had to get out of there. Now.

One item. The gown. Well, maybe two. The robe to go with it. Then a quick salad. Della kept her eyes focused on her purse and her purchases. Nope. Wasn't even havin' it. Wasn't looking out the glass behind the brother. No, no, no, no, no, no, no. Trouble, with a capital *T*. But damn, he was fine.

She made haste to the counter after she glanced around to be sure he was gone. Problem was, the three women at the register were in a huddle of whispered excitement.

"Ma'am," the young blonde who'd first spied her exclaimed. "That gentleman said to give you this when you came to the register."

The girl produced and thrust out a business card in Della's direction—DELTA AIRLINES, CAPT. J. BYRON FULTON.

An older woman in the group chuckled as Della refused to accept the card from the younger employee's hand. "Honey," she said slowly and with plenty of theatrical effect, "I'm an old doll, and I'ma tell ya this once and only once. You'd better take that card before I do."

Della had to laugh as she slid her lingerie onto the counter and grudgingly accepted the card. "Ladies, if you haven't noticed, he was in here buying undergarments for a girlfriend or a wife—it definitely wasn't for his momma, okay."

The shyest clerk giggled and peered toward the door, her warm brown face lit by mischief. "Wouldn't make me a difference if he was gonna cross-dress in it, so long as he was gonna take off that uniform, chile."

All of them glanced at each other and burst out laughing in unison.

"I can't believe you said that!" The young blonde slapped her coworker's arm, making the group laugh even harder.

"Honeychile, when you get to be my age, which I'm proud to say is way over fifty when I stopped countin', you become appreciative of the little thangs. Just the fact that the man walked in the store, stopped dead in his tracks, lost a piece of his brain to sidle up to you, and despite all odds to the contrary, was still tryin' to get next to you . . . *Humph,* darlin', I don't know your status, but married or not, I'd take that compliment with me to my grave. That's a porch rocker, if ever I saw one."

Through the chuckles, Della finally got out her question. She still had to get used to the local slang, which was often difficult to decipher. But she had to know: "A porch rocker?" She was waving them off as a new round of giggles erupted.

"Yeah, hon. A porch rocker. When you git ol' and gray, and don't nobody pay you no mind, you can be rockin' on the porch with a smile on your face, thinkin' back on the time you made a pilot crashland right in Lenox Mall in Victoria's Secret."

The women howled as other older patrons in line began adding in their two cents. A community of festive, raucous voices rang out, with each of them occasionally peeping toward the door.

"Baby, a compliment is a compliment," one elderly woman in line quipped.

"Sho' is, and my momma used to say, 'Consider the source.' And Lord have mercy, did you see that source?" a woman with a baby stroller added in.

"I been married twenty-seven years," another patron told her. "This helps." She chuckled, holding up a garter belt, thong, and Wonderbra. "But a little innocent flattery and appreciation every now and again don't hurt a girl, neither."

Even though Della had laughed the whole time they rang up her items and neatly folded her garments in tissue, with the final touch— placing them in *the pink bag*, a significant part of her was thrilled beyond measure. Okay, so he had a girlfriend. She was just window-shopping. Wasn't like she'd walked up to *him*. But the other women were right. It was nice to have a good-looking man, respectfully, get tongue tied and act a little simple in one's presence. Made a sister feel like she still had her old pull from yesteryear, even though she'd gained weight, had a kid, carried a significant load of personal baggage, and had stretch marks to boot.

For three minutes, standing in the aisle at Victoria's, she'd been twenty-one-again, free. And, it had felt so good.


What was on his mind? He was walking through a mall with a pink bag, and he had just made a complete fool of himself! No woman like that would speak to a guy buying lingerie. The whole thing was so stupid. Stuff a teenager would do. Byron shook his head. He'd grab a sandwich to go, head for home, and make that call he dreaded, to set up the last meeting with Ness. Yeah, it was time. He'd do this thing in Roswell, local—not at his apartment, but close to it. Asher, right on Canton Street, was intimate, not far from him, and he could just sit at a quiet table to do what he had to do. Maybe the women in his family were right—he needed to go to church.

He chuckled again as he continued to walk, shaking his head and hearing his sister's voice in his mind: "Flying ten tons of steel up in the air, believing that engines will hold, and don't give Father God no credit at all. Boy, one day you gonna be on yo' knees asking for divine intervention, and ya best hope he has some mercy on ya."

No lie. Coulda used some help from above this morning. Any store but that one. Why couldn't she have been on a bench, out in the mall, or anywhere else but there? Not that he had a reason to sweat it— although she wasn't married, she was obviously involved. Why else would she be in there, hooking up an outfit that would make a grown man turn sixteen again? And, one brother might have been a fool— her ex-husband—but certainly not the guy who had been lucky enough to scoop her up after all that. If there was a problem between them, she wouldn't have been holding silk to her face and daydreaming about how that brother made her feel. Lucky SOB.

Yeah. He had to get something to eat and shake the sense of defeat about the one that got away. Can't win 'em all.

The food court line wasn't long. Good. At least something was going his way. One day off, for a layover, then he'd fly for six straight days. Byron allowed his gaze to scan the sandwich board menu, working logistics in his head. Turkey club. Repack, get his other uniforms out of the cleaners, do some laundry, do the dinner thing with Vanessa. If they had to get deep, go to her place so he could leave. No drama in the Bat Cave. When he was tired, he needed to get some rest. Taking 240 people up in the air was no joke. Didn't do that on an all-nighter argument. No. Make it short and sweet and to the point.

His peripheral vision caught a glimpse of a shellacked pink shopping bag held by a blur of amber created by the woman who quickly walked by. Salad. Maybe he'd order a salad to go.

"Gillian," Della whispered into her cell, unable to stop laughing from her giddy high. "I almost got in big trouble back there, girl!"

"Oh, no," Gillian groaned. "How much damage? You were supposed to call me when you got to the register."

"Gurl, I couldn't," Della whispered through another giggle. "There were people around, and—"

"You know that's not important. The question is, how much did you spend?"

"Three twenty-five, and worth every penny!"

Gillian gasped. "On how many pieces?"

"Two. The gown was a hundred and—"

"Two pieces of lingerie?"

"Yeah, but, girl . . . listen—"

"Get out of the mall, now."

"Gil, sis, listen. It's what came with the gown."

"I don't care *what* type of special promotion they had that brought on delirium, you are dangerously close to ODing—"

"Gurl, he was so fine!" The words rushed out of Della's mouth as she turned away from the line to speak in a conspiratorial tone. She hunched over like a secret agent calling headquarters, trying to keep the nosy folks in line out of her business. But waiting till she got to the car to call her confidante was impossible.

"What?" Gillian's question came out on a slow whisper.

"Gotta go—call ya back!"

In an instant, she saw him, stood up straight, snapped her cell shut on her girl—oh no, and drilled her line of vision into the salad menu board. As though possessing a sixth sense, she could practically feel heat radiating off his body as he got on the line behind her, not that he was standing that close, but dag—she could actually *feel* him. But, she would not turn around.

Nope, because he still had that pink bag in his hand.

# Chapter 3

Now what? This was a bad idea, and he knew it. What had possessed him to get into the line behind this woman? He had nothing plausible to say to her, and she'd blown him off once already. But he wanted to know her name, at the very least. There was something about her eyes, too. The merriment in them, the amused confidence. The way she looked past all the trappings of what most of the women he'd encountered considered a good catch, to stare him dead in the eyes, point-blank.

As he watched her ignore him, knowing that she had glimpsed his presence, he studied the way deep red, bronze, and ebony strands ran through her shoulder-length blunt-cut hair. Natural. It was too full not to be natural. It reminded him of her face. Matte finish but radiant, just a hint of black eyeliner and thick, black lashes that weren't caked with mascara. A little blush, maybe, but her face was natural, smooth. Mouth damped just a bit by some type of gloss stuff, but the natural color of it came through, just like the colors in her hair did. That was it. Her voice, her eyes, and what she'd shown him thus far felt real, genuine. When she'd laughed, it came from down deep. When she'd raised an eyebrow at him, the expression was sharp, but not bitter. Her eyes said it all, as expressive as what she had not spo-, ken. All of it helped him make up his mind.

"I'm not a stalker, you know. Just a brother trying to get something to eat."

He'd made the comment in a low tone over her shoulder, and she rewarded him with a chuckle, although she hadn't turned around.

"I'm from Philly," she said in an amused voice, her head moving only slightly to glance back at him. "I'm not too worried about a stalker."

He laughed. "Okay. Busted. I saw you in this line and wanted to come over to begin again."

He watched her shoulders. They unsuccessfully gave way to what he knew was suppressed laughter as she shook her head. When she finally turned around, she graced him with a broad grin. Her eyes danced with mischief. He could have stood there and stared at her all day.

"Brother, you are so bogus."

He hadn't expected that, nor had he expected her to laugh after she blasted him.

Before he could say another word, she'd placed a hand on her hip. "Now, be honest. How are you going to stand here in the mall, trying to talk to me, when you have underwear—no less—for some other woman in a pink Victoria's Secret bag? Now, I know you probably get your share of play, and more than most, given you can do the 'Baby come fly with me' line. But do you really think that it's that bad out here that a sister has to allow a man to pick her up while he has a gift bag of panties for some other sister?"

He was about to try to defend his shaky position when she raised her hand, offered him a wide, dazzling smile, and said one word: "Pul-lease." Then she turned around and began studying her menu choices again.

"Aw'right, Philly," he chuckled, soundly put in check. "But at least you should give a man a chance to explain."

"Why would I need to do that? I don't know you."

Again, she'd given him her back to consider. He glanced down at the parcel he carried and laughed hard. This was ludicrous. She had a point.

"What is your name, sis? Just so I can nurse my wounds and remember who checked me this hard in the mall."

Begrudgingly, and on a long sigh, she turned around to face him. "If I tell you my name, will you let me eat my salad in peace—and go handle your bizness?"

"I promise." It was impossible to get the smile to vanish from his face.

"Della Mitchell."

He just nodded. Pretty. "Byron Fulton. And I'm from here, by way of Macon."

She just nodded, gave him the once-over lightly, with one eyebrow raised.

"I'm not married, never been, and don't have any kids—and yes, currently I'm in a complicated situation, soon to be rectified."

"Aren't we all? It was nice to meet you."

Just as quickly as the sun of mischief had lit in her eyes, her expression clouded over, she stepped out of line, and strode away— head held high. Damn. Something he'd said? He stared at her luscious form as it merged and disappeared into a crowd. Suddenly, he was no longer hungry.


Della put the key into the ignition and pulled out of the space slowly, making the turn to head out of the massive lot and go home. She glanced at the new purchase on the seat beside her. It had lost its allure. Kids. He said he had no kids. That was a good thing, rather than being a guy who had babies in every port—*if* he wasn't lying. But there was just something about the way he'd made the announcement to her, as though not having children was a badge of honor. It hurt. Rubbed her the wrong way.

On the one hand, she was glad he didn't have the complication of children, or a baby's momma in his life—but on the other hand, she was somebody's mother—Claire's—and maybe he'd be put off by her child. But all of that was totally stupid, because she didn't know this man, and wasn't going to get to know this man. In fact, it was shameless to be so taken with the mere physical presence of some guy she didn't know, and who obviously had someone special in his life. It was hoochie-momma action, snagging somebody else's man, and something she detested—especially after having had it done to her. Yeah, the brother had no shame. But damn, he was fine.

There had been just too many conflicting emotions running through her for her to stand there and deal with further conversation. Plus, that whole "soon to be rectified" mess replayed itself in her brain. Yeah, right. Wonder if the sister he's giving the draws to knew it was "soon to be rectified"? Whateva. Fact was, the good-looking ones always came with much baggage. Even her Urkel-looking, geek husband had gotten himself into trouble. See, sisters had to be united and stop behaving like this toward one another, she reassured herself, repeating the mantra she'd learned within her group meetings. There had to be a code of ethics, honor among sisters. Yeah. Right on!

She would *never* get back out there into the dating meat market, if this was what was waiting around every corner. In fact, she would never remarry, would never sleep with anybody again—unless she was 100 percent sure she wouldn't get burned. All physical and chemical stuff notwithstanding, a woman had to have her pride. Had to treat herself with dignity and respect. Anger made her grip the steering wheel tighter than was necessary. Damn Robert Mitchell for making her have to endure this crap again—and with a child!

Then she remembered Gillian. She'd hung up on her friend. Della slammed her cell into the hands-free unit and pushed Gillian's number on speed dial. Some solo girl's day out.

"Hey, lady," Della said in a flat voice. "Sorry I hung up. Mr. Bogus walked up to me in line and—"

"Girl, stop—"

"I did. Stopped his long litany of drama right in its tracks. I'm done, Gil, for real."

"Details, hon? You know it's not every day that we get a vicarious encounter. What did the man look like? Had to be seriously *all that* if you are acting like this."

"Girl, he's just some airline pilot or something, and he knows he's all that. So, I passed. I don't even want to think about it. And what pissed me off so bad was the fact that he had the unmitigated gall to walk up to me in Victoria's. Have you ever? Just thinking because he's all tall and handsome that that makes it okay to approach somebody who is minding her own business. Humph! I could have been a married woman, or engaged, or—"

"Okay," Gillian replied. "Look, I have an idea, because you sound like you're crashing. Post-shopping letdown, with a twist of man disappointment."

"Yeah. Something like that."

"How about if I get my neighbor, she's like a second mom—you've met her—to let Claire play with her grandkids for a few hours, so that me, you, and Ramona can go have a glass of wine somewhere nice? Because, lady, you haven't sounded this down in a long time."

Della glanced in the rearview mirror as she changed lanes on I-

85. "Yeah. Thanks, lady. But, let's do that another time, if you don't mind too much? I just need to go out by myself for a little while and get my head together. I can come get Claire so you don't have to keep—"

"Girl, please," Gillian said. "Why don't you let me keep this cute little bunny with me? As long as you promise to go somewhere nice that rejuvenates your soul, I'll even keep her overnight, and we can all go to breakfast in the morning. But no more shopping. Promise?"

"Promise. I am cured. I am not going back in there, except to do one thing—to return this mess I wasted money on and to collect myself. Period."

"Good. Then, get something sensible to eat, relax, go listen to some jazz, or go to the movies, whatever."

"Thanks, Gil. I don't know what I'd do without you guys."

Somehow her car had found itself winding back to Lenox Mall. Her strides across the parking lot were forceful, determined. She entered the mall pavilion without even a shudder. She was getting her money back. Period. What was the point of lingerie, anyhow?

Della pushed opened the store doors and went right to the register, where the friendly gathering of women still convened. Their faces lit up when they saw her. But she was ready for them. She was not dropping another wad to increase sales, and wasn't here to chitchat.

"Ladies, I'm sorry," Della began with a level gaze at their excited expressions. "But—"

"Ma'am, he came back!" the youngest of the store staff whispered hard.

"Yeah," the other one said, glancing around as she spoke and keeping her voice confidential. "He looked so sad, and brought back his purchase, said to turn it into a gift certificate and to give it to whomever we wanted. The man said he didn't need the things after all, and didn't even want his money back. Have you ever?"

Mouth agape for a moment, Della looked at the gift certificate the eldest woman now thrust in her direction, but declined to take it. "What?"

"You heard us, sugah," the older woman whispered. "Honey, I don't know what you did to that man in the half hour you left our store, but girlfriend, you need to bottle it." She held up the garment that had been returned with one hand and carefully set down the gift certificate with the other. "Look. It's not your size, so it was destined for somebody else, I do believe, if you will pardon my being so forward."

Against her better judgment, Della briefly peered at the returned item without touching it. Hell no, it wasn't for her—not at a size eight. Damn. He was dating a size-eight sister, and had rolled up on her? What was that about? The brother obviously had to be a dog that just liked women period, if he'd tried to talk to her. Pure canine.

"Well, none of this is my business, anyway, so I'll just—"

"Ma'am, I'm not trying to be funny or anything, but we have to tell you what happened."

Della sighed. How did this place of lingerie become a therapist's office? Yet curiosity had a stranglehold on her now.

"He dropped his parcel, said to convert it to a gift certificate, then took a very long look at the aisle you had been in, let his breath out hard, tipped his hat, and walked."

"That's deep," one of the younger clerks concluded.

"Ain't seen nothing like it in all the time I've worked here," the other agreed.

"Nope. Not from a man fine enough to make a girl wanna slap her momma, I haven't," the eldest admitted through a sigh. "Lordy, Miss

Claudy, ma'am. Listen, sugah. How about if we just hold this certificate in the store for thirty days with your name on it? If he comes back
and changes his mind, then fine. If not, we can even mail it to you—as
you are one of our preferred customers. Now, that seems fair, don't it?"

"But, no," Della stammered. "I do not even know this man, have
no intentions of getting to know this man, and all of this is just—"

"I would call him," the little blonde cut in. "Tell him you don't
want his gift certificate, and see what he says."

"Now, that's a plan," the older blonde murmured, nodding her
head.

"I would definitely let him know I had his card and access to his
certificate, but wasn't interested—as maybe a courtesy call," the young
sister said. "Or, we could call him from Victoria's and tell him that our
preferred customer, a Ms. Della Mitchell, came back a few days later,
and we offered her the certificate, since she had helped him with his
selection . . . but when you understood who it was from, you declined
his kind offer . . . so, of course," she drawled with a hearty laugh, "we
wanted to be sure he was absolutely certain there was no one else we
should mail this certificate to . . . as store policy, of course, and in the
interest of our maximum customer service."

"Saundra, you are pure genius!" the younger blonde squealed. Then
she turned to Della with a wide grin, using her thumb in the direction
of the girl named Saundra. "You've gotta always watch the quiet ones."

"I am not that bad, Sherie," Saundra giggled, "am I, Liz?"

"Mata Hari doesn't have a thang on that sweet-faced chile. Pul-
lease! Brilliant plan, darlin'. I, Elizabeth Hawthorne, could not have
done better. Now, that's what I call Steel-Magnolia plannin' in full
bloom."

All three women behind the register giggled as the eldest woman
gave Della a sly wink of encouragement.

"Honeychile," the older woman finally said, fluffing her bleached flip, "you can kill two birds with one stone. Information to find out for sure if no residual woman is around, or a wife—and you get to go shoppin', doll. You aren't the type to take sloppy seconds, if you don't mind my sayin', so we understand your hesitation."

Elizabeth Hawthorne fanned herself with her hand as she spoke, which made Della smile even harder at the theatrics of it all. "We women have to work together," the matron pressed on, "and must look out for each other's best interest. If he's single, you don't let a hunk like that get away."

The older woman chuckled and leaned in close to Della—who could only clutch on to her pink bag as a wild scheme with strangers unfolded. *How was this happening?*

"I wouldn't pass up this chance. Just let us do a bit of friendly female investigating? All harmless, I assure you, and we would never give your interest in said hunk away. Everything would be strictly confidential," said Saundra.

This was way out of control. Della blinked twice as three wide smiles waited for her decision. "Uh, uh . . . Tell you what. You give that certificate to the next person that walks in that has a baby in a stroller, please, ladies. Mothers need a little something special, and I can't accept it. In fact, I just came back to return my stuff, too."

Liz shrugged. "Oh, all right. But I can't see the harm in keepin' something for yourself, darlin', at least what you had intended to buy before Prince Charmin' walked in the door. Don't let a mere man turn around your wise purchase decisions. Be empowered. You have a husband, is that it?"

Each woman looked so defeated when the older woman spoke that Della found herself reneging on the earlier decision to return her items.

"No, I'm not married," Della whispered. "Or dating anybody at the moment, but I just can't conceive of some man walking up to me in this store and trying to pick me up."

"No, that's where you're wrong. I know—it was the size eight that threw you."

Della smiled and simply shook her head while the women fell into a companionable laughter.

"First of all, if you don't have a guy, and this one *definitely* found you attractive—which I might add, *you are*—then I see no harm in it at all, especially if he's not married, engaged, or livin' with anyone. Besides, you've got somethin' to fill up a thirty-eight D-cup, honey, and this size eight don't stand a chance against that. He's a Southern man, could tell from his manner . . . a healthy girl can get plenty of eligible invitations down here." The older woman folded her arms over her chest with a smile and sighed. "You must be newly divorced. Can always tell, sugah. Been there, seen it, done it."

She then nodded toward the young black girl who now had a customer to wait on. "I'ma have Saundra make that call, and we'll hold the certificate—and we'll tell him you declined it. However, if you pop back in here in a coupla days, we'll also have the scoop for you, guaranteed. . . . You don't have to do any of this, and we are only tending to normal policy to carry out a customer's wishes, namely, accept his returned merchandise and try to give it to another customer of *our* choice. You're our choice, so don't look a gift horse in the mouth—but we'll hold the certificate for thirty days, in case you have a change of heart. If not, no problem, and we'll give it to the first mother that crosses our threshold. Fair?"

Della finally nodded with amused defeat, smiled, and was about to leave when she was surprised by a big hug from all three store clerks. This was the weirdest shopping experience of her life. And the older woman had a point: Why should her decision to buy what she was going to buy be swayed by a chance encounter that temporarily depressed her? Ridiculous! The evolution of it all was just positively insane, but she found herself laughing, a little excited and a bit revived as each woman took a turn to give her a quick good-luck hug. Deep.

People just didn't do that where she was from. But all the fuss and merriment over something so stupid felt good. Even the mild female conspiracy felt good—if she dared call it fun. Now *that* was too shameless. She couldn't remember when she'd squealed and laughed and acted simple over some mystery guy. Life had gotten in the way of plain old-fashioned girl stuff. Della giggled as she hugged the women back. Elizabeth Hawthorne and her co-conspirators were a hoot.

"And, you ain't from down here, either, are ya?" the oldest clerk said. "That's all right, too. We Southerners are big on huggin' and hospitality—you'll get used to it in no time."


It had gone worse than planned. Women were psychic. Vanessa had launched into a diatribe as soon as his call connected to her cell phone—caller ID was a nemesis. She didn't want to do dinner, wanted to know who he'd taken out to Lenox Mall, then went berserk, and told him it was over.

Byron had held the telephone receiver in his hand and just stared at it. What, she was having him tailed? When the door to his condo buzzed, he let his breath out slowly.

He took his time going to the door and set the cordless receiver down as he passed the sofa, knowing that there was a woman as angry as a hornet ready to go ten rounds of verbal assaults on him just on the other side of the wood dividing them. She was ringing and pounding simultaneously—see, this was exactly why he didn't do deep relationships. This was the crazy way they ended. High drama. This was also why he'd moved way out to Roswell, instead of locating himself in the black professional zones of Dunwoody or Stone Mountain; he'd wanted to live anonymously, hidden where nobody would fall by, or know him well enough as a neighbor to speak as he came and went. Where nobody would show up at his door unannounced with theatrics.

Managing the locks, he opened the door and was about to tell Vanessa he was sorry that things had to go the way they did, but he didn't get a chance to. Her palm had slapped the spit out of his mouth before he could speak. Byron sighed. This was really bad.

"Vanessa, listen—"

"Don't you try to make some lame apology to me, you no-good, two-timing son of a bitch! How dare you be in Victoria's Secret buying some *cow* a set of lingerie in my favorite color! So this is who you've been seeing while you told me you were studying for three months—and made *me* wait, lying, telling me you had to focus? We couldn't have sex, couldn't go out, couldn't spend any time together because you had to study your stupid little airplane manuals, and I believed you!"

Her hazel eyes sparkled with tears and her light complexion had turned beet red.

"Ness, I wasn't buying—"

"Liar! My girlfriend saw you! She was in Lenox Mall this morning with her baby boy. She saw you in there standing next to her, buying her some black violet thing that cost a mint! Then you were in the Food Court all behind her buying her lunch, and whatnot—carrying her bag through the mall, Negro! So, I laid in wait for your no-good butt in my Jeep downstairs, knowing you said you'd call—thinking you had a couple of hours till we got together, but I was in my car. So, deny it. I want to know where this relationship is headed *right now,* damn it."

"You're right. We need to talk."

# Chapter 4

Serenity. That was the goal. She had gone home, cleaned, run a thousand errands to keep herself in perpetual motion, taken a shower to break Atlanta's bond of heat and humidity on her body, tried to get a jump-start on her work for next week—but gave up. There was no amount of frenetic activity that was going to shake this thing she was feeling way too deep inside her. It was embarrassing even to admit that to herself. Yet, it was all so basic and yet so very, very complex at the same time. She missed the touch, taste, sound, and smell of maleness in her space, and having only one of her five senses so thoroughly indulged today by a man who was pure eye candy had simply messed her up. Badly.

She'd steadied herself and taken the group's wise advice—go to the same places she would normally go on a date. They'd told her not to allow being single to keep her from anything she could enjoy if she were part of a pair. Movies, dancing, cruises, and so on were still within her domain. That's right. Damn right. Sometimes she could go out with other people—girlfriends, colleagues—or sometimes, like tonight, she could be content to walk into a nice establishment and dine alone. Why should she require an escort (female or otherwise) to entitle her to a sumptuous meal? She had to get past her inner issues and learn to just experience life to the fullest—alone.

Yeah. Problem was, that this thing called life wasn't designed to be lived alone, not indefinitely. If life were meant to be lived solo, then it would have been set up so that one didn't crave the other half of the species.

Della looked at the quiet street, which hosted a restored antebellum mansion turned exquisite restaurant. She needed to do this. To be able to walk in and sit down to eat in a pretty place that had pretty yellowed lace and smelled of magnolia blossoms in a grand old neighborhood with mature shade trees, banked on a still lane—just like back home. It reminded her of the Mount Airy–Chestnut Hill section of Philly, where she'd been raised. Maybe that's why she'd come to Asher: it was a house, not a glitzy chrome-and-glass establishment. Actually, it was more of a tearoom than a restaurant. It was upscale, but not so stiff that she'd really feel alone when eating alone. Plus, it was so close to where she lived, practically a stone's throw from her apartment.

The servers seemed like they were being extra nice to her, noting that she was dining solo, and were more than attentive. That was a special touch she appreciated tonight more than ever. She ticked off every positive attribute, hoping that would make being by herself more palatable. And it worked . . . a little.

Della surveyed the subtle charm of the environment, then checked out the menu. They served four-course meals here, but she'd order only one or two. Four courses were no fun alone—she didn't care what the group claimed about independence.

Maybe she should have relented, listened to Gillian, and gone out with the girls to Café 290 or Club 112 while she was still within Atlanta's city limits, places that offered some jazz or great seafood— but she just didn't feel like it tonight. She didn't need or want to see all the upscale couples at small tables in 290's jazz nook, or spend the evening watching people dance to romantic R&B at 112. It had been too long since she'd been able to walk into an establishment and know that she had someone to dance with her. Doing the wait-and-hope drill wasn't within her tonight. But, she did miss having the music to join her while she ate.

If she'd been thinking, she would have crossed the highway while at Lenox Mall to go over to The Ritz-Carlton to listen to live jazz in the lobby lounge. She could have eaten a salad or something light there. But that would have put her in too close proximity to Phipps Plaza—where the real divas, like Halle Berry, shopped. However, that would also have sent her right into the arms of Intimacy, a boutique that made custom-designed lingerie for women with fuller dimensions. Della sighed. Nope. She was sworn off exquisite boudoir fare, just as she'd given up fried foods, ribs, macaroni and cheese, and other soul cuisine dripping in butter, at least for now.

Instead, she'd have smoked salmon and white asparagus drizzled in green goddess dressing to go with the chardonnay she'd just ordered. It would have been nice to experience the wine pairings with dinner, but what the hell, she wasn't doing the full monty. She hated feeling like this. Out of sorts, all jumpy for positively no reason at all. Her gaze continued to rove over her choices, and sudden hunger from not eating all day gurgled in the pit of her stomach. That had to be it. Her blood sugar was dropping, and she'd been a whirlwind of activity since the morning.

"Oooohhh . . . but the desserts . . . Why did they have to have this apple bread pudding on here when I am trying to behave?"

Della shook her head and closed her eyes. Now she was talking to herself—a true sign of losing one's mind, or perspective. Abstinence. All things in good measure, she inwardly chided. She'd overindulged at the mall, but would not do so at the table. In fact, she would not overindulge in even thinking about what she might overindulge in anymore.

She snapped the leather-bound menu closed with conviction and moved the temptation to the edge of the table, without even opening her eyes.


For a moment, he hadn't been able to respond to the maître d' as he changed his reservation for two to a reservation for one. Three times in one day? His mother often talked of things like this—signs. Until now, he hadn't believed in junk like that. But as sure as he was standing at the podium now, momentarily dazed, there she was, her face toward the window, her eyes closed again, the candle turning her amber skin bronze and lighting the line of her jaw from beneath with gold.

Peach linen sheathed her, and a white cloth napkin was draped over her lap. Her long, curvaceous legs were crossed at the ankle and tucked under her chair, with a sheen of oil on them, tapering into her long, narrow feet that arched high in the little strapped sandals that exposed her perfect, manicured toes. The table was set for one, he noted as he passed, hesitated, and took a risk, leaving the server that was guiding him ten paces ahead of him.

"I've heard three is a lucky number," he murmured with a smile.

Della looked up and immediately caught her breath.

"I didn't mean to startle you," he said, his grin widening. "Seems I have a habit of doing that."

She cocked that one eyebrow again, and a slow smile eased its way out onto her face.

"Are you waiting for someone, or dining alone?"

She studied him, then glanced down at the table. The server that had been leading him was in midaisle.

"I was having a quiet dinner by myself," she said, her tone amused. "You?"

His smile broadened to give her a glimpse of dazzling white. She looked at his mouth. She shook her head and laughed. She couldn't believe this was happening.

"I was intent on a quiet dinner alone, but I'm flexible," he said pleasantly. "May I?"

She let go of an easy sigh. "Suit yourself. But I hope you aren't stalking me."

He took that as enough of an invitation to redirect the server to set up a place for him to join her. The server offered a nod and made arrangements for Byron to be seated at her table.

"I'm not stalking you," he told her with an gentle laugh as he sat across from her. "You can ask the maître d'. I've had a reservation for three days. Guess I'm just lucky, is all."

"Guess I was fortunate that I didn't need one, then."

Her smile was so pretty, but not half as pretty as the way she demurely slid it away from him as she lowered her lashes over those big brown eyes. Gentle. That was what it seemed like, what she seemed to have in her. A gentle spirit.

"You're having chardonnay?"

She nodded and glanced toward the window.

"Mind if I order a bottle for the table?"

She gave a small shrug. "Suit yourself."

Dang, she was tough, gentle spirit or not. Byron perused the wine list and settled on the William Hill Reserve. The sommelier waited for him to go through all the cursory formalities of accepting the bottle, inspecting the cork, and taking the first small swig with a nod. And she watched him go through these male rituals with a knowing smile, saying nothing, but intently focused on his every move. Finally with the two glasses before them, he leveled his gaze at her. His nerves were too frayed to play games, and the other axiom with the number three was, three strikes and you were out. He wasn't blowing this possible last chance. After a while, fate got tired of being tested.

"I said something today that made you walk away from me. What was it?"

Della looked startled. She'd been prepared for a line, for some man-bull, but not an honest "let's talk" vibe. She studied the man before her, his intense, earnest expression, the way his collarless, rust-colored silk shirt enhanced the gold and red tones in his ebony skin. There was something casual in the way his unstructured black suit jacket belied the muscular form beneath it. But his eyes were on her face, not strolling over her body as they had done earlier in the day. It was a noninvasive stare, one that asked questions but made no assumptions. She relaxed a bit.

"I didn't know how to take your statement," she murmured after a moment of contemplation. "You said you weren't married, didn't have kids—but it was the tone in your voice. I do have a child: a daughter, age three. I'm divorced, and have been through a lot of drama. I wasn't looking for any additional mess today. I was just minding my business and trying to shop."

He nodded. "My apologies on the tone. I wasn't trying to say anything about you. I was trying to let you know that I didn't have a life out there in the world that I hadn't taken responsibility for. That was it. No judgment."

She nodded. "Then my apologies, as well. I didn't know what to make of a guy carrying a pink bag." She smiled.

He chuckled and raised his wineglass to her, took a sip from it, and then set it down very carefully. "As you can see, I am no longer carrying a pink bag. Was that being blunt?"

She smiled. "Well, you most certainly were blunt today."

He nodded, his expression becoming warmer and more introspective. "I am also honest to a fault. When I said I was breaking up with somebody, it was the gospel."

She stared at him.

"For real. Still have the handprint on my jaw."

He laughed now, leaned closer, and turned his head so that she could inspect his cheek—which bore no sign of the alleged assault. But in so doing, he'd also given her an unintended whiff of him; it was a deep, woodsy aroma that made her stomach flip-flop.

"And you're out tonight solo, I suppose, just minding your business? Right after a breakup? Hmmm."

There was that eyebrow of hers again. But it came with a sly, sexy, lopsided smile. God, she was gorgeous. Encouraged, he pressed on.

"I sat in my condo for a while, thinking about all sorts of things. I was going to go listen to some jazz, had even contemplated getting wasted— but I have to take more than two hundred innocent people up in the air tomorrow morning. They don't have a thing to do with my mess, and they are all depending on the person in the cockpit to be operating with all his faculties. Then, for some reason, I figured, why not eat some real food, instead of ordering Chinese takeout or a pizza and drowning it with a six-pack of beer. Didn't want to stay in, but didn't want to go *out* out. Does that make sense? Decided to come to a place that looked like a home, for once. Didn't feel like a big crowd. Had a reservation. Found my way to where I was gonna go in the first place, sans date."

What he'd said was so basic and so honest that it siphoned the truth from her, as well. He was such an odd mixture of differences, too. His voice drawled Southern, and many of his figures of speech waxed extremely down-home; then he'd throw in something that she'd expect to hear from a Northern yuppie.

"Yeah," she finally said, her voice low and soft. "That's why I'm here myself. Tomorrow, I have to pick up somebody innocent, who is depending on me to be sane, responsible, and her mother. So, getting trashed or being tired or cranky is unfair to her. She, like your passengers, deserves me at my best."

He was glad that a server had approached the table. The draw to this woman was so strong at the moment, he would have covered her hand with his own, just to feel the connection to a sane human being. But it was way too soon to even go there. So, instead, he sat back and accepted a menu.

"I confess to being a hedonist," he said with an easy chuckle, his gaze trained on the menu. "I'm going to chow down, so please don't be offended—I haven't eaten all day."

Now, she really laughed. "You are going to make me stray off my diet, brother. But go ahead. Suit yourself."

"Diet?" He put the menu down slowly and looked at her sad smile. "You have *got* to be kidding me."

Somewhat startled by his intense response, she tilted her head, asking him to clarify his statement without words.

"I beg your pardon, but you're in fabulous shape. . . . I mean, seriously, Della. In my humble opinion, everything is more than where it should be, if you don't mind my saying. Don't mess with perfection, sis. Why are you dieting? I mean, tonight, can't you live it up a little?"

Both flattered and stunned by his directness, she outright laughed. "You know, I have come to realize that Southerners always seem to beg your pardon first and then say what they were going to say anyway."

"Well, that's our way," he replied, laughing, and very glad that she wasn't offended by his unplanned outburst. He wanted to reach across the table and touch her. Instead, he picked up his menu again and held it as a poor substitute to her hand as he spoke. "We eat. We tell the truth. And, we're very hospitable—and if we like you, you'll know it right off. If we don't, you'll know that, too—right off."

"Things are very different where I'm from, but Philly is the closest thing to a big down south in the Northeast corridor."

He loved the way she easily laughed with him and allowed the smooth lilt of her voice to waft between them. He dispatched his order of fresh mountain trout to the server and tempted Della to add a few more courses to her meal. It was not so much that he was interested in breaking her regime, but rather an attempt to order enough food to keep her sitting there, talking to him, and smiling as long as he could.

"Let me clarify the first point that got in between us," he said, letting out a long, patient breath. "My sister, Ruth, is thirty-one, and has a fifteen-year-old son. You do the math. It almost put my mother in her grave. My momma is real old school; raised us with a switch in one hand and a Bible in the other, and stayed married to the same man for almost fifty years. Me and my two younger brothers, Isaiah and Ezekiel, Zay and Zeek, helped my mother and father raise our nephew. They all have kids now, too. We all raised them. That's why I was so adamant about not making any that would not be connected to that support system . . . and after seeing what my sister went through, I didn't want to be party to that type of pain. Children are a blessing."

There. It had been said, and all he could do was hope that she got the message.

"Deep," she murmured, keeping her gaze focused on his eyes. "I just thought . . . No, correction. Let me say that I'm sorry I took it the wrong way. I didn't know you."

"That's cool." Levity returned to his voice. "Can I see her?"

"No. I don't let men I've just met meet my child like that, and—"

"I mean, a picture. Do you have a picture in your wallet of your princess?"

She had to laugh as she reached for her purse. "My bad. Yes, I do have a picture."

"You're tough, sis. Don't give a brother the least of a break, and definitely no credit." He shook his head as he accepted the wallet from her. "I've got enough home training to know you wouldn't let me see her unless Momma bear had done a complete inspection. I'm not crazy, you know."

"The jury is still out on that." She giggled, watching him as he gazed down at her child.

"She's a cutie . . . pretty, just like her mother. No matter what went down, her daddy must be proud."

His tone had lost its mirth, and his voice had gone to a reverent whisper as he took his time to study the photo. She was so glad that the waiter had come to pour more wine and to bring the first course. She'd wanted to reach across the table and touch the side of Byron's face, to just feel that smooth, clean-cut skin beneath her palm and to wipe away wherever slap had supposedly landed on it.

"No," she said softly. "She wasn't a boy, and her mother got fat while carrying her, so her father is not impressed by either of us anymore." She let out a long sigh, determined not to lay her soul bare in front of a person she just met. "Which is why I moved to Atlanta to take a PR job at Coca-Cola. New start."

Byron's gaze had not left her face. Even though she was pushing food around on her plate with a fork, she could feel his intense stare without looking at him.

"Then, I understand why you think men are crazy, because if you will beg my pardon, the man is absolutely out of his mind."

Silence fell between them for a while, and she was glad that Byron hadn't said more. Her nervous system was on overload, and she'd needed the few fragile minutes to blink back the sudden moisture that had filled her eyes. The man had said the nicest thing to her that any man had ever said . . . and the look on his face had actually said it all over again. He'd glanced down at Claire's picture, and looked at her child for a long time. Awe had dawned in his expression, something

Robert Mitchell, the child's own father, had never felt. And, coming from this wild, direct, very confident-bordering-on-arrogant man, it was too much all in one sitting. Half of her wanted to flee the scene, and the other half of her wanted to call the waiter for the check to take him home. None of what she was feeling made sense—being still and quiet was the best, and safest, bet.

"You have brothers and sisters?"

Byron's question came out of the blue on a chipper note, and it almost made her choke on a piece of salmon.

"I have two younger sisters, Caroline and Dianne. Mom and Dad gave up after three tries for a boy. I was first out the chute, so I was Dad's buddy. He passed a few years back. Heart attack. Mom still misses him. I almost didn't relocate here because of that, but my sisters are still back home."

"Sorry to hear that. Lost my pop last year, too. Stroke. They broke the mold."

"Yeah. They did. I'm sorry to hear about your dad, too. Nothing like it, when you've had a good one."

Both cast a glance beyond the window for a moment before allowing their lines of vision to settle on one another.

"How did you wind up with the name Byron, when the rest of your siblings have biblical names?"

He laughed at the unexpected question. "My first name is Joshua. But around the way, the fellas got used to calling me By . . . so Joshua dropped off into obscurity. I soothed my mother by using J. Byron Fulton for professional purposes. It was a compromise."

Della thought about his business card in her purse and smiled, taking a slow bite of her food.

He watched her pull the fork from between her lips with careful deliberation. Maybe it was the effect of the wine, or the three months of abstinence during the no-nonsense study required to pass the test for the next jumbo jet he had to learn—he wasn't sure. But the woman was having a decided effect on his libido as she ate.

"What do you like to do for fun?"

She smiled. He was interviewing her. But he had an interesting, nonstructured, free-flowing way about doing so.

"I like jazz and R&B, and like to dance . . . but I love the movies. Don't get a chance to go see flick, though, until they come on cable. Can't always send Claire to a girlfriend to watch her. That's one of the downsides in moving away from family. My mother has only one grandchild at the moment—my sisters don't have children yet. So, Claire is her heart. I got spoiled by the help to raise my little bird while in Philly."

He nodded, and she glimpsed the man who was devouring a plate as he listened to her. She noted how he seemed to be so comfortable in his own skin, and so content with what had been served. She couldn't remember a dinner out with Robert where he didn't complain or send something back.

"I never get to go to the movies, either . . . always working, so we'll have to rectify that. But, I like the oldies, and for jazz, I'm a purist. I can listen to a CD while I drive wherever I find myself. The smooth stuff is cool, but I grew up on the jazz masters." Byron spoke with his fork, gesturing with it to make his point.

"The masters?"

"See, now, girl, you done made another erroneous assumption. Just because I'm from way down here in Macon, doesn't mean I didn't listen to what y'all up North claim as your domain. And I also grew up listening to Billie Holiday, because that's what my dad played relentlessly while he was working under a car, or out in the yard, or fixing whatever was broken in the house."

"Sounds like you had a ball as a kid, come from good people."

Her eyes sparkled as she offered what he took as a genuine compliment. Her acceptance of him was conveyed in the reverent tone of her voice, and the way she didn't wrinkle her nose when he alluded to his parents' working-class background. Why had he wasted his time with anyone not like her? he wondered. That she was the type of woman he'd been searching for became so clear, so fast, as she drank in his memories and shared them with him like a good bottle of wine.

"We did, Del. You know, I used to get my butt whupped so much for being the adventurous one—beyond redemption, my momma would claim, but *we had fun.*"

"I can only imagine—three boys. Bless your mother's soul. But my sisters and I were no stranger to the switch. My mother had an old slipper she'd tan our backsides with, and as the oldest, I was always the first in line."

Her laughter was so rich, so thickly laced with natural resonance that he picked up his glass, needing to do something with his hands rather than reach for hers.

"Me and my brothers, we did it all. Ran the streets all summer, went exploring and getting into foolishness, worked like mules at crazy chores, too, as my parents didn't play, but there was always a family gathering. Was nothing like it. Swore to Jesus that unless I could duplicate that for my kids, I wasn't making any. That steadfast position also got me in a *lot* of trouble."

She had to laugh. The brother was making a heavy case, and she knew it. No matter. She just loved the rich, deep sound of his voice. She loved the way he'd just shortened her name without even thinking about it, as though a natural habit. It had been a long time since she'd been so flattered, or had been interviewed. Normally men talked about what was important to them—their careers, not what should be priority, their families. She liked this different shift J. Byron Fulton brought to the table between them.

"The adventurous one. I can see it," she replied in earnest.

"I was always curious. Made me learn to fly. Went in the military," he said quickly between bites of food. "Air force. Got out, did some small props for a while, crop dusting, whatever I had to do to get back up in the air—but couldn't shake turbines out of my system. Decided to take a chance on commercial jets. God blessed me. Case closed. I went all over the world." He looked up suddenly. "There are so many awesome nooks and crannies on the planet, Del. And there is *nothing* like flying."

For a moment all she could do was stare at him. The way he said her name ran all through her. His eyes, the intensity of his voice, and the sheer adrenaline that reflected in both, shot through her skeleton, connected to each vertebra, and ignited a spark between her legs. *Whew!* Maybe she would order dessert. He poured more wine, not even waiting for the server. Yeah, he could feel it, too. They both needed to cool this thing down.

"There's this place, Club Kaya, downtown . . . R&B—maybe, one night, when you're free, and I don't have to get up to fly in the morning, we can go?"

His voice had come out in a rush, in a half-invitation, half-assertive question, but she could feel what was in it, what hadn't been said. Brother was coming in for a landing before she'd turned on the runway lights, and he didn't give a damn. She wanted to laugh, but couldn't anymore—not with him looking at her like that . . . a Hail Mary in his eyes as he spoke and seemed to hold his breath at the same time. Heaven help her.

"Yeah, I guess—"

"You ever been to Bermuda?"

He'd dropped landing gear. Oh, shit. "Well, uh, no, I've been to Jamaica, and the Bahamas, but uh—"

"Good. Gotta show you Bermuda, and Saint Lucia, one day soon. Different, but awesome. Don't stay in a hotel—stay in a villa."

He was gonna hit the tower. This time, she had to laugh and look away from him. Oh, Lord. "What?"

"I'm not being fresh. I'm being real." He sat back, glanced at his watch, and took a sip of wine and set it down carefully, and returned his gaze to her. "I have to get up real early in the morning, and at the same time, want to stay here much longer than I know I should, so I'ma just say it plain. I like you. You come from good people; I can tell. Can I have a number, work or home, or whatever you want to provide so I can call you?"

"Uhm . . ."

"I've been wasting my time."

"What!"

"No, no, no. That's not what I meant about what I said, but I've been wasting time," he said, his expression sincere and perplexed.

She sat very, very still.

"I've taken people with me while I was working. Stayed in hotels all over the place. Sent them shopping, or whatever. But I have never gone to these places to just relax—isn't that crazy? Will you go? One day. Maybe. No pressure. But I'm not in Atlanta most of the time, is what I'm saying. This ain't coming out right at all."

She relaxed and looked away, a new tension replacing the one that just fled her. Yeah, she definitely needed some wine. "Uh . . ."

"Yeah. I know. Crazy. My buddies all take their wives and kids, or lovers, whatever, to stay in villas, relax—but I'm always moving. Looking for the next thing. Been wasting time. Just decided."

"Decided what?" Her glass was midair, her mind was trying to make sense of this quick, rapid-fire exchange, and only half of it was making sense. But what she was quite sure of was that this man had asked her to spend the night with him—halfway around the world somewhere, and sometime soon.

"Are you seeing anybody?"

"Well, uh, at the moment, no."

"Good. Me either."

"When's your birthday?"

"September twentieth. Byron, what—?"

"A Libra!" He slapped his forehead and laughed. "I should have known."

She was chuckling with him, but wasn't exactly sure why.

"Y'all take a while to make up your minds. Always balancing, making decisions. I'm a quick study. You like beauty, harmony, and peace. I listened to a card reader saying about the signs, one time. Yup. But y'all are also quite the sensualists, Libras. I have to tell you, if you don't mind me saying so, that in the store you blew me away when you were buying that gown. No wonder. I haven't been right all day, after that."

As he issued another intense appraisal of her, she felt her face flash warm. He'd seen her long before she'd wanted him to. And he was saying stuff that was rocking her resolve to remain distant. Oh, boy—this man was dessert overload.

"Can we back this up a few paces?" she hedged, trying to regain her former balance. "First of all, yes, I'd like to go dancing with you one night, but I need plenty of lead time to arrange for a sitter. And, I don't have a problem with giving you my number."

"Done," he said with a wry grin. "I will give you work, home, and cell phone—this way you can know there's no reason, whatsoever, that you can't call. If I'm in the air, then I'll call you back when I touch down. Fair?"

She let her smile answer the last part of his question. "Second of all, while I'm not seeing anyone, it has been a very long time since I've dated . . . and I'm very selective about entering into something that might wind up . . . uhm . . . I want to take my time with things, if I were to begin seeing somebody."

"Understood," he replied in a jovial tone. "I knew that when I saw you."

His statement made her laugh. "How, pray tell, did you *know* that when you hadn't even said a word to me?"

"Simple. It was the way you shopped. Very selective, very refined taste. Not hurried. Next question."

"You just, allegedly, came out of something. Am I correct?"

He smiled. Took his time, now. She'd made him fire his engines too fast. It was the way she'd really heard him, listened to his reminiscent stories about home, offered her own, and had not inquired once about his profession—but just drank him in with her eyes, and was able to backtrack and recall every detail of what he'd said. He'd never had a woman really hear him past his uniform. This one did, and it shattered his focus.

"Truth be told," he began at a slow pace, "it ended three months ago when I had to study for a new jet exam and refused to come out to play. Didn't see *anybody* during that period. That's the one thing I don't do, is play with lives. When it's time to learn something, it gets one hundred percent of my attention—then I can relax."

She nodded, but the smile hadn't vanished from her face. "Then, you play, right?"

"See," he murmured, leaning forward, "that's just it. Today, I was tired of playing."

"Oh, just like that, huh?" She chuckled and finished her wine.

He watched the residue of it leave a moist spot on her bottom lip, and then witnessed the tip of her tongue quickly wipe it away as the liquid slid down her slender throat. "Yeah," he replied, an octave lower than intended. Damn, this woman was fine.

"Why?" His voice was working her discipline. She discreetly pressed her knees together under the table.

Her doe eyes held him in an inescapable question that demanded a straight answer. "Because, I saw you . . . then talked to you, and now have had the opportunity to get to know you a little better . . . and my first gut hunch was right, like it normally is. I don't feel like playing anymore. Especially not right at the moment."

"I don't feel like playing games, either. I've also wasted a lot of time."

He watched those bashful lashes lower again as she twirled the crystal glass by its stem between her fingers. Della Mitchell could make a man bleed the truth.

"Del, every day I know, despite what my sister claims—just because I don't spend three hours a week in church like she does, that we are here only by the thin thread of Grace. Technology and engines notwithstanding, we take a lot for granted. You can't know that until you look out the front window and see nothing but clouds, or look down and see buildings and traffic that looks like ants. Been trying to tell Ruth for years that I have a daily religious experience when I go up for work and come back down without a bump or a skid. Somebody's watching over me, has to be more to it than steel and diesel. After seeing you three times today, I'm convinced."

She nodded, but could not glance at him. Not when she was feeling what she was feeling. Every pore in her body felt like he'd lit a match against it.

"Within the parameters of your own decorum," he chuckled, "one day, come with me. That's all I'm asking. Just consider it."

"I'll consider the offer," she murmured, wishing she had more wine, but knowing she didn't need any. Her mouth had gone dry when his request began as a forced chuckle and ended on a fervent rush of breath.

"I know I sorta jumped the gun, but after you've spent a lot of time wasting time, and everything you've always wanted is sitting right there in front of you . . . well, like I told you earlier today, it can make a grown man act stupid."

He was glad that she laughed a deep, down-home belly laugh of forgiveness for his assertive ways. He needed her to laugh to break the tension, to help him get his head together, and to back him up a bit. Oh, yeah. He needed her to be diplomatic and to remind him that he didn't know her that well, because in all honesty, he was really close to making a fool of himself.

"You want some dessert?"

"I don't think I can force another thing down." She looked up at him, but wished in a way that she hadn't. The air around her seemed thick, making it hard to breathe. Goose bumps rose on her arms as she stared at the blatant hunger he displayed; he looked at her like she might be dessert. If the man could read minds, he'd already know how much she was considering that option.

"Want to split the apple bread pudding with me that's calling my name : . . since you don't want to go all the way, tonight?"

Oh, shit . . . the man was definitely not playing. All she could do was nod.

He had not meant to say that to her the way he did, but his mind couldn't play games with what the rest of him was feeling. All he could do was hope that she hadn't been offended. Damn, he needed air, but he was in no position to stand up at present. He motioned for a server. Yeah, somebody come over here and break the tension, bring him a cup of coffee, and a tall cold glass of water. Her arms had goose pimples, and it was showing through the linen that held her cleavage, no disrespect intended. She'd lowered her lids all shy and took in a slow breath through her nose. Where was the waiter when you needed him? She was playing with the stem of her glass. God help him.

"Two forks?" The waiter asked with a smile.

All they could do was nod.

# Chapter 5

Della leaned on her apartment door once she'd locked it behind her and closed her eyes, not even bothering to flip on the light. Her mind kept replaying the chance restaurant meeting that had turned into a wondrous date, and for the life of her, she could not shake the sight of that man slowly devouring apple bread pudding. She shivered with the thought and wrapped her arms around her, the palm of her hand still burning from where he's put his card within it and kissed her knuckles as he'd folded her fingers closed over it.

His mouth had been a whisper against her skin, and as he stood too near her beside her vehicle, the scent of his cologne mingled with the wine and sweetness of dessert on his breath had practically made her dizzy. They'd walked awhile in the warm evening air, and as they'd leisurely strolled, looking at the homes and listening to the crickets, watching lightning bugs float a lazy path, he'd talked about the houses in Dunwoody and Stone Mountain . . . had told her that's where he'd like to go someday, if he stayed in Atlanta. *If* was a big word.

No matter what the girls said, all their wisdom and warnings notwithstanding, the question was not *if,* but *when* and *where*—

assuming he ever called her again. And, if he didn't, Lord knew it would be a battle for her not to call him. Whichever sister tossed this man back into circulation had to be missing her mind! God bless her, though.

She allowed her eyes to adjust to the moonlight. Somehow she didn't want to chase the feelings away with anything artificial. Although risk was not in her nature anymore, the man had flooded her system with a sudden willingness to take chances. For this one, yeah, she'd take a risk, no doubt. Dayum. In all her years of dating, she never had, but this felt so right. Byron wasn't like the staid, professional men she'd been with before. He was crazy. Impulsive. Real direct. But he also had a gentleness of spirit that was hard to define or wrap words around.

Her gaze scanned her apartment. Here? While Claire was gone, maybe? What was the protocol for that these days? What did one say? Your place or mine? That was so tired, too obvious, but dayum, three years was kicking her butt. Five, truthfully, if she counted the two years of sterile living with Robert . . . and God had dropped a hedonist on her? Was this a cosmic test? If so, she was failing like a mug. Della giggled. "I'm sorry, Lord," she yelled out. "Help me, Father, 'cause this one's gonna make me sin!"

Laughing and giddy, she twirled around in the middle of the floor in the dark. She felt so free. Yeah, she'd fly with that brother, anywhere he wanted to go. Her gaze landed on the coffee table, the sofa, and the art about her. It was neat, clean, adorned with prints from the motherland . . . and for the first time since her divorce, she was actually glad that she'd been granted the freedom to have a space all her own. Yes. She was single. Yes, she'd laid claim to this new place and had decorated it, put up curtains and miniblinds, and had turned it into a home for her and Claire. Had made a cute, pink rose-and-bunny-bordered place of comfort in her baby's room. Yes, Robert had wanted only things of value, not her collection of treasures and fabrics, and art, and things handed down from her generations of Mitchell women. Yeah, she could break her fast here . . . if he called. And, for the first time, she did not feel guilty.

Feeling light, she paced into her bedroom, and instead of flipping on the night light, she lit a candle, breathing in the fragrant vanilla. Then she laughed out loud again. *If* could work wonderfully here in her one room of pure decadence. Her gaze landed on the king-size bed that had four posts draped with sheer curtains. Her newly unmarried hand had picked every satin pillow on it. Every deep, rich golden color, like an Egyptian queen's lair, had been hers alone to choose, no matter the price. Every fern and stalk of elephant grass that made it an oasis did not have to be haggled about or fought over. Every masterpiece that graced the walls, she'd selected, just like the tall, wrought-iron candle holders—ones that Robert claimed took up too much floor space, or served no purpose other than silly aesthetics—she'd hunted for and found . . . and might just share with a fellow hedonist. . . . *If* he called . . . new black-violet silk might be his surprise. Della sighed.

The telephone rang. Her body felt sexy, lithe, and alive as she sauntered over to it to tell Gillian about her night. But a pleasant baritone filled her ear.

"I'm not testing the numbers you gave me," Byron chuckled softly. "Just wanted to say good night. Naw, truth is, I couldn't sleep. Real truth is, haven't enjoyed myself this much in anyone's company in a long time, if ever. So, indulge me for just a little bit."

She sat down slowly on the side of the bed, clutching the phone against her cheek with her eyes closed. "Yeah, I can do that," she whispered. "I had fun, too."

"Still think I'm stalking you?" His chuckle was warm and flowed through the receiver right into the marrow of her bones.

"No. Glad you keep turning up when least expected."

For a moment he said nothing.

"Me, too," he murmured. "Six days, then I have two off. Is that enough notice for a real, planned date?"

She chuckled. "Yeah."

"Good."

Again, heavy-laden silence fell between them. They were down to two-word responses. Her finger traced the gold threads in her comforter. Music in the distance clicked on. He was playing Billie Holiday's "God Bless the Child." She sighed and strained to hear the ballad.

"I touch down in Atlanta on Friday at nineteen hundred—I mean, seven P.M.—could get in from the airport and change, and come get you at nine, if that would be okay?"

"I'd like that."

"Good."

"But won't you need to rest, maybe? Wouldn't Saturday be better for you?"

"No. It'll be hard enough making it through the week. One more day will just make me nuts. Friday. Cool?"

Wow . . . what could she say to that except yes?

"Cool. But what should I wear, what do you want to do?"

Silence. She almost giggled, reading his profound answer embedded in his hesitation.

"Uhm . . . yeah, uh, dancing. You said you like to dance, right?"

"Uhmm-hmmm." She hadn't meant her voice to come out so low and sexy, but his embarrassed stammer did something to her. Let her know his thoughts had drifted, like hers, to the taboo subject underlying their conversation.

"Then how about dinner, dancing, something like that?"

"Something like that sounds great." She couldn't help but laugh. The man was repeating himself.

"Good."

"Okay."

"Yeah."

Silence. His breath sent a torch into her ear. Whew. Yeah, okay.

"That sounds nice, Byron. I'm looking forward to it," she forced herself to say. It was truth. Diplomatic. They needed to keep the conversation flowing, though. Anything to break the silence that was about to make her tell him to come over.

"Me, too," he finally replied.

"Don't you have to get up early in the morning?" It was time to get this man off the telephone. He was making her take breaths in shallow sips.

"Yeah . . . right . . . you're right. I should get off the phone, I suppose."

"Uhmm-hmmm."

"Okay, Del. You have a good night."

"You, too."

"Bye."

"Bye."

Silence. Neither of them hung up, and they both laughed.

"Okay, should we do this on the count of three?" he said.

"This is so silly."

"I know. Oh, I'll need your address, if I'm going to pick you up."

"Okay. Do you have a pen?"

"Naw. Tell you what; give it to me when I call."

"Okay."

"I don't trust myself with that information at the moment."

She laughed. "I hear you."

"Do you?"

"Yeah. Completely . . . because, neither do I."

"Was more information than I really needed to hear right now." He chuckled again low in his throat. "But I heard you. You hear me?"

"Yeah." There was a long pause. She lay down on the bed and shut her eyes. *Be strong, be strong—it is way too soon, and you know it,* she reminded herself. "Hang up, because I can't."

Silence. She'd expected him to laugh, but he didn't.

"Wanna give me your address now?"

"No." She giggled. "Yes, and no, but no. Not yet, right now, anyway."

She heard him let out a long breath on a low timbre of laughter. It carried hope and wistfulness, and a strand of disappointment ran through it. Oh, yeah, she'd heard him, loud and clear.

"Okay. I'ma call you from Chicago."

"Okay."

"Then I have to go to Denver."

"Okay."

"Then Dallas, L.A., Sisco, Seattle, Boise, then back South to hit New Orleans, and back to Atlanta."

Deep. The man was giving her an itinerary? "Your schedule sounds insane. Are you sure you're going to have the energy to go out on Friday night, for real, By?"

"Yeah, I will."

"All right, then, given your schedule, I want you to hang up and get some rest. You fly safe, okay. I'll see you Friday night, and if you need to cancel, no problem. I understand beat."

"All right, baby. Will talk to you later. But don't count on a cancellation unless Mother Nature decides to have a wicked sense of humor and holds me over somewhere. Friday, I'll be there. Promise. Good night."

"Good night," she whispered.

The phone went dead in his ear. That was the only way he could have gotten off the telephone. He stood and began to pace. He had to walk this off. Had to shake off her giggle, the voice, the way she breathed. Had to get that sigh out of his system, along with the image of her out of his head. Shit! Had he lost his mind? He'd called her *baby*, like he had the right to. In fact, he'd called this woman a half hour after leaving her, and he *never* did that. Plus, giving her his entire itinerary? Not even family got that much from him—he preferred to hang loose, unfettered by promises and fly into every city under radar. And, he was hankering after this woman that he'd just met like he was a lovesick adolescent. What the hell was wrong with him? If he hadn't eaten in a restaurant, he'da sworn the sister had rooted him—not that he believed in such nonsense, but dang. This just didn't make sense! But she'd called him By. Dang . . . his nickname sounded so good coming from her mouth to his ear. He wondered what it would sound like up close with no telephone between them?

He hit the remote to turn off the massive stereo system he'd wedged into his bedroom—his one indulgence. The ballads were messing with him. He had to get up early in the morning. Anyway, hope was moot. Should he be so fortunate as to get her to relent, where would he bring a woman like that? A hotel was out of the question. She'd think he didn't want her in his space and had something to hide, which he didn't. But he didn't bring women to his place, evidence of that was clear.

Byron walked the floors, going room by room, inspecting his domain. Damn. The spare bedroom still had boxes in it from his last move. The living room was a gym. Nothing but Nautilus equipment in it and a futon that doubled as a couch. His dining room was a home office—nothing but papers and manuals on the glass table, the chairs used as a bookshelf that he forbade the cleaning service to touch. Not a picture hung on the walls. The kitchen . . . He just shook his head as he paced through it and opened the fridge. Beer and old takeout containers. Yeah, the place was clean, but it was real spare. He opened his cabinets with disdain. Old cereal, a few bowls and plates from the dollar store, and mismatched coffee mugs. He closed the doors, and looked at the one pot and pan he owned that was resting on the counter. Juicer, coffeemaker. The woman would flip.

No. Her worst fears about him would be realized, if he were crazy enough to let her in there. The only room that he'd shamelessly adorned was the bedroom. Now that didn't make no kinda sense, even to him now. A sleigh king-size bed, the full monty, big-screen TV, and enough electronics to challenge Circuit City. He didn't even use the multiple fireplaces he'd insisted on when he'd bought the joint. What had been on his mind? Aside from his bedroom, the deck had more furniture on it than what was inside the condo.

This time he walked more slowly through his place. Okay, the powder room was clean, sterile, looked like a hotel's. But the bathroom off the master bedroom was ridiculous. Like the bedroom, he'd made that a private spa. Free weights were on the floor, shaving cream spilled over the can sides on the double sink, the Jacuzzi had a ring around it from the brown soap that hung from a rope like a dead man. The stacks of Turkish towels were all jumbled. Yeah, all right, so he'd put a bunch of stuff in there, should he have quick company— but nothing in his environment said, "Stay, baby, you're welcome to be here." And this was definitely not a place for a little girl to walk through, either.

Almost afraid to do so, he opened his medicine cabinet and cringed. "Oh, shit." A huge box of condoms just sat there, and had been clearly opened. He made a mental note: stash those somewhere, and call the maid from the first port. There wasn't much that could be done about his decor, but at least he could shape the joint up. The whole place needed to be beaten into submission, truth be told. Problem was, he wouldn't be here to do it.

His father's voice rang in his head, and it made him chuckle. "Yeah, Pop. I hear you," he whispered as he crossed the bedroom and began pulling off his shirt. "This ain't no place for a lady."

Della had acted so silly when she'd picked up her child that Gillian had forced a confession—not that she'd minded. Not that a confession was hard to wrench from her. And they'd laughed in Gil's kitchen until it just didn't make sense. But she'd sworn her to secrecy, too; however, she would tell Neecy in the group. The sister needed to know that twenty-five pounds did not change the allure of being a woman—not in Hotlanta, GA! And her little girl had giggled to see Mommy act so crazy as they ate ice cream and played and went to the movies. To hell with chores or structure. The sun was out today.

She'd run to the telephone like a teenager and was given the wonderful surprise of a deep male voice. She saved the message. Silly, but she did.

Monday, she'd dropped off her baby girl to the day-care lady and practically skipped to the car. When she got to work, even her coworkers who didn't know her well had questions. She felt radiant and was beaming like she had a secret—she hadn't realized how true that was until a dozen long-stemmed deep-violet roses appeared at the receptionist's desk. Curious faces gave her knowing glances and winks, as the ladies in her cubicle section ooohed and ahhhed, but she kept the card to herself. It was terse but laden with meaning. "Friday. I can't wait. By." She carried it in her suit-jacket pocket all day. Crazy. But it all felt so good.

Problem was, the week crawled like a snail, and each day a different shade of purple showed up. Irises, African violets . . . it just didn't make sense. Even the guys had commented, and their notice of her femaleness made her blush. Her boss raised an eyebrow, but what the hell. Her voice mail was pummeled with quick messages by a now very familiar voice. She no longer had to save them; she knew each day there'd be another one to treasure. This just didn't make sense.

The attention sent her to the mall—not to go shopping, but to loop back on her cohorts at Victoria's. They could call off the mission. She already knew the deal. The man was crazy—about her. God was good.

"You have got to be kiddin' us!" Liz Hawthorne had exclaimed, walking in a circle, laughing and slapping Saundra and Sherie's arms as she passed them, and they chuckled, too. "So, *I know* you are comin' back for the rest of the ensemble?"

It had been the magic question. Lord help her, but on *group night,* Wednesday, she'd bought the matching all-lace thong, Wonderbra, slip, and a pair of sexy hose—silk stockings not to be utterly confused with pantyhose, a garter belt, and a camisole. What could she say? *If* was weighing heavily on her mind, and she'd dropped half a dress size—sheer joy making it impossible for her to eat all week. By the time she'd reached Gillian's place, she was laughing and weeping in the same breath. It had taken three core members to calm her down and make her show them her loot.

But unlike other interventions, heavily dished out with warnings and wise sayings, a round of high fives and "You go, gurls," had greeted her. Then the meeting was much derailed, as they got into her business so hard, she had to laugh. It became a coming-out party.

"That's right, sister!" Ramona had said. "One day, I'ma hit lotto, too. Your apartment ready for reentry?"

"The bedroom, Mona." Neecy laughed. "Gurl, you got to have your pleasure palace in order."

"Now you know Miss Thang just spent the last year in credit detox because of her bedroom, most notably," Gillian, the voice of reason had added. "You didn't go overboard, did you?"

No. In truth, she hadn't and was proud of herself. She'd done it all in cash—no plastic. If things didn't work out, she wouldn't be looking at an insane bill for the next six months. But she would have to budget until the next check came. Whateva. *C'est la vie!* If he called, it was *on.* She and the girls had stayed up so late that everybody felt it the next day—but it was a good tired. A satisfied exhaustion. Byron's Thursday night call, when they connected, and when he'd written down her address, murmuring the words, "I can't wait," had nearly taken her over the top. She'd almost blown her cool and introduced the man to phone sex—something new she also wanted to try, with him. But she was smooth. Not yet. Too early in the mix. Friday couldn't get there fast enough. He was in trouble.

He'd never in his born days called a woman daily from every port he put in at . . . nor had he worried a florist to the point where they knew his voice. It was beyond insane. He needed to get a grip. Had to break the serious hold this woman had on his mind. It had to be fatigue. He'd studied too long and too much, maybe? That had to be it, because he was sweating her phone in a way that was humiliating. He'd literally blown up her voice mail, leaving long silences when he ran out of anything plausible to say. He knew she worked late sometimes, but he couldn't bear the thought that maybe she'd gone out—

with somebody else—on a Wednesday night. He had no right, really, to square off and claim territory, but damn. In his mind, she was definitely his. And, how in the world, or when in the world, did *that* happen? He never claimed anybody. J. Byron didn't do claims, or exclusives. He hadn't even slept with her, and he was acting a fool for her! Besides, everything was happening too fast, way off schedule. There was no balance. No. He had to pull it together. But, still, Friday couldn't come fast enough.

Then what?

# Chapter 6

Despite his better judgment, and his promise to take her out on a date, he found himself standing at her front door after she'd buzzed him into the gated lot. He could hear her moving inside her apartment, light jazz playing in the background. He could do this. He could be cool. Would go out, do a little dancing, eat, yeah. He was cool.

Then she opened the door and smiled.

Lord help her. The man looked better, and smelled better, each time she saw him.

"Hi." Yeah, be cool, Della. Just be casual, thank the man for the flowers, and then get your beaded clutch and bounce.

"Hi."

Why did he have to stand there like that, looking all good in a charcoal three-button suit—with that color of black violet shirt, huh, Lord? See, some things weren't fair.

"Come on in," she said in a quiet voice, and paced quickly away from him. "Make yourself at home. Just need to grab my purse and I'm ready. How was your week?"

"Fine," he said softly, watching her walk away from him, studying every single curve she offered in her retreat.

This was not how it was supposed to go. The burn was supposed to have worn off during the week with the distance. She was not supposed to blow him away at the door with a lacy knit dress the exact same color as that negligee he'd first seen in her hands. He was in trouble. Big trouble. The woman looked as good coming as she did going. The deep scoop in the back of the dress just teased his imagination with what it hid in the front. And tonight she had on black stockings so sheer that they looked like a thin shadow caressing her legs. Her dress stopped at the knee and offered a tasteful split up the back to expose just enough thigh to make a grown man wonder . . . stockings or pantyhose? The question nagged him. Her hair was swept up so that for the first time he got a really good glimpse of her neck. Gorgeous. But that pretty beauty mark on her shoulder was hidden away.

He walked over to the mantel, determined to keep his balance, all the while wondering how she had pulled everything in her apartment together in just a few weeks? This sister was a spell-caster. Had mysteries untold. The old dudes had spoken of women like this—all of them married them, too.

She had stunning art everywhere. He'd been in Atlanta for two years, and his place was a wreck by comparison. How did women do this? His gaze landed on her drapes, which matched a Queen Anne chair she'd covered in authentic mud cloth. Deep. He would never have thought to do that. Pillows on a black sofa that picked up hints of every color in the room, but none matched, but it all worked. Novel. In his mom's house, everything was a flower. Not a floral print to be found in Della's apartment—the only flowers being the ones he'd sent, which were all arranged in a single crystal vase. Very deep.

It felt good, he had to admit. She'd put a presence in there for any would-be suitors. He allowed his line of vision to study the photos on the mantel. Strong women, and an older man. Something inside him made him pick it up. Must be her dad. He heard her footsteps but didn't turn around.

"Is this your father?"

"Yup. That's him," she said pleasantly, easing up beside him. "Still miss him sometimes."

Her fingers caressed the edge of the frame as she accepted it from him and replaced it on the mantel with love. Her lips had a muted shade on them that drew out a hint of the hue in her dress, but also seemed to vanish right into her skin. Her mouth had formed into a sad smile that he wished he could kiss away, but decided not to. It was too soon. Her eyes had just a dab of dark violet at the edges, which gave them a smoky, mysterious look as she stared past him toward the frames. Her skin was radiant, and butter smooth. She smelled so good . . . light and intoxicating, and the fragile silver chain about her throat begged him to kiss her collarbone, as the long, slender earrings seemed to ask that he pay attention to her earlobes.

"That's my mom, and this is me and my sisters in high school." She chuckled. "That's my grandmom—we called her Nana . . . and this was all of us as little kids. And that's Miss Claire—too grown for her own good, and giving her momma the blues, but she's my heart. I keep these to show Claire how much she looks like the Mitchell girls. All of us together were a pistol—no wonder Dad finally gave up and went on to glory. Can't blame the man . . . He was outnumbered for years."

He studied her warm, sad eyes, and the sound of self-deprecating laughter in her voice. Never had he employed so much discipline not to kiss a woman in all his life—and he wasn't even sure why.

"You have a beautiful family," he heard his voice say. He was speaking, but his thoughts were a mile away; they had flown into the horizon of her eyes.

"Thanks," she said, bringing him back to earth as she glanced away toward the mantel again. "Well," she laughed, opening her arms and turning around. "This is my little place in the universe. Best I could do."

She had to be kidding? She was not apologizing for her place to him?

"I've been standing here, wondering how in the world you could do all this? My joint looks like it's been vandalized, and I'm ashamed to admit I've been in Atlanta for two years. How did you fix it up so fast?"

"Determination—and allowing necessity to be the mother of invention. You'd be surprised at what remnants and scraps can do.

"No doubt. This is awesome."

It was not an act; it was the gospel. He was impressed. Her environment was immaculate and seemed like a designer had shot a magazine layout in the joint. He walked around a bit, looking at all the prints and framed paintings, each one numbered as a limited edition.

"You like art?"

She'd sidled up to him as he stood before a Varnette Honeywood. There was a little girl getting her hair done in the kitchen, the old-fashioned way . . . just like his mom used to do his sister's hair.

"I love this one," he said quietly. "This one is for real home."

"Yeah," Della laughed. "It's one of my favorites. I use it to threaten Claire, when I tell her about the old days and how hard we sisters had it."

"You've been to the motherland? The masks are fantastic. Senegal, right—this one?"

"Yeah. And did the whole Gory Island thing. Needed to go for myself."

"It's good to see the world. Makes you appreciate just how small it really is—gives perspective. Ever been to East Africa? Madagascar?"

"Not yet."

"Then soon." He smiled and returned his gaze to her wall of treasures.

She had to get this man out of her apartment *now*, or they could forget going out—period. The man liked and appreciated art? Oh, Lord. Give her strength and resolve not to be a pure, shameless hussy. He'd looked so good when he'd walked through the door that she'd needed a minute in the bathroom to steady her pulse. Then he'd stared at her family with sheer adoration on his face? Have mercy!

"By . . . I also want to thank you again so much for all the flowers. You really didn't have to do that. They are lovely."

Was she crazy? Didn't have to do that? If she was gonna call him by his nickname like that, breathe it out all sexy while lowering those gorgeous eyes, she could have a whole flower shop.

"It wasn't nuthin' . . . I mean, I just wanted you to know how much I appreciated your letting me sit at the table with you. But I hope tonight I won't have to fight with you over the bill?" He laughed as she laughed. "Let's get it straight now, woman. You are in the South, and it is not politically correct for a sister to reach for the check down here. Some things ain't changed since dirt."

"I promise." She laughed.

Okay, she'd glanced at her purse. That was his signal that he was overstaying his welcome. He had to focus.

"Uh, you ready?"

"Yup. Where are we going?"

He'd fought with the concept of doing jazz at Sambuca out in Buckhead, so they could eat outside on the patio at Justin's off Peachtree Road in the same area, but the more he looked at her, the more he wanted to take her to an R&B establishment, where he could hold her in his arms. Jazz was more of a spectator's sport, but R&B meant moving together, dancing, and a chance for a slow song.

"How about if we do Club Kaya ... so we can dance? You like French food?"

"Do I like French? Please."

He smiled, having been rewarded with a blast of brilliance from hers.

"I know this little place on Cheshire Bridge Road, The South of France. Does that sound okay?"

If she had shot him, he wouldn't have felt the bullet. She had closed her eyes and placed her slender palm over her heart and sighed. Heaven help him.

"I have *always* wanted to go there . . . heard so much about it."

"Done."

She'd thought their easy conversation on the drive to the restaurant had been fabulous, but then the man had surprised her again by taking her to another country right in their own backyard. It had to be so, as they passed through lovely archways to enter a relaxed space that hosted exposed wood beams and fireplaces. She couldn't have prayed for a night out like this, and only a week ago, it was the farthest thing from happening to her. Now she was in a French cottage. She mentally talked to the butterflies in her stomach as they were seated in an intimate corner all to themselves.

"How about if we live it up a little and do champagne?"

For the moment, she could only nod and offer him a smile. She didn't trust her voice. She mentally threw a dagger in Robert's heart and willed him to disappear forever. Banished. Poof. Without blinking an eye, the man across from her had ordered Dom Pérignon just as casually as if he were ordering lemonade. It had been so long since she'd experienced the full dating treatment that she almost laughed. In fact, she really couldn't recall having been treated with such nonchalant flair—not without overt strings attached, and made crassly known by the brother who was ordering. See, now this was how a sister wanted to be treated. If a man would act like a man, and act like there were no strings attached, then he could attach a grappling hook. It was simple. Why didn't they get it?

"You're awfully quiet," Byron said after a moment, peering up from his menu.

Busted, she laughed. "I'm in shell shock, that's all."

He laughed. "What?"

"This goes against everything one is not supposed to say, but since we're friends, too, I have to say it. This is nice, and it's been a while since a real gentleman has treated me out. Thank you."

Her statement warmed him. No date had ever called him a friend, and he was very dubious about her claim that he was a gentleman. The night was still young, and she was chipping away at his home training.

"That's good . . . that we're friends, too, Del. But now out with it, and be honest. You saw the escargots on the menu and changed your mind? That's why you went mute on me, isn't it?"

His teasing made her chuckle harder. This man had such an easy demeanor, and he could make her laugh—which scored *big* points.

"No. In fact, my only worry, as much as I love them, is that they're cooked in garlic butter."

"Not the diet again . . . aw, baby . . ."

"No. Just don't want to be all up in your face with garlic breath."

He laughed, but his body had heard her loud and clear. Her chuckle had become a muted smile. The champagne came, and he was glad that he didn't have to immediately respond. Dang, he wasn't hungry . . . not for what they had on the menu, anyway.

"Everything in here has some form of garlic in it—the French way, I suppose."

"If you do garlic, then I'll splurge, too," she murmured with a wink.

She was messing with him, just like the way her voice had dropped was messing with him. She took a sip of champagne and allowed it to roll over her tongue. He could barely watch her take another sip.

"This is really good. You haven't touched yours, though."

He took a sip upon her prompting. "Was distracted."

"Really?"

"Been distracted all week."

She looked down at her menu, but not fast enough to hide the half-smile on her face. He knew as long as they held their menus, the waiter would hang back and give them time to talk, so he kept his open, as did she.

"You make up your mind about what you want, yet?"

"Yeah, Byron, have you?"

She had looked at him directly when she'd whispered the response. It made him swallow hard, but also had a paralyzing effect as his brain tried to process and separate what she'd said from what he wanted to hear. He wasn't trying to ruin the evening and piss her off by an aggressive move, but she had to cut it out, had to stop looking at him in a way that had many implications. He needed another sip of champagne, but she'd beat him to it, taking her glass by the stem first and bringing it to her lips, leaving that wet trail that had already been imprinted on his psyche.

"I know what I want," his voice said against his will.

"You sure?"

He just nodded. "How about you?"

She just nodded then smiled and looked down at the choices before glancing back up at him. "There are so many things here that I like, it's hard to pick just one thing."

"You can have whatever you want."

"You sure?"

He could feel himself going deaf as his pulse throbbed in his ears. "Yeah. If you're hungry, get whatever you want, baby."

The man had no idea. She was losing her mind. "I haven't done this in a long time . . . so, it's a difficult choice."

"Not if you know what you like."

He'd leaned in closer and set his menu aside. This was serious. She'd waited all week for this moment, and now he'd scared the doo-doo out of her. But that was crazy; she was grown, was a mother even. Evasion. Clarity.

"What do you want?"

He looked at her for a moment, and his smile vanished. "You want the truth, or the PC response?"

Oh, shit. "Gimme the PC response first." She chuckled, but couldn't break his hold on her gaze.

"I'll have the grilled filet mignon slathered in béarnaise with twin broiled lobster tails in hot drawn butter," he murmured without looking at his menu. "Now you want the non-PC translation?"

"No, I hear you," she said quickly, forcing her gaze to her menu.

"You sure you won't join me? It's really good. Been a long time since I've indulged, too."

"But, see, see, that's just it," she stammered, losing all sophistication. "I want a lot of things, and, uh, hot butter, and tails, are uh, momentary—that's a good description. I'll pay for it tomorrow, and it'll take weeks to undo the damage to my strict discipline. Do you understand?"

"I hear you," he said with a smile as he sat back and took a sip of his champagne. "Then why don't we simply share the plate? That way we can leave room for an appetizer and dessert. These entrées are really rich, and it might be wise to pace ourselves . . . so we'll feel good all night and not sick in the morning."

"Yeah, maybe we could do that." She could feel her knuckles losing color as she clutched the menu much tighter than intended. Her fingertips tingled. It was like putting a Thanksgiving banquet in front of a starving person. The person's body could go into shock if they ate too much after not having anything at all.

"Want me to order for you?"

His voice had come out on a ragged whisper, despite the fact that he'd pulled back. His eyes said it all. His mirage of coolness was evaporating fast. She loved it. She'd already lived with a control freak, and had dated far too many of them to count. Witnessing Byron's very primal response was beyond flattering; it totally turned her on like a flash fire.

"I'm not hungry," she heard her voice admit.

"Neither am I."

"You feel like dancing?"

"You want the PC answer?"

"No."

"Then, no, truth be told." He leaned in closer.

"Want to do that another night?"

"Yeah, Del. Later."

"Oh, boy." She let her breath out hard, closed her menu, and polished her champagne off in two quick swallows.

He smiled a slow, sexy smile. "Maybe I should have given you the politically correct answer."

"Maybe," she wheezed as an attentive wine server refilled her glass.

He gave the waiter a discreet glance, shook his head, and the man who was about to walk toward them stopped dead in his tracks. The action seemed to back up another server, who was approaching with bread. She wondered if it was some male secret code?

"All right, I'm sorry," Byron said, taking a deep breath and picking up his menu again with a sly grin. "You affect me this way, and I can't explain it—but I do apologize. Maybe after we eat, my gentleman status will be restored."

"Not all the way, I hope."

The thought had run through her brain, but was not supposed to leap out of her mouth! The statement had made him look up slowly and ease the menu down to where it had been. His expression was way too serious, and she was pretty sure that the man was holding his breath. The reaction was shredding every ounce of home training the Mitchell women had ingrained in her bones. Yeah, this was shameless—but oh well.

"Can you just ask them for a check?" she asked from a place low in her throat. "I need to get out of here."

Even though he'd raised his hand to gesture for the waiter's acknowledgment, his eyes searched her face.

"You sure?"

"Yeah."

"Uh, okay. Uhm. Yeah. I'll get the check."

"I can't do dinner and dancing . . . that's not what's on my mind."

What was she doing! The brother had almost knocked over his glass when he'd turned fast to hail the waiter. This had to be the most outrageous thing she'd ever done in her life, and the decision had been made quicker than she could snap her fingers. But things were in motion now. A server was at their table, inquiring about the service, the establishment's menu, and Byron wasn't even looking at the poor man.

"*Monsieur,* is everything to your liking?"

"Yes, just bring the check."

"The champagne?"

"Toss it."

"Bad bottle, sir?"

"Perfect bottle. Just bring the check. Now."

"As you wish. But nothing on our menu pleased you?"

"Yes. Everything. But the lady is ready to leave." Byron gave the man a silent, lethal glare, and the man nodded as though he'd finally received the telepathic transmission.

Then the server became calm and returned a smooth reply. "I shall dispatch your check at once, sir. Have a nice evening."

They said nothing as the man came back to their table with merciful swiftness. Byron flipped him a credit card without even glancing at the bill, his eyes trained on her. Never in her life had she felt so much adrenaline rush through her at one time. Anticipation made it hard for her to sit still while Byron signed the bottom of the check, and stood. She had to remember to allow him to come to pull out her chair—the server was long gone. It was as though some secondary, invisible words had exchanged between him and Byron, some male thing conveying the fact that Byron wanted to do the honors. The lady was in Captain Fulton's territory now—back off. Roswell seemed so far away at the moment.

This time, when they walked to the car, Byron's arm claimed her waist. Okay, she was knee-deep in this situation, and there was definitely no turning back. Half of her didn't want to, but the other half of her was shouting inside her head—*What the* hell *are you doing? You should be talking, learning more about this man, having dinner, then dancing, and kissing him good-bye at your door. Are you mad?*

The rational parts of his mind fought a losing battle with the primal sides of it. What the *hell* was he doing? This woman was dangerous. She'd unhinged him at the table in the restaurant, just broke down all his cool. Never in his life had he been so caught up in the moment that he'd flagged a waiter like that for a check. Half of her seemed so unsure, and then the other side of her became pure vamp.

And the crazy part was, he didn't give a damn. But she'd been so shy at first, then came out and flat-blasted him with the truth. Her eyes had told him everything he'd hoped for in one glance, and he could feel her body trembling to his touch as he walked her to his car. Raw, honest, it wasn't fake or fiction. This was the kinda stuff that would mess up a brother's mind and make him slip and fall in love. See, he wasn't ready for that just yet. This was a sister who'd make him make a baby, or something crazy. They needed to slow this down, but Lord knows, he was only human.

"Your place or mine?" he asked before his brain could stop him.

"Mine," she replied in a whisper, turning to him by the car door and stepping closer to his chest.

She'd opened those big brown eyes on him, turned up her chin, and parted her lips. That was all she wrote. His hands immediately found the sides of her face, which he cradled with care as his mouth captured hers. The taste of champagne and breath mints covered the soft tissue inside it, and his tongue tangled with hers, then slid over her teeth, tasting smooth porcelain, breathing in the cocoa butter and perfume of her skin. He swallowed her soft moan . . . Damn, Roswell was so far away. Perfect fit, Lord help him. Her lush body created a vacuum seal that he didn't have the willpower to break. But he had to back off, step back, and pull away, if he was going to get her somewhere not public.

As though sensing the logical aspects of his dilemma, she began breaking the seal herself. The cool night air felt like a knife as it carved a space between them.

"The sooner we get home, the sooner we get home," she murmured.

He was beyond speech. He'd heard her loud and clear, and just nodded as he moved away and opened the passenger's door to help her into the vehicle. Although he'd rounded his car quickly, jumped in, and started it, he had to remember that this was still Georgia. A brother pushing ninety miles and hour in a black Jag would not be the thing to do. He kept his gaze darting between the speedometer and the road. That was the safest bet; fly this transport in, under radar, and keep all passengers safe. He couldn't look at her, lest he lose focus and rev the engine to 120. Focus.

She watched his hands and the side of his face, and appraised the way the muscle in his thigh pulsed every time he accelerated. Oh, yeah, this night was going to be a porch rocker . . . one of those evenings that she'd have to take to her grave. A moment of personal history that she'd smile about as an old lady and she'd never tell a soul about: the night she gave in to shameless behavior and didn't even care. What the hell. The man had blown her mind, had done all this stuff, and she was supposed to act like it had no effect? Not in the new millennium. Shooot. Sitting there all fine. Sure she wanted more, but there was no denying wanting the basics he could provide. And she liked him a lot more than he probably even knew. But, she'd have to explain all that in the morning.

She glanced at him again, noting the way his hands gripped the steering wheel. He had the kind of hands that would definitely make a girl wanna smack her momma. Hands that took how many tons of steel up in the air every day? Jesus, have mercy.

"Uh, By . . . you've gotta slow down for the gate, or you're going to take it out when you hit the next speed bump."

Her voice was too calm, frighteningly so. He hit the brakes, leaving black skid marks on the asphalt.

"Sorry about that," he murmured. "What's the code?"

She smiled as she gave it to him, and he punched it into the gate security pad. The brother was breathing hard. This was pure female power. She chuckled as he drummed his fingers, waiting for the painfully slow gate to lift. *Now, Della Louise Mitchell, you oughta be ashamed of yourself.* But she wasn't.

He pulled into an empty spot and turned to her. She placed a hand in the center of his chest to stop the kiss that was surely coming. Not out here in her courtyard. She'd just moved there. She was a mother and had a reputation to preserve, after all. Some things just weren't done. No public displays of affection in her yard, yet—unless he was a permanent fixture in her life. After that, she couldn't care less about PDA.

"Let's go upstairs," she whispered.

He just nodded and opened his door fast. Oh, yeah, this one was going in her personal mind journal. She took her time getting out of the car with his assistance. How many years had she been left standing on the curb with a husband yelling for her to open her own damned door? Hmmm. This was nice, and all the aspects of it needed to be savored—just like having a man so turned on by her should be. The man had tossed a half bottle of Dom. Had practically torn up the under-chassis of his Jag just to get her home fast. Deep. And was now standing behind her at her front door, practically panting for her to fish out her keys and manage the locks. Dreams did come true, so she would not tempt fate to ask for much more than one night right now.

She wasn't sure what to expect from him as she bolted the door behind them. No doubt Capt. J. Byron Fulton had been with a lot of exotic women around the globe—and the realization was a bit sobering. Who was she to compete with that lineup? What was all too thrilling for her would probably make him yawn, she guessed.

Yet he stood a foot away from her, just staring at her when she tossed her purse on the coffee table. But he was in her domain, now, where her ego prevailed. She liked this man way too much to give him up to phantom women. Her hands went to her hair, and she pulled out the two long bobby pins that held it up, and let it fall to her shoulders. His eyes went to half-mast. She almost shook her head in wonder. If he had any idea how long it had been since she'd received such a non-verbal compliment from a worthy man . . .

The sight of her with her hair down, the way she'd done it, slow and sexy, never losing eye contact, had stunned him. In his soul, he knew that it had been hard for her to offer herself to him in that way, so openly; her eyes told him and held a quiet plea behind their faux boldness, asking not to be violated. He sent a silent promise back to her with his that he wouldn't. She was too much of a gift. Yet her eyes glittered with so much passion that he hadn't been able to cross the room for a moment, not wanting to break her spell, and definitely not wanting to do anything that would shift her mood. Then she walked past him, didn't say a word, but offered a glance over her shoulder that he followed.

Standing in the darkened doorway of her bedroom, he watched her walk around like a shadow, moving effortlessly within the domain that she obviously knew blind. He heard a small pop, and then light appeared as she lowered a long fireplace match to tall candles. Soft music soon filtered in between them, and his senses became over-loaded by the sight of her in the candlelight, the scents wafting around him, and the sound of a love ballad . . . Jeffrey Osborne. She'd gone there and hadn't even said a word.

All he could do was watch her as the blood within him rushed cell by cell through his body. He'd entered a sacred place, her sanctuary, and it looked like it belonged to an African goddess. . . . It did—of that he was sure when she dropped her dress and stepped out of it to stand before him in the color that was now his favorite on earth. Strapless wonder held her ample breasts . . . her belly was underscored by a thin hint of thong shielded by a garter . . . silk stockings with wide lace bands, and she was still in heels. *Have mercy.* If he lived till tomorrow, he'd marry her.

He unbuttoned his jacket, his hands trembling as he fumbled with it. She came to help, looking down as she worked. The beauty mark on her shoulder cried out for him to kiss it. The scent coming from her hair, and the touch of her hands, made him shut his eyes against the multiple sensations as he swept her soft shoulder, hoping to brand it with the heat of his mouth.

"You wanted R&B . . . then let's dance."

Dance? He couldn't breathe. She smiled and unfastened his belt; her hands sliding against his zipper produced a shudder that he couldn't conceal. He wanted to hold her so badly in that moment as her palm slipped into his, but he'd let her lead. He was in her house, and she'd taken clear control. She owned this space, and him with it. So, he danced, as the lady requested. . . . And was rewarded by touching hot drawn butter that was her skin. When he pulled her near, his palms slid down her arms and found her back—she shuddered. Yeah, they could share this plate till there was nothing left but sauce.

"You still worried about overindulging?" he whispered hard against her neck, keeping time to the music as they swayed to the song.

"No, but like you said, this is rich, and we can share it so it lasts all night."

She felt his Adam's apple move and was satisfied with his unspoken response.

He traced her supple spine with his fingertips and nuzzled her hair. When she gripped his shoulders tighter, he exhaled, remembering to breathe. The song had ended, but another ballad took its place . . . she'd made a tape . . . a planned seduction. He loved every minute of her intrigue, and he closed his eyes, almost unable to withstand the torture of her hand that had found a way beneath his pants after she slowly lowered his zipper.

The change of texture from fabric-interrupted friction drew a gasp that became a groan. He needed to get out of his clothes, to feel the skin-to-skin connection to her, but her touch felt too good to do anything to make her stop. If she had any idea what she was doing to him, how her hand was unraveling everything he'd ever learned, she'd have mercy.

His audible response made taking her time next to impossible. The tops of her thighs were wet; the thong was a weak dam to the current that swelled and overflowed her valley. All her plans to make it last were vanishing as she found his mouth, and he aggressively returned her kiss, deepening it while tightening his grip on her arms.

"I've gotta get out of these clothes," he murmured, no patience left in his voice.

She didn't say a word, but backed up as he stripped. That was the end of the game. There was no way she could keep it going as she practically went slack-jawed. She had to sit down on the side of the bed as she gazed at the man's body. Flawless ebony-colored stone came out of cloth and was standing in her bedroom, glistening with a light sheen of sweat—*for her*, no less.

But more than the six-pack of abdominals, or the way he sucked in air and let it out, making the cinder-block formation on his chest move with his lungs . . . more than the tree-trunk thighs that held him up and tapered into solid calves, or the shoulders that looked as though they could indeed carry the weight of the world on them with arms strong enough to cast off any such burden, it was the clear liquid that pearled and created a thin line that began with a drip and didn't break as it went to the floor.

Without a word, seeming oblivious of the music, he threw his pants away, not looking where they landed, his vision holding her transfixed. His lips had parted, and he was taking air in through both his mouth and his nose. His eyes communicated something she'd never seen. His expression told her that he didn't care what happened in the next thirty seconds, as long as she was under him. *Oh, shit . . .*

That's what made her reach for the drawer. Oh, yeah, this was serious. This was how babies were made, and the man wasn't rational. She had enough presence of mind to know that. He'd approached the bed much too slowly; now he was for real stalking her. She held out the foil package. He shook his head.

"Not yet."

She tensed. His dismissal of her offer had come from a place deep inside his chest on a ragged whisper.

"You trust me?"

"No. Not at all."

He chuckled as he climbed onto the bed on all fours and pinned her. "You should," he murmured, kissing her shoulder hard. "I'm not crazy . . . yet."

She relaxed, a little, and lay back, but kept the package in her hand. Immediate heat filled her skin; his mouth, his hands unraveled her brain at its stem. Piece by piece he removed all her trappings, anointing each bared area with the searing inside of his mouth. Teeth, tongue, lips, wetness found every untouched, unattended place on her body and cherished it till she cried out, but he wouldn't relent. He peeled away her stockings and took off her shoes, his mouth always in contact with her skin, somewhere, somehow, scorching her with pleasure wherever it touched her.

By the time he'd sought out her inner thighs, she was nearly weeping. This man was going to make her lose her mind . . . and then he did, plunging his tongue into her overripe valley, pulling at folds that had been ignored for so long she'd figured them dead. Their return to life was painful engorgement . . . exquisite renewal that arched her back and made her writhe to receive each lick. She could feel the small package crumple in her fist, but there was nothing she could do about that when the first hard convulsion hit her, triggering the next, followed quickly by another, her voice carrying much louder than she wanted, but she had no control over it—then sudden weight covered her, her fist opened, and a stronger hand interleaved her fingers with his. She tasted herself on a deep, full kiss; her legs had no choice but to part.

"Della, baby, your fingernail scored this package. Tell me fast, where another one is?"

She could only point to the nightstand with her eyes closed, he was too close, felt too good, was knocking on the door, and she couldn't speak. She heard wood scrape against wood, and then heard it clatter against the floor. Lord have mercy, the man had ripped out her drawer and toppled a lamp! Whateva. The primary question was, could he reach the box without moving from where he was?

"You got it?"

"Yeah. The nightstand—"

"Forget it. Just put it on," she said.

Impatience shook her. The anticipation of what he'd feel like was sending spasms through her womb. "Please, baby, hurry," Della whispered against her better judgment. Shame had been banished by his touch. She couldn't stand the wait much longer, if he didn't get that damned thing on.

She'd leaned up on her elbows and hadn't taken her eyes off him while he worked to create a barrier. His focus was in shreds. Had she any idea? Her voice, her skin, the way she'd convulsed in his arms . . . the wetness. Latex was killing him. Just like her expression was. All thumbs at this point, he'd dropped it by accident, his hands were trembling so badly. Blood was centralized in one place; his fingers were going numb. But she gracefully picked it up, put it in her mouth, and slid it down the length of him. Heat seared the barrier to sheath him, but her mouth and her hands stroked a small spasm up and out of him way beyond his control.

"You've got to stop . . . that feels too good. Del, baby, please. Gimme a second."

She showed mercy and planted long, slow kisses up his abdomen to his chest and then found his mouth, as he remained crouched above her on his hands and knees, not trusting himself to lower toward her yet. All night was out of the question. He needed to do algorithms in his head or she'd be really disappointed fast. She smelled so good; her nectar was still in his nose, and on his face. God help him.

Tangling his fingers in her hair, he kissed her hard and entered her the same way. He couldn't breathe as his eyes rolled back in his skull from the sensation of joining to her. Thick thighs created a vise around his waist as her heels caressed his butt, and his body moved in lunges against his brain's demands to be smooth and take it slow. Bullshit. Not possible. Not with this woman.

She had claimed him to the hilt, and her fast hard shudders went through his groin and up his spinal column, negating everything in his brain. Forceful spasms created a counterrhythm that felt so good he almost sobbed. Nails raked his shoulder blades. A hot kiss thrust her pleasure into his ear on a steam burst of air containing his name. Each breath that his body ejected now sounded like a chant.

Control was a myth once she'd urgently pulled his hips against hers and convulsed hard enough to nearly sit up. Her reaction instantly siphoned the same response from him as every muscle in his body braced for the impact of sudden release. Pleasure so profound that he was praying out loud against her neck, couldn't breathe, couldn't pull enough of him into her fast enough or hard enough, prolonged agony hurling pride aside as it poured from him spasm by immediate spasm until he dropped in her arms.

It took a long time for him to attempt to shift his weight. First he had to make sure that he hadn't suffered a heart attack. Pushing himself up in slow motion felt like an out-of-body experience as he attempted to roll off her. She was breathing quietly, hadn't moved, her eyes were closed. Hell, maybe they'd both checked out.

"You okay?" he whispered.

"Yeah . . . and how . . ."

Confirmation. He chuckled through heavy breaths. "I hear you."

"Never in my life," she whispered, awe in her voice.

He closed his eyes. Double confirmation. "Good."

She chuckled and pulled herself up to lean on one elbow, the other hand stroking his chest. "Good?"

He nodded, but didn't have the energy to open his eyes. "Very good." He smiled as her mouth swept across his. Pure contentment filled him, and he could feel himself drifting, losing consciousness.

"You hungry?"

"Starved. I feel it now."

"Take ten. I'll be back."

He didn't answer, couldn't, as he felt the bed shift when her weight moved from it. There was no clear way to be sure whether he'd blacked out, or just immediately rocked out to sleep. Three months of studying, one huge argument, six days of flying, and a week of wanting Della Mitchell had finally caught up to him.

But when he felt the bed shift again, there she was, just as he'd imagined. She had on the negligee that had stopped his heart in the mall, her hair was tussled all over her head, and a look of pure satisfaction graced her face. She had a black lacquered tray in her hand with a small knife, a wedge of smoked Gouda, and fruit. Maybe he had died in the throes. It sure seemed like paradise from his vantage point.

She smiled and set down the tray between them on the bed, and she leaned low to peel away the skin from the mango. He watched her work the knife in her hand, while juice drizzled drown her palm, creating a thin trail of sweet nectar down her forearm to her elbow. Pure reflex drew his mouth to her delicate wrist, just beneath where she held the knife as he followed the trail down her bent arm.

"Man, stop . . . I've got a knife in my hand." She giggled and switched the knife to the other palm.

"What am I going to do about this?"

"Eat the fruit, once I peel it."

He smiled. "You're not hearing me." He licked away the nectar at her elbow and she plopped a succulent piece of mango in his mouth. His body stirred from the taste of her as he closed his eyes and savored the natural sugar in both flavors, allowing the sweetness into every part of his mouth before he chewed the fruit wedge and swallowed it away.

She'd heard him, all right. But she also had some decisions to make. He was a free agent; she was a mother. This was *fantastic,* but would it last? Should she allow herself to be totally swept away? She'd have to decide that tomorrow.

"What am I not hearing?" Her question was a mere whisper as she worked on freeing another section of the mango to taste for herself.

He watched her eat it, and then sadly looked at the destruction of her nightstand and lamp. No woman had affected him like that, and none he could remember in recent history had responded the way she had. It was dangerous to get two hedonists together, that he was sure of, because one day one or both of them wouldn't reach for the box in the drawer.

"You're not hearing how crazy I am about you." His finger traced her jaw line as she closed her eyes to his touch.

"I hear you . . . heard you." She replied with a wide smile. "Did you hear me?"

"Yeah . . . most assuredly. Give me a few minutes and something to eat, and I'd like to hear you again."

She glanced at his handsome face and sweat-slicked body. He was still hard; it hadn't even gone down, and he was still talking yang. Men were so crazy—they didn't hear a thing a woman was trying to say. Especially not in bed.

He smiled at her as he watched her work the paring knife. She'd whittled away the tough skin and was making sweet strips of the tender meat inside . . . just like she'd done to him. He'd waited all his life for a woman like this to come into his life—women never heard what a man was trying to say . . . especially in bed.

"Then, eat your fruit, man, and enjoy it now before I do and it's all gone."

He just kissed away her words. She wasn't listening to him right now.

# Chapter 7

She awakened to her tummy being stroked by a strong, gentle hand that aimlessly wandered up and down her torso. Her spine was nestled against hard, warm flesh, and she nearly had to pinch herself to be sure that she wasn't dreaming.

"Good morning, sleepyhead," a deep voice murmured into her ear as she stirred.

"Uhmmm. Good morning, yourself," she whispered, snuggling deeper into his hold. "You want some breakfast?"

"Yeah . . . in a little while."

She smiled with her eyes closed, feeling a length of hardness pressing against her backside. "The box is empty, Byron. So, I repeat, you want some breakfast?"

"Oh, all right," he said against her neck. "Since you put it that way."

"Yes, I put it that way."

"You'd cook for me?"

"Sure, why not?"

"You can cook, too?" He let out a sigh. "I'ma hafta start going to church."

"Pullease," she scoffed, enjoying his lazy hold on her as the rest of her body began to awaken. "I've just sworn off my old recipes—but the Mitchell women can hold their own in the kitchen. It's a rite of passage."

"What can you make good?" His hand had moved to her breast, causing her to squirm a bit from the attention.

"Well, I used to make a butter pound cake with six eggs and a pound of putter with lemon drizzle icing . . . and peach cobbler—my aunt Julia taught me that. But I'm not too bad on macaroni and cheese, yams, greens—they take hours of coaxing to get right—I'm good with chicken, pork chops. I don't know. The basics. But I've learned a whole bunch of low-fat recipes," she added, slapping her hip. "Needed to."

"The basics. Ummph, ummph, ummph. The woman calls that the basics."

"Well just 'cause I'm from Philly doesn't mean North Carolina isn't in my bones."

He laughed, and she could feel the vibration of his chest melting into her back.

"Just keep me in the basics, baby, and I'll keep coming back."

His hand roved over her hip and back up to her waist. "Don't lose none of it, hear what I'm saying."

"Yeah, and you won't be happy if it gets any bigger either."

"Shoot, girl, you kidding? Especially the top and the bottom . . . have mercy."

"If my butt got any bigger, or my thighs got any chunkier, you'd—"

"Try me," he whispered, nipping her shoulder. "I'd lose my job for not being able to get out of bed. Damn, I'm home. Been wasting time."

She laughed, ignoring him.

"So, brother. What do you want—grits, eggs, sausage, biscuits?— my larder is loaded, and you'd better catch me while I'm in the mood."

"That's how this started last night. I asked you what you wanted, and caught you in the mood."

She laughed and tried to get up, but he held her fast.

"You sure the box is completely empty? Mornings are a killer."

Now she really laughed hard. "Man, stop. We have two choices if you want to do this—go to the store, or go to the store."

"Aw'right. Yeah. You're making sense, and I'm not." He released his grip and sighed. "Dang. Shoulda put one up for safekeeping. One day, soon, I hope I won't have to use one of those with you. I hate latex."

"Keep dreaming," she scoffed, still smiling and slapping away his hand as it crept between her thighs. "Aside from the obvious, is there anything *else* you want this morning?" She rolled over and leaned on one elbow to peer down at him. She expected to see him smiling, but instead his face was serious as he began to trace her cheek with his forefinger.

"Besides the basics? Yeah, there is," he said quietly.

"What?" Her body tensed, waiting for the "baby, there's something I have to tell you" speech.

"To always wake up like this with you when I can."

She let her breath out slowly, hoping he hadn't seen her do so. "Well, given your schedule, and my parental duties . . ."

"I know. But, we can fix those issues."

She pushed herself to sit up, but held the sheet against her. Some things looked much better in the candlelight than in sunlight. But he'd eased the cover from her, sliding it down her body until she was sitting before him, fully exposed.

"Don't do that."

"What?"

"Hide yourself from me."

She just stared at him and watched him drink her skin with his eyes. "Sure you want to see every flaw? Daylight takes away a lot of mystery, brother."

He shook his head and caressed her tummy again. It was riddled with stretch marks. "You have the prettiest skin."

"They let you fly jets without glasses?" She laughed and stood, fetching her robe.

"Yes. I have twenty-twenty."

"If you say so."

"I say so. And why don't you let me cook—while you shake the past out of your head."

She turned around and looked at him as he sat up to stare back at her.

"I don't know what he said to you, or did to you, but he and any-body else that let you get away, was crazy. I'm not them, and I don't dillydally with serious decisions. Up in the air, seconds matter, min-utes can cost you your life. So I don't play when it comes to making up my mind."

"You're thirty-eight years old and still a bachelor. Seems you've taken your time on some things."

He looked at her. "Because I hadn't made up my mind. Wasn't because I didn't know my mind—just hadn't made it up."

"Okay. So you have decided what this morning?"

"All I do know is, I spent last night in bed with a work of art, and this morning she looks prettier in the natural sunlight than she did in silk and candlelight. You hearing me, woman?"

Della didn't speak, but allowed her line of vision to travel out the window. He needed to get dressed or go take a shower before he made her cry.

"Look. I'll admit, last night was . . . but . . ."

"But what, baby?"

"There are things you don't know about me, Byron."

Silence stood between them for a moment.

"What terrible things about you could there be?"

She spun on him quickly and let it all come out in a rush. "I go to a women's group every Wednesday night—for shopaholism. I ran up ten thousand dollars of credit-card debt on lingerie, Byron. I don't know what was wrong with me, but the longer I stayed in the bad marriage I was in, the more I shopped, and it got out of control." She swept her arms around the room. "Look at this bedroom. I spent a mint on making a pleasure palace when I moved here, and I hadn't even had a date for three years!"

This *fine* woman hadn't had a date—translation, slept with a man—in *three years?* The concept was pure heresy to him. Three years . . . and she'd picked him to break her fast? Yeah, he was definitely going to start going to church with more regularity. A woman with that kind of passion within her had held out, waiting on the right one for *that long?* Oh, yeah, this was a marrying kinda woman. The decision was clear. Byron rubbed the line of his jaw, trying to wipe away a smile as tears ran down her face and she wiped them away with frustration.

"That is a showstopper, I'll admit." He stood and paced to retrieve his underwear. "Della, frankly, I don't know if I could work six days on, two off, or longer shifts in the air and touch down to a woman who has a fetish for sexy lingerie. I just don't know." He kept his back to her to conceal his grin. "Ten thousand dollars on lingerie is pretty steep . . . and how would a man react to the surprise of coming home to a butter pound cake drizzled in lemon icing, with a woman in a black garter belt who had the unmitigated gall to convert her bedroom into the Taj Mahal for him?" He turned and looked at her. "Some things some men just can't countenance. I'm so glad your husband left you—because it was shameless."

His beaming smile made her laugh, despite her desire to stay peeved at him. She sniffed and thrust her chin up, finally. "It's not funny, By."

"No. Your character flaw is tragic . . . but I'll help you through it. You can lavish all that sin on me. I'll take it like a man, baby."

"Yeah, right." She tried to pass him, but he caught her and held her face, and then he kissed her hard.

"Is that all?"

"Isn't that enough?"

"You're teasing me, right, Del? The man didn't appreciate *this* . . . and you bought stuff to turn him on, and he bolted?"

"No, I'm serious. He complained about everything I did, and the way I looked, hated that Claire was a girl, and I spent a lot of money, and—"

He kissed her again. "You want a line of credit at Victoria's? How much? Tell me the store, and I'll keep you in silk." His breath came out in a heavy rush against her neck as his palms slid down her arms. "Jesus, if that's a sin, I'm going to hell in a handbasket this morning. You want more baby girls? I'll make 'em. I ain't picky. Shit."

"Man, please." She tried to get away. "This is not the answer to—"

Another ardent kiss stopped her flow of words. "Come to Macon and meet my folks."

"What?"

"I know I've gotta pass inspection, 'cause you have a little girl. Bring her to Macon, next flight out. Meet my people, and let her see another grandma who will scoop her up and add her to the fold with pleasure. But, I have to warn you; my mother is out of control. She'll spoil your baby rotten, like all her grands, might even kidnap Claire from time to time, since Momma gets buddy passes to Disney World from her son."

"Uh, you've got to stop doing that so I can think."

"Don't think. Feel me talking to you." He placed several kisses down her neck and nudged the fabric away from her shoulder to find the beauty mark on it with his lips. "My sister is a trip, and she will tell you all my dark secrets, I'm sure—and will plot against me with my own mother in your behalf. . . . They've been waiting for me to crash and burn like this for a long time. And baby, I'm nose-diving."

"That's a serious move," she muttered quietly, leaning away from his attention at her neck. "Meeting the family, and all. You haven't even met Claire. What if you don't like her, or she doesn't like you?"

"I'll fly to Philly to meet your people. Will be on my best behavior. Claire is just a baby, what's not to like? And if I treat her like the princess she is, why wouldn't she like me back? I hope one day she'll love me. Your husband was crazy—let that nonsense with him go. Last night I told you I wasn't crazy. This morning, I'm sure I'm not."

Everything was happening way too quickly. She stared at this man whose expression was open, smiling, and singed with deferred passion. Pure desire glittered in his eyes. He wasn't thinking with the big head. No. Brotherman was still in some afterglow from last night. She wasn't about to get in this deep, this fast after coming out of what she'd come from. She needed time to assess, be sure, know his habits; let him learn hers.

"But—"

"Okay. Here's my flaws." He loosened his hold on her, sighed, and steadied his voice. "I travel a lot for the job. I'm a slob, but I make a decent enough salary to have a cleaning service come in and keep me civilized." Byron let his breath out hard. "I'm a chauvinist, true. But a recovering one. I've already deleted entries from my Palm that no longer need to be there, and—"

She placed her hand in the middle of his chest. "Hold up. I cannot go through falling in love—"

"You're falling in love? I needed to hear that part plain."

"Byron, let me finish."

"Okay," he whispered, his hands lazily stroking her shoulders. "I'm listening."

"I can't go through having my heart broken again . . . and I won't have Claire get attached to someone who has a lot of women, who might walk—"

"Fact. I *used* to have a lot of women. But, I wouldn't—"

"Byron, we are still reeling from last night. I have to think about all of this, and you have an erection—so I know you aren't thinking clearly."

He chuckled and dropped his hands from her shoulders to more gently place them on her hips. "Yeah, I am saluting you this morning, aren't I? Sorry, basic reaction to you in the bedroom half-nude. But you still aren't hearing me?"

She shrugged and glanced away.

"I heard you, though," he murmured. "Last night you said you wanted something to last for fifty years, without saying so directly. So do I. I hope you heard me, too. When I had to go to work, you told me to fly safe . . . of all the women I've been with, none of them ever said that to me."

She stared at him, her brow furrowed. "Nobody *ever* told you to fly safe? Get out."

He shook his head. "Only my family . . . and my friends. You said we were friends at dinner. You make me laugh, care about the little things. Yeah, you're a friend. I've had lovers, but not one that was also a friend."

Her hand stroked the center of his chest, and she looked at the earnest pain in his eyes.

He collected her fingers one by one and placed a kiss in the middle of her palm. "You have beautiful hands that don't grasp, but caress. You have beautiful eyes that see deep into the soul of a man, no matter what profession he's wearing. And you take ownership for your own flaws and fight with anybody that tries to help. . . . Your voice is so honest, Della." His lips found the bridge of her nose. "Let me help, and be a friend as well as a lover, and I promise not to get in the way of your independence."

She was going to speak, but her voice failed. "All my life . . . I've been trying to improve myself, trying not to put my problems on other people."

"Your biggest flaw is always looking for your biggest flaw. Just be, for once, woman. Is that so terrible?"

Strong arms held her as she'd never been held, with affection and gentleness, but also with support. She felt all the resistance in her drain away for a moment as she let go of fear and relaxed in this crazy man's arms, and she surrendered.

"My voice isn't always so nice, though. You should know that," she whispered, thinking back on the arguments she'd lobbed within dying relationships, and the way she'd struggled in professional situations. This man had no idea. "You don't want to hear my voice raised."

"If I have to build a soundproof bedroom to keep hearing the full range of your voice, then so be it."

"I'm serious." She lifted her head up to look at him.

"So am I. But I might just let the neighbors hear it all—I'll admit that male ego is a terrible flaw."

"What! Neighbors?"

He laughed. "Yeah. I could live with the embarrassment, as I walked out to get the Sunday paper off the driveway. Think I could stand the thumbs-up from the other husbands on the block as I drove off to work in uniform. I could withstand the humiliation."

"What did you say?" She pulled away from him and tightened the belt on her robe.

"Oh, woman, all right. All right. My bad. I won't have your business in the streets."

"No. That's not what I'm talking about."

"Then what, Del?"

She was pacing, and her eyes held panic. What had he said?

"Other husbands? Going out to get the paper. That was rhetorical, right? Just hypothetical, right? Byron, talk to me."

He stared at her and shrugged. "Why else would I want you to meet my momma, or to meet yours?" He didn't get it. Then it dawned on him. "Oh, yeah, definitely. You like to shop, so pick out the ring. Shoulda did it on knee and in a nice restaurant more romantic-like. Dang. Messed up, didn't I? Sagittarian flaw of directness. Sorry, baby. I'll do the whole nine yards; I jumped the gun. I'm always under time pressure, and that tends to also make me more direct—"

"What!"

"What, Del?"

"Are you insane?"

"All right. Maybe I'm doing this backwards—never did it before. Pick out the house first?" He gestured at the bedroom. "Clearly you're the decorator, so get whatever you want, and fix it however you like. My daddy taught me something—the woman gets to fix up the house however she likes, and the man fixes whatever in it that gets broken, and pays the bills. What, Del? You keep looking at me like I've slapped you, honey. If you want the bedroom soundproofed so the neighbors and Claire won't hear us, okay. No problem. I was just teasing about the thumbs-up in the driveway."

She stared at the man. He had a look of pure, honest confusion on his face. She covered her mouth with her hand. This could not be happening. "Wait. Let me make sure I'm *actually* clear—"

"Name the terms. Pick out the house in whatever neighborhood; I don't care. Dunwoody or Stone Mountain is nice, but if you want to stay in Roswell, fine."

He paced to the bathroom, and she remained glued to the side of the bed, where she sat in shock until she heard him flush and run the sink water. He came back in the room, still seeming pleasantly bewildered.

"What is it? I thought you heard me last night? And I *know* I heard you say *yes* in five octaves, didn't I?" Byron cocked his head to the side and began pulling on his pants. "So, since I'm cooking, where do you want to go for breakfast? Ray's by the River has a great view of the Mississippi and a stupid-crazy buffet."

"*No,* you didn't ask me to marry you last night!" She was on her feet and walking in a circle now, waving her arms as he laughed and found his belt and shoes. "I don't know this silent man-code stuff— I'm—I'm—Byron, I'm not a telepath!"

"Oh, my bad. Guess I was thinking it so hard, I thought you heard me."

"*Your bad?* Are you crazy?!"

"This morning, in a word, yes. Now that I think about it, definitely. But even a crazy man knows what makes sense, and what he likes, and he'd be even crazier not to take it off the market and stake a firm claim. I ain't about sharing you, Della. Nope. Told you I was a chauvinist. I like coming home to this."

Before she could answer him, he said, "Yup. You're right. Maybe I'm moving too fast. I don't know much about you, other than the basics. Only that you're educated, pretty, nice, artistic, come from good family, don't cheat, are honorable, have a beautiful baby girl, body to die for, or die trying to die in—plus, *can cook?* This woman I don't know, doesn't drink beyond a good wine and champagne, doesn't smoke, isn't into drugs, keeps a nice house, entertains well, has a good job and solid head on her shoulders, is a great conversationalist who makes me laugh at myself, has old-fashioned home training packaged in new millennium ethics, cares if I live or die, is a good mother, and knows how to handle money . . . her big splurge is lingerie at levels I can afford, if she does get into trouble. Makes love from her heart, and her body has done things to me that I can't tell Jesus. Says she's falling in love with me—I'm crazy in love with her. Happened overnight, and it's blowing my mind. Simple. I'm in the mood to do this now; glad I waited for you. Woman, I'm done. I gotta go to work tomorrow. What about this don't make sense? I'm hungry. Talk to me."

She stared at him as he started laughing. "You don't even know me."

"Okay, you're right. Some things I don't know yet. Aw hell, woman. Let the chips fall where they may. What's your favorite shape?"

"My favorite shape? What are you talking about!"

"I know your favorite colors, definitely know mine on you. But I do have just today to shop. Then it'll be Sunday. Need to handle my business before I jet again. So, what's your favorite shape for a diamond? I'm pretty sure of the size."

She looked at her hands and then looked up at him. This was insane, and she loved every minute of it.

"Four to five carats to let the other brothers know I'm not playing 'bout my wife—I think that'll fit just fine," he murmured. "Dang, woman, I'm starved. Aren't you hungry for some real breakfast, yet?"

# Please, Baby, Please

## MONICA JACKSON

# Chapter 1

Denise "Neecy" Ballard took the hair clip out of her hair and laid it on the bathroom sink. She licked the remnants of chocolate off her fingers and removed her rings. She laid her earrings beside them and carefully eased on the scale, her eyes squeezed shut. Then Neecy looked down and squinted with one eye at the numbers on the scale.

She gasped and almost hit the floor, scrambling off.

Horror filled her as the reality of how much she really weighed dawned. It was far worse than she'd thought. She grabbed her sweatpants and stretched-out T-shirt off the floor and pulled them on. Then she tore out of the bathroom, searching for her stepstool.

Twenty-five pounds of blubber was her reward for her hard-fought months of self-deprivation. All that nail-biting, meeting-attending, twelve-stepping, whine-mongering abstinence from shopping had gained her was twenty-five pounds of lard on her already too-generous rear. Enough was enough.

"Hello, my name is Neecy, and I'm a damn fool," she muttered to herself as she climbed up on the stool and felt frantically on the top of her kitchen cabinet. Where was the box she'd stashed?

Ah, there it was. She reverently opened the box, staring at the contents through the sudden moisture swimming in her eyes. With a trembling hand, she removed the forbidden precious plastic objects and spread them on the counter.

Neecy was done with denial that was transforming her into a fat slob. She was through with saying no to her inner desires. She was giving up on doing without what she really wanted.

She swept her credit cards from the counter and headed for the door. She, Neecy Ballard, was going shopping.

"How're you doing, girl? Long time, no see!" Pearl called out as Neecy entered the Funky Divas, her favorite clothes boutique. Funky had plenty of designer labels, but it was more about a certain unique style. All their clothes aspired to be one of a kind, and they suited women who cultivated their own special style, whether old-school soul or down-and-dirty funk.

Neecy smiled at Pearl, who looked like a high-fashion model. At first glance, the woman might seem aloof and rude. But Pearl was genuine and sweet. She always remembered your name, too.

"I know I haven't been in here for a while," Neecy said. "Honey, I've been on a money diet." Neecy patted her purse.

"I've just the cure for that. We're putting some Stella Sharon originals on sale tomorrow. I don't have them out yet, but for my best customer . . ."

Stella Sharon! Neecy's mouth watered.

"Tell you what; I'll meet you at the dressing room with some selections. I know you'll love them." Pearl sailed away.

Neecy drifted toward the dressing room. A display of dresses labeled with a famous movie star's name diverted her attention. Neecy had a thing for dresses. Sometimes she wished the long gowns of several centuries ago were still de rigueur for everyday wear. She loved laces, velvet, and lush fabrics in long, sweeping cuts. But if she were alive back in the day when that was the style for day-to-day wear, she'd probably be sporting slave muslin. There was good reason why she could never get into historical romances.

Pearl held an armful of dresses at the entrance into the dressing room. "They're only half price," she said with a grin.

Neecy drew in her breath and reverently took the dresses from Pearl's arms. Stella Sharon at half price, she thought as she stroked the rich fabrics. It didn't get much better than this. She moved into the dressing room feeling in a happy trance.

A velvet and black lace dress with long fitted sleeves lay on top of the pile. So elegant. Neecy's jeans and T-shirt dropped to the floor as she pulled the dress over her head. And pulled . . . and pulled . . .

No way was she getting this dress over her rear. Were Stella Sharon clothes running small lately? She peered at the tag. Size ten, as usual. The dress size wasn't running small; the size of her rear was running large.

Neecy wanted to sink down to the floor and wail. But she squared her shoulders and hung the dress back on the hanger, grabbed the armload of clothes, and went to find Pearl.

"I need a size twelve. It seems that prolonged shopping deprivation has caused my hips and thighs to expand."

Pearl bit her lip. "No prob. But the selection isn't as great in twelve."

A few minutes later, armed with another load of clothes, Neecy headed back to the dressing room. The dress lying on top was burgundy brocade shot with silver thread—low cut with a fitted bodice. Luscious.

She dropped her clothes to the floor again and unzipped the zipper. This time she stepped into the dress and pulled it up. She reached behind her to pull up the zipper and gasped. There was no way she was going to zip it up without tearing the zipper completely out from the seams. Lord-a-mercy. Could it be true she was a size fourteen? How humiliating.

She carried the dresses back to Pearl with a heavy step and even heavier heart.

"You didn't like any of them?" Pearl asked with disbelief in her voice.

"They were too small," Neecy's voice was as tiny. Size ten apparently was nothing but a faint memory.

"We have two dresses in fourteen. Would you like to try them on?" Neecy nodded, numb.

The size fourteens had no lace and no shimmer. They were plain and toned down, as if a woman that big had no right to feminine frills and frippery. Neecy tried the navy blue one on first, with some resentment. At least she could zip it up. But she gasped when she looked in the mirror and saw how tight it pulled across her hips and her rear, the fabric pulling into ugly horizontal lines.

That was when she panicked. No, no, no, it couldn't be. She rushed out of Funky Divas, leaving the dresses puddled on the floor.

Neecy slowed down when she hit the street and stared at Big Gals, a boutique across the street from Funky Divas that catered to bigger women. Stella Sharon didn't bother to pretty up her size fourteen dresses, so a dress bigger than a size fourteen would probably resemble an army pup tent and be just as pretty. Was this what she had to look forward to?

Weight Watchers loomed large in her future, but right now Neecy needed to shop like a junkie needed a fix. She wasn't ready to go into Big Gals, and her ego was too frail to face the size ten clodhoppers her big feet needed. She'd have to hit the jewelry and accessories. Accessories were like money—used wisely, there was no such thing as too much.

She headed across the street to Bon Bon's. She didn't have a diamond-size wallet, but Bon's specialized in fine replicas—expensive costume jewelry, really. Their hats, scarves, and purses were kicking, too. She'd spent many a contented time there. Maybe a few pairs of earrings or a hat would cheer her up.

Neecy had been at Bon Bon's a good hour before she finally felt like she'd achieved shopping nirvana. It was exactly what she needed. She tied a huge floppy straw hat with purple silk flowers and a purple scarf under her chin. She'd never worn exactly that sort of hat before. Tying the large purple bow under her chin, she peered into the mirror. It wasn't bad, really, and with a sundress, it would be— Her thought was interrupted by the *beep-beep* of a truck backing up. She glanced through the plate glass window and saw a tow truck backing up to her car.

Neecy felt as if somebody had dumped ice water down the back of her T-shirt as she recognized one of the two men who climbed out of the truck. She ran into the parking lot, the hat flopping in the wind.

"Hey, what are you doing to my car?" she yelled. Neecy had a good idea of what was up, but she wanted the rat to say the words.

The man pushed the baseball cap back on his head and squinted down at her. He was easily six-two with nut-brown skin and one of those lean yet muscled bodies. When Neecy first went into Joseph Vaughn's small used-auto dealership and met him, the man had almost given her a heart attack. He was so fine, her jaw had flopped to the ground and she had to remember to pick it up. She'd known right then that she was going to buy a car from him. If most of his customers were female, he was probably a millionaire, she decided.

"I'm repossessing my car," he said.

Those words made Neecy so mad, that his overall gorgeousness almost stopped registering.

"Re-repossessing *your* car!" Neecy sputtered. Joe Vaughn might be the handsomest man she'd ever laid eyes on in her natural life, but he couldn't get away with this. "I bought and paid for that car!"

"Maybe you bought it, but paid for it? Nope, don't think so," he drawled. "That's the problem."

"Lady, lady!" A plump saleswoman emerged from Bon Bon's. "You didn't pay for our hat."

Neecy gritted her teeth. "Can't you see that I'm having an emergency?" she said to the saleslady.

"So not paying is something of a habit for you, huh?" the man asked with a hint of humor in his voice.

She shot him a glance that she hoped would strike him dead where he stood, and dug around her purse. She found a ten-dollar bill and proffered it to the woman.

The woman looked at it as if Neecy had tried to hand her a dead rodent. "The hat is fifty-nine dollars and ninety-five cents," she said with a sniff. "Plus tax," she added.

Sixty dollars! They had to be kidding. "Tell you what, you can have the hat back," Neecy said, giving the bow under her chin a tug.

"The hat is clearly bent, and you're sweating. It's damaged. I'm sorry, but we have a policy of not accepting damaged goods as returns."

"Returns? I haven't even bought the darned thing."

Then she noticed that a hulking security guard had emerged from the store and was staring at her with ill-disguised anticipation. He brushed a hand across his club and stood at attention. And Joe the hunk and his buddy had commenced hooking up her car to the truck.

"Here, take my credit card and charge it," Neecy said, thoroughly outdone.

The lady took the card and disappeared into the store without a backward glance.

Neecy turned her attention back to the urgent matter of having her car snatched right under her nose. "Stop it! Stop it right now. I'm not allowing you to take my car!"

"Listen lady, you disappeared without a forwarding address, and you missed the second month's payment. If you needed the car that badly, you should have paid for it, like we agreed."

"Can't we work something out?" Neecy pleaded. How would she function without her car in suburban Atlanta? Folks' feet barely touched the ground around here. Heavens, there weren't even any sidewalks. "I have to have a car. What can I do?"

Joe pulled out a piece of paper from his pocket. "You can pay me seven-hundred thirty-nine dollars and forty cents," he said.

Then the store lady and the security guard came charging toward her. "This credit card was declined," she said. "We're calling the police if you don't pay immediately!"

Neecy's mouth trembled. "I must have given you the wrong card. Sorry." She searched in her handbag for her wallet, grateful for the opportunity to hide the shame she felt showing in her eyes.

"Try this one," she said, holding out another card to the lady. "And if that one doesn't work, try this one."

"Stay here, and keep an eye on her," the saleslady told the security guard, and she stalked back into the store, mumbling under her breath.

Neecy sank to the curb and sat there in defeat as she watched the two men hook up her car to the tow truck. She wasn't normally a crier, but this day had simply been too much for her. She rummaged in her oversize purse for a tissue.

"Here." Joe stuffed a tissue in her hand. Neecy gratefully took it and wiped her eyes.

"Tell you what. Why don't you ride down to the shop with us, and we'll sit down and see what we can work out," Joe said.

Neecy glanced up at him, surprised. The she blew her nose. "Okay," she said, feeling quite overcome.

The saleslady came out with her credit cards and a slip for her to sign. Joe held out his hand and helped her to her feet. It was with a sense of resignation and familiar shame that she slid inside the tow truck to sit sandwiched between the two men, her new hat thoroughly squashed like her spirits. How had she let things get so bad? Neecy wondered for the millionth time.

# Chapter 2

"Lady, you're a shopaholic," Joe said, eyeing Neecy, who sat in the chair across from his desk.

She looked utterly miserable, like a kitten drenched in a rain shower. "I thought I'd finally gotten it under control. I had budgeted to send you a payment, but when the refrigerator went out, I had to replace it."

Joe sighed. He didn't want to get into the whys and hows. He was a businessman with a bottom line, and now his business should be to collect the money owed him. In fact, he had no idea why she was sitting in his office now. A moment of weakness was his excuse.

His contemptible male weakness for a desirable woman had overcome him. And this woman was mighty desirable. She had a walk that could cause a car wreck combined with a brake-slammin' figure thick in that way he preferred. Her caramel-colored skin looked flawless, silky and so touchable. But the best thing about her was her aura of femininity. He'd never before met a woman who was so female, from her long fluttery eyelashes to her well-pedicured toes.

"Do you need a job?" he heard himself asking, and wondered what had gotten into him the moment the words left his mouth. And she looked just as stunned as he felt. He could kick himself.

Neecy blinked several times, as if trying to bring him into focus. *Yep, the same man who had taken her car away was now making her a job offer.* She jutted her chin. "I have a job," she said a bit more defiantly than she intended. Then with a bit less bravado, she added, "But I'm not working this summer."

Joe's right eyebrow arched in question.

"I'm a schoolteacher. I'm off summers." She twisted her fingers together. "I usually travel back home to the country for the summer, but this year . . ."

"You're going to get a summer job," Joe finished the sentence for her.

"Say what?" she asked, her neck snapping slightly to the left.

"Work for me for rest of the summer, and you'll get your car back."

"Work for you?"

"That's what I said. You obviously need money, and I need some work done."

"Work done?"

"Is there an echo in here?" Joe asked with a bit of exasperation in his voice.

Neecy frowned at him. "I don't want to work for you."

"You want a car for free? Right." Suddenly weary, Joe's attention was caught by the pile of paperwork he had to complete. He stifled a sigh as he picked up a paper from the top of the pile. Everybody wanted a free lunch. Why didn't more people understand that you had to earn—or at the very least pay for—what you wanted. He worked too hard himself to have much respect for anybody who thought they were entitled to free lunches—or free cars.

"Mr. Vaughn?"

He looked up into her eyes, such innocent yet intelligent eyes. Eyes you'd never think would belong to the type of person who skipped out on her bills.

"I'm surprised you're still here," he said.

She studied her hands. "I suppose I deserve your dismissal, but I was taken aback by your job offer. Surely it's not something you propose to everyone who has missed payments."

"No, it's not. Lady, you just came by at the right time. You need a car, and I need some help around this office." He eyed the stack of papers on his desk. "Badly."

"I just want to ask you this—is it standard procedure for you to go and snatch someone's car after they've missed a payment or two without contacting them or allowing them to make arrangements?" Neecy asked.

"I generally contact them first. But you moved and left no forwarding address. You skipped out on me." Her caramel-colored skin now had a rosy glow. Very attractive. Her voice was husky and suspicious. Nice.

"What sort of job do you want me to do?"

He supposed that the car would be easily valued as equal to a summer's worth of this fine woman's loving. He banished the wickedly appealing thought. "I need somebody for clerical work. Also to run errands related to the business, down to the courthouse or the Department of Motor Vehicles. I have a woman who works part-time, but she's off having a baby this summer."

"What does the job pay?"

"It pays your back car payments."

"And I'll get my car back now?" she asked.

"You'll get your car back when you pay me the back payments you owe me. We should be even by the end of August."

"So how am I supposed to get to work without a car?"

He suppressed a sudden grin. It sounded like she was biting the bait. He didn't know why the thought of this seemingly irresponsible and probably flighty woman working with him lifted his spirits, but it did.

"Atlanta has an excellent rapid transit system."

"You must be kidding," Neecy said, her voice dry.

"I don't think so."

"Look at all the cars you have on that lot! You'd make me take the bus?" Neecy's voice rose.

Joe didn't bother to reply. Instead he dug around in his file cabinet for an application. "Here, fill this out," he said. "And make sure you're here Monday at seven sharp."

Her head snapped up. "Seven in the morning! Now I know you're joking."

"Nope. Why would I joke? I always like to get an early start." Joe smiled at her.

Neecy glowered back at him, stood, and stalked out of his office, clutching the application.

It didn't bother him a bit, because he knew that she'd be back. And he could hardly believe how much he was looking forward to it.


Neecy walked into her home and immediately averted her eyes from the messy stack of papers overflowing on her desk. Her home was generally always well organized, because comfort was important to her, and clutter tended to work her nerves.

But the top of her desk was her downfall. It stood out, a sore spot, a gangrenous, cancerous, rotting, dripping mess despoiling the serene beauty and comfort of her home.

Her desk was a metaphor for her life.

She had an urge to sweep the entire mess away; the dunning

notices and the unopened bills she'd toss into a garbage bag and haul out to a Dumpster. But that fix would be temporary. She knew that rot always returned unless excised and thoroughly removed.

She'd been hanging on by her carefully manicured nails to her budget, and she'd just dropped off into free fall. Budgets were all well and good, but if the math didn't hold up, something had to give.

Neecy needed a more drastic fix. Bankruptcy? There was something so defeatist, something so *cowardly* about that route. She didn't want to go there.

But she couldn't escape the fact that her bills had surpassed her income. They had morphed from something resembling a manageable house pet, to an overgrown carnivorous monster that she couldn't afford to feed. It was only a matter of time until the damn things consumed her.

Neecy picked up an unopened envelope with no specific return address—a sure giveaway of a collection agency—and a letter opener. Before she could rip it open, the phone rang. She glanced at her caller ID and let the answering machine pick it up. Sure enough, the out-of-area unavailable number was a bill collector. She sighed as the caller left the long string of digits connected to a toll-free number and pleaded for her to call him back. She pitied those folks who had to handle bill collectors before caller ID and answering machines. She couldn't imagine.

That familiar overwhelming feeling came over her, and she sighed as she went to the kitchen to pull out the peach cobbler she'd made yesterday. Then she stopped in her tracks, her eyes squeezed shut as she remembered the state of her thighs. Size sixteen beckoned. Pretty soon her body would be like the state of her finances—out of control. She opted for a bubble bath, instead.

A few minutes later, luxuriating in the bubbly, silky water (*imported bubble bath, a bargain at $18.99 per twelve-ounce bottle*) she tried to figure out what to do. But that was too depressing so she just slid deeper under the bubbles.

The sudden, vapory vision of Joseph Vaughan filled her thoughts. Hmmmm. First, the memory of his tempting, crooked grin warmed her. Then her mind, as wayward as it tended to be, drifted sinfully below his waist, lingered there a while and settled on the inviting bulge of his . . . wallet.

She emerged from the water, gasping, the ends of her hair dripping soap bubbles. There it was—the solution to her financial problems in luscious, living six-foot-two caramel-cream color! Joe Vaughan had money. He reeked of it, in that understated Wrangler-blue-jeans-wearing, truck-driving way men with real money did. Flashy men sporting fancy cars, pricey watches, jewels, and expensive suits generally had nothing more than overextended credit. Just like her.

Joe Vaughan had cash, all right, and she was familiar with the way he'd studied her. He'd been cool with it, but he couldn't quite hide the unmistakable signs of male interest. He wanted her bad.

She'd shied away. He'd made her nervous. She'd felt overpowered and overwhelmed when she was near him. But he wanted to rescue her. So why didn't she let him? All she needed was a little help to get back on her feet. There wasn't a thing wrong with it. It was the way the way the world was supposed to work, and it made a man feel like a man.

She could handle Joe Vaughn. No way would she let things get out of control. A reasonable loan would save her, allow her a chance to get back on her feet. No way would she ask him for a thing. By the time she finished with him, he'd be begging to give it to her. It was the oldest trick in the book. *You mean the oldest profession in the book,* a little voice whispered to her.

Neecy frowned. That really wasn't her style. No, she definitely wasn't going to go there. But she felt herself warming at the thought of Joe's *there*. There was mighty close to that wallet—sinful, delicious, and oh so dangerous. She should stay away from both. Neecy bit her lip. Well . . . she might go *there*, but only if she really wanted to.

# Chapter 3

Neecy tapped her yellow high-heeled strappy sandals (*brand: Oscar de la Renta; cost: far too much*) against the asphalt as she eyed her watch and frowned. Her feet were already killing her. The sandals were cute but hadn't been the wisest choice for an early-morning commute on a crowded bus. But they'd been so perfect with the yellow sundress she'd picked to impress (and thankfully it had been loose enough to still fit). She couldn't resist the ensemble.

It was only seven in the morning, but the Georgia heat and humidity were already rising. She'd wanted to appear cool and professional, and maybe a little sexy, but she felt hot, grimy, and disheveled already. She longed to sit down, but all that was available was hard asphalt and scrubby grass full of anthills. She glanced at the chain link fence for respite, but the metal poles looked hot and forbidding, the fencing too flimsy to lean against.

Relief mixed with anxiety lose inside her as Joe Vaughn's navy blue pickup truck pulled up in front of her. He climbed out of the cab of his pickup, his movements graceful and loose, his form lean and supple as a dancer. She felt her temperature rise a few more notches, and she dug in her purse for a tissue. *Neecy, get a grip*, she told herself. *You wish*, a naughty voice in her head whispered back.

"You're late," she accused him, mainly trying to hide her own fluster.

He grinned at her. "I'm not late, you're early," he said, unlocking the gate that led to his lot.

She glanced surreptitiously at her watch, and since it was straight up seven, she had no answer to that.

Neecy followed him into the trailer that served as his office. He opened the blinds to the large picture windows in front, and a flood of sunlight illuminated the dusty room. Piles of papers seemed to cover every surface.

Joe Vaughn faded into the background as Neecy surveyed the room. She had been too tense yesterday to notice just how large a task this would be. She carefully dusted off a chair and picked up the nearest pile and sat. Then she set about trying to clear off a surface to sort. The first priority obviously was to—

"What do you think you're doing?" a peremptory male voice said.

"I'm doing exactly what you told me, I'm getting your office in order." She glanced around her. "And believe me, it looks like it needs it."

Joe snatched the papers from her hands and put them back on the precarious pile. "You'll only do what I tell you to do. I'm not going to have some airhead who can't keep track of her basic bills come in here and wreck my place."

Neecy felt a deep flush of shame, then fury. "Excuse me? I don't see how my personal business has anything to do with professional competence. I teach office skills and management to high school students, and I'm fully credentialed in my field. If you don't trust me to do the job you've given me to do, then you can take it and shove—"

"Hold on. I apologize, it's just that—"

"That you're an—"

"Hey! I said I was sorry."

"I'm out of here," Neecy said, getting up.

"What about the car?"

Neecy stopped at the door.

"Listen," he said, his tone contrite. Joe shifted his weight from foot to foot. "I want to help you. I know there are probably good reasons for the situation you're in now. Let me help you find your way out. I'm sorry for what I said. I'm more than willing to let you have at it at my office if you're willing to do so. I'm grateful for your expertise."

Neecy hesitated, her hand on the doorknob.

"Please?" he said.

A small smile crossed Neecy's face. He'd said the magic word. "I can understand how you could think that I'd be incompetent, given the circumstances," she said to him. "But I am good in an office."

"I'm sure you are," he said, his voice husky.

The tension between them turned to something else, something liquid and heavy, breathless, sticky-sweet, inexorable.

The world narrowed to the masculine, sexy curves of Joe's lips, and Neecy wanted him to kiss her more than anything in the world, but the thought overwhelmed her. She wanted to run and hide. She felt like a squirrel sitting in the middle of the road, undecided about which way to run, with an eighteen-wheeler bearing down on her. It was an unaccustomed and unpleasant feeling. Why now and why Joe Vaughn? She'd dealt with good-looking men before. Why was she losing it over this one? And it was then that she knew she was in trouble.

Joe looked away. Neecy sat down. It took a moment to get her breath, not to mention her nerves, under control.

She turned to a filing cabinet, pulled it open, and studied the filing system. It was a mess, and it would have to be redone. Good thing—

the task would give her the chance to focus on something else besides her fine new boss. She'd breezed in here, thinking that she could handle Joe Vaughn easily, and so far all she done was hope that he'd handle her.

The day was a routine one, with Joe at his desk and Neecy catching up with some filing.

Then Neecy heard a woman's voice ring out. "And who are you?"

Something about the tone got Neecy's back up, and she got off her knees where she'd been filing papers in the bottom drawer of the filing cabinet. She stood taking in the slender woman with the smooth chocolate skin, shoulder-length black relaxed hair, who was dressed neatly and casually in jeans and a crisp cotton blouse.

"My name is Denise Ballard," she said, offering her hands.

"Neecy's filling in for Trish this summer. Neecy, this is Grace—"

"Vaughn," the woman said, cutting Joe short.

Neecy's heart just about stopped. Joe was married?

"I thought you had gone back to using Shleppmann when our divorce became final," he said.

"It sounds so Jewish," the woman said. "And I don't look a bit Jewish."

Joe shrugged.

Divorced. So that woman was his ex-wife. Neecy stifled a sigh of relief, which turned to alarm when she noted the possessive hand the woman placed on Joe's chest. "I got an offer on the condo. It seems better than the last one," Grace said.

Joe pushed his baseball hat back and peered at her. "They have a hope at financing and all? Credit not down the drain?"

"Barely in the pipes, just a few blemishes, that's all."

Joe exhaled slowly and shook his head.

"I never carry a balance on my credit cards. It's a shame how people nowadays can't handle their money," Grace returned, sounding quite superior. "Carrying a balance on your credit cards is just like flushing money down the drain, don't you think?" she asked.

Neecy did have some notion of the concept, so she nodded in agreement. The conversation was headed in an uncomfortable direction, and it was time she got some fresh air. "I think I'm going to step out for a few minutes," she said.

"Nice meeting you, Grace."

Neecy closed the door firmly behind her. So Grace she never carried a balance on her credit cards! Well, there was no need to brag about it, Neecy decided, irked. If that was Joe's type of woman, she couldn't be more opposite from her—efficient, economical, edgy, and bladelike. She was the sort of woman that Neecy always felt she had to step lightly around or she might accidentally get cut.

Neecy nursed a cup of coffee at the fast-food restaurant across the street until Grace's car pulled away. Then she made her way back to the lot.

Joe pulled open the door and leaned against its frame, watching her hobble across the street in her too-high heels. "Concept of no balance on your credit cards rattled you, huh?" he drawled, with a grin.

"You're letting the air-conditioning out," Neecy said with a slight frown. "It's hotter than blazes out here."

"Seriously, don't let Grace bother you." He straightened and closed the door behind them. "She's a little holier than thou when it comes to finance. But she has a point." He paused. "If it stays slow, I thought we could take a little time this afternoon and sit down and start in on your budget."

She didn't want to go off on this man. Neecy drew in a breath. Yes, she did want to go off on him. She wanted to pick up that chair and—

"I did say that I wanted to help you," he said, his tone sincere.

She exhaled slowly. He wanted to help. And she wanted him to help her. Wasn't that the point? "Yes, I'd be glad to sit down and talk over my finances with you," she said.

Joe put the pencil down and rubbed his temples. "Let me get this straight. In your monthly spending plan, your hair appointments, your pedicures, your manicures, your various waxes, your facials, and your massages, which you say are all absolutely essential, you budget to spend five hundred dollars?"

"Yes."

"Not fifty, not five, but *five hundred dollars*," Joe repeated.

"Listen," Neecy said, "self-care is my priority. It's my therapy, so to speak. I've come to terms with the fact that I'm a high-maintenance sort of girl."

"Therapy might be cheaper. At least your insurance would cover that."

Neecy's lips thinned.

"I'm not saying you have to do without, but do you realize that there's not one of these things you couldn't do yourself instead of paying someone else to do them?" Joe leaned back in his chair. "Look, five hundred dollars would have paid your car payment and a few other bills to boot."

"What about my hair? What about my waxes? My massages?" Neecy said. The thought of kicking her salon habit almost made her break out in a cold sweat, nibble on her nails, and ruin her manicure.

"There's always the natural look if you're really looking to tighten your belt. And the Lord made razors to remove hair. As for your massages . . ." He got a wicked look in his eye. "I'd probably be willing to help you out there."

Neecy's stomach curled in pleasurable anticipation. Hmmm, kicking her salon addiction might be worth it, at least in one sense. But the natural look? She didn't think so.

# Chapter 4

Joe studied Neecy as she concentrated on the papers on her desk.

He couldn't quite understand himself. Joe understood physical attraction well enough. He had only to pass within a foot of her, and it was like he was sixteen all over again. It was all he could do to keep his hands off her. She could sue him for him for sexual harassment for his thoughts alone.

But it was much more than her body. Her presence was wonderful—warm, funny, and easy to be around. It was as if she were the piece of the puzzle he had been looking to fit into his life and make it right. She was that good. She'd just been here a few weeks, and already he couldn't imagine being without her.

But the way the woman spent money! She needed a good spanking. If a month ago somebody had told him that he'd have his nose wide open for the flaky, high-maintenance type, he never would have believed it.

He would just have to teach her better. He simply had been lucky to have had good home training. Many people didn't have that advantage. Neecy would be his new project. He'd start from the head down.

It wouldn't be an easy task, but he wasn't a man who quailed before a tough job.

"Neecy?" Joe said. Her head snapped up, and she looked at him, her brows arched in question.

"My sister braids hair. I think braids would look great on you." He leaned back in his chair and warmed to his subject.


A few days later, Neecy sat in Marjorie's buttery yellow kitchen, her neck aching. "We all expected Joe to marry Grace, but we do wish they had waited," Marjorie, Joe's sister, said, as her fingers flew through Neecy's hair.

"Why is that?" Neecy asked.

"They'd been together since grade school. They'd really never experienced anything else."

"I suppose getting married would be natural after being together that long, especially if they loved each other."

Marjorie's lips thinned. "Love has little to do with it if you're going to cat around with other men."

"Is that what happened?"

Marjorie shook her head. "I've said too much already. It's really none of my business."

Neecy was dying to question her further about Joe's marriage and more important, its demise, but felt that Marjorie had snapped that book shut. She stifled a sigh. "I need to stretch," Neecy said.

"As soon as I finish this braid," Marjorie said.

Neecy looked at her watch. She'd been sitting in this chair for five hours.

A few days ago, she and Joe had surfed the Internet looking at natural hairstyles. He'd showed her the attractiveness and ease of maintenance of the braided styles. He said that his sister was great at putting in braids. When he whispered in her ear how much he wanted to see her in the style . . . well, the man was a natural salesman.

"Okay, you can stretch," Marjorie said.

Neecy stood, groaned, and reached for the ceiling. "How much longer?"

"About fifteen minutes."

"You're kidding? We're finally almost done? Let me see."

"Not until I'm done. You know that's my rule."

Fifteen minutes later, Marjorie left to make a phone call, and Neecy was admiring herself in the mirror, wondering why she never considered braids before. She'd always ruled out extensions, choosing instead to keep her cinnamon-brown hair shoulder length by expensive and extreme hair salon babying. Marjorie assured her that her hair would regain its former thickness and health that had been ravaged by years of relaxers.

"Joe's here," Marjorie whispered, behind her. "He insisted I call when I was done. He wanted to take you out to celebrate. A surprise. I told him that women don't like surprises, but you know how stubborn men are."

Neecy smiled. She was discovering that she could deal with surprises from Joe. She sailed out to the living room to greet him.

He blinked at her. "You don't like it?" Neecy and Marjorie asked in an anxious chorus.

"No, no. You look great." He took a step forward and swallowed. "Really great." He put a hand out, as if to touch, then hastily withdrew it. Marjorie gave a satisfied smile.

"Are you ready to go?" Joe asked.

Neecy's pulse pounded. "Yes, yes, I am," she said, scurrying to gather her things.

"I wanted to take you somewhere nice. I knew this was was a big step for you. I don't think you'll regret it."

Neecy looked down at her casual khakis. "I have to go change."

"What you have on is fine."

"Not for somewhere nice."

"Trust me."

Since they weren't jeans, she supposed they'd do, although she doubted she'd be wholly comfortable at a nice place. But she'd trust him. He was an easy man to trust.

Twenty minutes later, Joe pulled into the parking lot, and Neecy pulled up an eyebrow. "Excuse me," she said, every high-maintenance, prima-donna alarm in her head ringing at full alert. "I thought you said you were taking me somewhere nice."

"This is somewhere nice."

"This is Shaney's Restaurant."

"I know where we are. This is one of my favorite places. Great fried chicken."

He'd bounded out of the pickup truck and was halfway to the door before he realized that she wasn't beside him.

Neecy tapped her manicured finger against the door of the pickup and waited for his return. The man was going to take a lot of training.

Joe returned, walking up to her side of the car. He opened the door, looking sheepish. "I was hungry," he said.

Definitely a lot of training, but there was hope yet, she thought and gracefully exited the car.

Once inside the restaurant and seated at the booth, Neecy peered at Joe over the menu. Training a man was not unlike training a puppy. Better to start sooner than later. She set down the menu. "Would you mind ordering for me?" she asked.

Joe frowned slightly. "I don't know what you want to eat."

"I like anything but liver and onions. And beets," she added.

"I don't want to order for you."

"It's customary for the man to order for the woman."

"Not at Shaney's."

"Speaking of Shaney's . . . Family-style dining with an average entrée price of less than ten bucks does not qualify as *somewhere nice*," Neecy informed him.

Joe sighed and laid down the menu. "Welcome to the real world. The world where you're not going to blow a hundred bucks on lunch and where you're going to order for yourself. Live with it." He picked up the menu.

Neecy inaudibly exhaled. So much for that endeavor. Oh, what the heck? She liked him the way he was anyway. Maybe Joe was less trainable than she'd first thought.

Neecy had barely finished the last bite of her fried chicken salad when he said, "Okay, whip them out."

"What?"

"Your credit cards. I know you're carrying again." He motioned the manager over, and the man approached with a large pair of scissors. He brandished the scissors and laid them on the table.

"Thanks, Eric," Joe said. "Could you send over dessert when we're done? How about the chocolate brownie special with double ice cream, two spoons, extra whipped cream and nuts? We need to celebrate the cutting of the cards."

"Cutting of the cards?" Neecy said, knowing he didn't tell this man, the Lord, and everybody else that she was going to cut up her credit cards in front of them, because she wasn't going to do it. No way.

"Cutting them isn't really enough. It's just ceremonial. You need to contact the creditors and have them cancelled. We'll do that tomor-row."

Neecy was speechless. "But—but what about emergencies?" she finally managed to get out.

"That's what savings are for," he patted her hand. "We'll get to that. Don't worry."

"I need my credit cards," she said, clutching her purse.

"No, you don't," he said, looking deep into her eyes, "You're bigger than they are. You're so much more."

"No, I'm not," she muttered, her thoughts a maelstrom of bills, shopping, Joe, everything.

"They're just plastic, Neecy."

His eyes were coffee, his lashes impossibly long. She didn't think they could grow that long on a man. But she was digressing. She shook her head to clear it.

Her credit cards! She worked so hard to establish—okay, to reestab-lish—her credit. "You have no idea how hard it was to get credit," she said.

"You said yourself that your debt was destroying you. It's an addic-tion, Neecy, like any other. Give it up, lady. You can do it."

He was holding a hand out to her—thin, long, sensitive fingers that could be soft and hard at the same time. She squeezed her eyes shut against their beckoning warmth. He wanted to snatch away her hard-won freedom to charge, shop, to buy, to have. More bling-bling. That *ka-ching* was the most beautiful sound in the world.

Neecy opened her eyes and reached out and touched Joe's fin-gers. He grasped her hand. His strength and warmth flowed out to her. She'd known this man only a short time, but that made no dif-ference. He was a rock, and she trusted him. Neecy picked up the scissors.

. . .

"It's been quite a day," Joe said as he pulled up in front of her apartment building.

"Yes, it has," Neecy agreed. "I love my hair, and . . ." She patted her purse. She didn't have words yet for what Joe had done for her.

He nodded, understanding.

"Will you come in? I'd love for you to see my place. I'll put on some coffee."

Joe hesitated, and Neecy's breath caught. She wasn't ready for the evening to end.

Then he smiled, and she almost sighed with relief.

"Nice place," he said, looking around as he followed her through the door.

"Make yourself at home. I'm going to put on the coffee," Neecy said, suddenly feeling nervous. He filled her small apartment with masculine energy.

"Do you mind if I put on some music?" he asked.

"Not at all."

A few minutes later, the mellow jazz notes of Najee filled her apartment.

Neecy took a deep breath and went into the freezer and took out her extra special coffee beans that a friend had given her for her birthday last year.

She pulled out her brand-new, never-used cappuccino maker (*clearance price, sixty-nine dollars*). She thought she had a coffee-bean grinder in the top kitchen cabinet. She dragged a kitchen chair over and climbed up on the counter. She stood and stretched up, opening the cabinet, which was stuffed full of unused small appliances. Where was that dratted coffee-bean grinder? She dug around. Then alarmed, she felt herself lose balance, and with a gurgled shriek, she started to fall. Strong arms gripped her around the waist and pulled her against a strong male body. The scent of Joe filled her nostrils. Her senses reeled.

"You need to be more careful," Joe said. His voice was rough, strained. He set her away from him carefully, like she was made of fragile porcelain.

He didn't meet her eyes. The atmosphere was heavy, almost oppressive. It was hard to breathe, to think.

"Uh, where's your bathroom?" Joe asked.

"Second door down the hall on your left," Neecy said, blinking rapidly.

Joe fled like a man who was one second away from losing control.

Neecy knew exactly how he felt.

But she should finish the coffee. She dug out the blender from a lower counter. It should do the job and just as well as the darned coffee-bean grinder.

Joe stuck his head in the kitchen. "Are you okay?" he yelled over the roar of the blender.

Neecy didn't bother to yell back. She made an OK sign with her thumb and forefinger and grinned.

Joe frowned slightly and withdrew. She turned off the blender and peered in. The coffee hadn't been grounded; it had been pulverized. Oh, well.

She approached her brand-new cappuccino maker with some trepidation. Now, where had she put the instruction booklet?

Twenty minutes later, she looked out and saw Joe leaning against the doorway, watching her as she tried to figure out the cappuccino maker. "Why don't you take a break? Let me finish up. The kitchen is my territory. Go pick out some new music."

Since at that moment Neecy had been torn between wailing in frustration or hurling the cappuccino maker against the wall, she gladly retreated. She took haven in the bathroom and wet a wash cloth with cool water and held it against her face. She'd wanted to impress Joe so much, but had come off looking like even more of a fool than she already did.

What must he think of her? She's shown him that she couldn't handle her own finances, and now she'd shown she couldn't even make a cup of coffee!

Instead of screaming, she lifted her chin and went into her living room. She put on a classic Earth Wind & Fire CD and went into the kitchen. The mess she'd made was cleaned up, the appliances had disappeared into cabinets, and a red can of Folgers stood by a full pot of coffee under her regular coffeemaker.

"I'm sorry for the delay. I was trying to be too fancy—to impress you."

"I know," Joe said. "I'm flattered."

He handed her a mug of coffee, fixed just the way she liked it, and took one of his own. "Let's go talk."

"I should be serving you," Neecy said.

"The kitchen is my territory, like I said."

Neecy couldn't argue with that. She sat down beside him and sipped the coffee, which was just like him, good, classic, strong, hot, steamy . . . She smiled to herself at the direction her thoughts inevitably took in regards to Joe and was surprised at how tired she felt. The song "Reasons" came on the stereo, and she leaned against his shoulder. His arm went around her. Easy, natural, like that was where it belonged, where she belonged.

"You're working for me," he said.

"Yes, I am, and—?"

"I don't want you to feel obligated to me. I don't want to cross lines that shouldn't be crossed."

She straightened and looked at him. "You're talking about sexual harassment, aren't you? You're afraid if you made a move on me that I'd up and sue you."

Joe said nothing, but his silence was eloquent.

A smile curved Neecy's lips. "Just don't sue *me*," she whispered, and touched her lips to his.

Joe's arms circled her and drew her to him. Her tongue stroked along the bottom of his lip in tentative exploration. His lips parted, and he took the kiss from her, tongues tangling. His lips were firm, hungry, sensual. Her body flamed in response. His cell phone rang. They both groaned. Joe pulled out his cell phone and looked at it. "I'm sorry, Neecy, but I have to take this, briefly. It's a franchisee."

He stepped away and listened for a moment. "I need to go. I had a great time," Joe said apologetically as soon as he clicked his cell phone shut. "See you tomorrow." He dropped a light kiss on her forehead.

Neecy blinked in disbelief, but knew better to protest. She got up and saw him to the door. She watched him pull off with her arms folded across her chest. Was that relief in his voice she'd heard when he said good-bye?

Joe lit out of Neecy's place like a devil was nipping at his heels. If it weren't for that phone call, he'd probably be in her bed right now, which would have been the point of no return. Once he had Neecy, he knew he'd never let her go. He wasn't sure, he wasn't ready—he might as well face it . . . he'd turned tail and run like a clean plucked chicken—cluck, cluck, cluck.

# Chapter 5

The next morning at work, Neecy sipped a cup of coffee at her desk. Phillip, the guy who helped Joe out around the lot, stuck his head into the office. "I'm going to take this guy on a test drive. I'll be back in a few minutes," he said.

She nodded. Joe was out for the morning at an auction, buying cars. She was grateful for the reprieve because being around him was like being a teakettle whistling its steam off. The man had yet to make a move to take her off the fire. Did he want her or not? He was driving her crazy.

She didn't know if she was coming or going around the man, he had her that confused and turned around. How much more was a girl to take?

Then like an answer, a good-looking man who looked a lot like Joe walked in, plopped in Joe's chair, grinned at her, and stuck out his hand. "Hi, I'm Harris, Joe's brother. You must be Neecy. I've heard a lot about you."

"Like what?" Neecy asked suspiciously.

"Uh . . . That you are very good at your work."

She didn't like him sitting behind Joe's desk. "Excuse me, but I need to get back where you're sitting," Neecy said politely. He moved, and she busied herself in one of Joe's file drawers, waiting for Harris to state his business and go away, hopefully in that order.

"Do you know when Joe will be back?" he asked.

"He said after lunch. He went to a car auction."

"I needed to talk to him." Harris sighed heavily, leaning elbows on his knees, his head in his hands. "My fiancée just dumped me." He dug in his pocket and pulled out a ring.

The gleam of the diamond in the sunlight darn near blinded Neecy. She moved to Harris and perused it. Two carats at least, a beautifully cut marquis set in white gold or platinum. "The girl is a fool," she said.

"That's what I think. She was a fool to dump me like she did. Every man deserves a second chance. . . ."

"I meant she was a fool to give the ring back."

"Excuse me?"

"Once it's on your finger, it's yours."

"Hey, she broke up with me."

"Still! You gave it to her. It was a gift. You can't take a gift back."

"An engagement ring is a symbol of a promise. Once that promise is broken—"

"Oh, c'mon, admit it. You lucked out when you got that ring back."

Harris sucked his teeth, scowling. Then a grin broke over his handsome features. "Okay, if she hadn't thrown it my face, I wouldn't have asked for it back. I'm thankful that she likes dramatic gestures. Do you realize how much this ring cost me?"

Neecy gave him a wry smile in return. "I have an idea."

"I can take it back to the jeweler for a full refund. I still have the receipt."

"You don't sound too heartbroken if you're so relieved about the money."

He shrugged. "She was as beautiful as this ring. I hoped it would work out."

He took Neecy's hand and slid the ring onto her left hand, fourth finger. She stared at it, the interplay of rainbows of light flickering and dancing against the intricate facets.

"You know the saying: There's always more fish in the sea," Harris said, and broke the spell.

"So you're a player," Neecy said, and pulled the ring off her finger.

"No, I'm not a player."

"You're hitting on me."

Harris laughed. "I hit on everybody."

"See, a player."

"A charmer."

"It must be the same thing."

"But, I was looking to settle down," Harris said.

"So why was the lady so eager to get free from such a charming hook?"

He grinned at her. "Maybe she wasn't the right fish."

"So you think you have to hook many fish in order to find just the right one, hmmm?"

"Maybe I do need to do that," he said with a roguish smile.

Joe's brother was a player of the worst stripe, a true charmer, the sweet type who disarmed with truth but still went unerringly for the kill.

But he was harmless to her, and she liked him. She smiled at him and handed the ring back.

She heard a small sound in the doorway. Joe was standing in the doorway. The man moved like a panther.

"Hello, Harris. I see you've introduced yourself to Neecy," he said.

"Yes, it was nice talking to you. Can we go somewhere private, man? I have something I want to discuss with you."

"As long as it doesn't have anything to do with what we talked about last week."

"Well, I wanted to touch base on that, too."

"Harris."

"All right."

"I'll be back in an hour or so."

Neecy looked after them, both wondering how two brothers could seem so different and worrying how similar maybe they both were. Joe seemed nothing like the player type his brother was.

A week had passed, and it was late Friday evening. A busy week, and it was finally drawing to a close. Neecy had hardly seen Joe at work, but it seemed as if the entire time had been foreplay. Arousal surged between them, sparked by a glance, a whiff of scent, an errant touch. She knew without a doubt that he felt it, too. More than summer heat lay heavy in the air; anticipation eddied around them, buffeting them like storm winds.

A couple came in the office to finish the sales paperwork with Joe. Neecy moved around on the periphery of the room. Time stretched. The transaction, which should have been relatively brief, seemed to take forever.

An eternity later, the couple left, and she and Joe were alone.

"So how have you been doing? We haven't had a lot of time to talk." He approached her, looking uncharacteristically nervous.

"I'm okay."

"That's good."

Their words faded away. The silence was awkward, vast. It angled her already taut nerves.

"Well, I better go," she murmured.

He touched her arm. "Wait," he said. "Do you have plans? We've never been on a proper date. I know it's short notice, but . . ."

Joe's words faded away, and her attention became focused on his fingers against the soft skin of her arms. They tingled, almost burning. She moved closer to him. His fingers tightened, moved, imperceptibly at first . . .

Then suddenly, she was in his arms. They gazed in each other's eyes, and she couldn't imagine being anywhere else, ever. His lips met hers, and the entire world except them ended. Her heart beating in time to his, she felt his firm lips, tasted the sweetness of his mouth, felt his tongue probing and learning the recesses of her mouth. Her body ached and throbbed in answer. They were stumbling toward the largest flat surface in his office, the desk. He slapped at the lights, and only the moon shining through the blinds lit them. Neecy couldn't think, all she wanted to do was feel, and what she wanted to feel was all of Joe Vaughn inside her.

He has so hard and . . . She opened one eye and peeked downward. *Huge.*

He shifted his package against her most sensitive part, and she lost all reason. All she could think and do was try to free what she wanted most. She reached for his waistband. With one arm, he swept the papers off the desk. The other pulled up her skirt and pulled down her panties. His tongue was circling the fabric above her nipple, his fingers everywhere, touching, tingling, electric.

"Oh, yes, now, put it in, please, please, please," she pleaded. And he did it like that, because he slid his huge thing home in her hot, wet, warmth and it felt so damn good she could sob. He pulled her to the edge of the desk and rock, rocked her in just the right way over and over until they both exploded to beyond there and back again.

. . .

Heavy satisfaction filled Neecy, who was replete, complete, and a little sore. She felt Joe's warm breath on her cheek. "Want to go over to my place?" he said. "We're not very comfortable here."

She became aware of her calves dangling off the table and the hard wood at her back. "I suppose not." They rolled off the table simultaneously. She gathered her clothes and went to the bathroom to freshen up. She viewed herself in the mirror: a woman thoroughly made love to.

They stopped by her house first and picked up some clothes and toiletries. Then shortly afterwards, Neecy followed Joe into his home, a comfortable house close to his car lot in the thriving area near Emory University in Atlanta. She looked around in surprise. The house was bare with stark white walls and beautifully finished hardwood floors. "You don't have any furniture," she said, stating the obvious.

"Grace kept all the stuff, and I've never got around to buying anything new."

"You do have a bed?" Neecy asked.

Joe laughed. "I do have a bed."

"I need to shower."

"There's a guest bedroom with a bathroom right over here. It's well stocked with soap, towels, and stuff, even a clean bathrobe. I'm going to shower, too. Don't worry; I have a huge water heater."

After they showered, Neecy snuggled in bed with Joe, who not only had a bed, but also had one of those big televisions in his bedroom.

Neecy was surfing channels when Joe kissed her shoulder. "I can't believe we are too tired already."

"Just right at this moment," Neecy answered. "It's been a busy week."

Joe yawned. "You're right.

"I hated it when I saw you standing in my office with my brother," Joe said suddenly.

"Why?" Neecy asked, suspecting the answer.

"He's a player. Did he hit on you?"

"No. He was telling me that his fiancée dumped him and showing me the ring she threw in his face."

"Don't think he didn't deserve it," Joe said.

"I think he does get that. He said he was ready to settle down."

"I'll believe it when I'll see it."

"What does he do?"

"He's a lawyer."

Neecy started to laugh.

"What's so funny?"

"You and your brother—a used-car dealer and a lawyer. You two should be used to bad jokes."

Joe cocked his head. "Not the bad ones. Folks don't have the nerve to tell those to our faces. We hear only the top-of-the-line used-car-salesman and lawyer jokes."

Neecy rolled over on her stomach. "Listen up. Here's a good one."

*A man has spent many days crossing the desert without water. Suddenly he sees a shiny object sticking out of the sand! It looks like an ash tray from an old used car. He pulls it out of the sand, and—poof!—out pops a genie! But this is no ordinary genie. He's wearing a shiny sports coat, has a pencil stuck behind his ear and a blue book in his coat pocket. This genie obviously used to be a used-car salesman.*

*"Well, G," says the genie. "You know how it works. You have three wishes."*

*"It sounds good," says the man, "But how am I going to trust a genie who was once a used-car salesman!"*

*"What do you got to lose?" The genie looks at him scornfully.*

*The man looks around at the endless desert sands and decides the genie is right. "Cool. For my first wish, I wish I were in a lush oasis with plentiful dishes of my favorite food and drink that are never empty."*

*The man finds himself in the most beautiful oasis he has ever seen. He's surrounded with bountiful forty ounces and grape soda and plates full of French fries, ribs, and hot wings.*

*"Okay, G, what's your second wish?"*

*"My second wish is that I was rich beyond my wildest dreams."*

*The man finds himself surrounded by backpacks filled with C-notes and winning lottery tickets.*

*Okay, you have just one more wish. Better make it a good one!"*

*After thinking for a few minutes, the man says, "I wish that no matter where I go, beautiful women will want and need me."*

"Poof! The genie turned him into a tampon." Neecy turned to Joe. "So, what is the moral of the story?" she asked him brightly.

"I dare not say," Joe answered, looking slightly appalled. "He turned him into a tampon?"

"Yes, a tampon."

"The moral of the story is that if a used-car salesman offers you anything at no cost, there's going to be a string attached."

Joe let out a mighty groan. "That was awful. I'm going to have to pay you back for that one."

Neecy shrieked with laughter as he tickled her tummy for revenge.

"Don't," she said, gasping. He stopped immediately. Neecy lay in his arms, breathing hard. "Payback can be a female dog, can't it?" he asked, a smile still in his voice.

"I guess so. Speaking of female dogs, how is Grace doing lately?"

"Ouch. Is that a cat scratch I'm hearing?"

"Sorry. I was being bad."

"There has been a lot of that going around the last few minutes."

Neecy lifted herself up on her elbow and stared at him. "And the last couple of hours?"

Joe gave her a silly grin that turned her insides to mush. "When she was good, she was very, very good," he said softly. "But when she told bad jokes, she was absolutely horrid."

# Chapter 6

It was a bright and sunny Saturday morning, and Joe was in the kitchen, cooking omelettes. Neecy was sitting on his dryer waiting for his single set of sheets to run through the spin cycle. Joe did indeed run a sparse and frugal household. Everywhere her gaze landed, there was something the man needed.

Her fingers itched, and she practically had to hold her feet back from running down to the mall. Shoot, not only the mall—Joe could use help from Wal-Mart, Kmart, anywhere. She didn't know how he stood the emptiness.

"Breakfast is ready," she heard his cheery voice call from the kitchen.

She climbed off the dryer and made her way to the kitchen to be greeted by two TV trays crowned by paper plates and cups and icy, hard, gun-gray metal folding chairs. The omelettes looked great, though. They were full of bacon, cheese, and vegetables with big crusty biscuits on the side that dripped butter. Joe Vaughn knew how to treat a girl well in more ways than one. Neecy kissed the hope of ever getting back into her size ten clothes good-bye, at least for the time being.

"Mmmm, looks great," Neecy said, picking up her fork. She closed her eyes as the omelette melted in her mouth. "This is wonderful, Joe."

The eggs were flavored perfectly with some mixture of herbs she couldn't quite identify. Maybe he'd been a chef in another life. She picked up the paper cup and took a sip of orange juice. Fresh-squeezed. Apparently, there were some amenities of life Joe didn't stint on. "You're a great cook," she said.

"It's a hobby of mine."

"Yet, you don't believe in furniture."

He grinned. "I'm not exactly against furniture. But I told you that Grace kept all of it, and I simply never got around to furnishing this place beyond the bare necessities. Shopping is definitely not one of my hobbies."

Neecy flashed him a bright smile. "It is one of mine."

"Oh, no—you're not dragging me to any stores."

"I'd be happy to do it for you."

He frowned at her. "You'd have this place done up in silk and hot pink."

"Oh, c'mon. Give me some credit. I have some sense of your style by now. Blue is your favorite color. You hate overly modernist styles, and you're also not too crazy about country looks. Any boudoir or feminine cutesy designs will have you running in horror to the nearest hotel room. You're a clean, traditional, minimalist type of guy. Trust me." She looked into his eyes. "Because I trusted you," she said.

He paused. "You did. You've trusted me quite a bit."

He went into another room and returned with a platinum credit card and lay it on the table. Neecy stared at it, afraid to touch it, afraid even to breathe too deeply. "Are you sure?" she finally asked.

"Ten thousand dollars—then we can evaluate what else may be needed."

A ten-thousand-dollar shopping spree! Had she died and gone to heaven?

"Let me go home and change first." Neecy started to pick up the card with only a slight tremor to her hand.

Joe slid the card back and put it in his pocket. "You'll need these." He held out a set of keys to his pickup.

"I'll be back in an hour." She grabbed the keys and hit the door running.

He was actually going to give her his credit card! Platinum, no less. Neecy felt a thrill go through her as she guessed at the credit limit. It was only the beginning. Joseph Vaughn could wipe away her debt with a wave of his well-off hand. Wasn't this what she wanted? Was it the end of her financial troubles? It had been so easy.

So why didn't her victory feel better then this? Neecy suspected the remnants of the warm glow she felt were from Joe's loving rather than from Joe's plastic, from Joe's trust in her rather than from the prospect of his bankroll. She wanted to go back and crawl into his warm strong arms rather than stroll through malls. Somehow Joe always managed to confuse the hell out of her one way or another.

Neecy had decided she'd needed reinforcement for this sort of foray and called up Ramona, one of her shopping cronies with the news. Girlfriend couldn't believe her good fortune in parting a man from his platinum plastic, and she was abuzz with ideas for her digs, too.

But Neecy was going to be on the strait and narrow with this one. Joe had trusted her. The plan was that she'd swing by the house, pick up the plastic, pick up her buddy, do the deeds, and by nightfall she and Joe would both be lounging in some decidedly more comfortable surroundings.

Joe met her at the door. "Okay, I'm ready," Neecy said brightly.

"So am I," he said. "Let's go."

Neecy was taken aback. "I thought you said you hated to shop."

"I do."

"Uh, you can just give me your credit card. I thought I'd pick up my girlfriend and we'd . . ."

Joe pushed back his baseball cap and was gazing down at her calmly. "I hate going to the dentist, but I do that, too. I told you I simply hadn't gotten around to the house yet."

"I thought you trusted me."

He raised an eyebrow. "I do trust you. You can do the shopping, choosing, and all that. But I haven't lost my mind. Give you my credit card? Woman, you must think I'm stone crazy. Please. You're driving." With those words, Joe headed out the door.

Neecy sighed. At least the man was direct. And like he said, apparently his mama had raised no fool. She reached into her purse for her cell to call Ramona and cancel.

All it took to blow the spending limit was a few good pieces of furniture. Ten thousand dollars hardly touched furnishing Joe's house. Neecy tried not to let her disappointment show. She'd looked forward to getting the house right for Joe so much.

"It's okay," he said.

"I know it'll take time," she said, focusing on the tips of her manicured toes. She had done them herself, and a good job she thought, and then frowned as she saw a chip on the polish on the fourth toe, left foot.

"I meant you can spend what you think we need to finish the house."

She looked up at him. "What did you say?" she asked, sure she'd heard him wrong.

"Spend what you think we need to get that house right."

"Joe, that's going to be at least fifty thousand dollars. Maybe a hundred. Probably more."

He shrugged.

Neecy stared at him in disbelief. "Daaaang," she whispered.

"Do we have time to do it once more before they get here?" Neecy asked, a little greedy—but hey, that was her style.

Joe looked at the clock. "I'd be cutting it short, and lady, you know I never like to cut it short."

He kissed her forehead. Joe had arranged for special delivery and set up for most of the furniture so they wouldn't have to wait. They had made love all Sunday morning and feasted on Joe's sumptuous brunch in between, so Neecy supposed she couldn't complain. "Let's shower," he whispered in her ear. "Sometimes I can make an exception in there."

"So the shower is quickie territory, hmmm?"

"That's supposed to be the rule."

Four hours and a lot of hustle and bustle later, the house was transformed. Neecy moved through the once bare rooms with a proprietary air. She'd done good. She'd done very good. Her choices fit Joe well. Best of all, they fit the house well. She'd always had an eye for spaces.

"I can't believe it! Joe!"

Ahhh, Grace's voice, Neecy thought. This was a moment she would savor. She took her time going to the foyer, allowing Joe ample time to make it there first from the other side of his roomy home. She thought he was in the kitchen, working his magic on dinner. She'd smelled deliciousness brewing.

"You furnished the house?" Grace was asking. "You must have spent an incredible amount of money. Why didn't you contact me?"

"Why should I?"

"We agreed that when major financial decisions are made that we should consult—"

"Newsflash, Grace. We're divorced. You no longer have papers of any kind on me."

"Excuse me? I have some financial interests."

"You got paid."

"We still own property together, and most important, the division of assets is still in question. Legal question."

"And will be until hell freezes over. The car lot was my father's business, and now it's mine. I built it from the ground up from virtual bankruptcy. I'm not giving it away to you or anybody else."

Silence.

Neecy started to silently back up. It didn't seem that now was the time to interrupt.

"You got a decorator. They did a good job." Grace asked, seeming to cast around for a change of subject.

"Thanks. Neecy did it."

"What?"

"Neecy did it."

"That girl you hired instead of repoing her car? Are you kidding? It's one thing to sleep with some slut, Joe, but to bring her into your home, your personal business—I thought you had more sense. She'll clean you out." Neecy heard the tap of heels against highly polished wood floors. "She seemed a little ghetto to me. I'd better take a look at the rest of the house."

Neecy withdrew, her heart pounding. Now definitely wasn't the time. She didn't want to confront Grace now, because she'd probably come off as ghetto as the woman thought she was.

She heard the rumble of Joe's voice. "You better leave, Grace," he said, matter-of-factly. "Neecy is here, and there is a high probability that she just heard your very untactful and rude speech. Let me assure you that the house isn't a bit ghetto, but Neecy has enough sistah in her to kick your skinny rear all up, down, and around it, so as amusing as the sight would be, for your own safety—"

Neecy heard the door opening.

A loud sniff and Grace's heels click, click, clicked out the door.

# Chapter 7

Late Sunday evening, Neecy let herself into her dark apartment and was greeted by the urgent red glow of her answering machine. She flipped through her caller ID. A couple of girlfriends, her mother, and bill collectors. Lots of bill collectors.

She opened the drawer were she stashed ner hew crop of unopened bills and closed it quickly as if it were filled with snakes. Neecy sat at her desk and cradled her head in her hands. The phone rang. She glanced at the caller ID. Another bill collector. They wouldn't even let you alone on Sundays.

Joe said as soon as she contacted them all and made the negotiated reduced payments, the calls would stop. She'd started on her list, but so far it had been disheartening. The few she'd called had finally agreed to her terms like Joe said they'd have to, but only after they'd done their best to discourage, bully, and threaten her. Her list was long, and the experience was so miserable, she'd been procrastinating. Next week, she needed to tackle contacting her creditors again. All of them.

The small voice whispered to her, the resentful one she'd been trying to ignore all weekend. She'd just spent enough money on Joe's home to pay all her creditors several times over. What would it be like to be able to buy anything you want? Neecy wondered. Then she remembered the condition of Joe's house, his office, his used, definitely not fancy pickup, and his Wrangler jeans. Being able to buy everything you want must come with a catch. Unless you're rich as Croesus, you don't get to buy hardly any darn thing—you have to save. What did Joe tell her? "*A penny unspent is as good as a penny earned.*" And he was dead serious. With Joe, pennies counted, spent and unspent. Could she live like that? And yet he dropped almost a hundred K in a single afternoon without a blink. A complicated man. She wanted to dig deeper. She wanted to understand more about the money thing, because she knew that understanding him would help her understand herself.

Joe was waiting for her when she got to the office. He kissed her cheek, and the mere brush of his lips and scent of his aftershave ignited familiar deep embers within her. "Good morning," he said. "Want to talk?"

Neecy nodded, thinking Joe must be a mind reader.

"When I thought about it, I wondered how all that shopping really affected you. I know you love to shop, but I also know that amount of money would have solved your immediate problems."

"It would have been better than winning the lottery, Joe." To Neecy's horror, her eyes moistened. "Excuse me, I have to go to the bathroom."

She went and took a moment to pull herself together. What was wrong with her? It was Joe's money, and her financial problems she had made all on her very own. Two entirely separate things that had no business mixing. To tangle them would have disastrous effects on any future relationship, especially given Joe's conservatism about money—but most important, her own self-respect. This sort of self-respect might be a new thing, but it felt good. It didn't come from Joe; maybe he gave her the idea, but she found it within herself all on her own. She could pay her own bills, and she would do so. She wanted Joseph Vaughn, and she'd have him, but she didn't need his money. What she needed was his character, his trust, his strong shoulders to lean on, and his loving.

What she'd give him was her all.

She left that bathroom feeling like a new woman.

"Are you all right, Neecy?"

"I'm fine, Joe. And that shopping trip was fine. I loved buying that stuff for you. There are people who try to find jobs shopping. I'm a natural."

Joe looked a little relieved, but still worried.

"I'm having a hard time calling my creditors, Joe. They are very nasty. I could use some help."

He took her hand and squeezed it. "I'd be glad to help you," he said.

"I've been wanting to ask you something. It's a little difficult," Neecy said.

Joe waited.

"What do you see in me? I mean really? We are so different. Is it just how I look? Is it that you find me attractive?"

Joe's eyebrows shot skyward. He obviously wasn't expecting that question. "I find you very attractive. But no, that's not all of it. I find a lot of women attractive, but I don't seek to spend the amount of time with them that I want to spend with you. There's more. I know we're different, but it feels like we belong together somehow." He looked anxious. "Do you feel the same?"

Neecy drew close to him and stood on tiptoe, winding her arms around his neck. "I do," she whispered, as their lips met for a tender kiss.

Grace wafted in the office at noon, smelling of Joy, the scent a little too cloying for a sultry summer day. But she looked cool in a breezy white dress. "Neecy, we need to talk," she said.

Joe, in that irritating way that men have when they sense females in their territory starting to circle each other, had disappeared.

"We do?" Neecy said. She had no need to talk to Grace, now or ever.

"I wanted to apologize for my hasty words at Joe's house the other day. That is, in case you heard them or Joe told you. I was so surprised. Well anyway, you did such a fabulous job on the house. I wanted to congratulate you. Have you worked in interior design before?"

"I teach office skills to tenth graders at Claymore High."

"Oh. That's why you're so great around here. I don't know what Joe is going to do this fall without you. . . ." Grace's voice trailed away. "Where is he, anyway?"

Neecy shrugged. "I don't know. Probably out on the lot."

"Harris wants to take us all out to lunch," Grace said.

"Why?" Neecy asked.

"I think he wants to get Joe out of the office. Joe will work nonstop unless you pull him away. But mainly, he's curious about you. He and his brother are pretty close, and Harris is nosy, in case you haven't noticed. Are you free? He's going to take us somewhere nice."

This might be interesting, if only to see Harris and Grace's conception of "somewhere nice." "Sure, sounds good," Neecy replied.

Harris drove a later model, silver Toyota Camry, with a leather interior. Neecy did a quick assessment. The car was good quality, held its value, wasn't too flashy, but not cheap either. He was educated, apparently worked, a solid type of guy, decent catch.

Joe and Neecy sat in the back. Harris drove them to a new trendy Afro-Caribbean restaurant that Neecy had been dying to try. Harris apparently did have a grip on what defined "somewhere nice" as far as a restaurant was concerned, and he was prepared to drop a few bucks. Well, good for him.

Joe held open the door for Neecy, and Harris escorted Grace into the restaurant. Joe had impeccable manners and was able to handle himself with ease. He seemed to have no problem ordering for her if called upon to do so. He asked if she liked snapper and ordered a light lunch of grilled fish, vegetables, and salad for them both.

The food was excellent, well prepared, seasoned with a light and skillful hand, fresh and flavorful. The conversation was surprisingly as light as the food.

Neecy observed them all from under her lashes. They had the easy familiarity of family. It was as if Grace were a sibling, rather than an ex-wife and ex-sister-in-law. Then Neecy noticed Harris's proprietary manner with Grace, his arm casually around her shoulder. She darted a glance at Joe's face. He appeared oblivious of the vibes between Harris and Grace. Stranger and stranger.

Neecy could sense nothing but brotherly and sisterly affection between Grace and Joe overlaid with a siblinglike hostility over shared property and money. But between Harris and Grace, there was something more. . . . Harris touched Grace too much. Their gazes slid away from each other's too quickly, as if afraid to linger.

Neecy wondered how long this had been going on. Had Grace married the wrong man? She remembered Marjorie mentioning there being some sort of catting around, apparently by Grace, and then quickly shutting up.

There was a mystery here that Neecy would love to solve. Or maybe not. Family drama could be terribly messy. If this drama spilled, it looked like it would take more than a few paper towels and spray cleanser to clean the mess up.

Grace stroked Harris's hand and was grinning up in his face over some remark he'd made. Well, well, nobody ever said that Neecy Ballard couldn't mind her own business, thank you very much.

# Chapter 8

Joe sat on the buttery soft leather couch Neecy had chosen for him in front of his large flat-screen television and couldn't get into the game. He still felt bad about spending all that money in front of her merely to furnish his house, when it could have lifted a heavy load off her shoulders.

He wanted to help her out very badly. Every time he looked at her, he wanted to whip out his . . . checkbook, and write the check that would fix everything financially for her.

But down deep, he knew that in the long run it wouldn't be good. It wouldn't help Neecy at all, who needed to learn how to deal with this sort of thing herself. A problem like this didn't go away on its own. It was sort of like smoking or any other bad habit.

For him, it was more complicated. It would feel good to help her, and he knew generosity was something that was eventually rewarded in one way or another. But Joe wanted to be with Neecy for the long haul, and it was the wrong way to start any long-term relationship. They were way too new.

But shouldn't a long-term relationship be built on trust? Joe swallowed. *Trust* was a long, hard word for him, especially concerning money. He hadn't been particularly rational concerning Neecy, but who said love was rational?

*Love.* Was that what this was all about? He wasn't sure, but it was something new, something different between Neecy and him. When he was with her, it was wonderful, magical, more than he'd felt before with any other woman. There was no comparison to the relationship he'd had with Grace.

Grace and he agreed that they had been a mistake. Grace felt like family, so it wasn't a bad mistake, although if she thought she was entitled to his auto business, she was sorely mistaken. He wasn't too worried, though. He always could handle Grace.

But he wasn't sure about Neecy. If he made a wrong decision concerning Neecy, it would be more than a mistake. It would be a disaster.

How could trust be the wrong way to start a relationship? If he wanted to be in it for the long term with Neecy, he would be sharing everything he had with her anyway, and that was the ultimate trust. Why should he make the decision for her?

Neecy and he had talked long enough so he had some inkling of the source of her challenges with money. He could see her changing every day, reaching inside to validate herself, rather than reaching for her checkbook. He should trust himself enough to know that a woman wouldn't draw him so strongly if she didn't have the sort character that he could admire and respect.

Joe nodded to himself as he made the decision to make that leap of trust and give Neecy access to all he had and all he was—and soon. Satisfied with his decision, he walked over to his computer to routinely check his bank account. When he reached the business account of his car lot, the one Neecy had access to, he literally felt his heart skip a beat. The blood drained from his face. No. It couldn't be true. How could the worst thing he could imagine happen to him so suddenly? For a second he didn't think he could breathe. Then his lips twisted in a bitter, terrible smile as his eyes filled. He should have known it was too good to be true.

The next morning, Neecy decided to go into work early. She'd been in a rush to get home from work last night. It was her friend's birthday, and she'd thrown this wonderful dinner party just for her girlfriends, and Neecy had to help her get ready for it.

Neecy signed on to her computer and updated the ledger entries in the spreadsheet. She frowned when she tried to get into the business account. Her password didn't work. She tried again. Then again. She stared at the screen in disbelief. Locked out. Joe had locked her out.

She tried another account. The same thing happened. She was locked out of all of them. She opened her desk and fumbled for a key. Neecy walked to a file cabinet and tried the lock with suddenly trembling fingers. The key didn't work. She was locked out of petty cash and the files.

She sank into a chair, her face frozen in shock, and waited.

Twenty minutes later, Joe walked through the door, looking grim.

"What's going on?" Neecy asked.

Joe sat behind his desk and rubbed his eyes. "Twenty thousand dollars is missing from this business account."

"Are you saying that I took it?"

"It's the amount you need to pay your bills."

Neecy didn't think she was capable of feeling such pain, breathing and keeping it together all at the same time. But she would. She would. "How dare you?" she whispered.

"I could say the same thing," Joe said, his voice raw. "You should have waited. A few more hours, and you would have had it all. I was going to give you everything, you know that? Everything I had."

Neecy couldn't speak. It wasn't the words he said that cut her like a knife; it was his voice, the disappointment, the pain, the scorn. It was the way he looked at her, as if she were a stranger, as if he didn't even know her. As if he hated her.

"Twenty thousand dollars is nothing, it's pocket change. How could you steal from me after I trusted you so much? After I let you into my life? I thought I knew you," Joe said, his tone accusing.

He did know her. Just like she knew him. Would she ever think he'd steal from her or lie to her? No. No, she wouldn't. And with that realization, a blaze of white, hot anger replaced Neecy's initial shock. "You know me. And if you think I stole twenty thousand dollars from you, you're the fool. You think about that for a while." She stood with a quick, angry motion, the chair moving backwards with a screech.

"And then if you still think I took your money, you know what to do." Neecy got her purse and marched out the door.

# Chapter 9

When he heard the door shut behind Neecy, he felt as if his coffin had clicked closed. He leaned back in his chair and closed his eyes. Time passed. Too much time. When he opened them, it was too late to go after her. He should have given her car keys back. She'd earned them and then some. Did it matter if she took the money?

He stared at her desk—the screen saver she'd loaded of coins and dollars was showering the screen. Raining money. It was too hard to believe she wasn't coming back. Too hard to believe he might never hear her voice, might never smell her sweet scent, might never hold her in his arms. It wasn't worth close to twenty thousand. Nope, it wasn't.

Two hours had passed since she'd gone.

He picked up the keys to Neecy's car and locked the office behind him.


Joe parked Neecy's car in front of her apartment. He stood in front of her door for a moment. He hoped she was home. If not, he'd just wait until she showed up. However long it took. He knocked on the door.

Neecy opened it immediately, like she was standing right behind it the whole time. "You," she said.

"Yes, it's me," he said.

She just stood there, staring at him.

"Uh, can I come in?"

"What do you want, Joe?"

"I want to talk to you," he said, stating the obvious.

"When you accused me of stealing your money, I think you said all you needed to say to me."

"I wanted to tell you it doesn't matter."

"What?" Neecy said.

"It doesn't matter that you took the twenty thousand dollars. I don't care. I just want things to go back to the way they were."

Neecy folded her arms across her chest. "So it doesn't matter to you if I stole twenty thousand dollars from your business bank account, is that what you're saying? You want to go back to rolling me in the sack and being all lovey-dovey, right?" she asked.

Joe shifted a little. "That's basically right."

Neecy's shoe tapped on the foyer floor. "Hmmmm, let me think about that for a moment."

Neecy's shoe tapped faster.

"Let me tell you what I think, Joseph Vaughn," she said a minute later. "You can kiss the caramel-brown crack of my ass!" And with those words, Neecy slammed the door in his face.

Joe blinked. Blinked again. Rubbed his nose. He felt an aftershock of the door impact. Maybe somehow, someway, he'd made some sort of mistake about Neecy taking the money. If only. If only . . .

A while later, Joe sat in his office, his head down on his desk, his heart full, and his mind spinning. He needed to talk. He didn't feel inclined to share his sad story with Grace or Marjorie. The rule was that a man's sad stories could only be shared with his woman or his father or brother—or maybe with the soldier in the trench next to him—but that was it. He was blessed to have a brother. Joe picked up the phone. It took Harris twenty minutes to get to the car lot.

"I told you that you should lock Grace out of the bank accounts ages ago," Harris said.

"You're always harping about Grace being out to get me on one hand," Joe said, "And then on the other it looks like as if you're out to get her, in more ways than one." He shrugged. "Not that I care."

Harris sighed. "I know. That was always the problem." Harris leaned forward and put his hands on Joe's desk. "You've always idealized Grace—out of guilt or something, I don't know. But she's not your sainted little sister. She's a real woman with desires, needs, and flaws. Bad ones. She has beef against you, man. That's what I've been trying to tell you all this time. Grace can be one evil woman, and she thinks you owe her."

"Owe her what?"

"Money."

"Please. Grace cost me plenty. Now that the deal on the condo is over and the money is split, we're done. My lawyer told me that he's shut Grace down as far as her claim on my business."

"Yeah, and that's what's pissed her off. She's complaining that she can't afford the fancy high-powered legal counsel that you can."

"Grace shouldn't be hurting for money. She always said she invested wisely."

"Please. Grace is in debt up to her ying-yang. Grace isn't straight-forward like that girl who's got your nose cracked open. Grace hides things and sometimes lies."

Joe took a deep breath and rubbed his face with his hands.

"You've got excellent business sense, you don't trust anybody,"

Harris continued. "But all along, I've always wondered why you trusted Grace."

"Because I married her. Obviously, I married the wrong woman. Screwed up both our lives."

"You didn't screw up your lives. You're both young. You'd been together since second grade. An understandable mistake."

"What about you, Harris? Your strings of women? Your strings of broken engagements? Has it been Grace all along?"

Harris looked away. "Maybe. She's always been there, my confidante, my best friend. I know her better than anybody, and she knows me."

"Why did you let her marry me, bro?"

"Like everybody else, including the both of you, I thought you two belonged together. All Grace and I were to each other were best friends, and I thought that's all we'd ever be."

Joe sighed heavily. "We wasted a lot of time."

"Everything's a learning experience. I'm going to stop wasting the time I have left. I'm going to confront Grace. We're going to settle this one way or another. Bro, let me tell you something. Sometimes there is only one right person for you. There is such a thing as your soul mate. And if you're lucky enough to find her, you better grab her. Don't let her get away. If Neecy is the one, you'd best throw yourself to the ground in apology and let her wipe her mud-crusted stiletto heels on you if that's what it takes."

"I already did. Apparently it'll take more than that. She told me to kiss her ass."

"Damn. So what are you doing sitting up here in this office? You better go get on your knees outside her door so you can be in the proper position to smooch in case she walks by."

# Chapter 10

"Hold up," Grace called in irritation and turned off the shower. It better be important. She'd tried to ignore whoever was leaning on her doorbell for the past few minutes, but the visitor was very insistent. She grabbed her white terry-cloth robe and wound a towel around her hair.

She looked through the peephole. If it was anybody short of the state troopers or UPS, they were going to get a piece of her mind. Harris stood there. She pulled open the door without hesitation, all irritation draining from her mind.

"I was in the shower," Grace said.

"Sorry to bother you."

"That's okay. Why don't you go put on some coffee while I get dressed?"

She dressed quickly. It was always great when Harris showed up. They talked for hours. She wondered if she should tell him what she did to Joe. . . .

She wound her hair up in a ponytail; she'd blow-dry it later.

When she walked into the living room, Harris handed her a cup of coffee. Grace took a sip, sat down, and crossed her legs. "What's going on?" she asked him.

"Neecy dumped Joe. He's taking it pretty hard. I think they really had the start of something special."

Grace shifted in her chair and studied her coffee. "So why did she dump him, then?"

"He accused her of stealing twenty thousand dollars from company funds."

Silence.

"You know Joe hasn't had it that easy either," Harris said softly.

Grace looked away. "I stood by him. I worked for him when I could have been going to school and getting mine—doing what I wanted to do. I sacrificed, Harris. You know that."

Harris caught her hand. "I do. But the sacrificing needs to stop here and now. The past is over. Let's start working on our futures." He brought her fingers to his lips.

Grace's breath stopped in her throat. *Harris.*

"Do what's right, Grace. I know that you're a good woman when it really matters. And Joe deserves happiness as much as we do. He's always done the best he could. Let it go, girl."

A sob came up from deep within Grace, and she got to her feet as if to flee. But Harris intercepted her, and he held her.

"I took the money," Grace said.

Harris drew her to him and held her close. She felt the warmth of his body melting into hers, and it seemed as if she'd finally come home.

"I know," he said.

"How can you stand me, then? You know what I am. I lie. I steal. I acted like I was looking down my nose at Neecy." Grace gave a short, bitter laugh. "She's got nothing on me."

"What you do, Grace, is make mistakes. We all do. What's important is that you own up to them. And you try to make them right. You are going to try to make this one right, aren't you?"

Grace nodded. "I am, Harris. I was feeling like crap over it."

"I know that, too, baby."

Harris held her for a while, and a new yet familiar comfort seeped into her bones, her soul. But the feeling scared her; it was almost too good, too right. "You can let me go now," she said.

"No. We're done with running away from what we feel." Then Harris lowered his head and touched his lips to hers for the first time ever in all the years they'd known each other.

In that instant, everything changed. They were blown across the line from friends to where lovers dwell, and they never looked back.

The phone rang. Neecy peered at the caller ID. She was working down her list, and the bill collector calls were dwindling; however, the calls from Joe were increasing. It was killing her to ignore him, but what else was she to do? The man thought she was a common thief but still wanted a taste of her stuff. Hell, he could get some thievish poontang if he got in his car and cruised down Peachtree Street with some loose twenty-dollar bills.

Neecy rolled over on her stomach and punched her pillow. The doorbell rang. She hoped it was her mama or one of her girls, because if Joe was showing up on her doorstep again, he was going to get seriously cussed out. If he kept on, she'd call 911 on his behind. She rolled out of bed, ready to do battle.

Grace stood there in the doorway. "What do you want?" Neecy asked, surprise eroding what little was left of her manners.

"May I come in?" Grace asked.

Neecy stood aside, feeling suddenly acutely conscious of her rumpled sweatsuit. She gestured toward the sofa, "Uh, please sit down."

Neecy sat in the loveseat adjacent from Grace and waited. She couldn't imagine what Grace had to say to her. Unless it was that something had happened to Joe. Her heart started to beat faster.

"I need to talk to you about Joe," Grace started.

"Is he all right? He's not hurt badly, is he?" Neecy blurted, fearing he was injured or dead.

Grace frowned. "Joe's fine. Physically, at least. What I wanted to say was . . ."

Neecy's eyes widened in disbelief. She knew that Joe had not sent this woman over here to plead his case to let him do the nasty with her.

"That I took that money from Joe," Grace finished.

Neecy choked on her own saliva.

After a minute or so of sputtering and coughing, she heard Grace ask, "Can I get you some water or something?"

Neecy motioned her toward the kitchen.

Grace returned with a glass of water, and Neecy took it gratefully.

"You stole twenty thousand dollars from Joe, and he still thinks I did it?" Tones of disbelief still tinged Neecy's voice after she recovered from her coughing fit.

"I'm going to tell him next, but I thought I'd come by and apologize to you first."

"Dear, it wasn't my twenty K."

"But you're a whole lot easier to tackle than Joe."

"I guess that's true." Neecy looked at Grace with new regard. "And here I thought butter couldn't melt in your mouth."

Grace looked miserable, so Neecy decided she'd be nicer. A little nicer, at least. "What did you do with the twenty thou?" she asked.

"I paid bills."

"Really?" Neecy said, feeling a bond of sisterhood with Grace.

"I have bills, too."

"I thought you were so good with money. You said you never carried a balance on your credit cards."

"I was lying," Grace said.

"Oh."

"Anyway, I wanted to apologize, but more than that—Harris said it was important to tell you that you need to forgive Joe for thinking that you took the money. He said you need to understand that Joe has issues, too, like everybody else."

"Oh, really?"

"He said that Joe is miserable. And you should realize that soul mates don't come around often."

"Harris said all this?" Neecy said.

"Yeah, Harris and I are . . ." Grace made two fists and touched them together.

Neecy looked at her in puzzlement. "You two are talking?"

"Noooo, we're not talking. Well, sometimes . . ."

"Meeting together, then."

"Sort of. But not really . . ."

"Oh, I get it! You're screwing!" Neecy said, light dawning. "I could see that when we were at the restaurant together."

"We were *not* screwing at the restaurant," Grace said.

Neecy looked at Grace like she was nuts. "Of course nobody screwed at the restaurant; we would have been thrown out."

"You know what I meant," Grace said, exasperated. "Harris and I were not lovers when we all ate at the restaurant."

"But you're screwing now?"

"Well, yes. But not then."

"But you wanted to."

"No! Yes! You're driving me crazy. Quit it!"

Neecy threw up her hands. "Hey, I'm confused, but I understand that it's a family issue," she said. "I'll leave who's screwing who and when you decide to screw alone. It's none of my business."

Grace rolled her eyes. "Just go on and forgive Joe, okay? He deserves a break."

"I don't know, for him to think to think I could do something like that . . ." Neecy's voice trailed away.

"Oh, please," Grace said, snorting.

Neecy had to laugh. "Okay, okay, I'll forgive him."

Grace shook her head. "I can't believe that you're going to be my sister-in-law," she said.

"Aren't you getting a little ahead of yourself?" Neecy asked.

"I don't think so," Grace answered.

Neecy took a long luxurious bath after Grace left. She massaged herself from head to toe in fragrant oil and dressed in a pure silk peach caftan that wafted and flowed when she walked, with nothing under it but her own silky skin. She manicured her nails, gave herself a deluxe pedicure, and waited for the phone to ring. It did, right on time. She looked at the caller ID and picked up the phone. "Hi, Joe," she said.

She listened for a while, and then she said, "Sure, come on over. I've missed you, too, baby. Oh, Joe, before you hang up, I wanted to let you know that I have the perfect joke to tell you."

Joe's groan echoed in her ear. A smile curved Neecy's lips as she laid the phone on the cradle. Love was the greatest gift in the world, along with forgiveness, trust, and understanding. She was truly blessed.

Neecy giggled softly to herself as she imagined Joe's reaction to the joke she was going to tell him. Sometimes payback could be a whole lot of fun, too.

# It Takes Two

## REON LAUDAT

# Chapter 1

"Yoo-hoo! Ramona! I got a whole crate of that body butter moisturizing prebath treatment you like," Mei Ling announced in singsong from the door of her beauty-supply store.

"I won't be stockpiling it by the crate anymore," Ramona told the petite Asian woman who ran the business next door to her own. "I'd go cold turkey if I could, but my skin turns to parchment without it. This time I'll need only a couple of jars that I plan to use sparingly."

"Still on that tight budget, I see." Mei Ling didn't bother to hide her surprise. "I really didn't think you'd last longer than a couple of weeks. I'm impressed."

Ramona blinked. "Thank you . . . I think."

Mei Ling was the kind of person who'd wave the most decadent peach cobbler under your nose right after you told her you were on a strict diet. The perverse thrill of sabotaging another person's attempt at self-improvement obviously made her feel empowered.

First there was that infamous fake smile that Mei Ling plastered on before she gestured with both hands. "Come on inside, and check out some of the beautiful new dresses I just got in."

*Fat chance*, Ramona thought wryly.

For several weeks now, Ramona's mail-order catalogs had hit the trash as soon as they had arrived. Spending hours on Yahoo! Shopping or punching speed dial for every handy-dandy device trotted out on late-night infomercials were things of the past.

Passing Mei Ling's shop each day to and from work hadn't posed much of a threat to Ramona's resolve to chill out on the shopping. Ramona wouldn't be caught dead wearing any of the "fashions" Mei Ling typically stocked, which included cheap hoochie-mama dresses, gaudy rhinestone jewelry, candy-colored pleather shoes, and trashy lingerie.

Phipps Plaza was another matter, however. The upscale mall located in one of Atlanta's ritzier neighborhoods was Ramona's biggest weakness, a Kilimanjaro Ramona had yet to climb. Just the day before, she'd come awfully close to losing her footing there again.

"The dresses are really cute. There's one cut in an A-line silhouette that would do wonders for camouflaging a—" Pointedly Mei Ling dropped her gaze below Ramona's belt. "—full derriere."

Ramona clucked her tongue, then shook her head. "Sorry. Can't right now. Gotta set up for Neecy. She phoned last night. Said she was coming in for a manicure."

"You sure I can't put that crate of moisturizing treatment on your tab? I can have my stock boy bring it over a little later?" Mei Ling asked Ramona just before turning her full attention to an old black woman entering the beauty-supply shop. "How are you doing today, Mrs. Turner? I have that set of green foam curlers you were asking about," Mei Ling said in a gratingly obsequious voice.

"Talk to you later, Mei Ling." Ramona was grateful for the opportunity to escape. That Mei Ling was a real piece of work. Her little veiled and not-so-veiled digs never failed to keep Ramona entertained since the day Ramona opened Nailz and Detailz three years ago. It was one of four minority-owned businesses housed in a fully renovated building that used to be a big 1930s church.

Ramona unlocked the door and stepped inside her shop. Light flooded the 1,700-square-foot space when she opened the blinds. The decor was sleek and modern, but comfortable. The furniture, a contemporary-style black leather and chrome. The spotless ceramic-tiled floor gleamed beneath a series of carved skylights.

Ramona turned on the stereo system, which piped smooth jazz through the place. She hoped to have about an hour of solitude to work on inventory before the seven nail techs she employed arrived, followed by their clients. But as soon as she slipped behind her desk, Erica entered her office.

"Good morning." Erica shrugged into the black work smock that all the nail techs wore. "What's on your agenda today?"

Ramona lifted a stack of papers. "Just going over these inventory spreadsheets."

"We're running low on acrylic powder." Erica removed something from the pocket of her slacks. "Here's that information you asked me to get."

Ramona accepted the brochure Erica passed to her. "Oh, yeah, the ten K for that breast-cancer-awareness campaign."

"You're still interested in participating, right?"

"Of course."

Erica had become involved in the fund-raising effort after the disease claimed her mother and sister a few years ago. Lately she had been desperately trying to recruit more African-American women to participate in the charity run.

Ramona knew she wasn't a runner. The last time she had made a mad dash for anything was the sales bin at Victoria's Secret's last big bra-and-panty blowout sale. But how hard could a ten K be? It was the least she could do to help Erica. Raising money for a good cause instead of spending it was definitely a big step in the right direction.

"It has all the info about the dates and how to handle pledges. If you have any questions after you read over everything, just let me know."

As Erica departed, Ramona scanned the text on the brochure. "Will do."

"Hey, what's shaking?" another voice called out.

Ramona's head snapped up.

Denise Ballard stood framed in the doorway to Ramona's office.

"Hey, Neecy, girl!" Ramona came to her feet to greet her friend and fellow recovering shopaholic.

"Didn't mean to interrupt." Neecy was wearing one of her many frilly sundresses that skimmed her full hourglass figure.

"It's always good to see you."

The two women shared a quick embrace.

Ramona's eyes went wide. "Hey, your hair!"

Neecy giddily ran her fingers through her mop of skinny, shoulder-length braids and did a full turn so Ramona could check her new hairdo from every angle. "You like? . . ."

"I love it! But quite a change from the relaxed glamour-girl coifs I'm used to seeing on you, but this look—"

"It's stylish *and* low maintenance," Neecy added.

"Hey, you're preaching to the choir." Ramona ran her fingers through her own no-fuss hair style—a short bob of silky twists.

Linking arms, the two women stepped out of Ramona's office and went to one of the vacant manicure stations. As the owner of Nailz and Detailz, Ramona usually filled her time handling the managerial duties. These days she performed manicures only on family and special friends who had given her their business when she was just a struggling novice toiling away in somebody else's shop.

"What are you getting? The usual?" Ramona took the seat at the small table.

"I really just wanted to come by and check on you." Neecy settled on the chair across from Ramona. "I'm skipping the expensive nail treatments and going the simplistic route. See." Neecy placed her hands on the table for Ramona. "I've been doing my nails myself. Cheaper that way."

"Great for you, bad for my business," Ramona groused in jest.

"You know how it is."

"Believe me I do, I just told Mei Ling I wouldn't be buying that expensive body butter by the crate anymore. But listen, I have a new polish I just know you're going to love, so this one's on the house, okay?"

Ramona plucked a bottle of Paradise Punch from the standing nail caddy nearby.

"Oooooh, pretty!" Neecy leaned in for a closer inspection.

"Thought you'd think so. Matches that floral print on your dress." Ramona went to work, removing the old clear polish from Neecy's nails. "So how's it going?"

"You mean with the shopping?"

Ramona nodded.

"I think I finally got a handle on things."

"That's great, girl." Ramona began shaping Neecy's nails with an emery board.

"And I have a new man now."

"Ooooh, do fill a sistah in with the juicy details."

"It's Joe."

"You mean *Platinum Plastic Joe?*" Ramona's voice hitched an octave.

"He's great."

"I'll bet." Ramona snorted. "Him and his huge money bags."

"Big bank aside, he's everything any woman could want in a man. True, he could fix all my money woes at the drop of a checkbook, but I'm not going to take the easy way out. I'm determined to work through things myself."

"Good for you!" Ramona smiled. "And you look so happy, too."

Neecy was practically glowing. "I am."

"Be sure to blow a little bit of that happy dust my way, would you?" Ramona rose to fill a glass bowl with water at a nearby sink.

"How about you? How are you doing?" Neecy asked.

"I can't complain, I guess," Ramona said unconvincingly as she sat down and squirted a cleansing and moisturizing solution inside the bowl so Neecy could soak her hands. "But I could use one of your corny jokes right about now."

"Say what?" Neecy's precisely arched brows hitched skyward. "Now I know something is wrong if you're requesting that I tell a joke. Spill it."

"I did go inside Phipps Plaza yesterday."

"Awwww, and you slipped up?" Neecy's eyes went soft with sympathy. "Oh, Ramona, we all will slip every now and then. What's the damage to your credit card?"

"I didn't really slip up, but I came awfully close. I figured I was ready to shop for a wedding present for Jalisa. I went to buy that gift and nothing but that gift."

"And?"

"I saw this fierce Dolce and Gabbana suit. I was practically hyperventilating as I admired its exquisite cut and elaborate detailing. I tried it on. It fit perfectly, and the sumptuous fabric—" Ramona sighed. "—heaven against my skin."

"And then what?" Neecy leaned forward and gulped, as if she were vicariously experiencing Ramona's big moment of weakness. "You cut up all your credit cards, right?"

"Yes, eighteen of them. I still have two left. One I keep for the convenience of ordering plane tickets on-line and for little emergencies. It has a credit limit of five hundred dollars."

"Surely that's not enough to splurge on a Dolce and Gabbana suit."

"No, it's not, but I have a second major credit card with a multi-thousand-dollar credit limit. That's the one I keep frozen inside a huge shoe-box-size block of ice in my freezer—in case of a major emergency."

"One of your more ingenious little tricks to head off potential disaster. At my weakest, I wish I'd thought of doing that. So then you what?"

"I told the store clerk I wanted to put the suit on hold until I got my credit card. By the time I raced all the way home, removed the block of ice containing the credit card, then waited for the thing to thaw, the urge to blow four grand on a suit had passed. As expected, that melting process—without the benefit of a good microwave zap—gave me a chance to think and reconsider the expensive mistake I was about to make."

"I say that's a reason to celebrate. Okay, so you wavered a bit, but you ultimately triumphed! Don't you see? This is a good thing."

"Maybe . . . But the true test of my will is to actually go inside Phipps Plaza and not go bonkers like that over anything so expensive again."

"You can always shop for Jalisa's wedding gift on-line."

"No, I won't feel as if I've beat this thing until I go back to Phipps Plaza alone and buy Jalisa's gift." Ramona lifted Neecy's hands from the solution and dried them with a small towel.

"Okaaaaaay," Neecy replied, obviously confused. "But why make it extra hard on yourself when you're doing so well right now? What's the rush with Phipps Plaza? Save it for a little later when you're stronger."

Ramona didn't feel like explaining her reasoning or urgency to Neecy right then. She'd already made a decision to return to Phipps Plaza that day right after work. "Enough about me. I need the four-one-one on this Joe."

Fortunately, Neecy didn't press, and proceeded to wax rhapsodic over her new man for the next half hour while Ramona relished the distraction of basking in her friend's richly deserved bliss.

# Chapter 2

Ramona Jackson circled Phipps Plaza three times, trying to ratchet up her courage to go inside. She pulled into the parking lot, her grip tightening on the steering wheel. Sucking in a deep, calming breath, she parked and reached for her designer leather bag. Apprehension skittered up her spine as she climbed out the car and made her way toward a department store's entrance, which spilled her into the shoe department. Sucking in another deep breath, she breezed right past what she knew were rows of the latest designs from Ferragamo, Stuart Weitzman, and Jimmy Choo.

The cosmetics counters bloomed with new summer palettes from MAC, Bobbi Brown and Estée Lauder. She glanced at them, then shifted her eyes forward, marching onward until she reached the escalators. Gliding to the second floor, she sighed with relief, and a little smile curled her lips.

In the housewares department, it didn't take long to fall in love with a large Waterford Crystal picture frame, which would be perfect for showcasing Jalisa's favorite bridal portrait. With the frame in hand, she headed for the gift-wrapping department. So busy admiring her find, she wasn't watching where she was going. She turned a corner and slammed into what felt like a warm brick wall.

Ramona wobbled on her high heels, but she kept her eyes and firm grip on the fragile glass frame in her hands. Realizing she'd crashed into a flesh-and-blood man, she sputtered, "I'm sorry. I'm . . . I'm such . . . a darn klutz." Her gaze traveled from the large black Pumas on his feet, up the long legs of his navy warm-up pants, and the broad expanse of his white T-shirt-covered chest to his gorgeous brown face.

A familiar gorgeous brown face.

"Kadeem!" shot from Ramona's mouth with a gasp.

"Ramona." To steady her, his large hands came up to clasp her upper arms. She relished the strength and heat from his touch. "Are you all right?"

She shook her head and blinked as though unsure this six-foot-three hunk of fabulously built man before her was just a mirage. "Yes . . . um . . . yes." Her hand stole to her chest as if the motion could steady the fierce hammering of her heart. "Just got the wind knocked out of me a little, but I'm fine." It wasn't just a physical jolt that rattled her, but also the visceral impact of suddenly coming face-to-face with the man who she had once believed was the one and only love of her life.

"How have you been?" Kadeem's ruggedly angular face broke into a brilliant smile as he gazed down at her. "Long time no see."

What an understatement. It had been four long years since Ramona exited the relationship that by the end seemed to be equal parts pain and pleasure. Now looking at his warm brown eyes and that bright sexy grin, all Ramona could think of was the pleasure.

Exquisite pleasure.

Kadeem taking her in his protective arms, latching on to her lips in that way that made her forget her own name. Ramona clinging to him while he pleasured her until the world blurred around her.

"I'm fine," she managed with a tentative smile, though she felt flushed by her memories. "And you?"

"Can't complain. It's all good." Kadeem looked down at the item in her hands. "Very nice picture frame."

She lifted the frame, grateful for the opportunity to focus on something else. "It's for Jalisa and Calvin."

"Of course, for their wedding, right? What a coincidence. I'm here shopping for Jalisa and Calvin, too. I'm one of Calvin's groomsmen."

"Is that right?" Ramona couldn't hide her surprise. Kadeem and Calvin had become friendly only because Ramona and Jalisa were close. Ramona had mistakenly assumed that when she and Kadeem broke up, Calvin and Kadeem would, too. Obviously the two guys had continued hanging out, but she couldn't recall Jalisa ever mentioning it. And Calvin had made it a point not to flaunt his friendship with Kadeem. She supposed that was fair. It wasn't as if they were all in third grade. Just because Ramona had decided she didn't want anything to do with Kadeem anymore didn't mean Calvin had to dump him, too.

"I gather Calvin didn't get around to telling you I'd be in the wedding party?" Kadeem asked with a tilt of his head.

Ramona was mesmerized by his mouth. He had a provocative way of moistening his full lips whenever he gazed at hers, as if he couldn't wait to taste them. "No, he didn't."

Ramona was forced to shuffle closer to Kadeem when a blond woman pushing a stroller built for her toddler twins nudged by.

Ramona held the picture frame securely between her and Kadeem as a much-needed buffer. But then her nose filled with the clean, masculine scent of his cologne. The same brand of cologne she'd bought him for their first Christmas together. The scent she remembered that made her woozy with longing. It still had that effect on her. Her knuckles skimmed the ridges of his diamond-hard abs. A familiar heat emanated from him. The man was still in awesome shape. As the memory of how hard he used to work to stay that way rushed to the front of Ramona's mind, she stiffened; then she summoned the resolve to retreat to get her bearings again.

There was still chemistry simmering between them—but, she recalled, lack of chemistry had never been the problem. And they'd made love all the time. No place—besides maybe the church cloak-room—had been off-limits. It was as if she could never get enough of him or he enough of her.

But it was that other obsession of his that wreaked havoc on their relationship. His fixation on honing that perfect body had torn them apart.

"Well, I'd better hustle my butt out of here." Ramona smiled nervously. "I told Jalisa I'd meet her for drinks at the Tavern in a half hour." She replaced the frame on a nearby display table and then lifted her wrist to check her watch, before scurrying away as if Kadeem were her kryptonite. After she'd put a few yards between them, she called over her shoulder. "It's good seeing that you're doing well."

Kadeem, obviously rattled by her abrupt withdrawal, lifted one hand for a limp wave. "Good to see you, too," he called out. "And I'm looking forward to the wedding rehearsal."

Ramona immediately tried to think of excuses for skipping rehearsals. But short of a deathbed situation, she knew that was out of the question.

"I was going to tell you," Jalisa insisted as she and Ramona stepped inside the Tavern, a trendy restaurant and bar located on the first level of Phipps Plaza near Saks Fifth Avenue.

They moved to two empty stools at the end of the bar.

"When? *After* I bumped into him at rehearsals?" Ramona was having difficulty keeping the irritation she felt out of her tone.

Jalisa pulled a stool away from the dark wood base of the bar so she could maneuver between them. "I was going to tell you today. I swear, which is why I invited you here for drinks."

"Oh, I get it now." Ramona's bob of silky twists swayed as she nodded. "You wanted to get me bombed before you dropped the bomb, right?"

"I wasn't going to get you drunk, but I figured a little buzz might ease the jolt a bit." Jalisa wore a sheepish smile. "Sorry, girl. I know you and Kadeem have a checkered past and all, but I figured . . . I mean, it's been a long time. I thought by now you two could tolerate each other for a few hours."

Tolerate each other? Though Kadeem and Ramona's relationship had gone sour, they had parted as amicably as two lovers could under the circumstances. Unlike the arguments that led to their breakup, when Ramona decided she'd had enough, there had been no hurling of insults or slamming of doors. In fact, when she had asked Kadeem to leave the apartment they shared, she got the impression that he'd been relieved. Much to her surprise and chagrin, she had expected him to put up more of a fight. But by then nothing and no else mattered but the bodybuilding, and she knew the breakup had been the right move.

But now, after seeing him again, he still had the ability to make her insides flip-flop. She had dated other men since Kadeem. Handsome, accomplished men, who had made it known they were into her. But none touched her heart and soul as Kadeem had.

"You're still attracted to him, aren't you?" Jalisa hefted herself up on a stool.

Before Ramona could reply, a bartender approached them to take their orders. She was in no mood for the little show à la Tom Cruise in the movie *Cocktail*. The bartenders here were famous for that sort of thing when whipping up mixed drinks. She went for something simple. "I'll have a chardonnay."

"I'll have the same." Jalisa reached for a toothpick in the jar in front of them, then plucked a maraschino cherry from a tray that also contained olives and slices of lemon and lime. When the bartender turned to get busy with their drinks, Jalisa didn't skip a beat. "So you're still attracted to him, right?"

"Of course, the man still looks good to me." Heat curled in Ramona's center, then settled between her thighs as she conjured up an image of Kadeem standing in the store, his long frame covered with sleek, rocklike flesh honed by religious weight training. These days, his sculpted body was more akin to that of a well-developed male gymnast or professional basketball player.

And it all appeared *100 percent natural*, which was one of the first things Ramona noted.

Her ex showed none of the telltale signs that would indicate he'd used steroids or any other physique-enhancing chemicals. In the past, she'd accompanied him to enough competitions to recognize the signs. Kadeem had no acne-ravaged skin, bloated barrel belly, freakishly huge muscle mass or vascularity. Some of the other competitors' pronounced veins striped their limbs like the highways on a road map. Kadeem was any female's vision of the perfect physical male specimen.

"I happen to know he's not involved with anyone," Jalisa added in singsong.

"And why is that *my* business?" Ramona reached for a toothpick and speared an olive.

"In case you're interested in—"

"A sequel to our first melodrama? Have you lost your mind?" Ramona gave Jalisa a sidelong glare.

"And he's not *competing* anymore, in case you didn't notice. He gave that up a while ago, according to Calvin."

"And why is *that* my business?" Despite her indifferent response, *not competing anymore* rang in Ramona's ears.

"Because I happen to know that's what broke up you two in the first place."

The bartender delivered their drinks. Ramona quickly reached for hers and took a big gulp. "There were more issues."

"True, but I know that was the coup de grâce."

Kadeem's obsession with the bodybuilding lifestyle had ravaged their relationship. There were the long hours, often as many as five a day, spent in the gym. Then there was all the stockpiling of every bally-hooed nutritional supplement that hit the market. The stress and wild mood swings he suffered from all the strict contest dieting. The carbing up, then leaning out madness. Kadeem's world grew smaller and smaller—focused on one thing—winning some stupid bodybuilding contest when Ramona believed he should have been putting his bachelor's degree in exercise physiology to better use. The day she came home and found syringes on their kitchen counter and vials of powerful, potentially dangerous physique-enhancing pharmaceuticals in their refrigerator she knew Kadeem had taken things way too far.

"Kadeem thought I never tried to understand what it all meant to him," Ramona admitted as she speared another olive. "And I suppose he's right. I didn't *want* to understand. It seemed so ridiculous and narcissistic."

Jalisa took a sip of her drink. "It's a fringe sport, my dear. Not a lot of people understand the appeal."

"Sport?" Ramona scoffed, twisting her lips in distaste. "There's no ball to shoot through a hoop, putt in a hole, or whack out of the stadium. Where's the sport in grown men pumping themselves up to gorilla proportions, stripping down to Speedos, then oiling up to preen and pose on stage in front of an auditorium full of people?" Ramona shrugged. "No, I guess I never *got* it."

"He's not competing anymore, so that's a nonissue," Jalisa repeated. "He's channeled that love of exercise into his own fitness center."

"A fitness center?" Ramona's jaw dropped.

"Yeah, he's had a successful personal-training business for the last few years now, and he used some of the money to buy the gym."

Ramona felt a flicker of renewed interest. "So when did all this happen?"

"Oh, it's been about a year since I heard him talk about doing any show. And he bought the gym about seven—no, eight months ago."

"Kadeem and me again—?" Ramona words trailed off as she considered this update on her ex. She popped the olive inside her mouth, then sighed. "I just don't know. Besides, he's shown me that he has that tendency to latch on to something and get really scary with his devotion. Call me selfish, but I need a man who is willing to make *me* a priority in his life. I'm not asking for more than I'm willing to give."

"I know you've both made some mistakes and bad choices, but you're older, wiser now. Who knows? Those years apart could mean you're better suited for one another than ever before."

Ramona didn't want to grasp on to Jalisa's optimism. It had taken her a long time to get Kadeem out of her system, but after seeing him again today and hearing this update, she began to wonder if she ever had gotten over him.

"So where are all your bags and packages?" Jalisa asked. "Or did you stash them in the car already?"

"I don't have any. Made it through the mall without purchasing a single thing," Ramona fibbed. After fleeing from Kadeem, she waited until the coast was clear, then circled back to housewares to purchase that crystal portrait frame for Jalisa's wedding gift. She stashed the gift in the trunk of her car before heading to the Tavern. "Thanks for the vote of confidence."

"You know I'm just kiddin' with you, girl." Jalisa wrapped an arm around Ramona's shoulder. "I'm proud of you."

"Today I conquered Phipps Plaza alone! And it feels so good!" Ramona raised her glass triumphantly. "It also helps to know I'm not abstaining alone." She took a big drink of her wine.

"Oh, yeah, that's right—"

"There's Della, Gillian, and Neecy."

"I think it's cool that you all are trying to get a handle on things— as long as you don't swap one compulsion for another one."

"Ain't that the truth," Ramona replied, thinking of a time when she thought she could never get enough of Kadeem Smith.

# Chapter 3

Kadeem was halfway home when he realized that he'd been so jolted by seeing Ramona again, he'd left the department store without purchasing a wedding gift for Jalisa and Calvin.

He pulled his Explorer into the driveway of his condo and climbed out, tapping the key fob to engage the SUV's alarm.

Inside he went to the fridge, removed a bottle of water, and lifted the cool plastic to his forehead for a minute before tilting it up to take thirsty gulps. Seeing Ramona again had practically set him on fire with need. The woman was even finer than he remembered. He loved her silky twists. Sexy. Ramona always had such great style, even during their high school days when she had little money.

Smiling to himself, Kadeem leaned against the marble kitchen counter as he recalled the first day he and Ramona had officially met in their high school gym. He'd seen her around school a few times, but knew she had been going with Jamal Phelps for what seemed like forever. He and Jamal weren't running buddies or anything, but he knew him from history and chemistry classes. Jamal seemed like a pretty cool dude, for the most part. As much as Kadeem had wanted to push up on Ramona, he tried his damnedest to steer clear until he knew she was available.

Kadeem had been wearing one of those nylon sweatshirts with a hood pulled over his head and matching nylon pants, which were supposed to help exercisers sweat more pounds away. At the time, little did teenage Kadeem know that the same pounds he'd sweated away came right back after he took his first drink from the gym's water fountain.

He had been maxing out on a series of cleans and presses with a loaded barbell when Ramona wandered over in her school-issued gym uniform. That day, she'd altered the T-shirt and shorts to damn near illegal brevity.

"Hey," she said, popping her gum so loudly, it sounded as if a bundle of lit firecrackers had gone off inside her mouth. He usually hated when girls popped gum like that, but that particular day, it wasn't annoying at all.

Kadeem dropped his barbell on the rubber-matted floor, sucked in a second wind, and then slapped his chalk-covered hands against his thighs. "Hey, yourself."

"I'm Ramona," she said, smiling.

"I know." He commenced to removing the elastic wraps on his hands and wrists that he used for support during his power-lifting sessions.

"You do?" Her eyes went wide with what looked like pleasant surprise. "And you're—"

"Kadeem Smith." He unbuckled his thick leather weight belt.

"You play football?" Ramona blew a bubble that burst before it grew past marble size.

"Nope."

"Basketball?"

"Nope."

"Baseball?"

"Nope."

"Run track?"

"Uh-uh."

"Why are you always working out so hard, then?" she wanted to know.

Kadeem didn't reveal that he sucked at every sport and was always cut during the first round of tryouts. " 'Cause I'm good at it. I like staying in shape."

She snapped her gum, giving him a long, appraising look. "So let me get this straight. You're working out so hard so you can work out harder?" When she plopped on a nearby padded weight bench, he admired her curvaceous calves and thighs. "So you're not doing all this heavy weight training to perform better at a particular sport or anything. Hmmmp."

That *hmmmp* was quite revealing.

Her reasoning made what he loved sound silly and pointless, but he had been much too attracted to her to take offense. He laughed instead. "All the *exercise* is not just an *exercise* in futility. My body stays strong and healthy. I think that's reason enough to incorporate it into one's lifestyle. Don't you work out?"

"Yeah, I can really work out a fried pork chop." Ramona laughed, slapping her thigh.

"You look pretty toned and fit, you must do something?" Brazenly, Kadeem let his gaze skim the length of her sexy legs.

"Chile, the only weight I lift is my fork to my mouth."

Kadeem checked her breasts, then moved on to her succulent lips that made his thoughts turn scandalous. He'd better cool out. After all, this was Jamal's girlfriend.

Ramona continued. "In fact, I'm supposed to be playing volleyball with my gym class as we speak."

"Why aren't you?"

"Stomachache." Ramona clutched her midsection and then grinned in such a way that let him know she'd pulled one over on Coach Nancy Dickerson, her gym teacher. "I'm supposed to be on my way to the school nurse to get some Pepto-Bismol."

"And why aren't you?" Kadeem asked, but not because he wanted her to leave.

"I thought I'd come over and bug you first. Aren't you hot in all that?" She lifted a hand and pointed to his workout gear.

He was hot, all right. And it was getting hotter by the minute 'cause her shorts rolled up an extra inch every time she moved.

"No, I like to dress warmly when I lift; the sweat keeps me oiled."

Ramona nodded as if she understood, fanning herself with one hand. "I see, but it's so hot in here already. If they'd let me, I'd wear a bikini to gym class."

"Looks as if you already do." Kadeem pointedly took in her brief gym outfit. "Wear a bikini to class, I mean."

"Ha. Ha." Ramona deadpanned with good humor, but didn't bother tugging her shorts down to a decent length. It was as if she wanted Kadeem to check her out.

He thought he'd better remind her that she was spoken for. "So how is Jamal?"

"The hell if I know. We broke up two weeks ago." She grinned.

That was all Kadeem needed to hear. "Oh, really?" he replied with a big grin of his own.

The cordless phone on the kitchen counter rang, snatching Kadeem from his jaunt down memory lane.

He reached for it and pressed the receiver to his ear. It was Calvin.

"I hear you bumped into Ramona at the mall today," his friend said. "How'd that go?"

"It was obvious she was taken aback when I told her I was going to be in your wedding." Kadeem leaned against the counter and took another drink from his water bottle.

"Yeah, Jalisa says she was going to tell her today, but who would have thought you two would finally run into each other after four years. What were the chances of that happening?"

"Maybe the planets are starting to line up."

"Which could be a good thing."

"Meaning?"

"I happen to know she's not seeing anyone seriously right now. There might be a chance for reconciliation after all. If that's what you want. Do you want—?" Calvin probed.

"I don't know." Kadeem said. "But *damn* she did look real good to me today."

"All right!" Calvin boomed through the phone. "My man Kadeem wants back in the game!"

"Hey, wait. Don't get ahead of yourself. I said she looked damn good. But I'm not so sure she's into me. She practically left skid marks, trying to get away from me at the mall."

"It's a whole different game. You two have changed."

Change. The question was how much?

The two friends chatted for a few minutes before Kadeem ended the call.

His thoughts lingered on Ramona. After class that day they'd officially met in the gym, he had raced home to phone her. They talked for two hours, and from then on they had been a couple straight through high school and college graduation. He and everyone else had assumed they'd eventually marry.

And they would have if Kadeem hadn't freaked Ramona out with all the bodybuilding craziness. He'd gotten so wrapped up, he'd frightened the hell out of her. And if he were completely honest, he had also frightened himself when he realized what he had seriously considered doing to remain competitive.

Before Ramona had spied those syringes and vials, he had decided that taking that chemical route to win a bodybuilding show was *not* for him. It flew in the face of everything he'd always stood for.

His devotion to exercise had not been just about achieving a certain look at first. It was about strength and good health. True, he'd almost lost sight of that for a while, but he had snapped to his senses *before* he did something stupid. Unfortunately, it had been too late. Ramona didn't believe that Kadeem had made an oath *not* to pump such vile substances into his body. She didn't buy it when he'd promised to become less fanatical about his workouts.

Ramona had never understood why all the exercise was so important to him in the first place. While she'd heard the stories, she had not been in Kadeem's life when he had survived the car crash that killed his favorite uncle and left fourteen-year-old Kadeem paralyzed from the waist down for a year. He had been told he'd never walk again, but he had refused to accept that. And through the grace of God and Kadeem's force of will, sensation eventually returned to his lower limbs—all that was needed before he embarked on a long, grueling physical-therapy program.

Eventually he not only walked and ran again, but he had transformed his body in the process. He'd gone from a gangly teen to one who was frequently mistaken for an athlete. And for the first time, he got attention from girls.

His determination soon turned to obsession as an irrational fear seized him and wouldn't let go: Slacking off or dropping his high intensity would mean he'd be wheelchair bound again. He had conquered the paralysis, but somewhere in the back of his mind he thought he would suffer a relapse if he didn't exercise like a demon *every single day*. He knew better now.

He'd dated other women, but Ramona was the only one he'd ever considered spending the rest of his life with. And after seeing her again today, he wondered—if she were open to giving their relationship another chance, would he take it?

True, he'd taken most of the blame for sinking their relationship, but Ramona wasn't completely faultless. His bodybuilding endeavors aside, Ramona could be an annoying know-it-all who was always primed to swoop in to fix everything—whether he wanted her to or not. She had difficulty trusting or giving folks a chance to figure out things on their own. And her perfectionist tendencies could thwart even those with the strongest sense of self. No man—especially a man such as Kadeem—likes to feel as if his woman thinks he's too weak to handle his business.

The time Kadeem and one of his college instructors, Mr. Lubeck, had butted heads over the theory explored in one of Kadeem's research papers came to mind. Kadeem had challenged his score, believing he deserved at least a grade higher, but the professor refused to back down. Things became more tense between Kadeem and Lubeck to the point where Kadeem feared their differences would affect how the instructor scored his future papers and projects.

Ramona knew Lubeck because he was one of the faculty advisers of a campus travel club with which she was associated.

Before the disputed matter could be settled in third-party arbitration, Ramona secretly took it upon herself to try to smooth things over between Kadeem and Lubeck. Kadeem ultimately got the grade he wanted, and Lubeck's prickly attitude toward him changed. But when Kadeem found out Ramona had a hand in it, he'd been thoroughly pissed. However, focusing on the fact that Ramona always had good intentions, he soon got over it. He'd never made much of an issue of what he'd dubbed her "tendency to rescue," but during their relationship, there had been several instances of similar interference on her part.

As much as Kadeem would love another shot at a relationship with Ramona, these days his tolerance for such meddling had lowered significantly. He took another drink of his water, chiding himself for not being more positive. After all, he'd grown and changed these last few years. Wasn't it possible Ramona had, too?

# Chapter 4

Ramona changed her outfit and shoes four times before she settled on a spaghetti-strapped top with a matching fluted skirt and strappy medium-heeled sandals. She stood before a full-length mirror, surveying her image.

Her selection was less about what she felt like wearing and more about what she knew Kadeem would like to see her wearing. Slacks were out because Kadeem always admired her legs. She went with red because on more than one occasion Kadeem had remarked how it was his favorite color on her.

En route to the church where the rehearsals would be held, butterflies felt as if they were dive-bombing inside her stomach at the thought of seeing Kadeem again. Ramona parked her car in the parking lot then climbed the steps to the small brick church. Once inside the sanctuary, she caught sight of Jalisa huddled with her cousin, Betty.

Betty had experience as a faculty adviser, coordinating school pageants, plays at the junior high school where she taught. This naturally made her the best person for the wedding coordinator duties, Jalisa had reasoned—not to mention the fact that her services came free.

Jalisa waved Ramona over.

As Ramona approached, she scanned the rest of the wedding party.

"He's running a bit late, but promised to be here shortly," Jalisa told her as she pecked Ramona's cheek.

"Who is running late?" Ramona asked, feigning ignorance.

Jalisa clucked her tongue. "Don't even try it." Then she whispered in Ramona's ear. "We both know who you were looking for, but I won't bust you out in front of Betty and the gang."

Ramona gave Jalisa a playful shove.

Betty clapped her hands. "Okay! Places everyone! Let's get this show on the road. Follow me. Jalisa, as ritual dictates, you must sit this one out."

"Aye, aye, captain." Jalisa lifted her hand in a salute. "You're in charge here."

As five bridesmaids and four groomsmen clustered in the vestibule, the front door opened, and Kadeem stepped inside, looking more handsome than ever. He wore a pair of black trousers and a slate silk T-shirt that did ridiculously delicious things to his tall, sculpted physique. His hair was cut in a neat fade, and his brown skin was just-shaved smooth. Ramona clamped her mouth shut to keep from drooling. There was no shame in the rest of the bridesmaids' games. They openly ogled him, drop-jawed. Then they began to jockey for more prominent positioning.

"Sorry, I'm a little late." Kadeem approached the group, instantly taking the spot next to Ramona. A combination of sandalwood and Kadeem's own clean, male scent made her want to climb his long frame and bury her face in that curve between his neck and strong shoulder—like old times.

"Hey, Ramona," he said.

"Kadeem," she acknowledged with a shy grin. Why was she suddenly so giddy and girly acting?

Before she could step away, he took the liberty of planting a peck on her cheek. What was probably meant to be a chaste greeting left her skin tingling.

It was as if they were the only two people there. Their gazes locked on each other, and all other conversation and activity seemed to fade away.

"Good to see you again," he said in that deep voice that had whispered a million and more I love you's when they were a couple.

Ramona gulped to take in air. "Good to see you."

"Hey, you two, do you have something to say that everyone else here needs to hear?" Betty made Ramona feel like a grade-school kid busted passing notes.

The heat of embarrassment crept from Ramona's neck to her cheeks.

"No, ma'am," Kadeem replied, obviously trying to smother a smile.

"Then I suggest you two pay attention. I would like to give these instructions once," Betty said crisply.

Betty called out names for the bridesmaid procession down the aisle.

Ramona would be paired with Kadeem. No surprise there. She had a hunch Jalisa and Calvin might pull such a stunt. Two of the other bridesmaids who had obviously been hoping for a different arrangement groaned.

"Betty doesn't play, does she?" Kadeem whispered to Ramona.

"No, she doesn't," Ramona quickly whispered back before she took her place in the bridesmaid line. "Before she moved on to a junior high school I hear she was an elementary school teacher. She's had plenty of practice wrangling the wild and unruly."

"Guess I'd better stay in line, then."

"Now, here we go. The groomsmen go down and wait beside the

groom's spot. When the music starts, I'll give the signal for each bridesmaid to begin making her way down the aisle."

Sounded easy enough . . .

Until Kristine, Jalisa's sister and matron of honor, was stopped by Betty midway down the aisle. "No! No! No! You're in a church wedding, not stomping grapes in some vineyard in the Old Country. Glide, ladies, gliiiiiiide!"

Uh-oh. Ramona rolled her eyes and released an impatient sigh. It was going to be a long rehearsal.

Three hours later, at the rehearsal dinner at Ruth's Chris Steak House, Ramona was glad when Kadeem made a beeline for her table and took the seat next to hers. She hardly had much of a chance to talk to him at the rehearsal on drill sergeant Betty's clock.

"We all survived Betty," Kadeem said.

"Yeah, but I think I'm gonna hear 'Glide, ladies, gliiiiiiide,' in my sleep for nights on end." Ramona chuckled, reaching to take a sip of her lemon water as the server placed plates of food before them.

"Wasn't Betty something else?" said Corinna, one of five bridesmaids in the wedding party. "I think I need a shot of whiskey. Scratch that. Bring me the damn bottle and a brand-new pair of Dr. Scholl's shoe liners to replace the ones that woman wore out—making us march up and down that aisle over and over again like we were preparing for battle."

Jackie, another bridesmaid, piped up. "She just wants Jalisa's wedding to be perfect, y'all. Cut the woman some slack."

"Why?" Corinna shot back. "She didn't cut us any."

Kadeem turned his attention to Ramona while the rest of the people at their table took off on their own conversations. He leaned closer, and Ramona felt herself getting lost in the brandy brown of his irises. He had the most mesmerizing eyes.

His gaze traveled from her face, neck, then down to her red top, and his lips turned up in an appreciative smile. Ramona got the impression he was picturing her naked. Her cheeks flushed because she was doing the same to him. Picturing him naked. She knew the exact location of a certain leaf-shaped birthmark. . . . Her fingers twitched to reach out and trace it. . . . But she managed to rein in that brazen thought. Such a maneuver would not only raise eyebrows, but also get them both thrown out of the restaurant. Kadeem still had the power to turn her on in an instant. She reached for her glass of water, took a generous drink, and then lifted her knife and fork to tuck into her steak and asparagus. She went through the motions of enjoying her meal, though it was another appetite that needed to be sated.

"So you about ready to put a hit out on Betty, too?" His playful question did not match that husky let-me-take-you-to-bed timbre of his voice or the glint in his hooded eyes. He slowly ran one index finger along the rim of his glass, and Ramona recalled all the times those same fingers were so adept at stroking all her erogenous zones.

Ramona quickly swallowed a bit of food in her mouth before she choked on it. "Nah, I . . . I . . . know I was complaining," she managed as if in a trance. "But I agree with Jackie . . ." Her words trailed off as she looked into his eyes. Their rapt attention to one another would be the talk of the bridal party if Ramona didn't try to snap out of this spell he had over her. It just didn't make any sense to her. She'd gone all this time, managing just fine without caressing Kadeem, kissing Kadeem and . . . She blinked, trying to get a grip. It was as if every moment of the last four years she'd spent denying that she missed him had not only rushed back full force, but quadrupled over the last three hours.

"You were saying . . . ," Kadeem prodded, as he finally lifted his knife and fork to cut his steak.

"Betty just wants the best for Jalisa. Everyone involved is working overtime and giving a little extra to make sure everything is perfect for the big day. And besides, I can use all the exercise I can get."

That seemed to catch him by surprise. "Oh?"

"I promised to run a ten K for charity soon, and I've basically been a couch potato. All that marching down the aisle in the church today, while nowhere near as grueling as running, got me off my fanny for a while."

"A ten K, huh?" His face lit up with amazement.

Ramona swallowed a bite of asparagus. "Yup."

A chuckle rumbled from Kadeem's broad chest. "Good for you. If I recall correctly, the old Ramona could only work out a fried pork chop."

Ramona couldn't restrain her smile. "You still remember that after all this time?"

"How could I forget? That was one of the first things I learned about you that day we met."

Ramona felt warmth inside. He remembered such a minor detail about their first meeting. "Well, the race is for a good cause. Proceeds will go to a local breast cancer research project."

"So what's your training regimen?" Kadeem reached for his iced tea and took a drink.

"Training regimen?" Ramona thought the answer was obvious. "I run, of course."

"But what else are you doing to condition yourself for that distance?"

"I figured I'd run around my block a few times every day until the race." She reached for her napkin and dabbed at her lips.

His thick brows hitched. "That's it?"

"What else is there?" Ramona shrugged. "It's just running. Though I haven't done much of it over the years, I think I know *how* it's done. You put one foot in front of the other—" She continued slowly with emphasis, then used her hands to demonstrate the idiot-proof technique. "—*then another foot in front of the other very quickly, over and over again.*"

"Ha ha. Cute." Kadeem smiled. "It's not just the actual running, but knowing *how much* to run each day to get your body conditioned for such a race. Ten kilometers is a little over six miles, lady. If you've never run much, that can be quite a stretch."

Kadeem's comments gave Ramona pause. She pursed her lips and got lost in her thoughts for a minute. Of course, he was an expert on such matters, and he seemed concerned that she might have bitten off more than she could chew. She already knew the distance in miles. She'd even gotten in her car and driven it, measuring the mileage on her odometer. The distance from her condo to that strip mall bordering the nearest highway was six miles. And seemed like nothing while cruising in her Lexus. In theory, it seemed doable. However, theory was far from the reality of lacing up her running shoes and actually hauling ass. "Hmmmm. I guess you have a point."

"You should have a training schedule, which will allow you to gradually and *comfortably* increase your mileage and intensity each week leading up to the race. When is it, by the way?"

Ramona, the chronic couch potato, was all for comfort. "About two months from now," she replied.

"If you get on a good program now and stick to it, you can still be ready in plenty of time."

"I can surf the Internet or buy a book with a good ten-K training schedule."

"Yeah, you can do that or . . ." He rested his fork and reached for the hand she had resting on the table and covered it with his own.

"Or what?"

"Let me train you." Kadeem squeezed her fingers. Little tingles moved from her fingertips and dispersed through her body. "Remember, I do have a degree in exercise physiology, and I'm a certified personal trainer."

"And competitive bodybuilder?" Ramona tossed out suddenly. She was fishing, trying to verify the information she had received secondhand. She needed confirmation from Kadeem that he was no longer involved in the activity that had torn them apart the first time around.

"No, I don't compete anymore."

Ramona released the breath she'd been holding since she tossed out the question. "So you have moved on?"

"Yes. Don't get me wrong. I still train hard and I always will, but I don't *need* it anymore."

Ramona didn't want to linger on this topic, which spurred negative memories. She had all the information she needed. "So you're willing to train me. What's your price?"

"For you, it's free." Kadeem lifted her hand to his soft lips. When he placed a moist kiss on her knuckles, she thought she would dissolve into a warm puddle. The air around them could not get hotter. Ramona struggled to catch her breath. Her insides fluttered. "So when can we begin? Working out, I mean?"

Kadeem leaned closer, his knee brushing her bare one, his warm breath caressing the sensitive shell of her ear. "Whenever you're ready . . . to work up a sweat."

Ramona felt more than ready. Heat had dipped to her stomach and settled between her thighs as an ache of longing. But her good sense urged her to slow the hell the down. They'd been apart for four years; hopping into the man's bed first thing could derail the progress they'd made today.

By the time dessert was served, Kadeem's body was taut with need as a result of sitting so close to the woman he'd desired more than any other for the past few hours. So when she rose to leave for the bathroom, rather than rise as a gentleman was supposed to do when a lady left the table, he sort of let his butt hover a few inches above his chair, then quickly sat down again. He didn't dare stand all the way up for fear that the rest of the table would notice how her proximity had done a real number on him.

He exhaled, biting his lip as he watched Ramona walk to the ladies' room. He couldn't believe his luck as he sat captivated by her full, curvaceous butt and the seductive sway of her hips. *Man oh man.* Ramona had only gotten more hot and stunning with time. It was all he could do to keep his hands to himself. Initially, at least, he had thought he'd exercise more suave restraint. Play it cool with her. After all, he hadn't seen Ramona in four years. But the moment he'd laid eyes on her again in the church vestibule, he knew he had to kick all game playing to the curb. He wanted to explore the possibility of a reconciliation. Helping her train for that race would be an excellent opportunity to get reacquainted. And to find out if she was open to the possibility. If her flirting this evening was any indication, he'd bet she was just as intrigued as he was.

Through more conversation, he could also determine whether those problems that helped torpedo their relationship last time would surface again. For his part, he didn't intend to return to the bodybuilding lifestyle. Now all that was left to do was determine if Ramona had reined in her swoop-in-and-rescue tendencies.

Just as Kadeem eased back in his chair, Calvin came by.

"How's it going?" Calvin slapped Kadeem on the shoulder.

Kadeem let loose a broad smile. "Couldn't be better."

"Yeah, it looked that way from my end." Calvin slapped Kadeem shoulders when they noticed Ramona approaching. "Ooops. Better go." With that, his friend slipped back to his chair at an adjacent table.

Holding a menu to block his front, Kadeem rose and helped Ramona with her chair.

"What's Calvin jawing about?" Ramona sat.

"Just making rounds to be sure everyone is enjoying themselves." Kadeem used his fork to cut a piece of his cheesecake.

"And are you? Enjoying yourself?" Ramona asked, shifting her body in Kadeem's direction in such a way that let him know she was opening to him again. He wouldn't blow it this time.

"Yes. Immensely." Kadeem's eyes made yet another slow journey from her impressive cleavage, up the column of her smooth brown neck to her face. God, how badly he wanted her again.

He would have her again, the thought filled him with a contentment he hadn't felt in ages as he sampled his cheesecake.

Ramona watched his mouth as he worked through his dessert. As he ate he discreetly, but deliberately did things with his tongue he hoped would spur memories of how he used it to tease and taunt her to a passion haze while savoring her.

Judging by the smoky look in her eyes, it was working. Then she suddenly blinked and reached for her water glass to take big gulps.

"Something wrong?" he asked, not bothering to restrain a confident grin.

"No," she replied quickly and then began fanning herself with her napkin. "It's hot in here. Think something's wrong with the air-conditioning?"

"I'm hot, too, but I don't think it has anything to do with the air-conditioning, babe," Kadeem replied, holding her gaze. He leaned in closer, just a breath from her lips. He didn't care about the rest of the bridal party, he was going to kiss her.

Before his lips brushed hers . . .

"Cheesecake," emerged from her mouth. A question or statement? He couldn't tell which.

He froze. Mission aborted.

Ramona continued, "I can't remember ever seeing you enjoy anything sweet that wasn't a Power Bar."

Kadeem merely chuckled, disappointed, but not defeated. He straightened and took another bite of his dessert. "Now do you believe me when I tell you I've loosened up? I'm not so militantly unyielding about my diet. I'm not a junk-food junkie either, but there's room for everything—"

"In moderation." Ramona swiped her finger across the whipped cream atop his cheesecake and slowly licked her finger as his thoughts careened where they shouldn't again in a roomful of people. Nights of erotic experimentation with whipped cream, honey, and fruit-flavored massage oils on his mind.

"So . . . think you can come by Peak Physiques on Monday?" Kadeem knew he shouldn't push, but he couldn't help himself.

"That's right. I heard you're the proud owner of a new gym," she said, sounding impressed.

Possessively, Kadeem let one arm drape along the back of her chair. "Well, it's not exactly shiny and new, but it's all mine."

"I'm sure it's great," she replied. "And Monday sounds good. I'll leave my shop around four. Expect to see me about an hour later. But until then—"

"There's that wedding and reception tomorrow. We'll be spending the entire day together practically."

"Practically," Ramona drawled, wearing a flirty expression filled with promises.

# Chapter 5

Jalisa's wedding in the small church that had an abundance of rustic charm was the stuff of dreams.

Amid candelabra and red roses, the bride and groom swapped beautiful, heartfelt vows they'd written themselves. Afterwards, the wedding party and seventy-five guests were whisked off to a dining and reception hall for a celebration that included a delicious five-course meal.

As Kadeem escorted Ramona to the dance floor, she couldn't help wondering if her special day would come. Funny, for the past four years she hadn't given much thought to if and when she'd get hitched.

But with Kadeem's strong arms encircling her, she found herself imagining that this was their first dance—as husband and wife. Silly, but she smiled anyway as they moved in time as Luther Vandross's "Here and Now" filled the air.

They danced like old lovers savoring sweet memories.

"Enjoying yourself?" Kadeem drew her closer to whisper in her ear. The vibration of his rumbling baritone sent the most glorious chills down her spine.

Ramona inclined her head to look into his eyes. "Yes. Very much."

He dropped his hands from hers and wrapped them around her shoulders to draw her closer. "I'm usually not much for weddings, but I'm enjoying myself, too."

"Oh?" Ramona pressed her cheek against the cotton of his crisply pressed shirt, her arms curling around his waist. He smelled and looked so good in his midnight black tuxedo, Ramona's breath caught. Hard, warm muscles held her tight. The teasing but pleasing scent of his cologne. The expert strokes of his fingers across her lower back. Oh, how she could get lost in this man.

"No, I'm not, but I'm sure the company has a lot to do with my newfound appreciation for this nuptial stuff." Like old times, Kadeem's hand stole up her spine and found that sensitive spot at the nape of her neck, then caressed it.

Ramona purred, "No fair . . . going for my weak spots like that."

"You mean like this," he whispered as his fingertips continued tracing small circles on her neck just beneath her hairline.

"You know that drives me crazy." Ramona gazed up at him, trying to keep her composure despite the thick haze of desire scrambling her thoughts.

"That's the point," he said, one corner of his lips turning up in a rascal's grin.

Ramona arced a brow. "Is that right?"

"I just wanted to show off a bit. I still know how to find all of your hidden treasures."

Ramona's body shivered. Her lips parted to protest, but when his mouth came down to settle softly over hers, her mind went blank.

The kiss was gentle. A brush of his moist lips only, but more than enough to crush the last of her equilibrium. The room seemed to spin around them as she melted in his arms, with a soft moan escaping her mouth.

"Hey, you two! Get a room, why don't you?" Calvin's brother,

Anthony, boomed—shattering the moment. But were it not for that intrusion, Kadeem and Ramona would have forgotten where they were.

Ramona's body involuntarily jerked away to force space between her and Kadeem.

"What's up, man?" Kadeem asked, trying to mask his annoyance.

"Looks like you two getting into a little somethin'-somethin'." Anthony chuckled with mischief.

"I think they're getting ready to cut to the cake." Ramona anxiously ran her hands over her silky twists that were gathered in an elegant cluster with a beaded ornament that matched her bridesmaid shoes. She scanned her surroundings to see how many other guests noticed their too-cozy display on the dance floor. "It's lemon with key lime frosting," she chirped before scurrying toward the other guests who clustered around the cake table. Before she departed, she heard Kadeem grumble to Anthony, "Thanks a lot, man. You and your perfect timing."

"Sorry, I know it must've looked like I was . . . well . . . blocking," Anthony said, flashing big teeth and giving Kadeem a slap on the back. "But Calvin sent me over."

Kadeem looked over near the cake table, where the groom stood with his beaming a bride. "Why?"

"He told me to remind you to pace yourself."

Calvin was probably right, but that was easier said than done, Kadeem decided, letting his recollections of the purest pleasures run roughshod over his willpower. "Check you later, dude." Kadeem snagged his third glass of champagne from a server and then made his way over to Ramona, who had already claimed a slice of cake.

Kadeem stepped behind her, slipping one arm around her trim waist that curved dramatically into the cushiest bottom. "So you still looking forward to our training session?" He sipped his champagne. As if he needed a buzz when he was so high off Ramona already.

"I don't know," she replied, not bothering to turn around.

Kadeem enjoyed the feel of her rear against him as he hardened. This time he didn't care. The alcohol must have lowered his inhibitions. And besides, he had a tuxedo jacket to conceal the evidence that he wanted this woman in the worst kind of way. He drank more of his champagne and continued rubbing the slight, feminine curve of her belly. Her warmth and the smooth satin of her gown were tactile treats for his fingers.

Ramona pressed against him, obviously now fully aware of the affect she had on him and loving every minute of it. "You sound as if you're looking forward to torturing me or something," she said, nudging closer still. A large centerpiece on a nearby table blocked what she was doing from view of the others, but Kadeem felt every spark she generated while rubbing against him so provocatively.

Kadeem bent to rest his chin on her shoulder and nipped at her earlobe. "I promise it'll be the sweetest torture."

She turned to face him. Her lips turned up in a sexy smile, she took the champagne glass from his hands and brazenly drained it before handing it back to him. "Can't wait," she teased, just before she left him standing there, on the edge of exploding.

She'd pay for that, he thought gamely with a smile as he watched her break into a seductive little shimmy on the dance floor obviously for his benefit. Kadeem took a chair. He just sat back and watched her work.

The next day, Kadeem watched Jason huff and puff through the cardio portion of his workout. "Ten more minutes in that target heart rate zone, and the rest is smooth sailing . . . or rather smooth pedaling."

The teen's hands gripped the side handlebars, and his beefy legs pumped the pedals of the recumbent stationary bike. "I feel like I've been on here for an hour already," he grumbled as perspiration rolled from his hairline, down his face to dampen the collar of his gray sweatshirt.

Kadeem checked his watch again, but this time he did it for Jason. Before the teen started his workout, Kadeem had been doing so every ten minutes as the time for Ramona's arrival drew near. "Try twelve minutes. That's all you've done so far."

"That's all? Man . . . you've . . . gotta be kiddin'," Jason sputtered in a winded voice. "Your watch must be broke."

"My watch is working just fine." Kadeem grinned.

"I didn't know you got off on inflicting pain."

"Stop grumbling. You'll thank me when you try out for your football team and finally make the cut. So keep pumping those pedals, my man. Looks as if you could use a refill on that water bottle of yours." Kadeem tugged the plastic squirt container out of the holder attached to the stationary bike's chassis, then crossed the gym floor to the nearest water fountain.

As he maneuvered through exercisers and equipment, he looked around Peak Physiques Gym, which was the culmination of an old dream. He smiled. The air was thick with the scent of sweat, Ben-Gay, and dedication. Grunts and groans of members maxing out on their sets mingled with the clings and clangs of metal weight plates. A frenetic DMX rap mix with much bass thumped through CD players positioned on each end of the gym. Kadeem couldn't afford a high-tech sound system just yet, but in time he planned to add one. There was no place in the world that felt more like home than his gym.

Kadeem had spent the last four years working extra-long hours at his personal training service and socking away as much of his earnings as he could—minus living expenses—in hopes of saving enough to buy his own fitness center one day. Peak Physiques was far from those super fitness centers that boasted large indoor tracks, lap swimming pools, juice bars, and gleaming state-of-the-art exercise machines. It was just a funky little neighborhood gym with ratty carpeting on the floor, cracked mirrors, and second- and thirdhand equipment. This hardly detracted from the joy Kadeem felt knowing it was all his.

"Hey, hurry up with that water! I'm dying of thirst over here!" Jason shouted.

"Coming right up!" Kadeem tipped the bottle's opening toward the stream arcing from the fountain. Though he spent a good chunk of his day taking care of Peak Physiques administrative duties—mostly on the phone making cold calls to sell gym memberships, he still carried a full roster of personal training clients because he needed the money.

Jason was one of the kids Kadeem volunteered to train for free as a way of giving something back to his old, underprivileged neighborhood. Two or three days a week, Jason would take the bus from the Perry Homes housing project to Peak Physiques. The boy, who already had high cholesterol levels, was about twenty-five pounds overweight. Kadeem had put him on a diet and exercise regimen not only so Jason could make his high school football team, but to hopefully head off the potential heart attack in the boy's future, as well.

When Kadeem first opened Peak Physiques eight months ago, he had new people joining almost every week. Lately memberships had tapered off, and the gym was still operating in the red because he had spent most of his cash reserves on the ceiling, roof, and walkway near the front door that required extensive repairs. The last thing he needed was getting sued by someone who had gotten crowned by a chunk of crumbling ceiling or taken a tumble after their feet snagged on the buckling concrete out front. Shelling out big bucks for repairs and such were just part of being a business owner, but he wondered if he'd ever get to upgrade the exercise equipment. That was one investment he was sure would draw more members.

He passed the water bottle to Jason, who immediately turned it upright and squirted some inside his mouth and then over his already drenched face. He shook his head like a wet Saint Bernard, flinging a mixture of water and sweat everywhere.

"Hey, watch it!" Kadeem widened the space between them.

Jason just chuckled. "Say, man, you given any thought to what I told you about my aunt Mavis?" Jason had obviously hit his target heart zone, because his speech was less choppy.

"Your aunt Mavis?" Kadeem echoed only to buy himself some time to think of a nice way to tell the kid he wasn't interested in dating his aunt. The woman had made it obvious she had the hots for Kadeem, after tagging along with Jason for one of his workouts. Mavis was as fine as they came with her big brown eyes, tight waist, curvy butt, and killer legs. He just wasn't into dating anymore for dating's sake. He'd done plenty of that the last few years. And though he'd cop to having some good times and good sex, he realized that a part of him would never be ready to move on until he got another chance with Ramona.

"Are you already off the market or something? If so, I can just tell Aunt Mavis you're already hooked up."

"Tell her I'm flattered and all, but yeah, I'm preoccupied right now," Kadeem replied, gearing up for Ramona, who would be arriving in another half hour.

The workday couldn't pass fast enough for Ramona, who closed her shop an hour earlier than usual.

In the parking lot of Peak Physiques Gym, she climbed out of her car, carrying a canvas gym bag stuffed with her workout gear.

Kadeem, who had just exchanged good-byes with a chubby boy who looked to be about fifteen or sixteen met her at the door.

"Welcome to my place!" Kadeem kissed her cheek. He made a sweeping gesture with his hands. "What do you think?" he asked, his eyes bright and full of pride.

The place was smaller than she'd imagined and filled with well-worn exercise equipment. Some of the cushioned weight benches had tears that had been sealed with black duct tape. What should have been textured belts on three nearby treadmills were bald from over-use. Trees of weights plates were starting to show signs of rusting. Paint chips from the cagelike apparatus to her left littered the floor.

"So what you think?" Kadeem prodded.

"It's nice . . . very nice," Ramona replied. It wasn't shiny and new and bursting with the best state-of-the-art equipment, but it was Kadeem's, and she knew he'd worked hard for everything in here.

"I see you're checking out the power rack over there." He nodded in the direction of the cagelike piece of equipment. "I got it at a steal. It's not new. As you can see almost all the paint is stripped off. It's supposed to be white, but it's turning black on me."

"Doing a reverse Michael Jackson, huh?" Ramona quipped.

"So she's got jokes." Kadeem laughed heartily, then tugged her into his arms so suddenly a gasp tore from her lips. "I've missed you, you know that?" Kadeem crushed her against his chest.

Ramona didn't bother fighting the emotion that was overwhelming her. "I've missed you, too."

"Good. We're on the same page again." Kadeem swept her with a hungry look that made her feel like the most desirable woman on the planet.

"Hey, Kadeem!" one of the gym members called out to him from a stationary bike a couple of yards away. "I can't get this doohickey thing here to move!"

"Be right with you, Mrs. Lawson," Kadeem said to the heavyset older woman struggling with the seat adjustment on the bike. He turned back to Ramona. "No matter, how many times I oil that damn thing, it's always getting stuck. I'll just be a minute."

"In the meantime, I should change into my running gear, right?"

"Yeah. The ladies' bathroom and locker room is that way." Kadeem pointed toward the right rear of the gym.

Kadeem was in the middle of spotting Sam, one of his members, who was pushing through his last set of "skull crusher" triceps presses with an E-Z curl bar. He stood near Sam's head as Sam tried to gut power through a final rep.

"C'mon, it's all you—all you. You got it," Kadeem coached.

Just as the bar stalled near the man's forehead, Ramona emerged from the locker room dressed in running shorts, tank top, zip-front sweat shirt, and sneakers. This particular woman lingering about in short shorts was not something any man should have to endure when his complete attention was required elsewhere. She smiled and lifted her hand for a little wave at Kadeem, who waved back, letting his eyes take a slow journey up her curvy body as heat rolled through his . . . He felt the lusty grin tugging at his own lips when . . .

"Hey, man! Will you help a brotha out here!" Sam bellowed.

Kadeem grabbed the bar just before it bashed Sam's brains out, then added with a guilty chuckle. "Sorry about that, dude."

Scowling, Sam jerked upright. "Where did you go just now? I thought you were supposed to be spotting me through that exercise! They don't call them skull crushers for nothing you know!"

"Got a little distracted, that's all." Kadeem's eyes were still on Ramona as she approached them.

Sam followed Kadeem's gaze to Ramona. "Oh, I get it now," Sam said with obvious appreciation. "Perfectly understandable, my brotha."

"I'm all ready to go," Ramona said, eliciting a chuckle from Kadeem, who was beyond ready as well, just getting a look at those killer legs in those shorts.

Kadeem left Carl, one of the college kids he'd hired to work at the gym part-time, in charge of overseeing things while he took Ramona outside to the patch of grass on the lawn out front. The gym was located in a mostly residential area that got little traffic. While still bright out, the sun had started to descend and the temperature had cooled to a pleasant seventy-six degrees. Perfect for a run.

Together they did some light jogging in place to prepare their muscles for light stretching.

"Because you've never raced before, I'm going to start you off training as if you were running a five K. We'll start today doing two miles; then we'll gradually work our way up each training day—alternating easy runs or hard runs, in which we will vary the speed, intensity, and mileage. Of course, because you're a novice, we'll start off at a low intensity—meaning if you find it a challenge, we'll break it up as a walk-run."

"Sounds good to me. I'm all yours."

"How are those muscles feeling?" he asked "Pretty tight after spending the entire day at a manicure station?"

"I don't do manicures all day anymore. Just here and there for special clients," Ramona told him as she jogged in place.

"Oh, that's right. Calvin said you opened your own manicure shop. Good for you!"

"Looks like we're both successful entrepreneurs."

Kadeem merely smiled, instead of revealing that Peak Physiques was hardly a big success just yet. It was still operating in the red— blood red. But hell, all small businesses struggled the first year or two. With a little time, careful money management, and a few new customers, the gym's financial outlook was bound to improve. "How are those muscles feeling?" he asked again.

"Nice and warm."

"Be right back," he said just before sprinting back inside the gym. He returned a couple of minutes later with a clean, beach-size white towel.

"What's that for?" Ramona watched him spread it in front of where she stood.

"For you. I know you don't want to sit directly on the grass. No telling what might crawl up those short shorts of yours." He grinned.

When he gestured for her to sit on the towel, she did as she was told. "What am I doing next?"

"Jogging is great for getting the heart rate up and the muscles warm, but if you really want to prime the muscles and rid them of knots that might be lurking, a massage is best." He rippled his fingers.

"A massage, huh?" Ramona cut her eyes at him playfully. "You ain't hardly smooth. I hope you know that. And I suppose you'll need to demonstrate how I should work the knots out?"

"I thought you'd never ask." He began gently kneading one calf, the other, enjoying the silkiness of her skin against his palms.

"Hmmmm. That feels great." With her hands planted on the ground, Ramona let her head loll back, and her eyes slipped closed in rapture.

"You always had such soft skin, Ramona." He worked his way up, bending her leg so he could massage the back of the thigh.

"Ahhhh," she moaned, sounding so orgasmic, Kadeem's mouth went dry. His own sweats were suddenly too snug in an obvious place.

"I'm supposed to knead your calf, hamstring, lower back, and—"

Ramona's head snapped back up. "You're *not* kneading my butt," she said, cleverly guessing where he was headed.

He put on a look of mock hurt. "Ahhhh, you're no fun."

"You not kneading my butt . . . in public, that is." She chuckled, obviously enjoying their little flirting game. It reminded Kadeem of the day he'd asked for her phone number in the school gym.

She cocked her head to one side with a soft smile on her lips. "So how long do I get to enjoy the pleasure of these magic fingers of yours before the real torture begins?"

"Five to ten minutes." He slowed his machinations along her hamstring. "Or for as long as you like."

When his fingers moved closer to the juncture of her thighs, her breath caught. Everything seemed to go still as they sat, looking at one another. He thought he saw something in her eyes that was urging him to go for it. But he thought better of it. After all, they were in public—in broad daylight. When he got this close to Ramona's sweet spot, he wanted to be all alone without the possibility of interruptions. A dog and its owner walked by. When they passed, Kadeem moved his hands back to the safety of her calf. "Nice shoes. They look new."

"I purchased them for training. Besides the gift I bought for Jalisa's wedding, they're one of my last splurges since I've restricted my shopping sprees."

"You call sneakers a splurge?"

"Now I do."

"And what about these restricted shopping sprees?"

"I got pretty crazy there for a while—buying all sorts of things whenever the whim struck. But now I think I've got things under control again with the help of my shopaholics group."

Now on his knees, Kadeem moved until he was positioned behind her so he could work the muscles in her lower back. "A shop-a-what?"

"Ahhh, that feels so good. A little to left. Lower. Lower. Ahhh, yeah, right there." When Ramona's head fell back again, his nose brushed silky locks that smelled like fresh apples. "Shopaholics, meaning we were spending way too much time and money in malls."

"I know you've always enjoyed shopping, but I don't recall you letting it get out of hand. How bad did things get?" Kadeem wanted to know, thinking maybe he could share his cash flow problem with Ramona after all—especially if she was facing a similar money challenge. "Did it start to affect your business?"

"Oh, gosh no!" she said quickly, flapping one hand. "My business is doing great. Fortunately, I had the willpower not to dip into my retirement savings or the funds needed to run Nailz and Detailz. I was able to keep my personal and business spending separate. It was my personal spending that got out of hand."

"How? Why?"

"I'd been doing some reading on the topic when I decided I needed to get to the root of the problem. At first I thought it stemmed from growing up so poor we couldn't even afford liquid milk, just the powdered stuff that came in a box."

"Hey, don't even go on that pity trip. Cause you know I can *out-poor* you any day with my childhood stories." Kadeem chuckled mirthlessly. "Ever tried to pop popcorn with mineral oil? That's all we had to eat in our house once. I practically lived in the bathroom for three days and left big oil slicks on every chair in the house."

Ramona gave him a wan smile, then continued. "My spending wasn't just about being poor and suddenly having money. I noted a drastic shift in my spending habits when my mother passed away four years ago."

"I was sorry when I heard about that. I wanted to reach out to you with more than the flowers I sent, but we'd just broken up. I wasn't sure how you would've felt about seeing or talking to me."

"I understand." Ramona stroked his arm with her fingers, sending more tingles of awareness through him. "Truth be told, I'm not sure your showing up would've been a good thing either. I felt so hurt and confused back then. I'd lost you—then I lost my mother. She wasn't the most perfect mom by a long shot." Ramona's voice cracked a bit, but she kept her composure. Kadeem could tell Ramona was still in pain about losing her mother. "She drank so much, I'm sure her liver must've been pickled by the time all that booze killed her, but I know she loved me and I loved her."

His hands moved to her shoulders. "Are you all right?"

She nodded, looking away in the distance. "Anyway, I think all the shopping became a way to fill the emptiness of losing two of the most important people in my life at the same time. But you know what? As much as I purchased, it was never close to being enough. That's when I realized I had a problem and had to do something about it."

Kadeem offered her a consoling smile, but nixed going into detail about the gym's budget woes. "Sounds as if you've taken the bull by the horns."

"More like taken the shopping bag by the handles." Ramona fisted one hand and raised it in the air. " 'Cause I've finally conquered Phipps Plaza!"

"Way to go!" Kadeem moved until he could look her in the face when he sat down beside her. "I'm glad you confided all that to me."

"Don't look so surprised. Part of my therapy is to share with people around me. The more people who know, the more likely I'm gonna be held accountable if I do something crazy around them."

"I'm not just surprised that you told me about it, but that you had that kind of problem in the first place."

"What does that mean?" Ramona plucked a blade of grass and idly rubbed it across Kadeem's bare forearm. "I am human."

The glass tickled; Kadeem took it from her hand. "Oh?" He tried to keep his tone light.

Ramona gave him a sidelong look. "And what does *that* mean, exactly?"

Kadeem averted his gaze as he watched the leaves on nearby trees shimmy in the light breeze. "When we were together, you always came off as a bit of a perfectionist. You know, Ms. Ramona *always* had all her ducks in a row. Always handling everything just so. You had this aura about you that you never screwed up and if there was a screw-up involved, it certainly wasn't Ramona's doing." Kadeem was careful to tread carefully, so he stopped short of tossing the part about that tendency being annoying as all get out. Especially now that he'd heard Ramona finally confess to a weakness—any weakness. That brought him up short. Maybe this was a new Ramona.

Ramona's jaw dropped. "I had no idea you felt that way about me. Why didn't you say something?"

Kadeem shrugged. "Why? So you could tell me I was the one with the problem?"

"Not to dredge up bad memories, but remember it was *your* obsession with bodybuilding that drove the biggest wedge between us."

Kadeem sighed. "No need to remind me. I'm willing to fess up to my mistakes, but you know what, Ramona? I know things got crazy there for a while. And I know you spied those vials and syringes. But I swear to you, though I had seriously considered using them, I *never* did. And after you asked me to leave, I pitched everything in the trash. If that stuff could destroy my life before I actually took it, I couldn't imagine the havoc it would cause had I actually started juicing up. I figured it wasn't worth it. I just wish I'd come to my senses sooner."

"Things happen for a reason," she said. "Maybe we both needed these years apart to appreciate what we had."

When Ramona let her hand rest on his thigh, he covered it with his own and squeezed. A long minute passed before either said a word as something healing passed between them.

Kadeem finally spoke. "We let so much time pass just sitting on our behinds, we'll have to do another warm-up jog in place." He added with a waggle of his thick brows, "Another warm-up complete with another therapeutic massage."

# Chapter 6

Over the next few days, Ramona made tremendous training progress with help from Kadeem.

By the end of the following week, Ramona was up to four miles. Two of which felt effortless, which was an accomplishment as far as she was concerned.

On this day, she and Kadeem had not only taken off for their run later than usual, but also had to cut their distance shorter than planned because of the nagging discomfort Ramona felt at the lower front region of her legs.

They made it back to Peak Physiques about thirty minutes before closing time, and Ramona practically limped inside the door.

With her arm hooked around Kadeem's neck, he helped her to one of the padded weight benches. He gestured for her to sit while he kneeled before her.

"So where do you feel the pain, exactly?" he asked, concern furrowing his brow.

"Right here and here." She pointed to the areas on her lower legs.

"Probably shin splints." He gingerly poked a finger along the fleshy area beside her shin bone.

"Ow!" Ramona bent and swiped his hands away.

"Just as I suspected. Did the pain just start today?"

Ramona considered fibbing, but decided against it. "No, earlier this week."

"Earlier this week?" Kadeem's annoyance tightened his handsome features. "Why didn't you say something before?"

"Because I was so psyched. I was doing so well. And you seemed so proud of the progress I'd made. I didn't want to start whining like a wimp at the first sign of pain."

Kadeem shook his head, then released a reluctant smile. "What am I going to do with you? You go from couch potato to devoted road runner just like that." He snapped his fingers. "You never cease to amaze me, woman. But if I had known you were feeling soreness in this area, I would've recommended we cut back to allow this muscle to heal before the inflammation got worse."

Ramona groaned. "That's what I thought you would say."

"Don't worry. Taking a few days off is not going to hinder your progress. It can actually help because you're obviously overtraining—a bit too much too soon."

"A few days?" Ramona balked. "What's a few days?"

"We're talking only about three or four. You'll be fine. It'll be good for you. In the meantime, I'm going to give you instructions for a gentle stretching program that should help, but not today."

"Anything else, doctor?" Ramona smiled.

"Yes, I was wondering if you'll have dinner with me."

Though they'd spent the last two weeks flirting, Kadeem's invite still caught her by surprise. Ramona had even begun to wonder if she'd imagined that kiss he'd given her on the dance floor at Jalisa and Calvin's wedding, the provocative warm-up massage he'd given her that first day she came here to train with him, and the heated looks she'd seen in his eyes. While it was obvious they were both still wildly attracted to each other, she felt Kadeem was putting forth a conscious effort to keep things from crossing a certain line. Truth be told, as much as she still wanted Kadeem, she was relieved things slowed down the second week so they could get reacquainted and comfortable with each other again. But now that she was satisfied with what she'd observed, she was ready to move forward and decided to put it all out there for clarification. "You're asking me to dinner? As in a date?"

Kadeem, who was still crouched on the floor, settled on his knees, then straightened his torso. "What if I am? Asking you on a date, I mean. Would you have a problem with that?" He leaned toward Ramona, caging her in, as he planted a hand on the weight bench, on each side of her.

Ramona got lost in his brown eyes again. She shook her head. "N-no. I thought you'd never ask," she said. "But I can't go anywhere like this. I'm all smelly from the run."

"Haven't you noticed? We do have showers in the ladies' room."

Ramona had noticed those showers the first time she slipped inside the ladies' locker room. The cracked tiles with hairy black gunk growing between them had been a turn-off, so for the past few weeks after her training she headed home to take her showers. "Yeah, I noticed the showers. I . . . um . . . I'm just real weird about showering away from home—especially in locker rooms with a lot of folks. That was the thing I hated most about school gym classes."

"With a beautiful body like yours, I know you can't be shy." Kadeem's dark eyes shone with appreciation.

Ramona smiled weakly, letting Kadeem believe that version. It was better than admitting that his showers gave her the willies.

"You're in luck." He came to his feet. "As you can see, it's closing time so you can have a shower all to yourself."

Ramona looked around the place and noticed that only two members remained. They were putting weights back on their racks, unhooking their thick leather weight belts, and removing their weight-lifting gloves. Obviously packing it in for the day.

"Dang, I didn't bring deodorant, soap, towels, or a shower cap." Ramona slapped her knee.

"I gotcha covered." Kadeem went to the front door and secured the locks after the last two members departed. "And you don't have to come out and say it. I know the showers are pretty skanky looking. I do plan to have them redone at some point, however. But until then, I do have shower flip-flops so your feet won't come in contact with the tiles. We definitely wouldn't want you getting some funky fungus or something like that, now, would we?" Kadeem added with a knowing grin.

Ramona smiled and sighed with relief. She was on her feet again.

"Need some help getting to the bathroom?" Kadeem moved from the front door. He opened a little closet adjacent to his small office. He passed white fluffy bath and face towels to Ramona. He reached for a little plastic bucket on a shelf, then placed a new bar of soap, shower cap, and mini-bottles of shampoo and conditioner inside."

"Thanks." Ramona reached for the bucket.

"Need some help to the shower?" He scorched her with his seductive gaze.

Looking up at him through her lashes, Ramona shifted her weight and struggled for air. "Nah, thanks. My shins are sore, but I can still walk without assistance."

"Well, I guess I'll see you in a few minutes, then. I'm gonna grab a quick shower myself."

They just stood there for a long minute, staring at each other. Ramona wondered if he was remembering all the baths and showers they'd shared. The images flashed so clearly in her mind, she felt the heat of a blush creeping over her cheeks.

"Guess I'd better hop to it," Ramona spoke first, then turned and headed to the locker room. She glanced over her shoulder before stepping inside. He was still watching her. He winked at her before she quickly slipped inside the women's locker room, where she stripped out of her running gear. She was about to step inside the shower when she noticed the cruddy cracked tiles at its base and realized Kadeem forgot to put the rubber flip-flops in with the rest of her stash. She wasn't about to step in that shower without them. She considered throwing her clothes back on to fetch them, but realized how silly it was to go through all that trouble when it was just her and Kadeem in the place. She secured her bath towel around her body instead and tiptoed to the closet, where Kadeem had retrieved the rest of the things he'd given her. She checked the shelves and found miniature bottles of shampoo, conditioner, mouthwash, tubes of toothpaste, disposable shower caps, but no flip-flops. She'd have to check with Kadeem. As she approached the men's locker room, she heard the spray of shower water. Steam slipped out the door and wrapped around her body, making her heated skin moist and tingly. Poking her head inside, she called out, "Kadeem."

He was singing an old Lionel Richie song in the shower, just like old times.

"Kadeem." She took two extra steps and peeked around the corner. Her belly went aflutter when she caught a glimpse of Kadeem's naked silhouette. His lines were blurred through the smoked glass, but there was no mistaking that his body was still an awesome sight to behold. Broad muscular shoulders, full-sculpted pecs, corrugated abs, trim hips, and a round but so very taut butt. Ramona gulped. She felt so woozy with need that she had to reach out to brace the wall to keep from losing her balance. For several minutes, she just stood there, admiring him. And he was blissfully unaware as he moved a bar of soap over the planes of his torso, belting out a not-half-bad rendition of "Truly."

"So arrrrrre you gonna stand there all niiiiiiight or will you join me?" he suddenly sang over the rush of shower water.

*Huh?* Ramona's rocked back on her bare feet. Since when was that a line in that song?

Kadeem suddenly angled his body to face her; then he pushed the shower door open in invitation, his rakish smile and huge hard arousal beckoning. Ramona went instantly weak in the knees. A yearning that throbbed double-time between her thighs, matched the accelerated beat of her pulse.

Ramona sputtered. "I—I . . . um . . . came for the flip-flops."

Desire gleamed in his dark eyes. "You mean these?"

Though Ramona's eyes were locked on the man's perfect physique, she caught a glimpse of the pink rubber flip-flops dangling from his wet fingers.

"Yes," she said, still struggling to pull air in and out of her lungs.

"See anything else you'd like?" He slowly licked his lips and gave her a sultry look as he ran his fingers along the deep trench between his carved pecs, down his tight abs until his hands found the dark curls circling the base of his penis.

Ramona bit her lip, wondering why she was stalling when every cell of her body screamed, *Go for it! Cracked, cruddy shower tiles be damned!*

"It's all for you," Kadeem whispered thickly as he began moving his large hand in long smooth strokes. "Come and get it while it's hot," he teased.

Ramona dropped her towel, then gingerly stepped over the clump of terry near her feet. If it weren't for those stupid shin splints, she would've sprinted over.

Once she was inside the shower, Kadeem's mouth came down open and hard over hers. She relished the feel of her breasts against solidity of his chest.

The warm water sprayed over them as their tongues tangled in kisses. Kisses so deep, it was as if neither could open enough to the other. Ramona's hands played along the flexing wet muscles of his back, then down to the rocklike curves of his bottom. Kadeem dropped his hands to the juncture of her thighs to softly and deftly manipulate the sweet spot that swelled and pulsed with a steadily increasing beat. It felt so delicious, Ramona strangled on a thick moan of pleasure. "Ahhhh, yes, just like that."

With his free hand, Kadeem latched on to her hips and pulled her closer, all the while working her into a passionate frenzy, but Ramona didn't want to slip over the edge this way. She pushed his hands away and wrapped her fingers around his hardness, using the pad of her finger to caress the delicate but oh-so-sensitive spot at the underside of its head. "You know that drives me crazy," he rasped against her ear.

Ramona wore wicked smile. "Turnabout is fair play. See, I remember your hidden treasures too."

Just then Kadeem reached down, palmed her bottom, and yanked her back in his arms. "Wrap your legs around me. Now," he demanded thickly, as if he couldn't wait any longer.

Once Kadeem had her pressed between him and the tiled wall, he used one hand to firmly cup one of her breasts. Then his tongue found the pebbled nipple that poked between his splayed fingers. Ramona buried her hands in his hair and guided him to the other one, which ached for the same attention. Then he reached for the foil packet inside the soap holder. He lifted Ramona, then brought the small square to his mouth and ripped the wrapper off with his teeth. After he protected them, he slowly circled her heat until she felt unhinged from the sheer pleasure of it. Sensations flooded her body as their passionate sounds reverberated off the shower walls. A sharp gasp tumbled from her mouth as she took him inside. Hungrily, his lips sought hers as he plunged deeper and deeper. Her tremors increased in intensity as she accepted each inch of him. Their tongues thrashed and tangled as he moved inside her, at first reverently, as if he were intent on drawing out every ardent moment. Deliberate and steady gave way to strokes increasing in speed and force. The soap on his skin sliding against hers made for a smooth, seamless ride. Just like old times. It was as if their bodies never forgot how perfect they were together. Like connecting pieces of the same puzzle. Ramona cried out, and soon they both shattered beneath a warm, steady spray of water.

"So you still famished?" Ramona secured her wet twists in a stubby ponytail, using a large barrette from her shoulder bag.

"Yes, aren't you?" Kadeem drew her into his arms.

Before they'd finally managed to peel themselves away from one another long enough to get dressed, they'd spent the last two hours in the men's locker room shower catching up in the most intimate ways. Kadeem's memories of great sex with Ramona had not done the reality of it justice. That much he knew for sure.

"Yeah," she replied in a subdued tone that made Kadeem wonder if she was already regretting what they'd done. She changed back into the work clothes she had worn to the gym. She seemed way too engrossed in securing the buttons on her blouse and the zipper of her skirt.

He lifted her chin to look in her eyes. "Are you all right?"

"Yes," she replied unconvincingly.

"Don't bullshit me. You're not having second thoughts, are you? I didn't rush something you weren't ready for, did I? It's just . . . well . . . the last few days I thought I'd read signals that you were as ready to take the next step as I was."

"I gathered from the condom that was waiting in the soap dish that you'd already planned for tonight to be the night," she said crisply.

"I'm not going to lie. I'd hoped and I thought it was best that I be prepared . . . just in case things worked out that way. . . . I've wanted to be with you again since that day we ran into each other in the mall."

"When you say 'want me' "—she cocked her head to one side— "what does that mean exactly? You want me as in just sex? Or you want me as in how we were before?"

"I want all of you," he said, never feeling more sure of anything in his life.

"Really?" Ramona's pretty brown face broke into a smile. "So this means—?"

"I'd like us to try again . . . as a couple, if that's all right with you."

"Oh, Kadeem! I want that, too." Ramona hopped up in his arms and wrapped her legs around his lean torso. She planted a series of kisses all over his face as he laughed heartily.

"What about those shin splints of yours?" Kadeem said.

"What can I say? It's a miracle! I'm cured." She laughed in that throaty way that had always made Kadeem feel all was right in the world.

"So what will it be tonight? Italian, Mexican, Greek, Chinese? . . ."

Ramona began tugging at his shirt again, unzipped his pants and dropped to her knees with a saucy grin. "I'll have another helping of Kadeem."

# Chapter 7

"I'm the one who is supposed to be radiating that well-tended glow. I just got back from a honeymoon in Aruba." Jalisa placed a pot of coffee and two cups on the elaborately carved kitchen table that was the centerpiece of her new sun-splashed kitchen.

Ramona shrugged blissfully, then settled back in her chair. "What can I say, getting back together with Kadeem has done wonders for my disposition."

"The way you're gushing and glowing, I'd say your disposition ain't the only thing Kadeem has worked his magic on."

"True, I ain't even gonna try to front. Now I know why I could never get into any of the guys I dealt with after Kadeem and I broke up. I was spoiled. He's ruined me for every other man. He's such a great lover."

"I remember you two always had great chemistry. Just watching you two devour each other with your eyes made onlookers shout, 'Get a room!' " Ramona took her seat and then filled their cups with coffee.

"Are we that obvious to everyone all the time?"

"Uhhh-huh." Jalisa wore a conspiratorial grin. "And I'm jealous."

"There's more to us than that. I hope people know that." Ramona suddenly felt the need to explain that their attraction to each other went much deeper than the physical.

"Hey, you don't have to convince me." Jalisa dropped two sugar cubes inside her cup, then stirred with a spoon. "After all, you two were together five years before the shit hit the fan. Some might disagree, but there has to be more than sexual chemistry going for you to hang around that long, right?"

"Of course, there's a lot more. I still love him, and I'm going to work extra hard to make sure we're together for the long haul this time. Now that he's put that bodybuilding nonsense behind him, there shouldn't be a problem," Ramona said confidently, then took a sip of her coffee. She couldn't imagine what could possibly go wrong this time.

At Peak Physiques Kadeem had just finished demonstrating a set of dumbbell chest flyes for Jason when his friend Smitty came through the front door, carrying a cardboard box.

"Whassup, dawg?" Smitty's thick country drawl made his street speak sound like hick speak.

Smitty dropped his box on the floor. Smitty was a former competitive bodybuilder turned bodybuilding-show promoter. He wore one of those shake-'n'-bake salon tans, a pair of baggy jeans, a faded NO JUSTICE, NO PEACE baseball hat crushed over his blond hair, and a black T-shirt with the sleeves ripped off to display the freaky-huge biceps that were still his trademark though he had given up competing around the same time as Kadeem.

"What's that?" Kadeem asked Smitty as he gave Jason the signal that their workout session was over.

"A box of flyers for the upcoming American Muscle Committee Classic. Man, you won't believe the purse that's up for the first-place winner this year."

Kadeem looked down to skim the flyer.

"Twenty Gs!" Smitty told him.

Kadeem whistled, crossing his arms over his broad chest. "Man, that's a lot of cheddar. They weren't giving away those kind of prizes on the amateur, local level when I was competing. What's the deal?"

"Well, you know Don Mangioni, right?"

"Yeah, he's the local businessman who just purchased Pecs and Pumps nutritional-supplement company."

"He's the main sponsor for the contest, and he plans to use the winner in magazine ads, hence the larger first prize this year. It will be compensation for endorsing his products."

Kadeem tried not to think about all the things he could fix or upgrade at his gym with that twenty thousand dollars.

"I know you're retired from competition and all, but for a moment I could've sworn I detected a gleam of interest in your eyes." Smitty lifted a flyer from the box and passed it to Kadeem.

Kadeem crumpled the flyer in his hand as a way of giving himself a mental shake. He wasn't about to go down that road again—especially now that he had Ramona back and things were better than ever. "Nah."

"Hey, dude, it's a drug-tested show—not randomly tested. Meaning *everyone* has to pee in a cup. Mangioni doesn't want to take the chance of having someone who is juicing winning the title. So you'd be playing on a level field. You could train *hard and naturally* without worrying that someone will have that pharmaceutical edge."

"Hard and naturally" rang in Kadeem's ears, but he still refused. "No, I'm retired. Just like you."

Smitty plopped down on a weight bench and lifted one of the twenty-five-pound dumbbells Jason and Kadeem had just used for their chest flyes. He began performing a set of one-armed hammer biceps curls and was checking out his form in a nearby mirror that had a big crack streaking through it. That crack was another thing on Kadeem's fix-it list.

"Shit, if I wasn't one of the co-promoters I think I'd do this show my damn self. That's a lot of moolah. And damn, man, look at you." He dropped the dumbbell and slapped Kadeem's midsection. "You stay in stellar shape. You could be ready for this one in no time at all."

Kadeem caught a glimpse of himself in the mirror.

"Go on and strike a double biceps pose! Show off those rockin' guns, man! Bam! Bam! Like the peaks on Mount McKinley. You know you want to do it."

"Naaah." Kadeem shook his head. "Those days are behind me, Smitty. So what else is up?"

Smitty came to his feet, studying Kadeem. "So you ain't gonna crack, huh? Something big must be going on if you're not even tempted."

A small smile played on Kadeem's lips. "Ramona and I are back together."

Smitty whistled. "I knew it. I knew it was just a matter of time." Then he paused. "Oh, I get it now. I remember Ramona hated the life."

"Yeah."

"Ramona doesn't have to know," Smitty tossed out.

"Oh, she'd know all right." Kadeem snorted. "She's nobody's fool, and she knows the drill. When I start existing on dry skinless chicken breasts and steamed broccoli, she'd get more than a clue. And what would I tell her if I suddenly started bulking up and leaning out at the same time?" Kadeem shook his head. "It's not worth the risk. Besides, I don't want to mess up by lying to her now that we have a second chance."

Smitty lifted his hands in surrender. "Okay, I get it, man. You're *not* to be convinced. Can I at least put some of these flyers up on the cork bulletin board over there and maybe leave a few at the front sign-in desk for Peak Physiques members who might be interested in winning this cool twenty grand?"

Kadeem almost said no because he didn't need a reminder of the opportunity he was passing up, but he ultimately decided that he was stronger than that. "Yeah, man, go ahead. Plaster the damn wall with them, for all I care." Kadeem was suddenly irritated at Smitty for trying to tempt him and at himself for momentarily feeling tempted.

"I gotta go talk to Jason before he takes off," Kadeem said, admitting to himself that he needed another distraction right now. En route to the men's locker room where he and Ramona had made earthshaking love on more than a few occasions after gym hours, he told himself it would take a lot more than a stupid flyer to get him to break the promise he'd made to himself and Ramona.

That evening, Ramona was running late for their date, so she asked Kadeem to meet her at Nailz and Detailz.

As Kadeem waited in a leather chair in the lounge, he surveyed the place. It was classy, just like Ramona. It made his business look like a shithole in the wall. He knew he shouldn't go there, but he couldn't help making the comparison.

Ramona was busy talking to one of her employees in her office. Kadeem picked up an *Ebony* magazine and tried to get lost in one of the articles as his feet kept time with the jazz that filled the place. Yeah, Ramona had done all right for herself, and he was proud of her. He wanted to make her equally proud of him.

"Hi, baby." Ramona appeared before him with open arms. "I've been waiting all day for a kiss and a hug."

Kadeem was more than happy to oblige, even sweeping her off her feet as her nail techs looked on in amazement.

"So this must be the reason for the boss's good mood lately," the nail tech wearing the short Afro said to the other one who wore a mop of skinny braids.

"Must be," the one with skinny braids replied.

A third nail tech looked up and laughed out loud.

"You got that right. I wish I could clone him and pass him out as party favors, girls. Ain't he fine?" Ramona joked with a bright smile when Kadeem released her. "Kadeem, this is Erica." Ramona pointed to the one with the short Afro. "And that's Danielle." The one with the braids smiled. "That's Lonette." That third tech had hair that was dyed a Crayola shade of red.

Ramona continued. "The rest of my staff is off today for various reasons, but you'll get to meet them all eventually."

Kadeem smiled at the women, who were brazenly checking him out from head to toe.

"Ladies, this is Kadeem, the love of my life." Ramona gave him an adoring look.

While her announcement in front of her employees caught him off guard, it also made him feel warm and secure inside. He and Ramona hadn't swapped the *L*-word again yet this second time around, but it was good to hear that they were feeling the same things. Weeks ago, Kadeem realized he'd never fallen out of love with Ramona.

"Ladies, if you have no more clients for the day, you're free to leave," Ramona said as she led Kadeem back to her office.

Erica surged to her feet and began clearing her manicure station. "Cool! You don't have to tell me twice!"

Danielle and Lonette soon followed, and in less than ten minutes Kadeem and Ramona had Nailz and Detailz to themselves.

Ramona sat on her desk and grabbed a handful of Kadeem's T-shirt to drag him closer for a deeper kiss than the one they'd shared in front of her employees.

"You don't know how bad I've wanted to do that all day," Ramona cooed. "I've missed you."

"I've missed you, too," Kadeem said, taking in the classy decor of her office.

"You like? . . ." Ramona asked with a sweeping gesture.

"Yes, it's very nice. It must have cost a fortune."

"It wasn't cheap," Ramona conceded. "But it could've been worse. I got a good deal because the guy who did a lot of the renovating in here goes to my church. Hey, I just got an idea. . . ." Her eyes got wide, and he could almost hear the wheels turning inside that pretty head of hers. "Why don't I call him up and have him take a look at the gym—specifically those locker rooms? You can get some estimates."

Kadeem didn't have the money for that right now, but he couldn't find the words to tell her.

"The consultations don't cost much," Ramona said, as if she'd read his mind. "And I'm sure when you're ready to actually move ahead on the work, I can talk him into offering you good deal."

Kadeem clenched his jaw and shifted his feet. This conversation seemed at once eerily familiar and uncomfortable. Before he could reply, there was a tap on the shop's front door.

He followed Ramona to the lounge. Through the glass door, he could see a petite Asian woman on the other side.

Ramona sighed. "That's Mei Ling. I have the closed sign on the door, and here she is still knocking," she grumbled as she worked through the locks, then opened the door. "Mei Ling, what can I do for you?"

"I thought you were still here. I saw Erica, Lonette, and Danielle leave. Closing up shop early again, I see." Mei Ling was talking to Ramona but staring at Kadeem with a curious twinkle in her eyes. "So who is your handsome friend, Ramona?"

"Who said he's a friend?" Ramona obviously felt like maintaining an air of mystery for this woman.

"He's certainly not your supplies guy, and he doesn't look like the type who'd come in for a cuticle treatment, silk wraps, and a French manicure."

"You never know," Ramona replied, mischief glittering in her eyes.

That's when Kadeem thought he'd better speak up. He didn't like the idea of anyone having ambiguous ideas about which team he was playing for. He was 100 percent heterosexual male. "I'm Ramona's man, Kadeem Smith." He offered the woman his hand for a shake.

"Oh, I love how he just claims that title, throws it out there all strong and sure, no hesitation." The woman's other hand fluttered to her chest as if she were a minute from a full-fledged swoon; then she put her small hand in his. "I'm Mei Ling. Charmed, of course." She batted her eyelashes.

"Again, what can I do for you, Mei Ling?" Ramona's tone had an impatient edge.

Mei Ling sputtered momentarily as if she couldn't recall why she'd come over. "I . . . um . . . I came over to see if you'd like to see the new shipment of shoes I just got in. I put them on the racks," she told Ramona, though her eyes never left Kadeem.

Ramona cupped Mei Ling's elbow and escorted her to the front door. "No, but thanks for thinking of me. My closet is practically bursting with all the shoes I need."

Once she had the woman on the other side of the threshold, she pleasantly said, "Good-bye. See you tomorrow."

"But—but—" Mei Ling tried to interrupt before Ramona

drowned her out with another pleasant but firm farewell, then closed the door and secured the locks.

Kadeem couldn't hide his amusement. "What was *that* all about?"

Ramona clucked her tongue. "She runs the beauty-supply business next door. And I'm sure she just came over here to snoop."

Kadeem shrugged. "A little flaky acting, but she seemed harmless enough."

"She is, for the most part, but sometimes it takes the patience of Job to deal with her." A shadow of a grin played on Ramona's lips. "So you decided where you'd like to go for dinner?"

"How about Chinese carry-out?" Kadeem joked, grateful that Ramona had obviously forgotten about trying to arrange a remodeling consultation for him.

"And dessert at my place." Ramona wore a suggestive smile that let him know he was in for a long, passionate evening.

# Chapter 8

The next day Kadeem was in his office, lamenting over the pitiful state of the Peak Physiques financial records when Carl, his assistant, poked his head in. "Yo, Kadeem. Something's wrong with another one of the treadmills out here."

"Great," Kadeem grumbled as he followed Carl to the treadmill at the end of the second row of cardio equipment.

"Of course, the first thing I did was check the plug. I thought maybe one of the members had accidentally unplugged it." Carl rested an arm on the treadmill's console.

Kadeem inspected the electrical hookup anyway, but he didn't find anything out of the ordinary. "Hmmm. Hit the ON switch."

Carl did as told, but the treadmill just stood there. Dead.

The last thing Kadeem needed to do was post yet another OUT OF ORDER sign on one of the gym's most popular pieces of equipment. Two days ago, he was forced to make another treadmill off-limits to members after its belt snapped.

"Should I phone the repairman?" Carl asked.

"Yeah, go ahead," Kadeem said before heading to the desk to greet a woman and man he didn't recognize. "Welcome to Peak Physiques. May I help you?"

"My wife and I just moved to the neighborhood." The man spoke for them both. "We're interested in checking out the place and possibly joining because it's so close to where we live."

The wife obviously didn't approve. She looked around the place, wearing a look of dismay. "I don't see why we can't join the Bally's. It's closer to where I work."

"But joining a gym closer to our home would be convenient for *both* of us, dear," her husband reasoned.

Kadeem could tell the wife was going to be a tough sale, but he geared up for the challenge. "I'm Kadeem Smith." He offered his hand to the man who accepted it with a firm shake, then to the man's wife.

"I'm Louis Stanford, and this is my wife, Earlene," the man said.

"Pleased to meet you Mr. and Mrs. Stanford."

"Please call us Louis and Earlene."

"You a personal trainer?" Earlene asked.

"Yes, but I'm also the owner of this place. Are you ready to tour the facility?" Kadeem always felt odd calling it a tour. The place was so small, they could stand where they were and he could point out most of the Peak Physiques areas of interest.

"Yes," Louis replied. "I like this place. Has a nice, relaxed feel to it. Reminds me of those little gyms I used to work out in when I was a young man training for Golden Gloves."

"You're a boxer?" Kadeem asked, instantly impressed.

"Used to be, a long time ago."

"Make that a long, long, *looooong* time ago. When he could still look down and get an unobstructed view of his feet," his wife zinged, slapping her husband's sizable gut.

"All right, all right, so I have a bit of a spare tire," the husband conceded, rubbing his belly.

"A bit of a spare? I'd say you're wearing a full set of Michelins."

"But you've gotta give me credit for wanting to do something about it," Louis parried. That's why I want to join a gym, so I can start working out again." He gave Kadeem the signal to proceed.

*That a boy! You tell her, Louis!* Kadeem cheered inwardly. "Which do you think you would prefer—free weights or Nautilus?" he said out loud, pointedly making eye contact with the husband and his wife. Winning the wife over was crucial if he wanted to sell *two* memberships today.

"Do you offer aerobics classes?" the wife asked.

"No, sorry. Don't have the space for that just yet, but I plan to build an addition. When I do, there's an aerobics room in those plans."

"When is this addition scheduled?" Earlene asked.

Kadeem didn't want to lie. Being vague was his best bet. "I'm still working out the particulars," he replied, hoping she wouldn't press.

"No aerobics classes?" Earlene harrumphed, letting Kadeem know he was losing her by the minute. "What about your cardiovascular equipment? I'd like to check it out." She turned and led the way toward the treadmills, stationary bikes, and Stairclimbers.

At that moment, Kadeem looked up and saw Ramona headed their way, dressed in her running gear. He'd been so engrossed in his books, he hadn't realized how late it was. She stood at the desk and waved at him.

"Can you excuse me for a second?" Kadeem asked the Stanfords. "Feel free to try any of the equipment that you feel comfortable operating." He closed the distance between him and Ramona.

Mr. Stanford had already mounted a Stairclimber.

Kadeem went to Ramona and pecked her cheek. "Hey, babe, sorry I lost track of time. I'll be ready for your training session as soon as I'm done with these folks, who are checking out the place."

"Potential members?" Ramona peered around Kadeem's shoulder.

"Yeah."

"Mind if I watch you in action?" she asked. "I'm interested in what you do here."

"Sure." Kadeem returned to the Stanfords with Ramona on his heels.

"So what do you think?" Kadeem asked Mr. Stanford, who was already huffing and sweating through the warm-up cycle on the Stair-climber.

"I—I f-feel like I'm about ninety-five years old," he said through winded breaths. "It's a d-d-d-damn shame how out of shape I am."

"If you join, I can design a diet and exercise program that can get you where you want to be," Kadeem said, fearing the man might keel over from a coronary any second. "But take it easy. You don't want to overdo it today."

"What's wrong with these two treadmills?" Earlene asked, scowling and standing on top of the one they'd just discovered had a problem. "One has an out-of-order sign on it. And I pressed the ON button on this one, and nothing happens." She tapped the console. "The lights won't even come on."

"The belt is broken on that other one, and we're not sure what's up with the one you're on right now. But a repairman is on the way," Kadeem said, relieved he didn't have to lie. He had given Carl the go-ahead to phone one.

Earlene pursed her lips disapprovingly before launching her complaint. "Two treadmills of four treadmills busted. This certainly doesn't look good. If I come in here to work out at peak hours, say right after work, I'd probably always have to tackle people to get to one."

Earlene was definitely up to the task. After all, she did have shoulders like a linebacker, but Kadeem forced a smile and went with, "As you can see, we have stationary bikes and Stairclimbers—"

"I prefer treadmills," Earlene said, cutting Kadeem off.

Kadeem glanced at Ramona, who was quietly taking in the exchange. "As I said before, we do have a repairman coming in," he said.

"How old is this equipment, anyway?" Earlene crinkled her nose. "Most of it looks as if it's seen better days."

Kadeem was determined to keep his cool. "I'll be updating a lot of this stuff—"

"When?" Earlene was relentless.

Kadeem sputtered. "Well—um—you see—"

Earlene flapped her hand at Kadeem. "I get it. You haven't worked out the particulars on that either, I'll bet." Then she dismissed Kadeem, stepped off the treadmill, and went to her husband on the Stairclimber. "Honey, there's no aerobics room, and half the treadmills are busted. Can we pleasssse check out Bally's now?" she sweetened her tone. "I'll make it worth your while."

Louis slowed his climbing motion and stepped off the machine. "Oh?" he said, his interest obviously piqued. He wiped perspiration from his brow with the sleeve of his sweatshirt.

"It's a surprise," she said, quickly cutting Kadeem a smug look that said she ultimately ran things around the Stanford home.

"You know I love surprises." Louis loped over to her like a big Labrador retriever wagging its tail.

"So can we go now?" Earlene asked, linking her arm with her husband's.

"Sure, anything for you, dear." Louis looked over at Kadeem. "Thanks for the tour, but I'll need more time to think."

Kadeem knew what that meant. No sale. "Thanks for coming in, and if you have any questions, don't hesitate to call," he said, trying not to let his voice reveal the disappointment he felt as he watched the couple walk out the front door.

"Sorry about that, sweetie." Ramona moved closer and rubbed Kadeem's back. "You'll get other sales. You wouldn't want that woman for a member anyway. I'm all for her being a savvy consumer and all, but I could just tell she's a shrew. And who still wears leg warmers to the gym, anyway? Wrong season. Wrong decade."

"Leg warmers?" Kadeem's mind was still on the money he didn't make.

"Yeah, didn't you notice she was wearing pink ones and a ripped sweatshirt, obviously a nod to *Flashdance*, to boot." Ramona chuckled. "*Très* eighties."

Ramona was obviously trying her best to cheer him up, but between the two busted treadmills and the two sales he had just lost, cracking on Earlene didn't improve his mood. "You ready for your run?" he asked, eager to change the subject.

"Yes. Kadeem, is something else wrong?" Ramona furrowed her brow with concern.

Kadeem needed to talk to someone, but he wasn't ready to reveal how he was struggling to make the gym a success.

"I'm fine." He forced a bright note into his voice and patted her rear. "Let's hit the road."

When Kadeem and Ramona returned from their run, the repairman was tinkering with one of the treadmills.

Kadeem went to the man. "What's the damage?"

The man straightened, tucking an oily rag in the back pocket of his cotton trousers. "Looks like the motor is shot."

"And a replacement motor . . . how much is that going to set me back?" Kadeem held his breath waiting for the answer.

"For this particular model? . . . Hmmm. They're not manufacturing these anymore, so it could be hard to track down a replacement. Then if we find one, it'll cost ya. It might be more cost effective to just replace the treadmill."

With all his other operating expenses, Kadeem didn't have the money for that right now. And he'd already maxed out the credit he could get from the bank. "What about the one with the broken belt?"

"I looked at that one, too. It's been ridden long and hard. I could replace the belt, and it'll be fine for a little while, but my guess is, it looks like it might have about six months before you start having trouble with the motor on that one, too."

*Damn. How am I going to entice new members with shoddy cardio equipment?* When he initially stocked the gym, he chose to cut corners and penny-pinch by purchasing more used than new equipment. Now that quantity-over-quality decision was coming back to bite him on the butt. The plan had been to replace all the used stuff with new after he'd sold a set number of memberships, a number he'd guesstimated he wouldn't reach until the year-and-a-half mark. Now here he was, needing new equipment ten months before he had planned.

The repairman broke into Kadeem's thoughts. "So you want me to fix that belt?"

"How much is that gonna set me back?"

The repairman reached inside his pocket and scribbled a figure on a pad of estimate sheets, then passed it to Kadeem, who scanned it, then gave the repairman the go-ahead.

At least one of the busted treadmills would be operable again—temporarily.

Kadeem left the repairman to his business and headed to his office to write out a check for him. Ramona followed Kadeem.

Once inside his office, she sat down in the chair in front of his desk. "Are you having money problems with this place?"

"I got it under control," he said without looking up from the checkbook, but his grip tightened on his pen. "What would you like to do tonight? I know you've been dying to see that new Denzel Washington movie."

"We can do that," Ramona replied. "So you going to buy new treadmills?"

"You want to go to the theater near my place or yours?" Kadeem carefully ripped the check from the checkbook along its perforated edges.

"That depends . . . ," Ramona said with a sultry gleam in her pretty eyes. "Are we spending the night at my place or yours?"

"Actually, I was thinking we probably should each go to our own places tonight." To avoid making eye contact, Kadeem swerved his chair toward his metal file cabinets and began rifling through the folders inside, not looking for anything in particular.

"Don't tell me you're getting tired of me already," Ramona replied, a hint of surprise and displeasure in her voice.

Kadeem figured he'd better clean it up and clean it up quickly. He pushed up from his chair, tugged her from hers, then gathered her in his arms, and kissed her lips. "You know I will never get enough of you. After we see a movie and grab a bite to eat, I probably won't be very good company. I have a lot on my mind, that's all. Just need some time to think."

Ramona looked at him as if she were gauging whether to buy that explanation or not. "You sure you don't need to talk?"

"I just need to think," he replied. He didn't need Ramona swooping in trying to rescue him again.

"Okay," Ramona didn't push.

. . .

Something was definitely up with Kadeem, Ramona decided as she settled between the covers of her bed—alone. The first time she'd slept alone since she and Kadeem reconciled. She supposed there would be nights when they slept apart, and if he hadn't been acting so worried and distracted, she would not have thought much of his suggestion that they each do the solo thing tonight.

She pulled the covers up to her shoulders. She hated seeing him this way—all uptight. And after observing him and hanging around his gym as much as she had, it wasn't much of a leap for Ramona to conclude that business wasn't going as well as he tried to pretend. Many days when she had arrived for her training at what should have been peak hours, she could count the members on one hand.

While the gym had potential, it still needed a lot of work.

*And* equipment. Kadeem would have a difficult time drawing in sufficient numbers he needed without it.

The way he'd skirted the issue when she had tried to ask if he would be replacing those defective treadmills any time soon spoke volumes. Money was obviously too tight. Most new entrepreneurs could use a little help now and then—especially that tricky first year of business. Shoot, if it wasn't for Deacon Fred Malloy cosigning that unexpected, second business loan Ramona needed to keep her shop open that first year, she didn't know what would have become of Nailz and Detailz. Ramona reached up to turn off her bedside lamp. She had an idea that was guaranteed to help Kadeem get over this hurdle.

# Chapter 9

The next day, Ramona arrived at Peak Physiques for her training session so hopped up on excitement, she couldn't get to Kadeem fast enough. She found him in his office, hunched over what looked like a pile of bills.

"I've got a surprise for you!" she sang.

"What?" Kadeem looked up and smiled, obviously finding her glee contagious.

"Check this baby out!" Ramona slapped the glossy, full-color brochure on his desktop.

"What's this?"

"Look at it!" She dropped in the seat across from his desk. "It's the brochure for the new TRUE 850 ZTX treadmill. I've been a busy bee today, doing a little research for you. I'm sure you already know the TRUE commercial and residential models are *the* very best. I also made a few calls. There's this very well connected businessman, Mr. Malloy. . . . Maybe you've heard me mention him. He's a deacon at my church. . . . Anyway, check this out: he has a business associate who can get you a set of these babies for a little less than wholesale! Isn't that great!" Ramona leaped to her feet, circled the desk, and then plopped on Kadeem's lap to plant kisses all over his face. "Did I do good, huh?"

Kadeem grasped her by the shoulders to peel her off him. "You what?" he asked, his tone sounding forebodingly low.

"I—I—did some research and made a few calls about the treadmills," she said slowly as Kadeem's displeasure became more apparent. Then she got what she thought was a clue. "Look, if you're worried about coming up with the money right now to take this guy up on the deal, don't sweat it. He said he's willing to do a six-months-same-as-cash thingy or if you need a little longer, *I* can float you an interest-free loan. I know you're good for it!" She was planting more kisses all over Kadeem's face when his grip on her shoulders tightened. He firmly pushed her away again.

"Why did you do that, Ramona?" he asked, then clenched his jaw until the muscles worked.

"Isn't it obvious?" She tilted her head, wondering why he wasn't happier. "I wanted to help you, help Peak Physiques."

"Because you figured I couldn't do it myself?"

Ramona saw the storm brewing in his dark eyes and wondered where all the hostility was coming from. He came to his feet so fast, Ramona had to grip the desk to keep from tumbling to floor.

"Kadeem, I wasn't thinking that at all. I just figured . . . well . . ."

"C'mon, Ramona, why are you stuttering right now? I thought you were never at a loss for words. Ramona always has the answers," he huffed, his voice growing louder by the moment. The few people on the workout floor peered through the office door.

"I thought we were team. Aren't we supposed to *help* each other?"

"Who said I needed your help?" He glared at her, nostrils flaring.

Now Ramona felt her ire igniting. "Well, excuse me for trying to do something nice. It's not a done deal or anything. You can say no when the guy calls you. It's up to you."

"Is it really up to me? If it really were up to me, you wouldn't have involved yourself. It was *you* who decided I needed those new tread-mills now—quick, fast, and in a hurry!" He couldn't pace his tiny office, so he took two steps and braced his hands against the wall. Then he released a humorless chuckle. "I should have known it wouldn't take long for you to start orchestrating and manipulating as usual. It's the same old MO, Ramona, the same old MO."

"What are you talking about? Why are you twisting my attempt to help you out of a tight spot into something ugly?"

"You really don't get it, do you? And that makes it even worse, 'cause if you don't get it by now, you never will. I'm supposed be your man, but you refused to let me be one. Have you ever wondered why I didn't fight harder for us when you broke up with me the first time around?" Before she could reply, he rushed in. "It was because of stuff like this. I didn't think I could take any more your compulsion to try to orchestrate every challenge for me."

"I . . . I didn't realize . . . ," she mumbled. "You never said anything."

"That's because deep down, a part of me knew you were just trying to help—then I'd start to beat myself up because another side of me began feeling resentful toward you."

"This time—I—well, just figured your money was tight and—"

"I have options, you know."

"Oh?"

Maybe Kadeem's anger had got the best of him, but he thought he heard skepticism in her voice. "Yes, I do." Just then he noticed the flyer for the American Muscle Committee Classic that Smitty had taped to his door. He ripped it off and slapped it on the desk. "Twenty thou-sand options."

Ramona quickly scanned the flyer. "You can't be serious," she scoffed, slowly shaking her head.

"What if I am?" he challenged.

"If you think I'm gonna hang around and watch you get sucked into that craziness again, you've got another think coming."

When he didn't reply, she looked at him as if she didn't recognize him. "If your plan is contingent on winning some stupid bodybuilding contest, that's not exactly a sure thing, ya know."

"It's a *shot*. Something that I can do on my *own*." He jabbed a finger at his chest.

Ramona shot to her feet. "Fine! And while you're at it, you can do everything else from now on all on your own because I'm outta here!" With that, she grabbed her bag and stalked out of his office, his gym, and his life.

When Ramona returned to her condo, her insides were still churning with anger and hurt. She'd tried hard not to cry, but a tear slipped down her cheek anyway as she muttered curses to herself. "What an ungrateful jerk!" She practically tossed her gym bag across the room and then dropped on her sofa, tearing at the laces on her running shoes.

She flumped back, chest heaving. She wanted to nurse her anger to drown out the pain she felt. Though she and Kadeem had been reconciled only a short time, the ache seemed to hurt just as much as, if not more than it had when they'd broken up the first time. Only this go-round, Ramona felt stupid. Stupid for allowing herself to fall again so quickly without hesitation. She knew Kadeem's behavior could sometimes skim a little too close to caveman, but she'd thought it was something she could handle. After all, nobody was perfect. Certainly not Kadeem and not her.

Kadeem's response when she'd opened up to him about her little shopping problem came back to her. When he'd expressed such surprise that she was actually copping to having a weakness, she should have explored his reaction and reasoning behind that observation.

Then there were there other comments: *Ramona the perfectionist with her ducks all in a row. Ramona always handling everything just so. Ramona never screws up.*

Ramona reached for a throw pillow on her couch then held it tight.

But she *hadn't* asked him to elaborate; instead she'd switched the blame back to his obsession with bodybuilding. Now she wished she had explored it, because she couldn't shake the feeling that his angry outburst today was tied to his obvious misperceptions about her. If they had hashed things out, then she could have set him straight. But now Ramona wondered if it was too late.

Later that evening at Peak Physiques, Kadeem struggled through a set of hack squats, but his form and concentration were all off. Soon pain pinched his knees. He climbed off the machine before he really hurt himself and used the towel around his neck to wipe the perspiration from his face. He reached down for his water bottle and took big gulps.

"Yo, dude."

Kadeem turned in the direction of the voice and saw Calvin coming toward him. His slim form looked more wiry than usual beneath a sweatsuit that was a little too big for him. His skin was a richer hue than usual. Undoubtedly a souvenir from his exotic island honeymoon. He wore the smile of a man who was content with newly married life.

"How was your trip?" Kadeem tried to force an upbeat note into his voice though he was still simmering from that argument he'd had with Ramona earlier.

"Great, but I overdid the wining and dining a bit." He patted his lean midsection. "Think I need to work some of it off."

"Looks as if you left whatever *it* was at home. Man, you couldn't grow a belly if your life depended on it."

"Hey, don't start with the Barney Fife jokes," Calvin warned, shifting into one of the stances he'd learned in his judo class.

Kadeem played along, lifting his hands in a defensive gesture. "Please, Hammer, don't hurt me."

The two friends laughed.

"Hey, I just noticed you had the walkway out front fixed." Calvin sat on a nearby weight bench. "Looks good."

"Yeah, it just about broke me, too," Kadeem replied distractedly, claiming the bench next to Calvin's. "The joys of business ownership," he added facetiously and leaned forward, propping his elbows on his thighs.

"It's a hassle sometimes, but I also know you love this place."

"Yeah, I do, but sometimes I wonder . . . ya know, if I was really ready to take the leap when I did. Maybe I should've waited another year or two, saved more money before buying this place."

"You got a great deal on this real estate, and if you had waited, you would have missed out. Hey, what brought all this second-guessing on? You know the first year of business is a challenge for most people."

Kadeem sat upright and released a weary sigh. "Yeah, you're right. It's just that . . . well . . ." He struggled to find the right words. "Ramona and I had an argument today, and I think I might have blown it—for a second time."

"What happened?"

Kadeem took the next few minutes filling Calvin in on the broken treadmills and how Ramona involved herself in his business without talking to Kadeem first.

"So if she *had* come to you first and asked if she could help, that would've made all the difference?" Calvin asked, studying Kadeem.

Kadeem propped his elbows on his thighs and then dropped his head in his hands. "Man, I don't know. All I know is her going behind my back like that and taking over just brought up all sorts of old mess."

"This mess you're referring to . . . Was it something you two talked about?"

"Not in much detail, but it caused a lot of inner turmoil for me the first time around."

"Well, hell, man, if you wanted to make a real go of it this time, that's the first thing you should've wanted to get out in the open."

Kadeem sat up and dragged his hand down the front of his face. "I know."

"But I have to add, while I agree Ramona should've talked to you first before making plans for you, I still think you would've gotten a bug up your butt about her extending herself this way. I remember how you got all prickly when I offered to float you a loan a few months back. Remember? Got all indignant like my offer to help was some kinda dig, as if I was saying you couldn't handle your business or something when that was the furthest thing from my mind. When you care about somebody, you just automatically want to help when you can. Wouldn't you feel the same way if I or Ramona was in trouble?"

"Yeah . . . I suppose . . ."

"You suppose?" Calvin snorted.

"All right. All right. I would go out of my way to help."

"While you're nursing your indignation over what Ramona did I think you need to figure out a way you, Ramona, and that huge ego of yours can peacefully coexist."

Kadeem knew there was truth to Calvin's words, but that didn't make them any easier to hear. "There's another problem."

"What's that?"

"Ramona thinks I'm gearing up for another bodybuilding competition," Kadeem added.

"Where in the hell did she get a crazy idea like that?"

"From me," Kadeem muttered, suddenly feeling childish for throwing that complication in the mix.

"Now I know you've lost it. I thought you wanted the woman back. Sounds to me like you're purposely trying to drive her away."

"Man, I'm not doing that damn show or any other show. I only said that out of anger. I just wanted to lash out and feel in control again."

"Did it work?"

"Hell, no. I miss her already," Kadeem admitted with an exaggerated sigh as his gut coiled in knots. What had he done?

The next morning, Nailz and Detailz was busy as usual. Every station but one had a customer getting full sets of acrylics, fill-ins, or elaborate nail art. At least a dozen were waiting their turns as they sat in the lounge area, flipping through magazines, chatting on their cell phones or among themselves.

Ramona was still in awe at how well her business was going. She was already well over her projected earnings for her fiscal year. At the rate the walk-ins were appearing, that day's tally would be a record breaker, but a healthy dose of glee regarding her good fortune was hard to come by—especially with her thoughts constantly circling back to Kadeem. When she wasn't obsessing over Kadeem, she thought she heard Phipps Plaza calling her. She'd managed to resist its siren's call, which was always strongest when she was depressed.

Ramona was relieved when Jalisa popped in unexpectedly.

"I was hoping you could give me a manicure," Jalisa said to Ramona just before taking a seat in the lounge area.

"You caught me just in time." Ramona gestured for Jalisa to follow her to the office. "I was going to duck out for a lunch break."

"Where? I can go with you."

"Phipps Plaza," Ramona admitted sheepishly. "And to be perfectly honest, I'm not sure the food court would've been my only stop when I got there."

"I thought as much, which is why I rearranged my schedule today to come and see you. Calvin told me what happened with you and Kadeem yesterday. You know I had to come by and put in my two cents."

Ramona lifted her hands in surrender. "I already know what you're going to say, so save your breath." She closed her door as Jalisa took a seat.

"And what was I going to say, Ms. Know It All?"

"You just said it."

"Huh?"

"I think I know it all, and I'm always trying to fix other folks' lives."

"Whoa! Where did all this come from?"

"Kadeem can be too proud for his own good—pigheaded and a bit chauvinistic at times, to boot. But after I got over my anger, I did some real soul searching last night. While I've always had good intentions when I go dipping . . . I haven't always gone about it the right way—especially when dealing with someone like Kadeem."

"Someone like Kadeem?"

"Yeah, he's the first one who really called me on what can be an annoying fix-it habit I have. You never did." Ramona crossed her arms over her chest and nailed Jalisa with a meaningful stare.

Jalisa eyebrows shot up. "Me? How did I get dragged into this?"

"That time I submitted your résumé to Somerson and Whitman behind your back . . . Why didn't you tell me to butt out?"

"Oh, that." Jalisa suddenly became interested in the watercolor prints on the office walls. "I'd complained about my job more than once. When I got passed over for the promotion to head of the public relations department, I was fit to be tied."

"Yeah, you were upset, but you weren't quite ready to leave there. But what did I do, anyway?"

"Took it upon yourself to find me another job."

"I know you had to be pissed when that human resources guy from Somerson and Whitman phoned you."

"Yeah, you should've given me the heads up on that."

"Not just that. I shouldn't have passed along that résumé without talking to you first."

"But you were just trying to help a sistah out."

"I was tired of hearing a sistah whine about her job and not do anything about it."

Jalisa shrugged. "Okay, so you thought you'd give me a little nudge."

"That was not even a shove, but more like a swift kick in the butt."

"I didn't realize . . ." Jalisa's words trailed off.

"Last night I got to thinking about some things Kadeem said. And I thought about the people I've found myself helping over the years. It's like I can't *not* get involved."

"But I think it comes from a good place, usually." Jalisa's eyes went soft with adoration.

No wonder Ramona felt so free to manipulate. Way too accommodating friends like Jalisa made it so easy. But if Ramona were holding up her end of the friendship bargain, she would not have been so quick to take advantage of that.

"You have a good heart, Ramona," Jalisa added. "I think you're being too hard on yourself."

"Of course I love helping people I care about, but there's more to it than that. Last night I started trying to figure out when it all began. I pinpointed things I was doing at age eight even. Eight! Can you believe it? I was a child who was never allowed to be a child because my mother was always so out of it, drunk half the time." Ramona shook her head as a sadness for the desperate little girl she'd been washed over her. "I was always scrambling around, trying to make sure the house looked orderly and clean, the dirty clothes were hidden away. I tried acting well fed when I was so hungry I could have eaten the damn box when we ran out of cereal. I had to take control because I always feared Child Social Services would take me away or I'd have to go live with my mean ol' aunt Marlene. Ma never could quite get herself together. She *needed* me." Ramona's eyes welled up as the memories filled her mind. "But I know she loved me."

Jalisa came to her feet, skirted the desk, and wrapped her arms around Ramona.

Ramona sobbed softly. "So you see, all this helping stuff started as a necessity for me. A way to control or hang on to my life with my boozing mother. But that same tendency can drive people away if I'm not careful. Look what I've done with Kadeem."

"Calvin talked to Kadeem last night, and he got the impression he's anything but done with you. Kadeem's got some things to say to you and sounds as if you have some things to say to him." Jalisa smiled, then proceeded to playfully scold Ramona. "This time around just make sure those things are hashed out before you hop *back* into bed together again."

Ramona's mood brightened as she broke into a watery smile. "You mean into the shower together again."

# Chapter 10

That evening after Ramona closed her shop, she considered driving to Peak Physiques, but reconsidered. And she wasn't so sure she trusted Calvin's interpretation of where Kadeem's head was at regarding Ramona these days.

All she could see was the anger in Kadeem's eyes. Maybe they both needed a bit more time to think things through. What if she showed up at his place and he greeted her with the cold shoulder? She couldn't take him pushing her away again.

Ramona walked inside her condo and began removing her work clothes as her brain wrestled with three options:

She could head to Phipps Plaza and put a dent in her credit card, take a nice leisurely soak in a bubble bath, or throw on her running gear and do the long run that was on her training schedule that day.

She'd experience a high if she went shopping right now, but she would ultimately crash and feel even worse about herself later. She'd already spent her monthly allotment for clothing and miscellaneous material goodies such as running shoes and Jalisa's gift. She'd have to wait until next month before she could shop guilt free.

The bubble bath sounded heavenly, but that would not push her closer to her goal to be ready for that charity ten K in a few weeks. The bubble bath would be a well-deserved reward for her discipline.

She quickly changed into her running gear and strapped on the heart-rate monitor Kadeem had purchased for her. *Kadeem.* She sucked in a deep breath as her heart squeezed painfully in her chest.

She stepped out the door, tucking her keys, ID, and spare cash in the fanny pack strapped around her waist. The mesh sling she used to carry a bottle of water dangled from one shoulder. She locked her front door, then lingered on the grass circling her building to do a light warm-up jog in place, which she followed up with a series of calf, hamstring, and lower back stretches, executed as Kadeem had shown her.

Ramona had taken off and was a block down the sidewalk heading north when she heard a vehicle approaching. It slowed to match to her pace. Ramona kept her eyes forward. *Damn! Another creep who makes a sport of hassling women who dare to jog alone.* She was about to do the quick U-turn in the opposite direction to lose the jerk as she'd learned in her self-defense course when she heard a familiar male voice. "Ramona!"

Ramona turned her head and saw Kadeem trying to steer and lean over the passenger seat to look at her at the same time. "You got a minute?" he asked.

"As you can see, I'm training. I have a very tough coach." She kept running at a steady pace.

"A tough coach, huh?"

"The toughest. He's the best."

"Is that right?" he said with a smile on his lips.

"Yup. He wouldn't like it one bit if I goofed off on my training today." She faced forward again, but couldn't help smiling back.

"So I guess I can't talk you out of your run, then?"

"Nope." When Ramona increased her speed, she lost sight of Kadeem in her peripheral vision. For a moment she fretted that he might have grown impatient with her again and given up.

She was relieved when she heard the sound of fast feet coming from behind. Kadeem jogged alongside her, catching her by the waist. "You didn't think I was going to let you get away from me *again,* did you?" He enveloped her in his strong arms, nearly sweeping her off her feet.

"I didn't know what to think. All I know is I still love you." She was winded, not from running, but from the rush of emotion she felt.

"I love you. And I'm sorry about behaving like such a jackass yesterday."

"Me, too. I should not have pushed, and I should've trusted you to do what was right for your own business."

"I want us to be friends, lovers, and partners. And I can learn a thing or two about what it really means when you truly *share* your life with someone. And that's what I intend to do."

"There's still a lot of work to be done . . . on both our parts."

"Well, you know that old saying, it takes two."

Filled with hope and happiness, Ramona smiled, then let herself melt into Kadeem's arms for a kiss that sent her heart and the monitor strapped to her body on wild tears.

# Promises

## NIQUI STANHOPE

# Chapter 1

Gillian Asher cast a sidelong glance at the woman standing just behind her as she bent to retie the laces on her running shoes. There was no way on God's green earth that she was going to allow anyone at all to force their way into the mall ahead of her. Not after the kind of night that she'd just gone through. From about 9 P.M. the night before until 6:30 this morning, she'd been rolled in an uncomfortable sleeping bag on an especially hard concrete ground. She had tried her darnedest to get to sleep during the overnight stretch, but had found achieving that goal next to impossible. With the incessant snoring of her neighbors, the constant attacks from bloodthirsty mosquitoes and other bug life, and the fact that she couldn't find a single solitary position on the ground that didn't cause her neck to ache like the dickens, she was completely certain that if she had gotten an hour's worth of rest, she'd gotten plenty.

Gillian straightened and pressed a hand to the center of her back. Great. Just great. The muscles in her back were beginning to tighten up on her. She cast a malevolent glare at the clerk just behind the double glass doors. What in the name of God is he doing back there? Couldn't he see the entire pack of women just behind the glass doors?

And wasn't it almost eight o'clock already? The store was way behind schedule and probably going extra slowly just to torture them all. She was certain that was it, and it wasn't just extreme tiredness talking either. The ad in the newspaper had clearly said

**Early Bird Designer Sale. 50% Off Everything. Free Grab Bag of Designer Goodies to the First Two Customers.**

A frown shimmered for a moment in Gillian's eyes. Did they have any understanding of what "early bird sale" meant? It didn't mean "We're going to open our doors at eight thirty in the morning. Or maybe even nine o'clock." It meant the doors would be sprawling open at the crack of dawn. The very crack of dawn.

She shifted restlessly from one foot to the next. Why didn't they just open up and let them through? Did the people running things have any appreciation of the kind of pain she was in? Her neck was so stiff, she could only just manage to turn it from side to side without experiencing excruciating pain. She knew her eyes were flushed a deep pink from lack of sleep, and she wasn't at all certain that, after spending an entire night in such a horrible manner, she would have the strength it would take to sprint ahead of the frenzied crowd of women now pressed in tight behind her. She needed to be let into the store, and she needed to be let in *now*. Her strength was beginning to wane, and she had to have all her wits about her if she was to get what she came here for.

"Excuse me," Gillian said to a woman who had begun edging up beside her. "I think I was here first."

The other woman gave her a sale-induced glare. "What?"

"You heard me," Gillian said crisply. She was in no mood at all to be nice and polite. Buying fever was rushing like hot lava through her blood. And she was absolutely not letting anyone into that mall ahead of her. That was all there was to it. She hadn't suffered an almost broken neck for nothing. As soon as the doors opened up, she was going to be right through them and running as hard as she could manage. She was going to get that free designer grab bag or die trying. And she had a better than even shot at getting it, too. On a good day, she could pull off a pretty decent eleven-point-five-second sprint over one hundred meters. Today, though, given the condition of her neck and back, she wasn't so sure that she could exactly manage a hundred-meter dash at that pace, but she was going to give it a good try, nevertheless. One way or another, she was determined to be the first person entering that roped-off sale area. And she was definitely going to be one of the two women who would have her pick of free Donna Karan, Versace, Fendi, Valentino, and whatever else she could manage to cram into her grab bag.

This particular sale came around only once a year, and on previous occasions, she'd always managed to arrive just a little too late. Not late by ordinary standards, mind you. Last year she had stepped onto the sale floor just an hour or two after the doors to the establishment had officially opened. By then, though, the shelves and racks had been picked almost completely bare. Gillian had made herself a promise right then and there to be supervigilant next time about getting to the sale before it even started. And this year she had an added inducement. This was more than just a simple shopping spree. Although there was nothing she enjoyed more than a good six to eight hours of hardcore shopping, this time things were a little different. Her willingness to brave the elements, wake at the crack of dawn, and then sprint like a crazy woman through a crowded Atlanta mall packed with other similarly inspired women had overtones of altruism and love written all over the endeavor. She was mostly doing all this for her beloved old grandmother. Her nana, as she had called her since she'd been old enough to speak. It was all for her. Because it was at this sale that she would find that right dress. The one that would convince her grandmother and everyone concerned that she, Gillian Asher, the career woman who hadn't had a stable relationship in at least two years, was actually a happily engaged and possibly soon-to-be-married woman. And it was imperative that her grandmother believe this farce.

Just two years before, her nana had been a robust and particularly feisty eighty-two. She had been plump and strong and had shown little willingness to slow the pace at which she had always lived her life. She had been happily organizing bake sales at the local AME church, volunteering for every cause under the sun, and generally keeping a watchful eye on all the children in the neighborhood. But ten months ago, everything had changed. And the suddenness of it all had taken everyone by surprise. It seemed to occur in almost a breath of time. One moment Nana Sarah was standing over a pungent pot of thick black-eyed peas, stirring heartily and joking as she was wont to do, and the next, she was being rushed to the hospital, strapped to a white fitted gurney, the victim of a sudden heart attack, one that would have taken a less stubborn soul. For days, Nana Sarah had lingered in a state of semiconsciousness, drifting in and out of a medicated coma, lingering on the verge of leaving them all. Gillian had practically lived in her hospital room during the first weeks of her recovery. She had gone home to her condo only to grab a fresh change of clothes, a bite to eat, and a shower. She had put everything on hold. Her headhunting business. Her constant but largely unsuccessful forays into the dating mishmash. Everything. Nothing else had mattered. Not even shopping. She had been numbed by the possibility that she might actually lose the only mother she had ever known. And when the extended family had begun to gather around, the aunts, uncles, grand-children, and great-grandchildren, Gillian had known that they, too, believed what the doctors had said. Nana Sarah had less than a 50 per-cent chance of survival. The bypass surgery was going to be a long and risky business, and given Nana Sarah's age, in all likelihood the opera-tion would be unsuccessful.

But Gillian had known what the doctors and all the other medical pundits could never know. Nana Sarah loved nothing better than a good battle. Give her a challenge and a little encouragement, and she would rise to the occasion. Nana Sarah was strong and a fighter, and no matter what was thrown at her, she could defeat it. She wouldn't go down without a struggle. But Gillian had known, too, that this was the most serious battle her grandmother had ever been in, and that it would take something special, something powerful to help her fight her best fight. So, while everyone else was out in the corridor crying, wringing their hands, and moaning, Gillian had wrapped her mind about the problem. What? What could she do? What special magic could she give her grandmother? What was that thing that would help her nana hold on through the long and difficult operation? She had sat at her bedside with her head bowed, praying for the right thought, the right inspiration. And then suddenly, it hit her. And the sheer bril-liance of the idea had excited her so much that it was all she could do not to get up and begin dancing right then and there in the quiet hos-pital room. For years it had been her grandmother's fondest wish to see Gillian married. Since the day Gillian had graduated from college, this desire had been made clear to her. But life, fate, and circumstance had not cooperated, and Gillian had found herself bouncing from one failed relationship to the next. And each time a relationship had not worked out, she had thrown herself deeper and deeper into her work and into her only real passion in life: shopping.

But in her grandmother's hospital room, on the eve of her bypass operation, Gillian made a firm decision. She would give her grand-mother the very thing she wanted. And it would be this that would help pull Nana Sarah through. It would be this that would give her the strength to fight off the darkness and come back to them all.

So, in the wee small hours of the morning, while everyone else slept, Gillian perched herself on the edge of her grandmother's white-sheeted bed, picked up her soft crepey hand, and lied her head off. Her whispered story had been so inspired, so utterly fantastic, that at the end of it all, Gillian almost believed it herself. She could very nearly believe that she was a happily engaged woman. One with a man who loved and cherished her as well as shared her love for shopping.

Her grandmother's eyelids had fluttered a bit during the half hour Gillian spent sitting on the side of her bed. And Gillian had known that somehow, her tale had been heard.

Over the next several days following the operation, although she had remained hooked up to an intricate network of tubes and moni-tors and other paraphernalia, Nana Sarah had begun to show signs of improvement. And Gillian hung at her bedside like a shadow, repeat-ing her story over and over again. Each time she told it, her grand-mother appeared to grow a little stronger, a little more willing to come back to them all.

Two weeks to the day after the operation, which she had not been expected to live through, her grandmother opened her eyes and pro-claimed in a whisper-thin voice, "Child, what're all those tears about? Don't you know your old nana is a tough old bird?"

From that point onward, Nana Sarah's recovery had been strong and steady. And so had the evolving plans for Gillian's nonexistent wedding. Just as Gillian had suspected, her story had been absorbed even though her grandmother had been deeply medicated. Despite Gillian's every attempt to keep a handle on things, her grandmother had insisted on thrashing everything out. There had been much debate over the venue for the wedding reception. The invitations. The cuisine. And of course, the dress.

And although Gillian had done her best to inject a modicum of control into the situation, her efforts had done little good at all. Nana Sara refused to be calmed, she had swept all Gillian's protests away with, "Now Gil, baby, you know this is the kind of wedding your mother would've wanted for you had she lived to see you grown . . . God rest her blessed soul."

So as not to send her grandmother into another attack, Gillian had given in and allowed the planning of the nonexistent event to continue at full steam.

By the time Nana Sarah was well enough to return home, it had been decided how many children Gillian and her husband-to-be would have, what names would be given to the brood, and where exactly the happy family would reside. Gillian had been in such a high state of nerves by the time she dropped her grandmother off and saw her properly settled at her brother's house in Hogansville, that she had headed straight for the first mall she could find and bought herself several hundred dollars' worth of Italian shoes.

Later, as she carefully placed the newly bought trophies into their little racks in the shoe closet, she searched her brain for a way out of her current predicament. Several wild ideas had come to her as she sorted and restacked her shoes according to color. Maybe she might pay someone to marry her? Why not? She had the money. She was a successful executive search headhunter. She could afford it. And, it was for a good cause. A very good cause. She could just go to one of those escort service places and lay her cards on the table. Maybe that wasn't exactly the business they did, but money was money, wasn't it? And they would be helping her sickly old nana get better. Or if that didn't work, if they refused to help her out, she could just put an ad in the personals. Someone suitable was bound to answer it. And whoever did would be well paid for his services. She would see to that. Why not? It could work.

But after several more hours of thinking the whole thing through carefully, the idea had begun to lose some of its luster. Holes that she had not seen before suddenly began to appear in the fabric of the plan. What would she do after the fake marriage? She didn't want some fake husband hanging about, hounding her for money at every possible turn. And, she didn't want to have to tell her grandmother, as she would have to at some point, that she was getting a divorce. The shock of that alone might be enough to kill her.

So, after much rumination on the matter, she had decided that that particular idea was probably not going to work out at all. There would be no fake marriage. It took several days of more deep thought before the perfect idea hit her. And, when it did, she laughed in delight at the simplicity of it all. What she needed to do was distract her grandmother temporarily. Turn her attention away from the planning of the wedding, to something that was almost as spectacular: a party. She would throw her grandmother a huge celebratory bash. Every single family member and friend she could round up would be present. There would be lots of food. Fun. Laughter. Love. Her grandmother would be the woman of the hour. And Gillian would bring along a man who would pose as her fiancé. Her grandmother would meet him. The man in question would charm Nana Sarah's shoes off. She'd be happy. Then, somewhere near the end of the evening, Gillian would mention in as gentle a manner as she could manage, that her engagement would be a long one. A very long one. The plan was genius itself. And, if she knew her grandmother at all, and Gillian was reasonably certain that she did, the plan would work. But she needed the right dress to pull everything together. A special "I'm engaged, and I'm so happy" dress to wear to her grandmother's party. Hence the reason why she was now standing outside the Phipps Plaza mall almost mashed up against a solid wall of glass.

"I think they're getting ready to open up," a shrill voice from somewhere behind Gillian said.

The crowd muttered in ominous agreement and surged forward. Gillian was flattened even further against the glass doors as a heavy knee came into contact with her posterior.

"Look lady," she said, turning to the woman with whom she'd been having words thus far. "Don't push okay? We're all going to get in there when they open the doors, so just back up off me."

Her adversary gave Gillian the kind of look that might have caused a less worthy combatant to back down, and then she turned to a petite woman standing somewhere off to her right to say, "Isn't it sad how ghetto some people are willing to get when free things are being handed out?"

"Uhmm-hmm," the other woman agreed.

Gillian bit down on her tongue. She wasn't going to get into it with them, because if she did get into it, she would really show them both what the science of acting ghetto was all about. But, she wouldn't. She would just focus on all the wonderful things that were waiting for her just beyond the glass.

She massaged the muscles in the backs of her thighs and watched the clerk through the double doors as he approached. Her heart beat in thick, heavy thuds. *He's coming. He's coming.* Hot adrenaline flowed through her now, and Gillian sucked in a preparatory breath. *This is it. This is it.* There was a loudspeaker in his hand. He was saying something or the other before pulling back the doors. Giving the teeming mass of women last-minute advice, no doubt. *Hunt hard, hunt well, probably.* Gillian squinted through the glass at the man. It was strange how quiet everyone had become. Or had she gone suddenly deaf? She couldn't hear a single word the clerk was saying. Not a single word. Was it the excitement? The anticipation?

It didn't matter, whatever it was. She shook her right thigh and got ready. She was poised. Focused. She was Marion Jones in the blocks waiting for the starter's pistol. She stared down at the clerk's busy hands. Locks were being thrown. *One. Two. Three.* The crowd was beginning to move. The savage beast was almost free.

Gillian tensed as the first row of dresses came into view. Her heart was beating like a trip hammer. Moisture pooled in the soft scoop of her palms. Her ears popped, and suddenly she could hear again. She caught a snatch of the clerk's tentative warning, "Now ladies, please take it easy."

The crowd moved as one, in preparation for a full-scale assault. And Gillian, perceptive as ever, anticipated them. She was off like a shot, her hair streaming behind her like a banner. Her stiff neck was all but forgotten. She ran like the wind, sprinting up the cobblestone walkway leading to the area set aside for the fifty percent–off sale. Behind her, she could hear the thunder of the herd. And nipping at her heels was her nemesis of the last several hours.

Gillian cast a look over her shoulder at the other woman and groaned with the sheer pain of the maneuver. *My neck, my neck! The pain. The horrible pain.* But the twinge was only a momentary spasm to be ignored. Determination fired behind her eyes. She was going to get that free designer grab bag. There were only two being given out this year, and she was going to get one of them or die trying.

She was almost upon the roped-off sales area now, and somehow she managed a fresh burst of speed. Already, beautiful visions of dresses and coats, pants and lingerie were swimming before her eyes. *But, where was the clerk responsible for handing out the free grab bags?* Gillian turned her head with great difficulty. *Where in the name of*

*God was the man?* There was an absolute stampede of women just seconds behind her, and two women in particular were dangerously close.

She made a beeline for the entrance to the sale area and bellowed at the first clerk to appear, "The bags. The bags. Where are they? Who has them?"

The man's eyes opened wide as he took in the crush of stampeding women. And, in an act born of sheer self-preservation, he tossed the two red bags into the air and then ducked beneath a display table. The crowd changed direction with little effort, but Gillian, again, anticipated this and made a wild grab for one of the floating red objects. She snatched the sack out of the air and held on for dear life as she was tackled solidly from behind and brought down in a flurry of limbs. Two women had come out of nowhere. She hit the carpeting and stuffed the bag neatly beneath her. No one, but no one was getting it away.

"Get off," she panted as soon as she was able to get her breath back. "I slept out in the open for this bag, and I don't even *like* camping, okay? So, there's no way on earth that I'm giving it up to any of you."

One of the women tried to get at the bag, but Gillian tucked herself into a ball, rolled, and then bounded to her feet. She was immediately swallowed by the crowd. And there were women everywhere. Some were pulling things off padded velvet hangers and stuffing their prizes into already overflowing shopping bags, others were struggling in the aisles over the same garment, and others still were rushing up and down between the rows of clothing, screaming at each other in the language of true frenzy. It was a madhouse, and Gillian knew that if she was to survive it intact, she had to be surgical about things. She had to get in, and get out. No daydreaming, no browsing. She had to put herself into seek-and-find mode and then just buy, buy, buy.

Her eyes darted around the teeming area. God, life was beautiful. There was nothing better than a sale. And not even sex was better than a good nine-to-five session of hard shopping.

She spied the size-ten clothing racks and muttered, "Bingo." Her special dress would be somewhere in there, and it would be black, soft, and gorgeous. And when she put it on, everyone would look at her and say, "Who're you talking about? Gillian? Gillian Asher? Of course she's an engaged woman. Doesn't she look like an engaged woman? Is there a single redblooded man in the world who wouldn't want to own that booty? Of course she's an engaged woman."

Gillian trod heavily on the right foot of the clerk still cowering beneath the table, but in her excitement, she failed to notice. She jostled her way down the first aisle and began grabbing up designer dresses in every shade and fabric she could find. A Versace silk in burgundy. A Valentino mesh dress with a deeply scooped back, Vera Wang in soft turquoise.

She exhaled softly. *God. I've died and gone to heaven. Heaven. And, as many things as I can fit into my grab bag will be free. Free.* Gillian smiled at no one in particular. *Yes. Yes.* Now *this* was pure happiness.

She went down the next aisle in as thorough a fashion, stuffing dresses and pants, shirts and blouses into her red bag. When it was obvious that little else would fit, she picked up a regular shopping bag and began work on the items that she intended to purchase. And now she was clinical, precise. Like a particularly gifted virtuoso, she smoothed and folded, plucked and secured. Fendi handbags. Donna Karan slacks. Fashion Fair lipsticks and face creams. Dolce & Gabbana perfumes.

In only minutes of steady shopping, she was literally struggling beneath the weight of the two bags. But she was not through yet. Not yet. She still had to find the dress. The perfect dress.

She forced her way between two arguing women and stood on tiptoe to see into the next aisle. A frown darted across her face. Where was her dress? It had to be here somewhere. And, she would know it when she saw it.

Dozens of items called out to her as she walked by, and she tried her best to ignore them, pausing for only scant seconds to drop a few knickknacks into her overflowing bags. She trudged down another aisle and up another, her eyes hunting rack after rack, her enthusiasm for the chase never waning even once.

And then suddenly, there it was. The exact dress that she wanted, *needed*. It had been hiding in the next aisle over all along, just between two beige monstrosities of indeterminate purpose.

Gillian's mouth went dry as she gazed in wonder at the beauty of it. Could it be true? Could it be real? This was the very dress she had imagined in her mind. Had dreamed of for countless nights. Black gauze full-length sleeves smoothly blending with a crushed velvet bodice. A low-cut transparent back with tiny black pearl buttons running the entire length of it. And a wonderfully cut hemline that just screamed Sex Goddess.

Her heart thundered in her breast. She had to get to it and fast. It was calling out to her, "Mama. Mama. Come and get me. Come and get me."

She darted around the lip of the aisle, and pounced with a triumphant, "Here I am, baby."

But, her triumph was short-lived. There was someone else standing right before her prize—the crazy woman who had stood right behind her in the line outside. And she was running her hands all over the soft and silky fabric.

Gillian closed her eyes for an instant and took a deep steadying breath as incoherent thought rattled through her. *I can't stand it. I won't stand it. This can't be allowed to continue. This woman has to stop what she's doing. And, she has to stop right now. The crushed velvet number is taken. It's mine. Mine. Mine.* She almost felt like just ripping it out of the woman's hands. But, she wasn't like that. She would ask her for it nicely. *Nicely.*

Gillian cleared her throat. "Excuse me."

# Chapter 2

Her nemesis looked up. "And what do you want?"

Gillian swallowed. This woman really didn't want her to let loose the ghetto boiling just beneath the surface of her seemingly calm face. What did she want? What did she want? She was from west Philadelphia, born and raised. And, people in her old neighborhood routinely took things to the street, and over infractions of much lesser importance.

"That dress you're holding. It's mine. I was just about to put it into my bag. I already tried it on and everything. I just stepped away for a second to get another bag." Okay. So that wasn't strictly true. But, the dress was hers. She'd dreamed it. And, she'd seen it first.

"And this is supposed to mean something to me?" And, the other woman removed the velvet-and-mesh dress from its hanger and proceeded to spread it against her body.

Oh no, she didn't say that. Gillian's chin tilted up, an involuntary sign that she was preparing to do battle. Why did this have to happen to her now? And with the very dress she really, really wanted? And why was this strange woman haunting her every footstep anyway? How did it come to be that she wanted the exact dress that had the name Gillian Asher written all over it? What was wrong with the woman?

"Look, lady," Gillian began, and her voice went into a sharp and dangerous register. "I'm trying to be nice about this. I don't want to start anything with you. Okay? So, I'm asking you politely, just let me have the dress. I need it. It's for a special event. My grandmother's—"

The other woman cut neatly across her explanation with, "What about this conversation are you not getting?" And she began making signs with one hand. "I do not care about your boyfriend or your mother or your grandmother, for that matter. This is the dress I want, and guess what? I'm taking it." She turned and prepared to walk off up the aisle.

Gillian nodded her head and muttered: "Uhm-hmm. Okay, fine. If that's the way you want it. Fine." She set her two bags down. She would give diplomacy one final try. *One final try.* Then she would just have to resolve things *Philly style.*

"Lady, please, can I have the dress? There're a lot of others here for you to choose from. You know you don't even really want it either. You're just doing this out of sheer spite. Come on, do something nice for once in your life." It was an interesting twist on standard diplomacy, Gillian acknowledged, but it was clear that no standard approach would work on the she-wolf standing just a few paces from her. Guilt though, was a powerful weapon in most situations. And who knew, maybe there just might be a decent bone lurking somewhere in the woman.

But, this time, the gamble did not pay off. The other woman turned. "You know what?" she said. "I've had just about all I'm going to take from you." She threw the dress across one shoulder and then began removing her earrings and her shoes.

Gillian sucked in a breath. All she'd wanted was the dress. Now look at all of this mess. A woman was all up in her face, and for what? Was it worth it?

"Lady," she tried again, "you don't want to do this. Okay? Just have the dress. Force yourself into it, if it'll make you happy. God knows you probably haven't been able to fit into a size ten in years."

"What you need," the other said, stepping forward with challenge sparkling in her eyes, "is a good old-fashioned beat down. When's the last time you had yourself one of those?"

And, before Gillian could even think to respond, the other woman had launched her attack. A football-style tackle that would have done any NFL player justice drove Gillian back against a long rack of clothing.

"You crazy b—!" Gillian bellowed as several dozen garments crashed to the floor. The suddenness of the assault had taken her a bit by surprise, but Gillian was soon in full command of the situation. She accepted the gauntlet offered so recklessly by the other woman and allowed *the ghetto* bubbling just beneath her skin to boil over. *West Philly was now officially in the house.*

Over the next several minutes, pandemonium reigned. There were clothes falling everywhere. Things crashing and breaking. Women screaming and throwing garments of every shade and description, as they, for some unknown reason, also decided to join the fray. Alarms just as suddenly started going off. And finally, inevitably, there were the sounds of running feet as a team of security personnel came thundering into the mix.

Gillian and her adversary were yanked apart by several pairs of thick and burly hands.

"Someone get my bags!" Gillian hollered above the din. "Get my bags." And she struggled mightily to get to the red grab bag, which sat amidst the twisted wreckage of clothes racks, hangers, and other sundry items. "I'm not leaving without at least the red one," she said as several more men tried to restrain her.

Her red bag was retrieved in an attempt to keep her calm, and then both Gillian and the other woman were marched forcibly to separate elevators and taken up to the executive floor of the establishment.

On the way up in the wonderfully fashioned bullet elevator, Gillian, who was still hanging on to a fragment of the black velvet dress, had ample time to ponder what had just occurred below. She hadn't behaved in this manner in years. My God, she was a professional woman with a highly successful business, not some street fighter. Why had she let things get out of hand like that? It wasn't as though she didn't have more than enough clothes either. She had nothing but clothes. She had at least one hundred pairs of designer shoes, two entire closets filled with almost every garment imaginable. But, whenever she found herself in a shopping situation, a strange fever entered her blood, and the urge to buy everything in sight swept over her in the most vicious way.

Her three girlfriends had been after her for months to join them in their shopaholic support group. But each time the subject had been raised, she had turned them down with a laughing comment. *A group for shopaholics? Ridiculous.* Maybe they had a problem, but she certainly didn't. She just shopped for fun anyway. And, she could stop shopping anytime she wanted to. She didn't need to shop. She didn't live to shop. If she really wanted to, she could just stop. Cold turkey. She just didn't really want to right now. Why should she, after all? She was a thirty-five-year-old woman without a life. Without a man. What else was she going to do with her time? And, besides, the only reason she had come to this particular sale in the mall in the first place was to get herself that dress. The very one, or what remained of it, that she was now hanging on to.

Gillian looked down at the velvet shred in her hand, and a rueful expression clouded her eyes. *God just look at what that crazy woman has done to my little black beauty.* What a spiteful, spiteful woman she was.

The elevator doors opened smoothly on the top floor, and Gillian was hustled off and into a large office at the end of a narrow white tiled corridor. Rick Parker would be in to see her shortly, she was told. Her escort left her standing in the middle of the room with the comment that he would be standing right on the other side of the door. The implication being, she'd better not try anything funny inside the office.

Gillian frowned heavily at the man as he closed the polished brown door and left the room. God in Heaven, they were treating her just like a criminal. What had occurred downstairs had not been her fault. She'd been attacked. Attacked by a woman who was obviously dealing with some really serious mental issues.

She walked across to one of the ultramodern sofas and sat with the grab bag on her lap. She had lost the other one, so there was no way on God's green earth that she was going to lose this one, too. And she sincerely hoped that the mall security people were now in the process of carting her attacker down to the police station. It would be the best solution for a woman with such obvious instabilities.

Her eyes darted about the office, taking in the plush surroundings. Well, they'd brought her to a nice enough office. That was a good sign. It probably meant that they understood what had occurred and whose fault it had all been. They probably just wanted to take a statement or something like that from her. They hadn't brought her here because she was in trouble. Because, in all seriousness, how could she be in any trouble at all? She had just defended herself. If someone attacked you, you didn't just lie down and take it. Did you? What else could she have done in the circumstances?

Her brow furrowed. But just in case they didn't understand, just in case they didn't exactly see things her way, what was she going to say to the mall director when he put in an appearance? She couldn't be stumbling around like a fool, trying to get him to understand that none of it had really been her fault. She had to be poised, professional, ready with some kind of explanation that he would buy. And, it wouldn't be a good idea at all to come across as a half-crazy virago. So, there'd be no attitude. No smart remarks. And if pressed, she was even willing to offer some sort of an apology for what had happened. That way, he would understand that she was a dignified and respectable woman, not one who went around starting brawls in shopping malls.

Gillian rested her forehead on her palm. Yes, that was exactly the right approach to take. That was precisely what she would do. She would be nice and sweet to this Rick Parker, he would take her statement about the crazy woman, and then she would take herself off downstairs and right out of this madhouse. And, the first thing she would do once she got home was find a very large ice pack for her poor aching neck.

She was gingerly massaging the back of her neck when Rick Parker walked into the room and quietly closed the door.

Gillian's eyes darted over him in a quick assessing little glance. He was a tall man. Six feet three inches tall at the very least. And, he was simply the most utterly gorgeous specimen of manhood she had seen in a very long time. Coal black eyes. Smooth milk-chocolate skin. A sculpted nose rising above a generous mouth. A neatly groomed mustache of just the right length and thickness. And, a butt you could just bounce quarters off of.

He came to stand directly before her, and Gillian's eyes lifted to meet the inky black depths of his.

"So," he said, after a moment spent just looking at her. "You're the one responsible for starting this ruckus."

# Chapter 3

Gillian came defensively to her feet. Her heart had begun to beat in a strange and lopsided manner in her chest, and her breath as he continued to stare at her, came in short shallow rasps.

Hot words flew to her tongue, but she stilled them instantly. *No.* She'd already decided that she was not, under any circumstances, going to lose her temper again. Really terrible things always happened whenever she lost her temper. She wasn't going to make a fuss about his assumptions. He was completely wrong about what he'd just said, so, calmly, rationally, she would just let him know this.

She tried a tentative smile. "I can't tell you how very sorry I am about this—this little misunderstanding downstairs. You see—"

But, he didn't allow her to finish. His smooth baritone cut neatly across her well-thought-out attempt at mollification.

"I'm really not interested at all in your version of the commotion you started downstairs. I don't even want to know whether or not you usually run all over Atlanta getting yourself involved in similar situations. What I'm most concerned with right now is how exactly you intend to pay for the damage to the showroom down below."

Gillian's mouth flopped open, and she watched speechlessly as he pulled a sleek-looking calculator from his jacket pocket and, in a completely unfeeling manner, began doing a long sequence of calculations.

"You don't mean—" Words failed her again, and she swallowed away the dryness at the back of her throat. *This was unreal. This was absolutely not happening. Not to her.* "You don't mean to say," she tried again, "that you—that you really expect me to pay for what that woman did downstairs? You can't be serious. Surely?" Was he completely out of his mind? Had every single last person in Atlanta suddenly gone straight to la-la land? That woman and now the mall director, too? What was going on? What in the name of Heaven was really going on?

Rick concluded his calculations and then lifted his head to look at her again. "I am very serious. Unless you would prefer me to file formal charges against you for any of a variety of reasons, I fully expect you to make good on—" He looked at the face of his calculator. "—fifteen hundred fifty-five dollars and two cents' worth of damages."

Gillian blinked. "Fifteen hundred and what? Are you crazy? Have you been smoking something up here in this office? That woman is the one you should be asking to pay for things. Do you even know what happened down there? Or are you just using your psychic powers of deduction to figure things out?"

Rick held up a hand, and Gillian's flood of words came to an abrupt halt.

"We're not here, Miss—" And he gave her an expectant look.

"Asher," Gillian said.

"We're not here Miss *Asher*, to insult each other. Or anyone else, for that matter. And, I think I should let you know that the *woman* you so brutally assaulted downstairs is the wife of a local councilman. So, I really believe that you should count yourself lucky that she isn't filing charges against you herself."

Gillian pressed a hand to her chest. "*I* assaulted *her* brutally? Is that what she said? *I* was the one?"

"There was no need for her to say anything at all. I believe that headlock you had her in when security arrived on the scene was pretty self-explanatory."

Gillian drew herself up, and prepared to launch into speech, but Rick cut her off yet again.

"As I said before, there is little to be gained from rehashing what you think happened down there. So, I really don't want to hear any of it. Every year, it's the same thing—"

"Look," Gillian said, "I'm trying to tell you what actually happened out there, but since you're not interested in hearing anything that I have to say, fine. But let me tell you this: That crazy woman was the one who jumped on me and tried to tear my clothes off. And unless the rule of law has changed in the past twenty-four hours, I should be the one pressing charges against her. But"—and she was the one to hold up a hand now—"as you said, there's nothing to be gained by discussing any of this. I think you should tell your *friend* the councilman, though, that he should look into getting his *wife* some serious psychiatric help, because the witch is just plum crazy."

Gillian fiddled for a minute in her pocketbook and then withdrew a neat leatherbound checkbook. "Although I wasn't the one responsible for the damage, I'm not going to drag myself down to her level. I'm going to be the bigger person about this. I'm going to pay your fifteen hundred fifty-five dollars and just let it go at that."

She wrote out the check quickly, tore it from the checkbook, and then handed it to him. Rick accepted it without comment and proceeded to inspect it.

Gillian's eyebrows lifted as the inspection continued for just a little longer than it should have. "It's good. Don't worry," she said with a tinge of ire in her voice.

"I'm going to need your driver's license and your home phone number on the check," he said with what Gillian could only interpret as a strong note of suspicion in his voice.

Gillian provided the number and then handed over her license. If possible her anger was beginning to build even more. And all because of Mr. Rude Rick Parker. She might not be the wife of a local councilman, but she was most definitely one of the best customers any mall could ever dream of having. She spent literally thousands of dollars every month on various purchases. But because of what she had suffered here today, she would never ever shop in his mall again.

She tapped a foot impatiently as he stared at the license. *He did think she was a criminal*, Gillian fumed.

"It's not my best photo, okay? Actually, I don't take good pictures. But it is me. And if you'd like to make absolutely sure, you can call my office." She opened her bag again and pulled out a nicely embossed business card, which elegantly proclaimed her as the President and CEO of *The Asher Group*.

Then she snatched up her tattered red bag and stormed out of the office, thinking that she never wanted to lay eyes on Mr. Rude Rick Parker again.

# Chapter 4

Several days later, Rick Parker sat at his lacquered wooden desk, going through a particularly frustrating sequence of calls. He glanced at his watch, flipped a page in his desk calendar, and then barked a vaguely irritable, "Come in," in response to the knock on his office door. He would be a happy man once the mall's annual supersale week was officially over. Shoplifting grannies, free-for-all brawls between hitherto law-abiding housewives, and a never-ending litany of problems with everyone from the big chain stores to the food court vendors. The supersale was undoubtedly good for business, but the general havoc that it wreaked was almost enough to drive any sane person completely out of his mind.

"I've got the security tapes from the twenty-fifth, boss," his assistant said, poking a head in the doorway.

Rick pointed to a small pile of tapes already sitting on a round corner table. "Put them over there with the rest of them, Raoul. . . . Oh, and before you go—" Rick covered the mouthpiece of the phone with a hand. "Has the Asher woman returned to the mall?"

Raoul frowned. "Asher woman?"

"The brawl on the twenty-fifth. The woman with the very short hair and—the interesting face?"

Raoul nodded. "Right. I'm sorry, boss, didn't know who you meant for a second. No. We haven't seen her. Do you expect her to cause any more problems? I know the councilman was very concerned for his wife's safety."

Rick waved a dismissive hand. "No, no. I wouldn't worry about her." He placed long fingers against his forehead and massaged his temples. "It's nothing to be concerned about. I just wondered if she'd come back."

When Raoul left, Rick switched his attention to the phone in his hand. "Yes, I'm still holding, Jessica. No, it's fine. Yes, as I was saying before you went off, I'm afraid we can't shut the mall down for even one hour." He nodded and made the appropriate sounds of sympathy. "I understand that your client would be mobbed if he attempted to shop in the open mall, but I'm sure you understand that there are certain things we just can't do, not even for celebrities."

The voice on the other end yammered on, and Rick shot another glance at his watch. He would never be able to review those security tapes over lunch unless he could get this woman off the phone.

"May I make a suggestion, then, Jessica?" Rick interrupted after weathering several minutes of her droning voice. "We have an entire crew of very capable personal shoppers here. We could arrange for one of your people to work with a designated personal shopper." He nodded. "Yes. It's done all the time. Some of the biggest personalities seem to prefer this method." He paused. "No, I'm sure he will be pleased with the service." He listened again and then said with a pleasant but final note in his voice. "I'll arrange it myself. Yes. Do you have my cell number? Good. I will let you know when we're ready. And, can I say how much we appreciate the business."

He hung up and went immediately into another phone call. "Is Maria available between two and five today? Great. Ask her to come up when she has a minute."

Another knock on his office door coincided with the click the receiver made as it settled again into the cradle. Rick bade the person enter while making yet another call, this time on his cell phone.

Charles Fearing, a very capable man with a long history in law enforcement, entered and closed the door. At the look on the security head's face, Rick took the phone away from his mouth and said, "What? Another brawl?"

"We've got a code seven in progress," he said.

Rick flipped the phone closed and stood. "No chance the mother could've misplaced the child in the excitement of the sale?"

The other man shook his head. "It wouldn't seem so this time. The poor woman's hysterical. She said she left the little boy for just a minute in her shopping cart. When she returned, he was gone."

Rick nodded. "Okay. We'll go to a standard Adam alert. Shut down every exit. Notify local law enforcement. And, bring the mother up. We'll need to keep her calm if we're to find the child. I'll see what I can get from her." He came around to pat the security head on the back. "We'll find the little tyke. Don't worry. Your team has trained for exactly this kind of situation. We'll find him."

Rick sighed. It was another day at the mall.

Halfway across town, in the thick of traffic, Gillian was dealing with a situation of her own.

"Are you sure you're up to doing this, Nana? I mean, you're not fully recovered yet." It was the umpteenth time the very question had been asked, and Gillian's grandmother gave her an implacable stare.

"Gil baby," Nana said, "what do I always say?"

"Never put off for tomorrow what you can do yesterday," Gillian repeated obediently. It was her grandmother's favorite saying, and what it meant right then, was they were definitely going shopping for a wedding dress.

Gillian, by dint of sheer terror had hitherto managed to avoid the entire subject of her impending nuptials. But in the last two weeks, her grandmother had become relentless. She'd begun to insist that they start a search for at least the dress. This, she had told Gillian in a tone of voice that brooked no argument, was the most important item in the life of a bride-to-be. She had also begun to insist that she be introduced to the man who had managed to steal her baby's heart. It was probably because of this reason alone that Gillian had given in and agreed to go wedding-dress shopping. She had figured that shopping for a wedding dress was infinitely more doable than having to produce a nonexistent fiancé.

"You know," Nana Sarah said now with a dreamy expression in her eyes, "your mother always wanted you to have a big wedding." She smiled at Gillian. "And of course, she wanted you to wear white lace. But I think ivory satin is much more modern, don't you, Gil baby? I see you in a beautiful ivory gown with a long line of baby fine pearls running down the back. But, that's just me. What do you think?"

Gillian swallowed. "Ivory's nice." Her brain was churning like a restless ocean, strong waves of guilt battering her. This had been a bad thing she'd done. A very, very bad thing. At the time, it had all seemed so simple. So straightforward. She had thought only of finding a way to save her grandmother's life. Now, it seemed that her horrible latticework of lies and half-truths was more likely than not going to be the contributing factor in her grandmother's having another attack.

She turned a corner sharply and stepped on the gas. Traffic in downtown Atlanta was terrible during the noon hour.

"Here's a nice mall, Gil," her grandmother said as they passed the multistoried structure. "I think they're having a big sale there this week, too. Maybe we should stop in and have a look through one of the bridal boutiques?"

Gillian cast a quick glance at the building in question. Not on her life. She was never, never shopping at that mall again. Besides, Rick Parker would probably find some reason to have her further humiliated if she were to show up on the premises again.

"There's a little place just around the corner, Nana. I thought we'd stop there." Her grandmother gave her a pleased nod. "So, you have been looking already, then? You saw something you like there?"

The prickle of sudden tears caught Gillian by surprise, and she wiped a quick hand underneath one eye. Her grandmother was such a warm, trusting, and altogether wonderful person, but she had a terrible, terrible granddaughter.

Gillian blinked and dabbed the corner of her other eye. As terrible as she was, though, she did love Nana Sarah. And, there truly wasn't anything that she wouldn't do for her.

She pulled the Jeep Cherokee into a parking spot just vacated by another car, and cut the engine. She was going to have to find a man to marry. That was all there was to it. And she was going to have to do it fast. Because nothing but nothing was going to derail her grandmother's progress toward good and stable health now. Theirs was a family with good long life genes. With a little care and lots of love, her grandmother might live well into her nineties. So no foolish stunt on her part was going to cheat Nana Sarah out of the joy of spending years more with her family.

Gillian's forehead crinkled into worry lines as she reached across to help her grandmother out of her seat belt. Where was she going to find a man who would agree to go along with her plans? A long engagement was as far as she was willing to take the farce, but it still required that she find a man of good character. A decent man who would agree to her terms, take the money she would pay him, and then drift willingly from the scene once he was no longer needed.

She climbed from the Jeep and walked around to the passenger-side door.

"You're going to take it easy now, Nana. Remember the doctor said you could go on this shopping trip, but only if you didn't get yourself overtired."

Nana Sarah waved Gillian's supporting hand away and stood unaided.

"All of this nonsense," she said with the beginnings of irritation in her voice. "No one's going to stop me from helping my only grand-daughter shop for one of the most important days of her life." And she shot Gillian a bright little look. "You know that you can choose any dress you want, don't you, Gil baby? Your Nana's been planning for this day since your good mother was taken from us."

"Oh, God," Gillian muttered.

"Speak up, child. My ears aren't what they used to be."

"Nothing, Nana. I was just thinking out loud."

Her grandmother cackled. "Leave that till you're my age, honey. You're way too young for any of that foolishness. There's no reason at all to be talking to yourself."

"No, Nana," Gillian said, taking a firm grip of her grandmother's elbow. "Everything will be all right. You're going to be fine."

Nana Sarah nodded in agreement, and she turned to regard Gillian with eyes that sparkled with happiness and tears.

"Gil, baby, I've never said this to any of the others, because you know I don't believe in having favorites. Your Nana loves all of her family exactly the same. But, I think this is the reason why the good Lord spared your nana's life."

Gillian stood firmly on the fear in the pit of her stomach and asked in a very steady voice, "What do you mean?"

"The good Lord let me live so I would get a chance to experience this day. This one day that I've waited for, for so many years. So many years." And she stopped in the middle of the pavement to give Gillian a warm hug. "My Gilly," she said, emotion thick in the back of her throat. "My Gilly's finally getting married."

Gillian closed her eyes and uttered a silent prayer. *Help me please, God. Send me a man. Send me a good man. Soon.*

# Chapter 5

Rick Parker leaned back on the soft black leather couch and closed his eyes. He would allow himself ten minutes of shut-eye. He had been working at a steady pace since 6:30 this morning. But, it had been an effective morning, everything considered. The missing little boy had been recovered without further incident. Apparently, the little tyke had grown tired of sitting still in his mother's shopping cart and had wandered off in search of adventure. A security team had found him after a full hour of search, curled up beneath a rack of cashmere coats, fast asleep.

The celebrity shopping problem had been solved very effectively, too, by having one of the mall's best personal shoppers, Maria Serrano, assigned to take care of the matter. There had been only one problem that cropped up in the last several hours that had caused Rick any concern at all.

The brawl on the twenty-fifth was continuing to be a source of worry. A spanner in the works of the smoothly oiled giant shopping-mall machinery. Councilman Rogers had put in a personal call and had made Rick promise that he would do his all to prevent the news of his wife's involvement in the supersale fracas from reaching the press.

The councilman had edged his request with a veiled threat. Should his wife's involvement ever become public knowledge, he would see to it that the mall's business suffered. And that Rick Parker's unblemished reputation as a mall boss also suffered.

Rick had absorbed the threat with equanimity, and had, in his usual professional manner, assured the councilman that all necessary steps would be taken to ensure that such a scenario never played out. He had hung up the phone and spent several minutes turning the problem over in his mind. His staff was trustworthy. And only a small handful of the senior security people had even known that one of the women involved in the brawl was the wife of a public official. So, there was only one loose cannon in the equation as far as he could see. Only one person whose actions he couldn't vouch for. One person who could possibly cause them all some problems.

Rick's eyes opened to narrow black slits now, and a thoughtful furrow ran from one side of his forehead to the next. *Gillian Asher.* As unpredictable and volatile a person as she seemed to be, there was no telling what she might do. *Why, in the name of God, did the woman come into my mall on that day?*

He rubbed a hand across his eyes and stood. He had to have a look at the security tapes from that day. Gillian Asher was, after all, a person of some professional standing in the business community. So, there was every possibility that she might have an even greater interest in ensuring that the entire situation be hushed up. But, to tie off that particular loose end, he had to be absolutely certain of what had occurred during the melee. Then, and only then, would he know how to properly handle the situation.

Rick reached for one of the security videotapes, slid it into the machine, and then settled back on the couch to watch.

. . .

"Gil, baby. How about this one?"

Gillian took a look at the sweeping white gown. Lordy. Lordy. Lordy. Now that was the right kind of dress to get married in. It almost gave her hope that she might find her own real man to truly marry. It was elegant and old-fashioned with just a touch of modern couture. The train was a sweep of fine gauze, several yards long at the very least. The dress itself was a wonderful blend of satin and silk with a covering skirt of transparent mesh adorned by beautiful whorls of handmade lace. And a surprise awaited as the dress was turned. Soft transparent mesh ran from the high neckline all the way to the waist, giving a tantalizing glimpse of neck, shoulder, and back. And, baby fine pearl buttons sweeping from neckline to just above the waist completed the picture of supremely wicked elegance. It was, without question, a beautiful gown. And it was exactly the one Gillian would have chosen had she really been an engaged woman on the verge of marriage.

"You like it," her grandmother said with great certainty. "Go on, then. Try it on."

A cold shudder caused a rash of goose bumps to pepper Gillian's arms. The fever to buy was beginning to creep into her again. And it didn't matter at all that she had a mere five hundred dollars in her checking account. That money was clearly earmarked for food, utilities, and other sundry considerations over the next month. She still had two credit cards with spending limits of ten thousand dollars each. And, if pressed, since her credit was still afloat, she could probably get herself another two, with maybe even higher limits.

"It's beautiful, Nana. But I don't think I should look—" Gillian cleared her throat and stood squarely on the ripple of excitement that darted like hot lightning through her blood. "I don't think I should look at one this expensive."

"Nonsense, child. Didn't I say I would be buying it for you? Now, go and try it on. And, don't you argue with your nana." She spoke the final words in a winded manner, and Gillian shot her a worried look.

"Nana. I think you'd better sit down. I think you need to rest for a minute." Her grandmother sank without protest into a padded pink chair and then said, "See that you try it on right now, Gil. I want to see what you look like in it."

Gillian sucked in a breath. She would just try it on then. Just to make her grandmother happy. Of course, if it was a good deal, she could always buy it now and then pack it in mothballs in preparation for whenever her happy day did present itself. Good deals were not to be passed up these days.

"You sit here then, Nana. When I'm ready, I'll come back out."

Gillian raised a hand and signaled the couturiere, who had until now been standing at a polite distance.

"A wonderful choice, mademoiselle," the couturiere said as she approached. "I am Madame Boucher. Come with me, please."

Gillian nodded her thanks. Her body temperature had risen several degrees within as many minutes, and a strange feeling of certainty was beginning to block rational thought. *I'm going to buy the dress. I have to. It's probably one of a kind. There's never been another like it.*

"It is lovely, isn't it?" the couturiere said as she carefully lifted the dress from its perch and led the way into one of the fitting salons.

"Yes," Gillian said in a hoarse voice.

When the door to the fitting salon closed softly behind her Gillian forced herself to take a deep breath. The way she was feeling right now, she could very easily buy every single dress in the entire store. She would control herself, though. If Della, Ramona, and Neecy could see her now, if they could only listen in on the wild thoughts running through her head, they would say that she needed to come to the shopaholic group—and fast. But, it wasn't true. She *didn't* need the group. She *could* control herself. She would buy herself only one dress. Maybe two.

She rubbed the skin of her arms and began taking large shallow breaths as the wonderful perfume of silk and satin scented the air.

"I will help you with your clothes, *oui?*" Madame Boucher said. "This is a special time, is it not, *cherie?* To have found that one right man to spend the whole life with after looking for such a long time?" The couturiere gave Gillian a lavish smile.

"Yes. It's a wonderful feeling," Gillian mumbled as she clambered out of her black-and-yellow sundress. She was almost beginning to believe that she did have a fiancé, a man to rub her feet, listen to her problems, and care about what the devil she was really going to do with her life.

"And, how did you meet him?" the couturiere continued in a light conversational manner.

Gillian stuck an arm through the cloud of white silk and muttered a confused, "Who?"

"Your fiancé, *chérie.* You have not forgotten about him so soon?"

"Oh. Him," Gillian said a little wildly. The feel of the fabric against her skin was beginning to make her crazy. She could hardly breathe, let alone concentrate on making polite conversation with a woman whose sole purpose was to sell her a dress that she didn't need and definitely could not afford.

"Move this arm a little for me, please."

Gillian wiggled a bit as the sheaf of white floated about her and then came to rest snugly against her body.

"So, you will not tell? It is a secret how you have met this wonderful man?" Gillian looked down at the gorgeous creation. She did look like a bride. Like a happy woman. Like a woman who had found her significant other.

"I—ah—it was one of those strange things. Totally unexpected. I was . . ." She struggled for the right story, the perfect romantic fable that would satisfy this very inquisitive woman. "I was . . . shopping. I love to shop. I find it therapeutic. And I just . . . Well, he was there. Shopping, too. Looking for a gift for his—" She swallowed. "—Sister. And, you know how clueless men are when it comes to buying the right gift for a woman."

Madame Boucher nodded in sympathy. "*Oui*. It is a sickness they all have, I think. They will buy you the broom. The mop. But never the lingerie. Never the diamond."

"Yes," Gillian said, warming to the story. "Well, he was going to buy his sister something completely ridiculous. Something that she would never ever have used. So, I helped him find the right thing. He was so grateful that he invited me out to dinner. And, one thing led to another—and—"

"Ah, *oui*," the couturiere said in a pleased manner. "My niece, she had one of those strange encounters, too. Now she is a married woman with twin girls. You know that it is a miracle whenever these things happen that way. It is the hand of God in your life. A blessing from Heaven." Madame Boucher pulled at the waistline of the gown and then began very nimbly to fasten the tiny pearl buttons running down the back.

"These things . . . ," she continued after only a moment's pause, "whenever they happen this way, they always last. Because it is something that was meant to happen."

The couturiere turned Gillian, bent to fluff the skirt, and then straightened to say happily, "You, mademoiselle, will have a very good and long marriage. Trust me *cherie*, Madame Boucher knows."

Gillian's brows crinkled. Maybe, under ordinary circumstances, Madame Boucher might be in the know when it came to marriage and other matters of the heart. But, her radar was horribly off on this occasion. Because, this time, she definitely didn't know what Gillian Asher knew.

"You like it?" Madame Boucher asked finally, after much pulling, fixing, and gathering. "It is, maybe, a little large at the waist. But, that is no problem. I will fix for you. Come, see how beautiful you look. It is the dress for you, I think."

Gillian stared at herself in the floor-to-ceiling mirror. She swished slowly to the left, turned sideways, and then looked at herself over the round of one shoulder. The fever that had been building in her was so strong now that she could almost feel the rush of hot blood as it pounded its way through her veins. She closed her eyes for a moment, and fought hard for control.

"It's . . . nice."

"Nice? *Cherie*, this dress is not *nice*. This dress is a creation. This dress is elegance itself. *And* it fits as though it was made for only you. Come, we must show your—mother?"

"Grandmother," Gillian said. *My poor frail grandmother. Oh, God.*

She took a deep steadying breath as Madame Boucher pulled back the salon door and loudly declared, "Madame, here is your lovely bride. . . ."

It was almost seven o'clock when Rick Parker inserted his key into the front door lock of the town house he owned in a neat little section of Sweet Auburn. It had been a long and particularly trying day at the mall, and judging by the shrieks he now heard tearing through the upper rooms of the house, it was apparent that things were not likely to improve any time soon.

"Isha, Darren," he called out as soon as the door was firmly closed behind him, "whatever you two are doing, I want you to stop it right now."

His bellow brought a tiny face surrounded by wild uncombed hair to the head of the banister on the level just above.

"Hi, Dad." The little girl grinned. "You'll never guess what Darren did this time. He took all of my paints and poured them down the—"

"She started it first, Dad!" An identical face with much shorter hair appeared beside the first. "She broke my ant farm, and now Jimmy Jam and Terry and all the rest of them are gone."

Rick set his briefcase down. "Are you telling me that there are ants running all over my house?"

"I found the big ones," Isha chimed in, a cherubic smile on her face. "It's the little tiny ones that're kind of tricky. They can run really fast, and they hide in strange places, like Mrs. Thompson's underthings."

Rick bit hard on his inner cheek and tried his damnedest not to laugh. Raising ten-year-old twins would be a handful for any two-parent household, but for him, a single father with an extremely demanding job, it was nearly impossible. The twins needed discipline. A firm hand. A parent who was there when they got home from school. He tried his best to do that as much as possible. But he wasn't a wealthy man and, to give them both the kind of future that they deserved, that their mother would have wanted for them, that he wanted for them, it was necessary that he work long, hard hours.

He looked up at the two faces that so resembled his own and dug down deep for that thread of parental steel that was always needed in situations like these.

"Where is Mrs. Thompson?"

"Gone," both voices said in near unison.

Rick beckoned the two with a hand, and they came down the stairs toward him with such innocence shining in their eyes that a tremor of dread slid up Rick's spine.

"What do you mean she's gone?" he asked as they came to stand before him with hands clenched behind their backs. "Gone where?"

"Oh, she just left a little while ago, Daddy," Isha said, a consolatory note in her voice. "You don't have to worry that we were left alone all afternoon. She knows you usually get home at seven so she—"

"She said she wouldn't stay another minute in this house," Darren added with a wiser-than-his-years shake of his head. "And she also said that she wouldn't wait around until you got home either, so you could talk her into staying. She even left some of her clothes behind."

Rick pressed a hand to his forehead. Mrs. Thompson was the second nanny in as many months to quit on the job.

"What exactly did you two do this time? Besides the ants and the paint?" Rick asked. And he looked at them both without a flicker of humor in his coal-black eyes.

"Nothing," they both said.

"Almost nothing," Darren, the more honest of the two, amended after a moment of looking at his father's face.

Rick met his son's eyes. "Almost nothing?"

"Well, it might have had something to do with the lizards."

"It wasn't my idea to get them, Dad. It was Darren," Isha piped in quickly. "He put some of the really big ones into Mrs. Thompson's undy drawer."

"That's only because Jimmy Jam and Terry were hiding in her pantyhose," Darren hissed, throwing his sister a dark look. "I thought they'd get scared and come out of there if they thought there was a lizard around. Ants don't like lizards, Dad."

Rick nodded. "Uhm-hmm. Okay. Last time it was water balloons filled with paint. Now, it's lizards." He splayed his hands to stave off another round of explanations. "I've heard enough. I don't even want to know where you got the little reptiles you used to scare poor Mrs. Thompson half to death. Both of you are going to march right upstairs, find all of those ants . . . and lizards. And then, you're going to sit down and write a letter of apology to Mrs. Thompson." He paused to draw breath and then said, "Now off you go, and I don't want to hear a peep out of either one of you until it's time for dinner."

He watched his children's retreating backs and sighed again. He bent to retrieve his briefcase and muttered darkly beneath his breath, "What you two need is a mother."

# Chapter 7

"There's Neecy," Gillian said to the two women already seated in the corner booth of the Sambuca Jazz Cafe.

Ramona made a little sound of mock disgust. "Gil, you'd better go get her. You know how she can get when she's in a restaurant. She might just wander into the kitchen or something."

Gillian exchanged a grin with the woman who had just spoken, and then got up to wave.

"Neecy!" she shouted. "Over here. We're over here."

"Look at those shoes she's wearing," Della said in a hushed undertone. "They look like—"

"Prada," Ramona cut in. "They're Prada shoes. And I *know* they're new."

Gillian's gaze found the strappy sandals amidst the crush of dozens of pairs of feet and a shimmer of heat skittered through her. They *were* Pradas. And Ramona was right. The leather was soft and pungent, and she could almost smell its characteristic fragrance from where she stood. Where had Neecy gotten them? She'd been looking all over downtown Atlanta for just those very shoes.

"Girl, where did you get those shoes?" Gillian said as soon as Neecy was close enough.

Denise Ballard did a little twirl before the booth. "Like them? I found them in the back of my closet just the other day."

"Yeah, right," Ramona muttered and shuffled farther into the booth so that Neecy could sit down. "You know those shoes were not just sitting there in the back of your closet. Okay?"

Neecy opened her eyes wide, and Gillian sucked in a breath. As important an issue as the Prada shoe mystery was, there was another topic of much greater urgency to discuss. And unless she did something right away to call a halt to the wayward direction the conversation had begun to follow, there would be no getting back to the real reason she had asked her three friends to join her for drinks.

"Okay, ladies, everybody. Just take it easy for a second. There's something I've got to figure out here, okay? So, can we forget the shoes for a second?"

Ramona rolled her eyes. "What's the matter with you?"

Neecy reached across to squeeze Gillian on the arm. "What is it? Your grandmother?"

Gillian wiped a glimmer of perspiration from the peak of her nose. "Yes. Kinda sorta."

The others leaned in now, and all eyes were on Gillian.

"Gil, I'm so sorry," Della said. "What happened? Did she have another heart attack?"

Gillian picked up a bread stick, broke it neatly in half. "Not yet. But, she will for sure unless I find myself a fiancé within the next two days."

Ramona cackled. "Find yourself a what? By when? Girl, are you having a nervous breakdown?" And she turned to address the other two women. "Now, this is what I've been saying. How many times have we asked her to come to the shopper's anonymous group? You see what too much shopping can do? She's gone and lost her mind."

Gillian shot Ramona a hard look. "I'm serious. I've got to find myself a man. A good one. And right quick. That's why I asked you all here on a Wednesday night. I can't do it by myself. There's just not enough time. I've been trying to come up with all kinds of ideas, but nothing's working. Nothing's exactly right."

Ramona smiled. "Oh. Is that all you need? Well, that's easy. Let's see—" And she began looking around the crowded café. "Look. There's one over there, and he's not wearing a ring. Let's find out if he's available." And before Gillian could even think to stop her, she had made eye contact with the bald man seated at the bar and was beckoning him over.

"Excuse me, sir," she said to the towering hulk, once he was close enough. "Are you married?"

Gillian gritted her teeth and tried in vain to locate Ramona's ankle beneath the table.

"No, ma'am," the bald-headed stranger said, a good-natured smile lurking at the corners of his mouth. "But, I'd like to be when I get out of the Navy."

"Oh, the Navy," Ramona said. "Well, that's not gonna work. I'm sorry, sailor," she said, and raised a hand to give him a brief salute. "We need a land-bound man for this assignment. Carry on."

Della and Neecy began to chuckle as the sailor made his way back across to the bar. But, Gillian was far from being even mildly amused.

"I can't believe you did that," she whispered to Ramona. "Calling that poor kid over here when I'm trying to explain the trouble that I'm in."

"You mean you're really serious about this 'needing a man right away' thing?"

It was Gillian's turn to look exasperated. "*Of course I'm serious.* Like I said, I need a man, and I need a man no later than Friday. This week Friday."

Neecy bent forward to whisper. "You sure you're feeling okay, Gil? I mean you're—you're talking kind of crazy. You know that, right?"

Ramona exchanged a look with Della, who until now had remained completely silent.

"God knows we all need somebody, Gil," Della said now, in a calm and perfectly reasonable tone. "But, you can't let the need of a man make you go to pieces like this. You'll find your man—we all will. Eventually. It might be next week. Next month. Even next year. But, trust me, you'll find him. You have to keep your stuff together though." She wagged a motherly finger at Gillian. "You know what I mean? So, getting all hysterical and screaming about how much you need a man right now, really isn't going to do much good. You know? They tend to lock people up for a long time and give them shock therapy, chemicals, and all sorts of mess when they start talking crazy like you're talking right now.

Gillian sighed. "You don't understand. None of you understand what I'm trying to tell you."

"Okay, honey," Neecy said, reaching forward to squeeze Gillian's hand. "Tell us again why you need this man . . . and by Friday this week. We're listening." She turned slightly to silence Ramona with a look.

"I think we should order something to drink first," Gillian said. "And maybe some appetizers. 'Cause, really, this is gonna take a while."

# Chapter 8

It was after midnight before Rick finally made it to bed. He had spent several hours working with the twins on various homework assignments. Isha, whose passion was mathematics, had pressured him for dozens of algebraic problems, even though the rest of her class was just beginning to grasp the intricacies of pre-algebra. And Darren, a truly artistic soul at heart, had insisted that they spend an equal amount of time discussing the ins and outs of jazz composition.

At just before 9 P.M. Rick had decided to call it a night, and had sent them off to bed with the promise of a bedtime story. They were both neatly tucked in and ready for sleep half an hour later, when he kissed each cheek good night, turned out the lights, and gently closed the door.

The next hours were passed in his little study, bent over a stack of paperwork. Under the yellow glow of a bronze desk lamp, he carefully unraveled the problems of the day and made plans for the weeks to come. There would be meetings with the chain stores, a mall-wide book festival, and a huge bridal show, all within the next month. And, in order for each event to occur with appropriate smoothness, careful planning would be necessary.

He bent to his papers for two hours, making copious notes, checking and rechecking long columns of figures. At just after 11:30, when the middle of his back began to ache, he decided to put the many documents away and reward himself with a steaming hot shower. He allowed himself fifteen minutes of this luxury, and then he shut the water off, toweled himself dry in long brisk strokes, got into a pair of light cotton pajama bottoms, and climbed between clean linen sheets.

He lay with his head cushioned against the flat of his palms, watching the white face of the moon through the beveled glass of his bedroom window. And, as the noises of the city began to quiet, only then did he allow his mind to wander to her, Gillian Asher. After years of convincing himself that his heart had become a completely dead thing, it was strange and unwelcome to be hit by this burgeoning adolescent infatuation. He had tried his level best to push all thought of her completely from his mind, but in his quiet moments when he was relaxed, his thoughts now went inevitably to her. How and why this foolishness had struck him, he was unclear of. But, he had been aware, from the moment he walked into his office on that very disturbing day, that Gillian Asher would spell nothing but trouble for him. And, the sudden clarity of the realization had been so sharp and so profound that he had been unable to do much more than just stand there and look at her for several seconds. He had found his voice after a pause and had dredged up something fitting to say, but what exactly he had said was beyond him. He had come down extra hard on her but only because she had so rocked his equilibrium.

His brow wrinkled in thought. There was probably no possibility of simply asking her out to lunch or dinner, either. Since their first meeting, he'd been aching to give her a call but clearly, after his heavy-handed treatment of her, she would have no interest whatsoever in spending any time in his company. But, what he could do, what he certainly could do was return her fifteen hundred fifty-five dollars to her. She had been completely correct about what had transpired between herself and the councilman's wife. She had clearly not been to blame for the furor that had broken out on that day. And, had he spent any time at all listening to her explanation of events, he might have realized it then. But, at the time, all he could think was to get this woman out of his office before he embarrassed himself by doing something like . . . touching her.

Rick turned onto his side and closed his eyes. He would fix things though. And he would start by returning her money personally. Then maybe, as an extra touch of contrition on his part, he would invite her out to perhaps *dinner and a movie?* Yes. Dinner and a movie should work out quite well.

He fell into a satisfied slumber, dreaming about the lovely Gillian Asher.

At a few minutes to midnight, Gillian pulled into her one-car garage and cut the engine. Her friends had ended up being no help at all. So she was going to have to find a man to present to her grandmother on her own.

She hurried up the stairs, inserted her key in the lock, and turned. Before she went to bed that very night, she would have the problem all worked out. She would find herself a man, and a good one, too.

She went to sit at the center island, which divided the kitchen neatly in two.

Gillian reached into a drawer for a phone book and began to thumb vigorously through the many pages. Her fingers ran rapidly down the print until she came to *E: Escorts—male escorts. Excellent.* She would call and place an order. Her description would be general enough to make it easy for them to locate a man quickly, but specific enough that the man who was chosen was the sort to easily impress her grandmother and her entire family.

She cupped her chin in a palm and thought on the matter for a moment. He would be tall and slim with smooth black eyes. He would have thick, strong, capable hands. The kind of hands that were unquestionably masculine. He would be businesslike. Professional. But not greedy. He would be well spoken and intelligent, with many interests. But, most of all, he would be the type of man who would be able to convince her grandmother, without considerable effort, that he was in fact the man who had conquered her heart.

Gillian went down the yellow phone book page, circling numbers at random and muttering to herself, "Not a difficult thing. Not a difficult thing at all. There's got to be somebody good out there somewhere."

# Chapter 9

Gillian looked at the clock on the bedroom wall. *Great. He's going to be late.* She had already called the escort service more than once in the last hour. And on both occasions, she had been given the same bland response, *Her date for the evening was on his way. She shouldn't worry.* But, everything was not fine at all, and she was worried. Very worried. Because of the speed with which arrangements had been made, there had been no opportunity even to have a look at the man who was going to play this most important part. So, she had no idea whatsoever what he even looked like, let alone anything else. The escort service had given her only a very general description of the man, and had assured her that one of their best candidates had been selected. But, their concept of who was a good candidate and her concept of it were two entirely different things, she was sure. For all she knew, they might very well send over a man who looked good on the surface but who was completely incapable of even stringing a decent thought together. And, if that did happen, if such a man did show up, there would be no way on earth that her grandmother would be fooled by the charade.

She smoothed the front of the Valentino dress and gave herself another look in the mirror. It was gorgeous. A smooth turquoise creation that hit her at midthigh and yawned, in the most pleasing way, to the midsection of her back. She had been right to buy it. True, it wasn't the exact dress she had envisioned wearing, but the crazy woman at the mall had put an end to that little fantasy.

A frown creased her brow. Well, Rick Parker had had a lot to do with it, too. If he hadn't insisted that she pay for damage—which she had not, in any real sense been responsible for—she might have been able to buy another little black dress at one of the other boutiques. But he had ruined everything with his ridiculously inflexible attitude. She really despised the man. But, it didn't matter, because she wouldn't be seeing him again. So, she didn't need to dwell on the sorry mess any longer.

Gillian bent to fix the seam on her stockings. If the escort didn't show up soon, they were definitely going to be late. It would take them more than an hour to get to Hogansville in normal traffic. And, should the traffic on this particular Saturday afternoon be much more than what they bargained for, they would never arrive at her brother's house in time to be part of the gathering of relatives who would bellow the word, "*Surprise!*" as her grandmother returned from her usual Saturday afternoon drive.

Gillian walked down the narrow hallway and out into the sitting room. She was going to call the agency again. And this time, she was not going to be nice about things. It was scandalous, just scandalous the way paying customers were being treated these days. Like being wrestled to the ground in crowded malls, hustled up to the offices of extremely rude men, and then insulted.

She snatched the phone from its cradle and punched in the number to the escort service. They didn't know who they were playing with. But, they would soon find out.

"Yes, hello," she said, as soon as the phone was answered. "This is Gillian Asher calling again." She drew in a sharp breath and prepared to launch into battle just as her front door bell chimed.

"Wait a second," she said to the voice on the other end. "That may be him now. Let me check."

She went to the window and peered out. There was a tall man standing on the top stair, his back to the door. She dropped the curtain back in place and hustled back to the phone.

"Never mind," she said. "He's here." *And, it was about time he showed up, too.*

She hung up the phone, and then paused for a scant second more before the large gilt-framed mirror adjacent to the door. She looked good. Her short cap of Halle Berry–styled hair, with its recently touched-up honey-brown highlights, gave her face a sharp but appealing beauty. And, the dress, the dress fit her body like a custom-made glove.

Gillian fixed a shining curl, gave herself a smile of encouragement, and then walked across to open the front door.

"You're late," she said as soon as she had managed to pull back the dead bolt and fling the door open. "I'll fill you in on everything on the way over," she said, ducking for an instant behind the face of the door to grab her purse off a nearby table. "The limo's been waiting for at least half an hour. Didn't they tell you—?" But the words she had been about to say stalled in her throat as she straightened and came face-to-face with the man who had, until now, been standing with his back to the open doorway.

"Y-you," she stuttered, staring up at Rick Parker wide-eyed.

Rick met her sparkling eyes and for several seconds, he was at a complete loss. He felt around in the top pocket of his shirt to remove a neatly folded cashier's check. "I came to give your fifteen hundred dollars back to you. I had a look at the security tape. You were right and I was wrong." He smiled. "And I'm big enough to admit it."

Gillian accepted the check with fingers that had gone suddenly numb. "You're—you're not my escort." She sucked in a tight breath. *God, he must think I'm a complete maniac.*

Rick shoved both hands into his pockets and rocked back on his heels. "Uh, no. But, I understand how you might've jumped to that conclusion." He shrugged. "I showed up at the right time—or the wrong time—depending on how you look at it. Strange coincidence." And he gave her a smile. "Maybe it means something."

Gillian nodded. "It means something, all right. It means that I'm going to be showing up at my grandmother's party without my, ah, fake fiancé."

Rick stared at her. "Your what?"

Gillian waved a hand. "It'll take too long to explain. Oh, God, I don't know what I'm going to do. I'm going to give those agency people a piece of my mind!"

"Well . . . I could come along—as your, ah, escort?" Rick said.

"Why?" she asked suspiciously, then winced at the harshness of her tone. "I mean, why would you do something like that for me?"

Rick looked her in the eye and said, "Because I haven't been able to get you out of my mind."

"What?" Gillian asked, stunned.

"I haven't been able to get you out of my mind and I would very much like to escort you to your grandmother's party?" He smiled. "You do still need someone to escort you, don't you?"

Rick put a hand beneath her arm and led her down the stairs. "Are we very late?"

Gillian snapped out of her daze and glanced at her watch. "Uh, if we hurry, we might just make it. There's a lot I've got to tell you before we get there, I mean. This whole thing is very complicated," she managed to say even though she was still reeling. Had he really said he couldn't get her out of his mind?

"Uhm-hmm," Rick agreed.

The limousine driver stepped out at their approach and walked around to hold the passenger side door open. She shook her head. She didn't have time to question him further. She had an impending disaster on her hands.

"Good evening, miss—sir," he said, nodding at Rick.

Rick reached across to pat her hand. "Just relax."

Gillian opened her pocketbook and removed a white linen handkerchief from its velvet interior. "I can't relax. I've got to tell you about this evening. It's important. Very important."

"Okay." Rick nodded. "Tell me, then. I'm listening."

# Chapter 10

Almost an hour and fifteen minutes later, Gillian was again reaching into her purse. But this time, she felt around the velvet interior until her fingers closed on the cashier's check Rick had given back to her. After tonight, she was really going to need to do some serious shopping just to relieve tonight's stress.

Rick reached across to squeeze her arm, and Gillian started in surprise.

"So nervous," he said huskily in her ear. "You're not still worrying about how things are going to go this evening, are you?"

Gillian met his deep black eyes and smiled. He was turning out to be such a nice man. Not at all like what she had originally thought.

"Are you sure we're going to be able to pull this off?" she said now, a little frown spoiling the smooth perfection of her brow.

Rick tilted a black brow and asked with a smile flickering about his lips, "Now, who would dare say that we're not completely taken with each other?"

Gillian laughed. "You make everything seem so—easy somehow. Doesn't anything ever worry you? Don't you ever get stressed out?"

Rick shook his head. "When you're raising two kids on your own, you don't have the time to be worried—or the energy to be stressed out. You just solve the problems as they hit you."

Gillian turned in her seat. "You have two kids?"

"Twins. A boy and a girl. A handful. Believe me."

"Twins," Gillian said, and fiddled aimlessly with her purse. It was strange, but she never would have thought of him as a parent. He seemed too suave, too sophisticated, too smooth to be a father. And a single father, at that. If he hadn't told her himself, she never would've believed it.

"Where's their mother, if you don't mind me asking?" she asked.

Rick placed an arm along the back of the seat so that Gillian was forced to either lean against it or sit slightly forward.

"My wife . . . passed away years ago. When the twins were just babies. Cancer."

"Oh," Gillian said. "I'm sorry. I shouldn't have asked."

Rick looked down at her with steady black eyes. "It's okay," he said. "I've had some time to get over it. For years I never thought I would. But, time evens out the pain. It still hurts . . . but not as much as it did five, seven years ago."

His chest moved in a silent sigh, and a deep wave of feeling washed over Gillian. For the first time in a long time, she felt the need to wrap her arms around a man and just hold him.

She reached for his hand and held it. "I have a big mouth," she said. "But, maybe it's good to talk about her . . . get everything off your chest."

"Hmm," Rick agreed, and he reached a hand to tilt her chin. "I don't know about a big mouth, but you have great lips. Do you know that?"

A smile dimpled Gillian's cheeks. "Oh, I see. Trying to distract me so that you don't have to tell me any of your deep, dark secrets?"

Rick laughed. "You make me sound a lot more complicated than I really am. I think Isha would like you, though. You both seem to have a similar way of thinking."

"Your daughter?"

"Uhm-hmm. A fiery little beauty if I ever saw one. And devious, too. If you let her get away with a single thing—well." He laughed again.

"I think you probably spoil them rotten," Gillian teased, a sparkle in her eyes. "Whatever they want, you let them have. Right?"

Rick chuckled. "I'm probably too strict with them. What they need is a mother. Someone who'll spoil them rotten. And be their friend."

Gillian's heart stopped dead in her chest and then commenced a frantic beating. Was he telling her this for a reason? Was she completely crazy even to think so? Why, they hardly knew each other at all.

"Well, we *are* supposed to be 'in love,' right?" It was just too big an opportunity to pass up.

Rick lowered his head, and before Gillian could even begin to guess what he intended, his lips were on hers. And they were hot and firm and . . .

Gillian sighed softly from between her lips, and Rick cupped the back of her head and deepened the kiss. His tongue wrapped around hers in a slow languorous rhythm, and Gillian held him with trembling fingers as a hot incoherent thought wrapped itself around her. *God, this was impossible. It was too perfect. Too beautiful. Too everything.*

"Yes," he husked against her ear after countless minutes.

"What?" Gillian asked, her voice raspy around the edges.

"I knew I was right about you."

She sat back slowly, reluctant to let go of him completely. "What do you mean, right about me?"

"You're going to be nothing but trouble for me. I knew it the very first time I saw you."

"Right," Gillian said. "You knew one thing and one thing only the first time you saw me. And that was—"

"What exactly?"

"That I was some sort of maniac who went around to all the shopping malls putting women in headlocks. You said so yourself."

Rick threw back his head and laughed heartily. "You had that woman down on the floor in less than two seconds. What're you, anyway? Some sort of kung fu master?"

Gillian cast a glance out the window. "The woman was crazy. That's all I'm going to say. And you—"

"I know. I know. I should have listened to you. But, I apologized for all that already, remember?"

"Hmmph." Gillian fought not to smile. "You're lucky I'm a forgiving kind of woman."

Rick glanced at his watch. "We should be there in a few minutes, I think."

Gillian nodded. "God, I'm beginning to get nervous again. You made me forget about all this—" She waved a hand. "—for a little while."

"Well," Rick said, and lifted her left hand to inspect her fingers. "That's not all you forgot."

Gillian stared at her hand and then groaned. "Oh, no. I forgot to get a ring. How could I have done that? And I know my grandmother's going to notice, too. She's already asked me a couple of times now about it. I told her you were poor . . . and couldn't afford to get me the one you wanted right away."

Rick removed his arm from the back of the seat. "Gillian Asher, you are definitely not making this easy for me, that's for sure."

Gillian waved a hand dismissively. "What'll we tell her about the ring?"

"You can tell her that the diamonds are being specially cut. And that you'll be picking it up in a couple of weeks."

"She won't believe that," Gillian said. "Try to think for a minute. You're supposed to be poor, remember? I mean really, really dirt poor."

"Would she believe you if you told her that I just won the lottery?"

Gillian held on to a giggle. "Can you please be serious?" She shot a look out the window and gasped. "Oh, my God, we're here."

Rick held both her hands in one of his. "We'll distract her."

"Distract her? How?"

"By telling her that we've decided to set the date."

"No!" Gillian almost shrieked. "We can't do that. You don't know my grandmother. She'll be booking reception halls and churches and all sorts of other stuff if you tell her that. It'll be like waving raw meat in front of a hungry bull."

Rick caressed her cheek. "Bulls don't like raw meat. In fact, they don't like any kind of meat."

Gillian waved a hand. "Well, whatever. You know what I mean."

"You know," Rick said as the big car pulled slowly into the short driveway. "I have a feeling everything's going to be okay."

"And I have a feeling that I'm going to have a nervous breakdown."

"You'll be fine. You have nothing to worry about," Rick said, and he wrapped an arm around her. "Just think like an engaged woman."

Gillian held on to a shudder. He was right. There was nothing to worry about. So what if she had neglected a few little details. This was her grandmother's special night, and she was going to be happy. That much she would make certain of.

# Chapter 11

Before Gillian inserted her key into the front door lock, she turned to him and said, "You ready? Remember, we're supposed to be crazy in love with each other, now."

Rick smiled down at her. "Got you. Crazy in love. That shouldn't be too difficult to do now."

Gillian gave him a playful little tap on the arm, and said, "Okay, Mr. Parker. Here goes nothing."

She pushed the door open slowly and steeled herself for the interrogation that she knew was surely to come. But her heart stopped on a dime and then commenced a mad pounding in her chest at the collective shout of, "Surprise!"

Gillian's eyes darted over the crowd of grinning relatives. She saw aunts, uncles, cousins she hadn't seen in years, as well as her big oversized brother.

"No . . . ssh . . . ," she admonished with a finger held to her lips, "Nana's not here yet. It's only me and my—ah—Rick."

But, before she could get any further, the crowd parted much as the Red Sea must have in a different time and place, and to Gillian's horror, her grandmother came slowly forward.

"I *am* here, Gil baby."

Gillian looked wildly about the room. What was going on? Why was her grandmother here? And, why was everyone smiling at her in such a very peculiar manner?

"What's—what's happening?" she managed to ask over her rapidly beating heart.

Her grandmother came forward to hug first her and then Rick.

"Child," she said through gleaming and slightly moist eyes. "This is for you." Gillian blinked. She was completely at sea. She and her brother had planned the party for her grandmother. What in the name of Heaven was happening?

"What—what's for me, Nana?" she babbled.

Her grandmother held on to both Gillian and Rick and said very warmly. "This is your engagement party, Gil, baby."

"No, no Nana," Gillian said, and her voice rose just a fraction. "This is your party not mine. Tell her, Charley," she said, casting a desperate glance in her brother's direction.

"It is for you, Gil," her brother said, coming forward and beaming at her in a manner that made Gillian long to slap him solidly. "It's like Nana said. We've been planning this for weeks. This is *your* engagement party. We got you, huh?"

Gillian felt her legs tremble, and at the exact moment that she felt certain that they were going to give way, she felt Rick's long fingers wrap themselves about her shoulders. Her brain was churning like a wild thing, and for several seconds she wondered if she was going to just black out.

"Come in, come in," her grandmother said. And, Gillian, because she could do little else, allowed the crowd to hustle her from the lip of the door and into a soft settee in the living room. Once they were all comfortably seated, her grandmother turned to Rick and said, "My, you're such a fine figure of a man. Just the kind I thought my Gil would choose, too. You both have made an old woman very happy. Very happy."

Rick wrapped a long arm about Nana Sarah, and Gillian allowed him to take over for the next several minutes as she tried to control the strong waves of fear that threatened to overcome her. Things were bad. That was undoubtedly true. But, she would think of a way out of the tangle somehow. All wasn't lost. Because, really, how much worse could things get?

She turned her gaze to Rick again. Rick. Dear, dear Rick. He was doing such a wonderful job holding everything together. Covering for her, as she sat like a solid lump of ice beside him, not able to do anything more productive than just breathe. Anyone at all would think that he really was in love with her. How could he manage to be so composed, under such horrific pressure?

She forced herself back to the matter at hand. What was that? What was her grandmother saying now? And what exactly was that that she had in her hands? It looked like . . . She squinted. A Bible.

Gillian shot Rick a look that reminded him very much of a trapped hare, and then curled her fingers into tight fists as everyone crowded in to listen to Nana Sarah's little speech.

Gillian felt a fresh rush of blood surge through the skin of her face, and she struggled hard to keep track of what exactly her grandmother was saying. She caught the words: ". . . been planning this since you came to me at twelve . . ." And then, ". . . this is a promise Bible that all the brides and grooms in my family have signed for the last ten generations . . . dating all the way back to plantation days . . ."

And Gillian stared with severely blurred vision at the thick leather-bound Bible with its precious age-yellowed pages.

"This Bible," her grandmother continued, "has always been passed from mother to daughter, Gil, baby—and now, I pass it to you and ask that you and Rick, who feels like my grandson already, sign and date the promise statement in the front. Then repeat the prayer with me so that you will both have a long and happy life together, with many, many babies."

Nana Sarah proffered a pen and added, "Thank You, Jesus. Bless this promise made here today."

Gillian accepted the pen and dark spots began to dance before her eyes. There was no question about it, she was going to black out.

Her grandmother pointed. "Gil, you sign here—and Ricky, baby, you sign over there."

Gillian exchanged a look with Rick and prayed hard for salvation. But, when it came, she could hardly believe it. The doorbell. The doorbell was ringing in the most insistent manner.

She gripped the pen and muttered, "Thank you, *God*."

"Doorbell," she said, and prepared to rise.

Her brother Charley, who on any normal day could not be persuaded by a team of wild horses to answer his doorbell, sprang from his seat saying, "No—no. I'll get it. You stay and sign the promise, Gil, sweetie."

Gillian shot her brother a look that could incinerate and wondered abstractly what everyone would do if she suddenly keeled over stone dead on the floor.

Rick signed the promise with a flourish and said in a manner that made Gillian wonder if he wasn't secretly laughing at her, "Your turn, honey."

Gillian's hand shook a bit as she signed the sacred document. There was no doubt at all in her mind now, she knew that with this final act, she was going straight to hell.

So focused was she on what she was doing that it was almost a full minute before she realized that her brother was making frantic signals at her from somewhere near the environs of the living-room doorway. She raised her head to frown heavily at him. *What did he want now?*

*Didn't he understand that she had quite enough to contend with at the moment?*

"Gillian, I need to speak to you over here," her brother finally said when it became apparent that Gillian was intent on ignoring him completely.

Gillian got up with the beginnings of a frown huddling somewhere just behind her eyes. If her brother had ordered a singing cablegram or anything like that, she was going to have to slap him. Hard.

"What?" Gillian said as soon as they were out of earshot of everyone else.

Her brother bent to her ear and whispered, "Your—ah—other fiancé is at the door. And he insists that you're expecting him."

# Chapter 12

"Sweet Jesus," Gillian muttered beneath her breath. This could not be happening. First the engagement party and now this. The silly fool of an escort had decided to show up at her grandmother's house. Why, why was she being punished like this? Was it because of the shopping? Was that it? Could that be it?

"We have to get rid of him," she said to her brother. "He's not supposed to be here. I gave them both addresses, but I never thought for one second that they'd be—that he'd be stupid enough to actually—God."

"Gil," Charley said in a very calm voice, "what exactly is going on? Have you gone and gotten yourself engaged to two different men?"

Gillian waved a hand at him frantically and said, "Ssh—keep your voice down. I'll tell you what's going on later. Right now, we have to figure out how to get rid of this guy."

"What's all that whispering about out there?" her grandmother called suddenly. "Gil? What're you doing? We haven't said the prayer yet."

"Nothing. Nothing at all's going on, Nana. I'll be right there."

Gillian marched across to the door and yanked it open.

"What're you doing here?" she asked the stocky man standing on the stairs.

"I'm from the Julian Escor—"

"Okay, okay," Gillian said, waving a hand to quash what he'd been about to reveal. "You have to go away," she continued. "You're too late, and you're in the wrong place, okay? Nothing can be done now."

"Look, lady," the man said in a tone that indicated he would not be sent on his way lightly. "I've just traveled for two and a half hours by bus and walked a good mile in from the bus stop. You hired me for the day—so, you got me. And I ain't about to leave here without my tip."

Gillian gritted her teeth. *Tip? He wanted a tip? If things had been just a little bit different, she would have given him a tip he would not soon forget.*

"Lower your voice," Gillian said instead, her voice a hushed undertone. "My grandmother's just inside. Look," she said, and raised a hand to wipe away a bead of sweat from her brow. "I shouldn't even really be paying you anything—but, okay—I'll give you two hundred dollars if you just turn around and disappear without making a scene. How's that?"

"Three hundred dollars," the man said, "and I'ma need somewhere to wait until the next bus. You know what I'm saying?"

Gillian pressed her lips together. *Okay. Fine. He had her back to the wall.*

"Wait a minute," she said, and shoved the front door almost closed so that she might whisper to her brother.

"Charley," she said, "we're going to have to hide him."

"What?" her brother said. "Gillian, what's going on?"

"Just do what I say please, Charley. I'll explain everything later. I promise. And— Please go get Rick. But, don't let Nana know what's going on, okay?"

Minutes later in hushed conference before the front door, Gillian, together with the two men, decided, "There's no other way. We're going to have to put him in the bathroom."

And, before either could question the wisdom of the suggestion, she had pulled the door back open.

"Come with me," she said to the escort. "My grandmother can't know that you're here. Get me? So, until you're ready to leave for your bus, you're going to have to wait in the bathroom."

She hustled the man into the front toilet, closed the door, and then said to Rick, "Stand here, and don't let anybody—anybody at all—in or out."

Rick gave her an unreadable look. "And what about the promise we're about to make to each other? How're we to accomplish that with me guarding a bathroom door? Should I just bellow my agreement from here, or what?"

Gillian groaned and wrung her hands. "Oh, God—I don't think I can take much more of this. Okay, okay, Charley, you stand here. Rick, let's go make that damn promise—then—then—we'll handle the rest of this mess."

"Gil," her grandmother called from the sitting room. "What're you doing, child? What's going on?"

"I'm coming, Nana. I'm coming." She lifted her eyes to the heavens to pray silently. *God, if you get me out of this one, I promise you I'll stop all of the binge shopping. And not only that, I'll go to the shopaholics' meeting. I swear to you I will.*

"You two had better go right now before she comes looking for you," Charley said.

"Let's go," Rick whispered in her ear.

"Charley, I'm serious. Don't let him out of there. Okay?"

"I don't understand anything that's going on, but okay," Charley agreed.

Rick reached across to clap Charley on the shoulder. "Join the club. I don't think anyone but Gil has any understanding at all of what's going on here."

Rick and Charley exchanged a grin, which was totally ignored by Gillian. "If he tries to come out, just—just wrestle him to the ground or something. All right?"

The remainder of the evening passed in a horrific blur for Gillian. First there was the promise made over the bound Bible, and then a good length of praying from the entire group, punctuated with cries of "Amen," and "Bless them, Jesus," from Nana Sarah.

Then, the true festivities began. At some point during the entertainment, though, the escort, having tired of sitting atop a particularly rickety commode, and egged on by the smell of creamy macaroni and cheese, fried chicken, corn bread, and any of a variety of other niceties, attempted to emerge from his hiding place in the bathroom. This unwise decision prompted a short scuffle between himself and Charley, which then succeeded in convincing the man that he was really being held captive for some nefarious purpose. In a fit of complete fear and panic, he then attempted to squeeze his bulk through the narrow bathroom window, which, given his general size and deportment, turned out to be a very bad idea.

At a few minutes before eight o'clock, with the escort firmly wedged halfway in and halfway out of the bathroom window, a decision to call the fire department was made.

Several hours and many convoluted explanations later, Gillian stumbled from her brother's house. How she had managed to explain away things to Nana Sarah, she would truly never know. And, in the height of the confusion, her tongue had become unhinged, and she had broken down and confessed all to Rick, explaining in great detail how her uncontrollable urge to shop had contributed to the very precarious state her life was now in.

She sat beside Rick in the limousine now, a severely subdued look on her face.

"I'm sorry," she said for the umpteeth time, "but I truly had no idea at all that any of this was in store for me tonight."

Rick reached across to hold her hand. "Gil, you made me a promise tonight, and I made you a promise. If you keep yours, I'll do my best to keep mine. Deal?"

Gillian sucked in a breath. "Okay."

"Do you understand now that you have a shopping problem?"

She nodded. "Yes. It seems so."

Rick gave her a little squeeze. "Come on, don't look so weather-beaten. You're going to get yourself some help—and you've got a man now who will stand by your side and help you through the rough spots."

Gillian blinked at him. "I do?"

Rick smiled. "You definitely do." He wrapped an arm about her. "Tomorrow, I want you to come meet my kids. Can you make it?"

Gillian swallowed. "I'd love to meet them."

She snuggled against his shoulder and closed her eyes. Things were going to work out for her, after all.

# Epilogue

Almost two years to the day following their first meeting at the shopping mall, Gillian Asher and Rickford Parker were married in a lavish traditional ceremony at the first Baptist church in Atlanta. Nana Sarah gave the bride away with tears shining in her eyes. Isha did her duties as flower girl, and Darren carried the two gold rings up the aisle on a gorgeous satin pillow edged with lace. Gillian was resplendent in white: the very wedding dress which she had so unwisely purchased two years before.

Rick smiled into his bride's eyes and whispered, "I promise to spend the rest of my life making you happy."

Gillian moved closer to him. "And I promise you I'll never shop again."

"Well, don't overdo it now," Rick said, his black eyes shining down at her.

"I mean it." Gillian nodded. "Never again like I used to."

Rick wrapped an arm about her waist. And Gillian's heart expanded in her chest. Because no Prada shoe, Versace gown, or Valentino dress had ever made her feel like this.